A Christmas
Bride

JESSICA GILMORE

KANDY SHEPHERD

NICOLA MARSH

MILLS & BOON

First Published in Great Britain 2021
by Mills & Boon, an imprint of HarperCollins*Publishers* Ltd,
1 London Bridge Street, London, SE1 9GF

www.harpercollins.co.uk

HarperCollins*Publishers*
1st Floor, Watermarque Building,
Ringsend Road, Dublin 4, Ireland

A CHRISTMAS BRIDE © 2021 Harlequin Books S.A.

Proposal at the Winter Ball © 2015 Jessica Gilmore
Gift-Wrapped in Her Wedding Dress © 2015 Kandy Shepherd
Wedding Date with Mr Wrong © 2012 Nicola Marsh

ISBN: 978-0-263-30256-1

MIX
Paper from
responsible sources
FSC™ C007454

This book is produced from independently certified FSC™ paper to ensure responsible forest management.

For more information visit: www.harpercollins.co.uk/green

Printed and bound in Spain
by CPI, Barcelona

PROPOSAL AT THE WINTER BALL

JESSICA GILMORE

For Charlotte and Flo

Charlotte for so selflessly allowing me to pillage her commuting woes and for being such a brilliant sounding board, co-plotter, and very patient (and talented) editor.

Flo for making 'The Call' that changed everything, for guiding me so patiently through the whole publishing process, and for being a fab co-presenter extraordinaire and late-night wine-drinking companion.

Thank you both x

CHAPTER ONE

'A GLASS OF white wine and make it a large one.' Flora sank onto the low leather seat and slumped forward, banging her forehead against the distressed oak table a couple of times. She sat back up and slouched back in her chair. 'Please,' she added, catching a quizzical gleam in Alex's eyes.

'Bad day?' He held up a hand and just like that the waiter glided effortlessly through the crowds of office-Christmas-party escapees and Friday-night drinkers towards their table, tucked away in the corner as far from the excited pre-Christmas hubbub as they could manage. Flora could have waved in the waiter's general direction for an hour and he would have ignored her the whole time but Alex had the knack of procuring service with just a lift of a brow; taxis, waiters, upgrades on flights. It was most unfair.

What was it about Alex that made people—especially women—look twice? His messy curls were more russet than brown, his eyes undecided between green and grey and freckles liberally splattered his slightly crooked nose. And yet the parts added up to a whole that went a long way beyond plain attractive.

But then Alex *was* charmed—while Flora's fairy

godmother must have been down with the flu on the day her gifts were handed out. Flora waited not too patiently, ready to finish her tale of woe, while Alex ordered their drinks. A humiliation shared was a humiliation halved, right?

Finally the waiter turned away and she could launch back in. 'Bad day I could cope with but it's been a bad *week*. I think I'm actually cursed. Monday was the office manager's birthday and she brought in doughnuts. I bit into mine and splat. Raspberry jam right down the front of my blouse. Of course it was my nicest white silk,' she added bitterly.

'Poor Flora.' His mouth tilted with amusement and she glared at him. He was still in his work suit and yet looked completely fresh. Yep, unfairly charmed in ways that were completely wasted on a male. Flora's seasonally green wool dress was stain free today but she still had that slightly sticky, crumpled, straight-from-work feel and was pretty sure it showed…

'And then yesterday I left work with my skirt tucked into my knickers. No, don't laugh.' She reached across the table and prodded him, his chest firm under her fingers. 'I didn't realise for at least five minutes and…' this was the worst part; her voice sank in shame '… I wasn't even wearing nice knickers. Thank goodness for fifteen-denier tights.'

Alex visibly struggled to keep a straight face. 'Maybe nobody noticed. It's winter, surely you had a coat on?'

'I was wearing a jacket. A *short* jacket. And judging by the sniggering the whole of Holborn noticed. But even that was better…' Flora stopped short and buried her face in her hands, shame washing over her as she mentally relived the horror of just an hour ago.

'Better than?' Alex leaned back as the waiter returned carrying a silver circular tray, smiling his thanks as the man put a pint in front of him and a large glass of wine in front of Flora. She picked up the glass, gratefully taking a much-needed gulp, the cold tartness a welcome relief.

'Better than tonight. I didn't mean to...' The old phrase tripped off her tongue. Flora's mother always said that they would be her last words, carved onto her grave.

Here lies Flora Prosperine Buckingham.
She didn't mean to.

'I was just so relieved to see a seat I all out ran for it only I threw myself in a little too vigorously, misjudged and I ended up... I ended up sitting on a strange man's knee.'

She glared at Alex as he choked on his pint. 'It's not funny! The whole carriage just stared at me and the man said...' She stumbled over the words, her cheeks heating at the memory. 'He said, "Make yourself comfortable, pet. I like a girl with plenty to grab hold of."'

She took another gulp, ignoring the guffaws of laughter opposite. The words had stung more than she cared to admit. So she was tall with hips and a bosom that her mother called generous and her kinder friends described as curvy? In the nineteen fifties she would have been bang on trend but right now in the twenty-first century she just felt that bit too tall, that bit too wide, that bit too conspicuous.

Of course, sitting on a strange man's lap in a crowded Tube carriage hadn't helped her blend in. There had probably been people from her office in that very carriage on that very train, witnesses to her humiliation. Thank goodness her contract ended next week, although the thought of even one week of whispers and sniggers was bad enough; if only she could get a convenient dose of flu and call in sick. A week of rest, recuperation and isolation was exactly what she needed.

Though sick days meant no pay. Flora sighed. It was no fun temping.

Alex finally stopped laughing. 'That was very friendly of you. So you've made a new friend?'

'No!' She shuddered, still feeling an itch in the exact spots where the large hands had clasped her. 'The worst thing was I just had to sit there and pretend nothing had happened. No, not on his lap, idiot! On the seat next to him. I'm surprised I didn't spontaneously combust with mortification.'

How she would ever get back onto that Tube, onto that line, even onto the entire underground network again she had no idea. Maybe she could walk to work? It would only take a couple of hours—each way.

'Will you go back there after Christmas?' It was as if he had read her mind. Alex was far too good at that.

Flora shook her head. 'No, I was covering unexpected sick leave and she should be back after the holidays. Luckily January is always a good time for temps. All those people who decide to *carpe diem* on New Year's Eve or do something outrageous at the Christmas party.'

'Come on, Flora, is that your grand plan? Another

year temping? Isn't it time you *carpe diem* yourself? Look, it's been two years since you were made redundant. I know it stung but shouldn't you be back in the saddle by now?'

Flora put her glass firmly on the table, blinking back the sudden and very unwanted tears. 'It's not that easy to find design work and at least this way I'm paying the bills. And no...' she put up her hand as he opened his mouth '... I am not moving in with you and I am not moving back home. I don't need charity. I can do this on my own.'

Besides, it wasn't as if she wasn't trying. Since she had been made redundant from her job at a large but struggling pub chain she had sent out her portfolio to dozens of designers, retail head offices and agencies. She had also looked for freelance work, all too aware how hard it was to land an in-house position.

Most hadn't even bothered to reply.

Alex regarded her levelly. 'I'm not planning on offering you charity. I'm actually planning to offer you a job.'

Again. Flora swallowed, a lump roughly the size of the *Titanic* lodging itself in her throat. Just great. It wasn't that she envied Alex his incredible success; she didn't spend *too* much time comparing the in-demand, hotshot team of architects he headed up with her own continuing search for work. She tried not to dwell on the contrast between his gorgeous Primrose Hill Georgian terrace, bought and renovated to his exact design, and her rented room a little further out in the far ends of North London.

But she wished he wouldn't try and help her. She didn't need his pity. She needed him to believe in her.

'Look,' she said, trying to stop her voice from wobbling. 'I do appreciate you offering me work, just like I appreciate Mum needing a runner or Dad an assistant every time I'm between contracts. But if I learned anything from the three years I was with Village Inns it's that mingling the personal and the professional only leads to disaster.'

It *could* have been a coincidence that she was made redundant shortly after breaking up with the owner's son and heir apparent but she doubted it.

And yes, right now life was a struggle. And it was more than tempting to give in and accept the helping hands her family and best friend kept holding out to her. But if she did then she would just confirm their belief that she couldn't manage on her own.

At least a series of humiliating, weird or dull temp jobs kept her focused on getting out and getting on.

'I'm not offering you a role out of pity. I actually really need you. I need your help.' His mouth quirked into a half-smile.

Flora gaped at him. Had she heard right? The cheesy blend of Christmas tunes was already pretty loud and amplified even more by the group at the bar who were singing along a little too enthusiastically. 'You *need* me?'

That potentially changed everything.

'You know the hotel I designed in Austria?'

Did she know about the high-profile, high-concept boutique hotel Alex had designed for the über-successful, über-exclusive Lusso Group? 'You might have mentioned it once or twice.'

'I've been offered an exclusive contract to design their next three. They pick stunning natural locations, like everything to be as eco-friendly and locally sourced as possible and each resort has an entirely unique look and vibe. It's a fantastic project to work on. Only the designer I used for Austria has just accepted a job with a rival hotel brand and can't continue working with me.'

This was a lot bigger than the small jobs he had been pushing her way for the last two years. It was too big to be a pity offering; his own reputation was at stake as well. Hope mingled with pride and for the first time in a long, long time Flora felt a smidgen of optimism for her future.

Only to be instantly deflated by Alex's next words. 'I'm flying out tomorrow for the launch of the Austrian hotel and while I'm there I plan to present my initial concepts for the Bali hotel complete with the interiors and overall look. I thought Lola had at least made a start on it but when I called her today to ask her to fax her scheme over she told me cool as anything that, not only hadn't she started, but thanks to her new job she wasn't intending to.' He blew out a long breath, frustration clear on his face. 'This job better work out for her because there's no way I'll be recommending her again, no matter how insanely gifted she is.'

Ouch, ouch and ouch again. Flora's fingers tightened on her glass stem. So it wasn't her talent he was after, it was her availability?

But maybe it was time to swallow her pride. A job like this would propel her into the next league. She leaned forward, fixing an interested smile onto her face. 'So what do you want me to do? Study your plans and email my ideas over?' Her tiny box room of a bedroom, already crammed with material, her sewing machine and easel, wasn't the most inspiring surroundings but she could manage. Or she could travel back to her parents a week early and work from there—at least she would be warm and fed if not guaranteed any peace and quiet or, indeed, any privacy.

'Email? Oh, no, I need you to come to Austria with me. That way you'll get a real feel for their taste.' He fixed her with a firm gaze. 'You need to follow the brief, Flora. There's no room for your whimsy.'

Her whimsy? Just because her private designs were a little fantastical didn't mean she carried her taste into her professional work. She knew the difference between indulging her creativity in her personal work and meeting a client's brand expectations, no matter how dull they might seem. She narrowed her eyes at him. 'Of course, I *am* a professional.'

Alex held her gaze for a long second before nodding. 'Good. I'll talk you through my plans on the flight to Innsbruck'

The reality of his words hit her. A trip abroad. She hadn't been on a plane since her redundancy. 'Tomorrow? But I have another week of my temp job to go.'

'Can't you get out of it?'

'Well, yes. Although my agency won't be best pleased.'

'It's a temping agency. I'm sure they will be able to replace you.'

'Yes. Of course.' A fizz of excitement began to bubble through her. No more Tube trains and oppressive offices. No, she would be spending the next week in a gorgeous hotel. No more spreadsheets or audio typing or trying to put salespeople off, she would be flexing her creative muscles instead.

'It's a shame it isn't Bali. I could do with some winter sun.' Flora shivered despite the almost oppressive heat in the overcrowded wine bar. Her last holiday had been a tent in the Cornish countryside. It had all sounded idyllic on the website, which had deliriously described the golden beaches and beautiful scenery. The reality had been freak storms and torrential rain. She didn't think she'd been truly warm since.

Alex set down his pint. 'This isn't a holiday, Flora.'

'I know.' She leaned forward and grabbed his hand. 'I was teasing you. I'd go to the Antarctic for a chance like this. What do I need to do?'

His fingers curled around hers, warm and strong, and Flora's heart gave the all too familiar and all too painful thump at his touch. 'Be ready tomorrow morning, early. Pack for snow and some glamorous events, you know the kind of thing.'

No, she didn't. Not recently but there was no way she was going to tell him that. 'Warm yet dressy. Got it.' A thought struck her as the group by the bar began to roar the chorus of yet another overplayed Christmas classic. 'When are we due back? Mum and Dad are expecting both of us home on Christmas Eve. They'd be gutted if you don't turn up. Horatio is on duty at the hospital so it'll just be Minerva, her perfect spouse and her perfect twins.'

She could hear the bitter note in her voice, feel it coat her tongue and took another sip to wash it down. What she meant was she couldn't cope with Minerva and her Stepford family without Alex.

'No Horry?' Alex raised his eyebrow. 'That's a shame. I do like watching your mum trying to fix him up with the local eligibles. He's so beautifully oblivious.'

'I think it's a defence mechanism.' Flora eyed Alex speculatively. 'Anyway, you should be glad he never takes the bait. If Mum wasn't worrying about her permanent bachelor son she might turn her matchmaking skills onto you.'

'You're her youngest child,' he countered sweetly. 'I wouldn't worry about me, Flora. It'll be you she'll be launching forth next.'

'Don't be ridiculous.' But she wasn't as sure as she sounded. Now thirty was just a year away there had been ominous rumbles about settling down along with the usual thinly veiled hints about getting a proper job, buying her own house and why couldn't she be more like her elder siblings? 'You're one of the family. Better. The Golden Boy. You know they think you can do no wrong.'

Alex had spent every single Christmas with the Buckinghams after the year his father and new stepmother had chosen to spend the festive season in St Bart's leaving eleven-year-old Alex at home in the housekeeper's charge. The next Christmas Flora and her family had taken it for granted he would join them, a stocking with his name on the chimney breast, a place set at the table.

Five years later he had packed his bags and left his father's house for good, taking up permanent residence in the attic bedroom next to Flora's own. He'd never told her just what had led up to his bitter estrangement from his father and Flora had never pried.

Turned out there were places even best friends didn't dare go.

'Don't worry, we'll be back for Christmas. There's no way I'm missing out on your father's Christmas dinner. He's promising goose this year. I watched him prepare it on a video on the Internet. Nothing is keeping me away.'

'That's all right, then.' She took a deep breath of relief. One day surely even Alex would manage more than six months with one of his identikit, well-bred girlfriends and would have to spend the holiday season with *her* family, not the Buckinghams. Each year they managed to hold onto him was a bonus.

She stared at her empty glass regretfully. 'If I need to pack, find my passport and be ready before the crack of dawn I'd better get going. What time shall I meet you?'

'Oh, no.' Alex pushed his chair back and stood up, extending a hand to Flora to help her out of her seat. 'I'm not risking your timekeeping, Flora Buckingham. I'll send a car for you. Five a.m. sharp. Be ready.'

Alex looked down at his tablet and sighed. So much for briefing Flora on the flight—although to be fair he should have known better. It was a gift he envied in her. No matter where they were, what the time was, she would fall asleep at the first sign of motion. She'd slumbered as the taxi took them through the dark, wintry pre-dawn streets of London to the airport, waking long enough to consume an enthusiastic breakfast once they had passed through passport control, only to fall back asleep the second the plane began to taxi down the runway.

And now she was snoozing once again. She would definitely give Sleeping Beauty a run for her money.

He elbowed her. 'Flora, wake up. I want you to take a look at this.'

'Mmm?' She stretched. 'I wasn't asleep, just dozing. Oh! Look at that.' She gazed, awestruck, out of the car windows at the snow-covered mountains, surrounding them in every direction. 'It's just like a Christmas card.'

'What do you think—is it as pretty as you imagined?'

She turned to him, mouth open in indignation, and he stifled a smile. She was far too easy to wind up. 'Pretty? It's so much more than mere prettiness. And look, there are actual chalets. Everywhere!'

'Well observed, Sherlock.'

She didn't react to his sardonic tone. 'I didn't realise Austrian people actually lived in them. I thought it was like thatched cottages. You know, people assume England is all half-timber and cottage gardens but in reality you're far more likely to live in some identikit house on a suburban estate. Oh, I wish I lived in a chalet. They are utterly beautiful.'

'I hope you feel the same way about the hotel.' It was the moment of truth. She had a keen eye, could always see straight through to the heart of his ideas. Would she appreciate the stark simplicity of the hotel, or think it too modern, anachronistic in this natural paradise?

'I always love your designs but this one sounds even more exciting than usual; I have to admit I am really looking forward to seeing it in all its finished glory.'

The car had been steadily taking them along the busy roads that led towards the Tyrolean capital, Innsbruck, but now it veered away to follow a smaller road that wound ahead, climbing into the footholds of the

Alps. The snow lay inches upon inches deep on the sides of the roads.

'Just look at it, look at the light.' Flora's fingers flexed. 'Oh, why didn't I pack my sketchbook? Not that I could really capture it, not the way the sun plays on the snow. Not that light—it's like a kaleidoscope.'

A knot unravelled in the pit of Alex's stomach. She saw what he saw. The interchange between light and the snow. She would get the hotel.

'I have never seen so much snow in my life, not if I took every winter and added them together.' Yep, she was fully awake now, her dark eyes huge as she stared out at the mountains. 'How come England grinds to a halt at just the hint of snow and yet everything here is running normally despite tonnes of the stuff?'

'Because this stuff is what keeps the local economy ticking over. You can't market yourself as a winter wonderland without the cold white stuff.'

'It's like Narnia.' Flora leaned back and stared with enraptured eyes as the car took them higher and higher. On one side the mountains soared high above them, on the other the town was spread out like a child's toy village, the river cutting through the middle like an icily silver scarf. 'How much further? I thought the hotel was in Innsbruck itself.'

'No, it's above the town, close to the ski lifts. The guests are transported in and out at will so they get the best of both worlds. That's the idea anyway, nothing too much effort for them.'

'They are paying enough for it,' Flora pointed out. 'I cannot believe I get to stay somewhere this luxurious. Even the staff quarters are probably one up on a tent in the rain.'

'You're not in the staff quarters. Could you really see Lola in anywhere but a suite? You're doing her job, you get her room. Tomorrow is the soft opening so nobody who stays at the hotel this week is an actual paying guest. We'll be helping to wow travel journalists, bloggers and some influential winter sports enthusiasts.'

He paused, searching for the right words. He knew how awkward she felt in crowds and amongst strangers. 'Flora, it's crucial that they all leave at the end of the week completely bowled over. And it's equally crucial that I leave with fully approved designs. You can manage, can't you? I can't emphasise enough what a big deal this week is. For me, for my firm as well as for Lusso Hotels.'

'Really? How good of you to warn me. I might have put my foot in it otherwise.'

Warning bells tolled through Alex's mind. She sounded frostier than the branches on the trees outside. It was the same tone she'd used the day he'd told her that one day she would grow out of boy bands, the tone she'd used the day he had told her that her first boyfriend wasn't good enough. The same tone she'd used the never to be forgotten day she'd chopped her hair into a pixie cut and he had agreed that, yes, she did look more like a marine than like Audrey Hepburn.

'I only meant...'

'I know what you mean: be professional, don't mess this up. Well, I won't. I need this too, Alex. I might not have founded a "Top Ten Up and Coming Business" while in my twenties, I might not be the bright young thing in my profession. Not yet. I have a lot to prove and this is my big chance. So don't worry about me. I've got this covered.'

Alex opened his mouth to point out that she hid in the kitchen at every single party she attended and would rather face a den full of lions than make small talk but he shut it again. He needed to warn her just how much networking lay ahead of her but not now. He'd wait until she was a little mellower.

Luckily the car turned down a single-track road, cut into the side of the mountain, a dramatic drop on one side showcasing the valley spread out below. 'We're here,' he said instead with some relief. The car slid to a stop and Alex unbuckled his seat belt. 'This *is* Der Steinadler—The Golden Eagle. What do you think?'

She had been looking at him intently, forcing her point home, but at his words she turned and looked out of the window. Her mouth fell open. 'Holy cow. You did this? This is it?'

'Yep, what do you think?'

'I…' She didn't answer, clambering out of the car instead, muttering as her trainer-clad foot sank into the snow and pulling her quilted jacket more closely around her as the sharp chill of the wintry mountain air hit. She turned to him as he joined her. 'All that time spent playing with building blocks as a kid wasn't wasted, huh?'

The hotel was built on the narrow Alpine shelf and looked as if it were suspended above Innsbruck spread out in the valley below, the mountains opposite a living, breathing picture framed through the dramatic windows. Alex had eschewed the traditional chalet design; instead he had used the locally sourced golden wood as a frame for great sheets of glass. The hotel should have looked out of place, too industrial for the tranquil setting, and yet somehow it blended in, the trees and mountains reflecting back from the many panes of glass.

Every time he saw it, it was like being punched in the chest. He couldn't believe he had made his ambitious vision a reality. 'You like?'

Her cheeks were glowing and her large, full mouth curved into a smile. 'I love it. Alex, it's wonderful.'

Relief flooded through him. He wasn't sure why her opinion mattered so much. It wasn't just that she was his oldest friend. No, he trusted her taste. If she didn't get it then he wouldn't have communicated his vision properly. 'Come on, then. Let's go inside. I think you might combust when you see the swimming pool.'

CHAPTER TWO

'SHOW ME AROUND, ALEX! It's not every day a girl gets the architect providing the grand tour.'

'Don't you want to see your room and freshen up first?'

She shook her head. 'No, I'm quite fresh, thank you, and you can conclude the tour at my room.' Flora watched the bellboy pile her bags and coat onto his trolley and sighed happily. 'This is a lot better than lugging a tent over three fields—and then having to go back for the beds. Besides, you want me to get an idea of what the client wants? The best way is for me to take a detailed look around.'

Her first impression was of luxurious comfort rather than cold, chic elegance. The whole interior of the hotel was the same mix of glass and wood as the outside but softened with warm colours and plenty of plants, abstract prints and comfy-looking cushions and sofas to mellow the potentially stark effect.

Alex shrugged off his designer ski jacket, a coat that had probably cost more than Flora's entire suitcase of clothes, and gestured. 'Where do you want to start?'

'Bottom and work our way up?'

'Okay, then, get ready to combust. We're heading down to the pool.'

If Flora didn't actually burst into excitable flames when she saw the swimming pool it was a close-run thing. Housed a floor below the hotel entrance in a space carved out of the alpine shelf, the high-ceilinged pool was enclosed by a dramatic wall of glass. Swimming up to the edge of the pool must feel like swimming to the very edge of the mountain itself, she thought, staring out at the white peaks, as if you might plunge over the side, dive down to the valley below.

The lights were low and intimately flattering, padded sofas were dotted around in discreet corners, and whirlpools, saunas and steam rooms were hidden away behind glazed sliding doors. Tables held jugs of iced water and inviting platters of fruit; thick fluffy towels were piled up on wooden shelves.

'Oh.' She pivoted, taking in every single detail. 'I just want to grab a magazine from that beautifully overstuffed bookshelf, pull on a robe and move into this room for ever. May I? Please?'

But Alex ignored her. 'Come on, next stop the lounge and then I'll take you to your room.'

By the time they reached her room Flora had scribbled down plenty of notes and photographed enough details to give her a good place to start. Obviously the designs she came up with for the Bali hotel would need to be unique, to marry with Alex's vision and the setting, but it was good for her to have an idea of the owner's tastes. She could see why Lola had used the palate she had; it was warming, sumptuous and complemented the natural materials prevalent throughout the building. The soft furnishings and décor were all shades of soft cream, gold, bronze and orange, whether it was the bronze and orange stripes on the cushions or the subtle champagne of the robes and the towels, the same colour in the crisp blouses and shirts worn by the staff.

It was clear that whatever look she designed for the Bali hotel would have to flow through every single detail, no matter how tiny.

'Okay.' Alex stopped at a cream door and gestured. 'This is you.'

Flora held her breath as she slid her keycard into the slot and turned the handle. Yes, she was here to work but there was no reason why she shouldn't enjoy it and after a few long years of penny-pinching and worrying it was rather splendid to be in such indulgent surroundings.

She stepped in and stopped, awestruck. 'Wow. Oh, Alex.'

At one end was the ubiquitous wall of glass and the ubiquitous stunning winter-wonderland view—not that it was getting old. Flora thought she could live here for ever and it would still be as breathtaking as the very first heart-stopping glimpse. The ceiling was high, arched and beamed, the walls a pale gold. The bed, a floating platform, was made up in white linen accented with a bronze silk throw and matching cushions.

Her suitcase had been placed on a low chest at the foot of the huge bed, the cheap, battered case more than a little incongruous in the spacious, luxurious suite. A reminder that this luxury was borrowed, that she had to earn her place here. Now she was here the jeans, jumpers and one good dress she had packed didn't seem enough. Not for the weather or for the hotel itself.

'You like it?' Alex stepped into the room, a smile

playing on his lips as he watched her dart around, peering into every door.

'Like it? Do you realise that this walk-in wardrobe is bigger than my bedroom? In fact this suite is bigger than the house I live in—and I'm including the garden!'

She stopped by the glass screen that separated her bed from the small seating area and stared at the other screen, which stood between her bed and the bath, a huge tub affair perched on a dais right in the centre of the room.

'Thank goodness the toilet's in its proper place and not on show, otherwise this would feel more like an oddly luxurious prison cell than a hotel room!'

'It's looking good.' Alex took a few steps further in and turned slowly. 'I haven't seen most of the suites since they were decorated and the fixtures installed.' He stopped by the bath and ran one finger along the bronze trim. 'At least you'll be clean while you're staying here. It can be so difficult to drag oneself away from the bed to the bathroom, don't you find?'

Flora tested out the sofa, wincing as the rigidity of the cushions rejected her attempt to relax. It looked good but she wasn't sure she would want to actually sit on it for any length of time. 'Was the bath in the centre of the room your idea, Mr Fitzgerald? Have you been watching *Splash* again because I don't think there are many mermaids in the Austrian Alps.'

He grinned. 'Nope, not guilty, the fixtures are all Lola's vision. Apparently this particular suite is the epitome of romantic.'

'That's where I've been going wrong, all that old-fashioned bathing in private nonsense. Although it could be just a *leetle* awkward if I was sharing a room with a friend, not a romantic interest. Is this…erm… motif in all the rooms?'

'Not at all,' he assured her. 'In most of them the baths are tucked away respectably in the room for which they were intended. Okay. If you are ready, they are laying out *Kaffee und Kuchen* for us. I thought we could go and look through my design ideas in the lounge while we have a snack.'

'*Kaffee and Kuchen?* Coffee and cake?' Flora jumped to her feet. 'Never did words so gladden a girl's heart. I'm ready. Lead on, Macduff. Take me to cake.'

The coffee and cakes were laid out in the lounge, the social heart of the hotel, situated on the ground floor at the very front of the building to ensure it took full advantage of the stunning views. Once again Flora stood by the huge floor-to-ceiling windows and her stomach fell away at the terrifying illusion that there was nothing between her and the edge of the mountain.

Clusters of comfy bronze and red velvet sofas and chairs surrounded small tables, bookshelves full of books, games and magazines filled one wall and a huge wood-burning stove was suspended in the middle of the room. Somehow the lounge managed to feel cosy despite its vast size, easily capable of seating the sixty people the boutique hotel was designed to hold.

'Right.' Alex seated himself on one of the sofas and laid out his sketch pad in front of him. It would, she knew, be filled with exquisite pen-and-ink drawings. This was just the first phase, the visionary one. From here he would proceed to blueprints, to computer models, to hundreds of measurements and costings and attention to a million tiny little details that would transfer his vision from the page to reality.

But she knew this, the initial concept, was his favourite part. In many ways neither of them had changed that much from the children they had once been, designing their dream houses, palaces, castles, tree houses, igloos, ships in absorbed companionship.

But in other ways… She ran her eyes hungrily over him, allowing herself one long guilty look at the bent tousled head, at the long, lean body. In other ways they had both changed beyond recognition—not that Alex had noticed that.

No, in his eyes she was still the dirty-faced, scabby-kneed little girl he had met the first time he had run away from home. He'd only made it half a mile along the lane before bumping into Flora and together they'd built him a den to stay in. Planned for Flora to bring him bread and milk and a blanket.

He loved her, she knew that. And there weren't very many people who could claim that. Outside Flora's own family probably none.

He just wasn't *in* love with her. There had been a time, way back when, she had wondered. But her one attempt to move things up a level had ended messily.

Flora curled her fingers into fists, trying to block out the memory. Block out the way he had put his hands on her shoulders, not to pull her in closer but to push her away. Block out the look of utter horror in his eyes.

He had kissed a lot of girls that summer and subsequent springs, summers, autumns and winters. But not Flora; never Flora.

And here she was, all these years later, still hoping.

Pathetic. One day she'd stop being in love with him. She just had to try a little harder, that was all.

Neither of them noticed the light outside fading, replaced by the gradual glow of the low, intimate hotel lighting. It wasn't until the huge Christmas tree dominating the far corner of the lounge sprang into brightly lit colour that Alex sat back, took off his work glasses and rubbed his eyes.

'So, what do you think?'

Flora chewed on her lip. 'I think I really need to take a trip out there to fully get your vision,' she said solemnly. 'At least three weeks, all-expenses-paid.'

'Play your cards right, convince Camilla Lusso that you can do this and you will do,' he pointed out. 'I told you that part of the brand promise is ensuring each hotel is both unique and part of its environment—and to leave as small a carbon footprint as possible. You'll need to source as much from local suppliers as possible.'

'Very worthy.' Flora pulled the pencil out of her hair and allowed the dark brown locks to fall onto her shoulders. 'Will the guests arrive in a canoe, paddled only by their own strokes with the help of a friendly wind?'

He bit back a grin. Trust Flora to see the big glaring hole in the whole eco-resort argument. 'Unlikely. But it's a start, don't knock it.'

'If I get to travel to Bali I promise not to give it as much as a second thought. Do you think they'll go for it? The glass-bottomed hotel?'

'I don't know. They've already decided to set the hotel in the rainforest—which is a pretty interesting decision. After all, most people expect a sea view in a place like Bali, so I really want to still have that water element. And although it would be nice to build out over the sea the local laws won't allow it—and the whole "surrounded by the sea" concept is a little "honeymoon in the Maldives" obviously.'

'Obviously.' Flora sounded wistful and he nudged her.

'Come on, work with me here. If I can't convince you I'm doomed. I actually think this might be even more breathtaking. Not just building over the lagoon but using glass floors to make the lagoon part of the hotel—the water as one of the design materials.'

'And I can bring that detail to bear inside. The lovely local dark woods and the natural blues and greens. Yes.' She nodded. 'I can work with that. Thanks, Alex.'

Alex pushed himself to his feet and walked over to the bar, a long piece of polished oak on the other side of the room. 'Glass of wine or a stein of Austrian beer?'

'I'm not sure what a stein is. A glass of white wine please.'

Alex ordered their drinks from the barmaid who was hovering discreetly at the far end.

He carried their drinks over and handed her the wine, taking a long appreciative gulp of his own cold beer, a heavy weight in the traditional stein glass. 'Cheers, or should I say *prost*?'

She raised her glass to his. 'Cheers. You were right. A job like this is just what I need.'

Alex paused. He knew it wasn't easy for her, younger sister to such high-achieving siblings, daughter of well-known experts in their fields. He knew her mother's well-intentioned comments on everything from Flora's hair to her clothes cut her to the quick. He knew how self-conscious she was, how she hated her conspicuous height, her even more conspicuous figure, her dramatically wide mouth and showy Snow White colouring. She really truly didn't know how stunning she was—when she wasn't hunching herself inside one of the sacklike dresses or tunics she habitually wore.

But she was twenty-nine now. It was time she believed in herself.

'You could have had work before,' he pointed out. 'How many times have I asked you to freelance for me? You were just too proud to accept—or too afraid.'

Her mouth shut again, her lips compressed into a tight, hurt line. 'There's nothing wrong with wanting to stand on my own two feet.'

'No, there isn't.' He fought the urge to backtrack; he'd always hated upsetting her in any way. 'But there's nothing wrong with accepting a helping hand either. Sometimes I think you're so determined to prove yourself you actually hold yourself back.'

Her eyes blazed. 'I can't win, can I? Once you accused me of not knowing my own mind, now you're telling me I'm too stubborn.'

'If you mean I told you not to apply to vet school then I stand by that. Just like I stand by telling you not to take that job at Village Inns. I still don't know why you did.'

Flora set her wine down on the table and glared at him. 'Why were you so set against it? No one lands the perfect job straight from college. It made sense to get some experience.'

'No, but your heart was never in that job, just like it wasn't in veterinary medicine. You applied for that to please your mum.'

Flora jumped to her feet and walked over to the window, staring out at the dark before turning to face him. 'So you were right that I wasn't vet material. Right that I couldn't hack it. So it took me a while to work things out. Excuse me for not being driven, focused on the goal like you, Mr Super Architect of the Year.'

He ignored the dig. So he was driven. Wasn't that the point? It was why they were here after all. 'Art school was far more you—but then you took the first safe job you could find even though designing those trendy pubs and twee restaurants drove you crazy. And when that didn't work out you went into lockdown mode. Took it personally, as if *you* had failed.'

'No, I didn't!' She paused, looked down at the floor. 'Well, maybe a little.'

'Look, Flora. You know the last thing I want to do is hurt you. In any way.' It was truer than she knew. Alex didn't know where he would have ended up, what he would have been without Flora's friendship. It was why he had never been able to confide in her, not fully. He had never wanted to see the warmth in her eyes darken and chill. To be judged by her and found wanting.

God knew he judged himself enough for both of them.

'Thank goodness.' She looked at him directly then, her blue eyes shadowed. 'I'd hate to hear what you would say if you wanted to hurt me.'

'I just want you to follow your dreams. *Yours*, not your mother's or mine or trying to beat your sister at her own game. I want you to go for what you want. Do what makes you happy. Not hang back for fear it doesn't work out or in case you get knocked down again. Take each rejection as a challenge, get back up and try again. Harder each time. Here is your chance. Seize it.'

'I was trying to before my temporary boss and arrogant best friend decided to have a go at me.' But the anger had drained out of her voice. 'I'm not so good at the seizing, Alex. We didn't all get the Masters of the Universe education, you know.'

Alex had hated every single day at his elite boarding school. The only thing in its favour was that every day he had spent there was a day not at home. 'I dropped out of sixth form to slum it at college with you so I missed the Advanced World Domination course. But I tell you what I do know, Flora. We're all mostly faking it. Tell yourself you can do it, tell yourself you deserve it and make yourself go for it. That's the secret. Now, I don't know about you but those cakes seem like hours ago and I know the kitchen is hoping to do a last trial run on us before the guests arrive tomorrow. Let's go eat.'

'That was amazing. Although I don't feel I can ever eat again.' Flora patted her stomach happily and curled up on the velvet sofa.

'Not that cosy though, just the two of us in a room set for sixty.'

'Oh, I don't know.' It had felt a bit incongruous at first, the two of them waited on alone in a vast room, but a couple of glasses of the delicious wine had soon set her at her ease and when Alex suggested they went back into the lounge for one last look at the plans and a *digestif* her original plans for a bath and an early night were forgotten.

She had only drunk schnapps once before and it

hadn't been pretty. But it was the national drink, after all; it would be rude not to sample it.

Alex was leaning back in his chair, his glass held loosely in his hand. Flora was usually so very careful about how she looked at him. If he ever caught her staring. If he ever guessed how she felt…

Alex was her oldest and best friend. His was the shoulder she cried on after break-ups and heartbreaks. He was her go-to person for advice. He knew all her vices and nearly all her secrets. But there were two things that lay between them. Two secrets; a chasm that could never be bridged.

He had never confided in her why he had left home, and why he was so against any kind of reconciliation with his father.

And she had never told him that she loved him.

Not as a friend, as a confidant, but in every way it was possible for a woman to love a man. Sometimes Flora thought she had fallen for him that very first day, that skinny red-headed boy with a look of determination on his face—and desolation in the stormy eyes. The hair had long since darkened to a deep auburn, his body had filled out in all the right places, but he was still determined.

And he hid it well, but at heart he was still as alone as he had been then. Not one of his girlfriends had ever got through to him. Was that why she had never told him how she felt? He was right, she *was* afraid.

Afraid of not being good enough for him. Afraid he would turn away in disgust and horror, just as he had all those years ago. Afraid that this time she would lose him for ever.

Flora downed the schnapps in one satisfying gulp,

choking a little as the pungent, sharp liquor hit the back of her throat. Hmm, not as bad as she'd thought. In fact, that warm feeling at the pit of her stomach was really quite pleasant. She refilled her glass.

She gazed into the amber depths as his words rolled round and round her mind. *'Get back up and try again. Tell yourself you deserve it.'* He was right. She never had. She took every rejection as a final blow whether it was work or her heart. It was easier not to put herself out there. Easier to lock herself away and hope.

Hope that somebody would see her Internet site and say, 'Hey, you amazing talent, come work for me!'

Hope that Alex would turn round, look into her eyes and realise, just like that, she was the only girl for him.

Hope that her parents would tell her that she made them proud.

She just sat back and let life pass her by. Hoping.

Flora raised her glass and downed the schnapps. It wasn't quite as fierce this time. Not as hot. More…mellow. She had definitely underrated schnapps.

She reached out and closed her hand around the bottle, wondering why it took a few goes to clasp it properly, and pulled it towards her.

'Another one?' Alex's eyebrows rose. 'We had quite a lot of wine at dinner. Are you sure?'

'Yes, Dad.' She grinned at him. 'I like your hair like that.'

Alex touched his head, staring at her in confusion. 'My hair?'

Flora put her head to one side. 'It's all glowy with the Christmas lights behind you. Like a halo. Angel Alex.'

She didn't see him move but the next thing she knew

he was by her side, one firm hand on hers, removing the bottle from her grasp.

'If you're talking about angels then you have definitely had enough. Come along.' He slid the bottle out of her reach and pulled at her hand, helping her rise to her feet. Flora swayed and caught his shoulder and he grimaced. 'Bed time for you. I forgot you and schnapps don't mix.'

'We mix just fine.' Flora regained her footing and stopped still, her hand still on his shoulder. She loved that Alex was taller than her. She looked up at him, his dearly familiar face so close to hers. The greeny-grey of his changeable eyes, the long lashes, the faded freckles on his nose, the curve of his cheekbones. The curve of his mouth. So close. Kissing distance. Her stomach clenched, the old exquisite pain. And yet all she had to do was stand on her tiptoes, just a little, and move in.

His words ran through her mind. *Try again. Harder each time.*

Maybe that was all she had to do. Try again. Maybe Alex was waiting for her to step forward, to make the move. Maybe it had always been within her power to change things but she had just never dared.

Maybe…

Before she knew it the words were tumbling out, words she had spent the last thirteen years keeping locked up deep, deep inside, more plaintive than demanding. 'Why didn't you kiss me back?'

'What?' His eyes widened in alarm and he took a step back. She moved with him, still holding on as if he were all that kept her anchored. He was lean, almost rangy, but there was a solidity when she touched him, the feel of a man who was fighting fit. 'What are you talking about?'

'All those years ago. Why did you push me away? Have you never wondered what would have happened if you hadn't?'

'It's never crossed my mind.' But his eyes shifted to her mouth as he spoke.

He's lying. Her throat dried as she realised what that meant.

He *had* thought about it. And that changed everything. Almost unconsciously she licked her lips; his throat tightened as he watched the tip of her tongue dip onto her top lip and, at the gesture, her heart began to beat faster.

Emboldened, Flora carried on, her voice low and persuasive. 'All those nights we stayed up talking till dawn. When we visited each other at uni we slept in the same bed, for goodness' sake. The tents we've shared... Have you never wondered, not even once? What it would be like? What *we'd* be like?'

'I...' His eyes were on hers, intent, a heat she had never seen before beginning to burn bright, melting her. 'Maybe once or twice.' His voice was hoarse. 'But we're not like that, Flora. We're more than that.'

Flora was dimly aware that there was something important in his words, something fundamental that she should understand, but she didn't want to stop, not now as the heat in his eyes intensified, his gaze locking on hers. If she pushed it now, he would follow. She knew it; she knew it as she knew him.

She also knew that whatever happened the consequences would be immense. There would be repercussions. Last time they had pretended it had never happened. It was unlikely that would happen again; their friendship would be altered for ever. Could she live with that?

Could she live without trying? Laugh it off as lack of sleep and too much schnapps? Now she had come so far…

No, not when he was looking at her like that. Heat and questions and desire mingling in his eyes, just as she had always dreamed. *I want you to go for what you want.* That was what he'd told her.

She wanted him.

'Kiss me, Alex,' she said softly. And before he could reply or pull away Flora stepped in, put her other hand on his shoulder and, raising herself on her tiptoes, she pressed her mouth to his.

CHAPTER THREE

HE SHOULD HAVE walked away. No, he *should* walk away, there was still time. Only there wasn't. Time was slowing, stopping, converging right here, right now on this exact spot, somewhere above Innsbruck. All that was left was this moment. The feel of her mouth against his, her hands, tentative on his shoulders. He shouldn't, he couldn't—and yet he was…

Because it was all he had dreamed it might be, those shameful, secret dreams. The crossing of boundaries, the touching the untouchable. Her touch was light, her kiss sweetly questioning and despite everything Alex desperately wanted to give her the answers she was seeking.

He stood stock-still for one long moment, trying to summon up the resolve to walk away, but the blood hummed through his veins, the noise drowning out the voice of caution; her sweet, vanilla scent was enfolding him and he was lost. Lost in her. Lost in the inevitable.

With that knowledge all thought of backing off, backing out disappeared. One hand slipped, as if of its volition, around the curve of her waist, pulling her in tightly against him, the other burying itself in the hair at the nape of her neck; a heavy, sweet smelling cloud.

And Alex took control. He kissed her back, deepening, intensifying the kiss as the blood roared in his ears and all he could feel was the sweetness of her mouth, the softness of her body, pliant against his.

Her touch was no longer tentative, one arm tight around his neck. Holding his head as if she didn't dare let him go. The other was on the small of his back, working at the fabric of his shirt, branding him with the fevered heat of her touch.

If she touched his flesh he would be utterly undone.

Like the animal he was he could take her here and now. Not caring about the consequences, not caring that they weren't in a private space. That the staff could walk in any minute. That once again there would be no going back.

That once again he could take things too far. And once again he could lose everything.

He had learned nothing.

Alex wrenched his mouth away; the taste of her lingered, intoxicatingly tempting on his tongue. But he had to sober up. 'Flora.' His breath was ragged as he stared into her confused dark eyes. 'I...'

'Am I interrupting something?' Both Alex and Flora jumped slightly as the rich, Italian tones, tinged with a hint of mockery, floated across the hotel lounge. Alex didn't need to look around to know who he would see—the owner of this hotel and the woman who had employed him to design three more, Camilla Lusso.

'*Buongiorno*, Camilla.' He took a deep, shuddering breath, willing his overheated body to cool, his spinning brain to slow. 'I wasn't expecting to see you until tomorrow.' He turned, fixing a cool, professional smile on his face as he greeted his biggest and most influential client.

'That's rather clear.' Still that hint of mockery in her voice, her eyes assessing and cool as she looked at Flora, clearly not missing a single detail as she took in the mussed hair, the swollen lips, the wrinkles in the baggy dress.

Camilla Lusso could have been any age between thirty-five and fifty-five although Alex suspected she was at the top end of the age range, but her expensively styled hair, subtle make-up and chic wardrobe made her seem timeless. A glossy, confident and successful woman. A professional woman who demanded top-class professionalism from everyone who worked with and for her.

Flora was supposed to be impressing her, not being found drunkenly making out with the architect.

Why now? Why tonight after all these years? He could blame the schnapps, he could blame the mountains framed through the windows, the warmth of the fire burning in the stove. It was a scene out of *Seduction 101*. But the only person he could really blame was himself. He should have backed off, backed away, laughed off the conversation—not been struck dumb with the thought of an alternate world. A world in which he might have been worthy of the adoration and desire shining out of Flora's dark eyes.

He had to fix this. Camilla's eyes had narrowed as she assessed Flora. If she found her wanting in any way then Alex knew she'd turn her away, no matter how good her work.

'I owe you an apology, Camilla. When I recommended Flora to you I wanted you to appreciate her for her own talent and so...' He paused, searching for the right words, the right way to make this all right. There was only one way. To make the whole embarrassing scene seem perfectly normal.

'I didn't tell you that we're dating. I'm sorry, I should have mentioned it but we agreed to be discreet this week, to put our relationship on the back burner.' He allowed himself a wry smile. 'Starting from tomorrow.' He took Flora's hand in his, pinching her in warning, hoping the shock of the last five minutes had sobered her up. *Play along.*

To his relief she picked up his cue. 'Pleased to meet you. I am very excited to be working with you and to help breathe life and colour into Alex's designs. I didn't realise I would have the honour of meeting you this evening otherwise...' Flora gestured at her wrinkled dress, at her mussed-up hair '...I would have made more of an effort.'

'But no.' Camilla's face had relaxed—as much as her tightened skin would allow—into a smile. 'The apology is all mine. I should have warned you that I had changed my plans. I have interrupted your last evening of privacy.'

'Oh, no.' Flora's cheeks were pink and her hand hot in Alex's. 'Not at all, we have mostly been working...' Her voice trailed off at the knowing look on Camilla's face as she said the last word.

'It all looks absolutely fantastic, just as I envisioned.' Alex took over the conversation, taking pity on Flora. 'And the staff seem to know their roles perfectly—not that I would expect anything else from a Lusso Hotel. What time can we expect the guests tomorrow?'

Camilla accepted a glass of wine from a discreetly

hovering waiter and sat down on one of the chairs by the stove. 'We're expecting the first to arrive after lunch tomorrow. I am so pleased you agreed to spend this opening week with us, Alex. The majority of the guests are influential travel journalists and bloggers and I am sure they are going to have lots of questions about your inspiration for this beautiful building. But please, not all work, eh? You must take full advantage of the facilities while you are here.'

Again she swept a knowing look up and down the pair of them. Alex gritted his teeth. 'It's my absolute pleasure. It's not often I get to spend so much time in a building I designed after completion. It will be really interesting to watch it fulfil its purpose.' Alex stole a glance at Flora. She was no longer flushed, rather she had turned pale, as if all the life had been leached out of her apart from the dark circles shadowing her eyes. 'However, if I'm to ensure the Bali designs are perfect for our meeting at the end of the week and socialise appropriately I think we'd better turn in. We were on the road at five a.m.'

'Of course. I look forward to seeing your designs, Miss Buckingham. Alex has been singing your praises. I can't wait to be impressed.'

Flora had thought she knew all about humiliation. She was the high priestess of it, dedicated to short sharp bursts at regular intervals. There was the awful day her university boyfriend announced he was in love with her sister; the even more awful day her subsequent boyfriend admitted he was in love with Alex; the time she thought her last boyfriend had been proposing when he had, in fact, been breaking up with her.

She had been going to refuse him, of course. But that *so* wasn't the point.

Her redundancy and the nasty smile on Finn's face as he had watched her gather up her pitifully small box of belongings and get escorted from the building like a thief.

Yep. High priestess of humiliation. Case in point: the week of catastrophes she had just experienced.

But, nope. None of them equalled the scene just now. She would rather sit on a hundred strange men's laps on any sort of public transport than relive the scene she had just left.

Flora squeezed her eyes shut as if she could block out the memory by will alone. *Kiss me, Alex.*

Oh, but he had. And it had been…it had been…

Flora flopped onto the bed and searched for the word. It had been wonderful. Right until the moment he had pushed her away with horror in his eyes and disgust on his face. That bit had sucked.

No. That had been the worst moment of her life. Bar none. Much, *much* worse than last time. At least she hadn't asked him, *begged* him to kiss her then. She'd just misjudged a moment. She should have learned her lesson. She wasn't what he wanted. Not in that way. Not then, not now.

She could never face him again. She should pack her bags and escape down the mountain, at night, in thick snow. She couldn't ski, didn't have a car and Innsbruck was several miles below. But that didn't matter, the exit plan itself mere details. The important thing was that she needed to escape and to pretend she had never ever laid eyes on Alex Fitzgerald with his crooked smile and red-brown curls.

But then he would spend Christmas alone. And without her family what did he have? He would never show it, of course, never say anything but she *knew*. She saw the look of relief when he stepped through the front door into her parents' hall. Saw him almost physically set down whatever burdens he carried around along with his overnight bag. Watched him relax, really relax, as he talked sport with Horatio—not that Horry had much of a clue but he tried to keep up. Watched the laughter lurk in his eyes as he half teased, half flirted with Minerva in a way no other mortal, not even her own husband, could get away with.

He helped her dad in the kitchen, talked through work problems with her mum and was on Flora's side. Always.

No, he couldn't be allowed to leave them. She would just have to grin, bear it and blame the schnapps. Not for the first time.

And she would work hard. She would blow the caramel-haired, caramel-clad, tight-skinned Camilla Lusso's designer socks off with her colour schemes, materials and designs. She would make Alex proud and this would be just a teeny footnote in their history. Never to be mentioned again. Never to be...

What now? A knock on the door interrupted her fervent vowing. Flora pushed herself off the bed, smoothed down her hair. *Please don't let it be Camilla Lusso.* There was no way she was ready for round two. 'Come in.'

A bellboy pushed the door open and smiled politely. 'Excuse me, Fraulein. I have Herr Fitzgerald's bags if now is convenient?'

If now was *what*?

'I beg your pardon?'

'Frau Lusso asked me to move Herr Fitzgerald's bags into your room.' He opened the door a little wider, pushing a trolley through heaped with Alex's distinctive brown leather bags.

'But…' Flora shook her head. Was she dreaming? Hallucinating? Had she been drinking absinthe? That would explain a lot. Maybe the whole hideous evening had been some weird absinthe-related dream.

'Mr Fitzgerald has his own room.'

'Not any more,' Alex stepped into the room, just behind the bellboy. His voice was light but there was a grim set to his face, his eyes narrowed as he stared at her. 'Camilla very kindly said there was no need for us to be discreet and we absolutely shouldn't spend the week before Christmas apart. Nice bath. Do you want first dibs or shall I?'

'You can't stay here.' Flora sank back onto the bed and stared at the pile of bags. It was most unfair; how did Alex have proper stuff? They were more or less the same age. How had he managed to turn into an actual functioning grown-up with matching luggage filled with the correct clothes for every occasion?

'What do you suggest?' He seemed unruffled as he opened up the first, neatly packed suitcase and began to lay his top-of-the-line ski kit out onto the other side of the bed.

'Well, we'll just say we're not ready for this step. Say we're waiting.'

'We're waiting?' An unholy glint appeared in his eye. 'How virtuous.'

'People do…' Her cheeks were hot and she couldn't

look at him. All desire to discuss anything relating to love or sex or kissing with Alex Fitzgerald had evaporated the minute she had caught the disgust in his eyes. Again.

'They do,' he agreed, picking up his pile of clothes and disappearing into the walk-in wardrobe with them. 'Why haven't you unpacked?'

Flora blinked, a little stunned by his rapid turn of conversation. 'I have. Those clothes there? They're mine.'

'But where are your ski clothes? You can't hit the slopes in jeans.'

Flora winced. She had a suspicion that hitting would be the right verb if she did venture out on skis—as in her bottom repeatedly and painfully hitting the well-packed snow. 'I don't ski.'

Alex had reappeared and was shaking his tuxedo out of another of the bags; somehow it was miraculously uncreased. Another grown-up trick. 'Flora, we're here to mingle and promote the hotel. In winter it's a ski hotel. I don't think staying away from the slopes is optional. Did you pack anything for the dinners and the ball?'

The what? 'You didn't mention a ball.' Unwanted, hot tears were pricking at her eyes. Any minute he'd inform her that she needed to cook a cordon-bleu meal for sixty and she would win at being completely inadequate.

'You'll have to go shopping tomorrow. You need a ski outfit, another couple of formal dresses for dinner and something for the ball.'

Flora leaned forward and covered her face with her hands, trying to block the whole scene, the whole evening, the whole day out. If she wished hard enough then maybe it would all go away. She'd wake up and be back on the train, squashed onto the knee of a leering stranger, and she'd know that there were worse ways to make a fool of herself.

'I can't afford to go shopping for things I'll only wear once. I cut up my credit cards so I wouldn't be tempted to go into debt and until I get paid next Friday I have exactly two hundred and eight pounds in my account—and I need to live on next week's pay until I go back to London after New Year. We don't all have expense accounts and savings and disposable income.'

It was odd, arguing over clothes and money when so much had happened in the last half-hour. But in a way it was easier, far better to worry about the small stuff than the huge, shattering things.

'You're doing a job for me so you can use my expense account. We'll go into Innsbruck tomorrow morning.'

His tone suggested a complete lack of interest in pursuing the subject. It just ramped up Flora's own annoyance.

'How very convenient.' She was going for icy hauteur but was horribly afraid she just sounded sulky. 'Typical Fitzgerald high-handedness.' She glared at him. 'Will you stop that, stop unpacking as if you are planning to stay here? Just say you need the space to work and there simply isn't the privacy in this room.' She cast a desperate look at the bath. She'd never dare use it now.

'I tried that and Camilla offered me her office. Look, Flora…' Alex put down the pile of jumpers and ran a hand through his hair. 'If we act like this is a problem then she'll get suspicious. I probably shouldn't have lied but I didn't want her to think badly of you. She's very strict on first impressions and professional behaviour from everyone she works with. You and I know that what happened didn't mean anything, it was just a silly moment that got out of hand…'

Whoosh. His words kicked Flora right in the stomach.

'But look at it from her point of view. It'll look even worse if she thinks we lied. What's done is done, it's only a week.' He was so dismissive, as if this was no big deal. But then it wasn't a big deal for him, was it? 'I'll take the couch. Your virtue is safe with me.'

That was only too clear. Unfortunately.

'Come on.' He grabbed a pillow and a quilt from the wardrobe and took them over to the sofa. 'Let's grab some sleep. It was an early start and we've a busy day tomorrow. You can have first go in the bathroom and tomorrow…' He smiled but it didn't reach his eyes. 'Tomorrow we'll figure out a privacy rota for the bath.'

Flora might have got the bed rather than the low, modern, 'easy on the eye but far less easy on the body' sofa but that didn't make sleep any easier. She'd shared rooms with Alex before. Heck, she'd squeezed into a misleadingly named two-man tent with him many times at festivals. But tonight, hearing the slow, easy sounds of his breathing, sleep eluded her.

Flora was more aware of Alex than she had ever been before in her entire life. She had known him as a lanky, red-headed, freckled boy, sleeping on her floor in his striped boarding-school-approved pyjamas, crying out for his long-dead mother in his sleep. She had watched over him as he began to grow into those long limbs, as muscles formed in his shoulders and legs, as other girls began to cast covert—and not so covert—glances at him. And she had watched him learn to glance back.

But she didn't know him at all tonight.

And yet she couldn't stop sensing him. Sensing the strength in his arms, the artistry in the sensitive fingers. She knew without looking just how his jaw curved, how his hair fell over his forehead, how his eyes were shuttered, hiding his thoughts even from her. Especially from her. She felt every movement as if he were lying right next to her, not with what might as well be acres of polished floorboards between them.

She had to stop loving him once and for all or else she risked losing him for ever. And if she lost him then where would he go? Would he lose himself in short-term relationship after fling, trading one gazelle-like blonde for another as carelessly as if they were new shirts? This whole nightmare was a wake-up call. Alex was right. She had to grow up.

And grow out of loving him.

CHAPTER FOUR

IF ALEX EVER needed a new job then he could always audition for work as an actor. As long as the role demanded he was asleep throughout. He'd spent an entire night rehearsing for just such a role.

Lying still but not so still it seems unnatural? Check. Breathing deeply? Check. Resisting the temptation to add in the odd snore? Check. Playing word games, counting sheep and alpine cows and blades of grass? Oh, yes. Very much check.

Doing anything and everything to keep his mind away from the bed just a few feet away—and from the warm body occupying it? Check. Not dwelling in miserable detail on the long limbs, the tousled hair and the wide, sensual mouth just made for kissing? No, no check. He'd failed miserably.

It was all too reminiscent of his last summer in his father's house. Lying in his bed at home during the long school holidays, wishing he were in the little attic room that Flora's family only half jokingly called his or even, on the worst nights, wishing he were back at school in the dorm room filled with the cheesy, musty scent of adolescent boys.

It wasn't as bad when his father was at home. Then

he just had to listen to the noise. The drinking, the laughing, the noisy lovemaking. But his father was so seldom home.

He didn't know what was worse. The way he had dreaded the creak of the door when his stepmother came in to 'check on him'—or the way he had anticipated it. The musky smell of her shampoo. The way the bed dipped where she sat. The cool caress on his cheek. Her whisper. *'Alex, are you awake?'*

And so he had practised his breathing, kept his eyes lightly closed and pretended that he wasn't. He didn't think he ever had her fooled. And in the end she stopped asking if he was awake. Stopped waiting for permission.

In the end he had stopped pretending.

No. He rolled over, the narrow sofa uncomfortable beneath his hip. No. He mustn't think of his stepmother and Flora in the same way, at the same time. They were nothing alike. He couldn't, wouldn't taint Flora with that association. She was better than that. Better than him.

Far too good for him. He had always known that.

And that was why he had to step away. Just as he had all those years ago. He'd broken up his childhood home with his out-of-control desires. He'd been so lucky that Flora's family had stepped in and offered him a second home, an infinitely better home. He couldn't, absolutely couldn't let desire infiltrate that space. No matter what.

He opened one eye, relieved to see the room turning grey with the pre-dawn light. Slowly, stealthily he slid off the sofa, wincing as he straightened his legs; he felt like the princess must have after her night sleeping on a pea—if her bed had also been too narrow to allow her to turn and a good foot too short. He tiptoed to the door and slid it open. He could have sworn he heard a sigh of relief from Flora as the door slipped shut behind him.

He needed a run. He needed a swim. And most of all he needed a very long and very cold shower while he figured out just how he was going to survive the rest of the week.

'I hope you slept well?' Camilla smiled in welcome when Alex walked into the dining hall two hours later. Darn, he had hoped to have more time to gather his thoughts but it was too late. They were on. Time to be convincing.

'Like a baby,' he lied, searching for a subject that didn't involve sleep, Flora or the suite they were now sharing. 'Look at the morning light in here. It's spectacular.'

'It should be. You designed it that way.'

'That's true, I did.' And he had. But it was always an unexpected joy to see his dreams made real.

The hotel was on the western slopes facing Innsbruck and so the huge windows were always most effective in the evening when the sun hung low in the evening sky and began to set. To counter this and to ensure the dining room didn't feel too dark during the day, Alex had designed it as a glassed-in roof terrace with dramatic skylights positioned to capture as much morning sun as possible. Balconies ran around the entire room so summer visitors could enjoy the warm Alpine sun as they ate.

Like the rest of the hotel the floor was a warm, golden oak, the same wood as the tables and chairs and the long counters that ran along one side. Guests could help themselves to juice, fruit and a continental breakfast; discreetly hovering staff were there to take orders for hot breakfasts. There was no menu; the kitchen was prepared for most requests.

Alex strolled over to the counter and poured himself some orange juice before spooning fresh berries into a bowl. 'Coffee, please.' He smiled at the hovering waitress. 'And scrambled eggs, on rye bread. That's all, thanks.'

He took his fruit and drink over to the square table where Camilla sat, basking in the sunlight like a cat. Her plate was bare and she had a single espresso set in front of her. In the two years they had worked together Alex had never seen her eat. He suspected she ran off caffeine, wine and, possibly, the blood of young virgins.

Camilla took a dainty sip of her espresso. 'I think I made the right call on the mattresses. I know they were expensive, but a hotel like this needs the best, hmm?'

Alex nodded, wishing he had had the opportunity to sample the mattress himself. 'Of course. Your guests wouldn't settle for anything less.'

Camilla eyed him shrewdly. 'A hotel tracksuit? Very good of you to live the brand, Alex.'

He speared a blueberry on a fork. 'Early morning workout. I didn't want to wake Flora. Good idea to have them where anyone could borrow them. I wonder how many people will slip one into their suitcase?'

She shrugged dismissively. 'Let them. They pay enough—and it's all good branding.' She looked over at the door. 'Good morning, Miss Buckingham.'

'Good morning.' Flora wandered over to the table,

a glass of juice in her hand. Alex gave her a quick critical look. She had on more make-up than usual, as if she was trying to conceal the dark shadows under her eyes. It might fool anyone who didn't know her. It didn't fool him for a second.

Had she been pretending to sleep as well?

A little belatedly Alex remembered his role as adoring lover and got to his feet to give her a brief peck on the cheek. He closed his eyes for a brief second as her warm, comforting scent enfolded him. 'Morning.'

Her eyes flew to his. He couldn't read her expression at all. He expected anger, discomfort maybe. Instead all he saw was determination.

Interesting—and very unexpected. She looked different too. Her dark hair pulled back into a loose bun, the dark green tunic belted over her jeans not left to hang shapelessly. She'd accessorised the whole with a chunky silver bead necklace and earrings. She looked smarter, more together.

And, yep, she looked determined. For what he wasn't entirely sure.

'I need to go into Innsbruck this morning,' Flora said after giving her breakfast order to the waitress. Alex's coffee arrived as she did so and he gratefully poured a cup of the delicious, dark, caffeinated nectar, offering it to Flora before pouring his own.

It was all very domesticated.

'I only brought work clothes. I didn't realise that I would be participating in the week's activities.' She smiled over at Alex. 'Apparently I won't be able to avoid learning to ski any longer although I'm sure I'd be far more useful concentrating on all the lovely après-ski activities.'

Camilla drained her cup. 'I think learning to ski is an excellent idea. You really should look at the hotel's ski lodges. I'd be interested to hear what you think of the materials and colours. They're accessible by ski lift but the only way back down the mountain is on the slopes.'

Flora grimaced. 'I can't wait to see them but I have to admit I'm a little nervous about the whole "two bits of plastic on snow" part. I can ice skate but other than that my balance is decidedly wonky. But hey, *carpe diem* and all that. It's good to try new things.'

Alex looked up. What was going on with her? Something was definitely different. Her tone, the way she was dressed. Did this have anything to do with yesterday? Their disagreement—or what happened later?

He should step back. This was what he wanted for her, right? For Flora to be more confident, to start living. And he could do with his space too. To make sure he cleared any lingering sentiments from that darned kiss from his system so they could go back to being easy with each other.

He looked out of the window. It was a glorious day, the sun already high in the blue winter's sky, lighting up the snowy peaks in brilliant colour. He should stay in and work—but the contrast to the damp fog he had left behind in London was almost painful. He yearned to get out, to clear his lungs and his mind in the cold, clear air.

Besides, Flora had never skied before; she had no idea what she needed—an easy target for anyone wanting to hit their sales targets. And it *was* his company's expense account on the line. 'I'll come in with you. Unless I'm needed here, Camilla?'

'No, no.' His client shook her head. 'You have a lovely day. Visit the Christmas markets and enjoy Innsbruck. I'll be doing the tour of the hotel when the guests arrive. I don't need you for that. This evening I am planning a mulled-wine reception and sledge rides for my guests. It would be nice if you were here for the reception so that I can introduce you.'

'Absolutely. Sounds great.'

Flora didn't say anything while Camilla sat with them but as soon as she sauntered away Flora pushed her plate away and narrowed her eyes at Alex. 'I don't need a chaperone. I hate shopping enough as it is. The last thing I want is you hanging around looking bored.'

'I love shopping,' he promised her, reaching over and nicking a small Danish pastry from her plate. 'Don't worry about me. I'll be absolutely fine.'

She smacked his hand as he carried the pastry away. 'I wasn't worrying about *you*. I'm going to try out the swimming pool first while I can be sure of having it to myself if you want to go and get changed.' Her cheeks flushed pink and she avoided his eyes. 'I'll be at least an hour so you have plenty of time to, you know… Change.'

He did know. She didn't want to walk in on him. Last summer when they had shared a tent at the festival she'd been content to stand outside the tent flap and yell an imperious demand to know whether he was decent or not. Those more innocent days were gone, maybe irrevocably. He tried for a light humour. 'We should have a code. Like college students—a ribbon on the door handle means don't come in.'

'I'd be tempted to keep one on there all the time.' But she smiled as she said it, a welcome attempt at the old easy camaraderie. 'I'll see you in the foyer at around eleven. You bring the credit cards and arms ready to carry lots of bags. I'll just bring me.'

It was annoying. She was annoying. Annoying and pitiful. Annoying, pitiful and pathetic. Yep, that just about covered it. Flora grimaced at herself in the half-steamed-up changing-room mirror. She shouldn't be glad that he wanted to spend the day with her. She should tell him to stick his pretend relationship and his begrudging job offer and his expense account—and then she should go spend the day sightseeing before jumping back onto a plane and heading home to re-evaluate her life.

All of it.

But instead she was taking extra care drying her hair and reapplying the make-up she had swum off—and not just because this wide room, tiled in bronze and cream, was the most comfortable and well equipped changing room she had ever set foot in. It was going to be very difficult going back to her local council gym with its uncomfortable shared changing facilities and mouldy grout after the thick towels, rainforest showers and cushioned benches.

No, she couldn't deny it; she was looking forward to the day ahead. Because when all was said and done he was still Alex Fitzgerald and she was still Flora Buckingham. Life-long best mates, blood brothers and confidants and surely one embarrassing drunken episode and one insanely hot kiss couldn't change that.

She wouldn't let it change that.

And she wasn't going to sulk and dwell on his words from the previous afternoon either. Flora's hands stilled as shame shot through her, sharp and hot. He knew her too well, knew how to hit a tender spot, how to pierce right through the armour of denial she had been building up. She was too afraid of messing up. So scared of getting it wrong that she had ignored her instincts and selected purely science A levels in a bid to show her parents that she was as clever as her brother, as her Oxford-educated, high-flying sister.

But in the end what had she proved? Nothing. Quitting her vet course might have been the right thing to do but in the end it had just confirmed all their ideas. That she wasn't quite as robust as the rest of her family, not quite as determined.

Flora resumed drying her hair. For once it was going right, the frizz tamed, the curls softened into waves. Maybe this was a good omen for the weeks ahead. The truth was even now she wasn't sure she knew what she *really* wanted, deep down inside. Was she so determined to find more work as an in-house designer simply because that was easiest, hiding behind somebody else's brief, somebody else's brand? Or should she be trying to step away from the corporate world and indulge what he called her *whimsy*?

The little designs she played with might indeed be whimsical, fantastical even, but they had their fans. After all, her little online shop selling scarves and cushion covers in her designs ticked over nicely. Imagine how it would do if she actually gave it all her attention.

She smoothed some gorgeous-smelling oil onto her hair and twisted it back into the loose bun. Three hotels, three design briefs. This could buy her the time and income she needed to find out where her heart lay.

Or was she going to wander from dream to dream for ever, never quite committing? Always afraid of failing. Of falling.

No. This week was a wake-up call in all kinds of ways. And she was going to make the most of it.

She smiled her thanks at the chambermaid who was already collecting her towels and returning the changing room into its pristine state ready to wow the expected guests. Flora knew that along with the journalists and bloggers a few influential winter-sports fanatics had been invited; a couple of ex-Olympians and several trust-fund babies. They would expect only the best even from a free jolly like this one and Camilla and her staff were determined they would get it.

Maybe that could be her career? Travelling from luxury hotel to luxury hotel to be pampered and indulged in the hope that she would say something nice about it. How long would it take to get bored of that? She was more than willing to find out.

She wandered up the stairs to the large, high-ceilinged foyer. It would be the first impression of the hotel for all future guests and so it had to set the standard: light, spacious, with quality in every fitting. Would the people expected here later notice—or did they take such attention to detail for granted? It would be nice to be that jaded…

Yes. Nice was the word. Although she was a long, long way from jaded. Driven into Innsbruck, attentive service in all the shops and, best of all, the hotel driver stayed ready to collect her bags and whisk them back. If only she'd been buying something useful like fabric rather than over-priced, over-stuffed shiny clothes.

'I could get used to this,' Flora confided, watching her bags get loaded into the small hotel city car, ready to be delivered back to her room—their room—and hung up ready for her return. 'I think I was always made to be part of the other half.'

'It's not the other half,' Alex pointed out. 'It's the other one per cent and, I don't know, I think it would do them good to carry their own bags some of the time.'

'Don't spoil my fairy tale. Expense accounts and my every whim taken care of? I feel like a Christmas Cinderella.'

'And who am I? Buttons?'

He hadn't cast himself as Prince Charming. Flora ignored the stab of disappointment and linked arms with him, just as she usually would. *Act normal, remember?* Alex gave a barely susceptible start before falling into step with her.

'No,' she said sweetly. 'You are my fairy godmother. I can just see you in pink tulle.'

He spluttered a surprised bark of laughter and despite herself her heart lifted. They could get back on track even if they did have to share a room. As long as neither of them used that darned bathtub. It had been the first thing she had seen when she opened her eyes that morning, taunting her with its suggestion of decadence.

'I don't remember the fairy godmother having such a hard time convincing Cinders to try on clothes.'

'That's because she wasn't making Cinders wear clothes that made her arse look huge, her bosom matronly and her hips look capable of bearing triplets. Ski clothes and curves do not mix. In fact, winter clothes and curves don't mix.' She had allowed Alex—or rather

Alex's firm—to buy her the thermal turtle neck and leggings, the waterproof padded trousers and jacket, the fleece neck warmer, hat and gloves but had felt the whole time like a tomboy toddler being forced into a frilly bridesmaid dress. At least she had talked him out of the hot pink and gone for a less garish turquoise and white look. But she was pretty sure she'd still look and feel like a child playing dress up.

At least she was fairly happy with the dresses she had bought, even the formal dress for the ball. Actually, if she was honest with herself, she was secretly delighted with it—although whether she'd actually have the courage to wear it in public was a whole other matter. The sales assistants had been enthusiastic but then again that was their job. Just look how gushing the saleswoman had been when she had tried on the Bavarian-barmaid-inspired bridesmaid dress for Minerva's wedding. Even her father hadn't been able to summon up a heartfelt compliment for that particular outfit.

A little part of her wished she hadn't sent Alex away for what he rather insultingly called 'a restorative coffee' when she had started dress shopping, But it had been bad enough having him there assessing her while she tried on padded trousers. The thought of his eyes skimming over her in dress after dress was far too uncomfortable an image.

Innsbruck had no shortage of designer boutiques and stores but Flora had felt even more out of place in them than she had in the bustling board shops. It had been such a relief when she had stumbled on the vintage shop with floors and floors of second-hand and reproduction clothes. Usually she felt too self-conscious to wear anything that drew attention to herself—and with her height vintage always made a statement—but in this town of winter glamour it had been a choice between vintage inspired or designer glitz. No choice at all.

And it *was* a glamorous town. The old, medieval streets surrounded by snow-capped mountains gave Innsbruck a quaint, old-fashioned air but there was a cosmopolitan beat to the old Tyrolean town. People came here to shop at the Christmas markets and to enjoy the myriad winter sports aimed at all levels. There was a palpable sense of money, of entitlement, of health and vigour.

'Look at them all.' Flora stared down the main street at what seemed like a sea of glowing, youthful faces. 'It's like they've been ordered out of a catalogue. I've never seen so many gorgeous people.'

'Even him?' Alex indicated a man sitting in the window of a café, his sunglasses perched high on his unnaturally smooth face, his skin the colour of a ripened orange. Flora bit her lip, trying not to laugh.

'Or her?' He nudged her in the direction of a skeletally thin woman, swathed from neck to ankle in what Flora devoutly hoped were fake furs, incongruously bright yellow hair topping her wrinkled face.

'Maybe not everyone,' she conceded. 'But most people seem so at home, like they *belong*.' No one else bulged out of quilted jackets, or had hair flattened by their hats. The girls looked wholesomely winsome in thick jumpers and gilets, their hair cascading from underneath their knitted hats, their cheeks pink from the cold. The men were like Norse gods: tall, confident as they strode down the snow-filled medieval streets. Alex fitted the scene like the last piece of a jigsaw. Flora? She was the missing piece from a different jigsaw that had somehow got put in the wrong box.

'What did I tell you, Flora? No one really belongs, they just act like they do. You just need to stand tall and look people in the eye.'

'Not easy when everyone is wearing shades.' It was a feeble joke and Alex just looked at her, concern in his eyes. She winced; somehow she had managed to provoke almost every response going in the last forty-eight hours. She made herself smile. *See, joking.*

'We don't have to be back at the hotel for a few hours yet, you're respectably kitted out and I have even managed to clear my emails while you were dress hunting. What do you fancy doing?'

Flora pulled at her coat. 'I should work. What if Camilla wants to see my ideas? All I have are a few online mood boards.'

'That's all she wants at this stage. I can promise you, she'll change her mind a million times and in the end your first concept will be the winner.'

'Then why drag me here for the week?' Oh, no. He hadn't forced her over here as some sort of intervention, had he? He could just imagine him on the phone to her mother, reassuring her that he had it all in hand. That he would put an end to this temping nonsense quick smart.

'Not that I'm not grateful...' she added unconvincingly. Just think, if he'd left her alone she could have been cosying up to the man on the train again tomorrow morning. Maybe she'd misjudged him and his grabby hands. He might just be plain-speaking and tactile. They could have told their kids and grandkids about how they'd met on an overcrowded commuter train a week before Christmas. Just like a film.

'Flora, Camilla can snap her fingers and have the best at the touch of a button. It's the story, the package that she needs to see. She loves that I'm young, terribly English, well educated, have my own firm and I'm tipped for the top.' His laugh was a little self-conscious. 'It's an easy sell, makes a good interview, adds that extra little detail when she's publicising the hotel. You're here so she can see that you can do the same—that's why it's so important that you look right, that you say the right things.'

That she what? Panic churned in her stomach, the snow dazzling as she stared at the ground, her eyes swimming. 'I'm here to schmooze? You didn't tell me that!'

'I didn't hide it. You know who the invited guests are. Look, Camilla knows I wouldn't recommend anyone who wasn't talented and creative. She needs to see that you can mingle with the right people, chat to journalists, help sell her creations. And, Flora, you can.'

'But I can't...' He wanted her to what? *Chat to journalists? Sell?* Flora gulped in air, rooted to the spot, oblivious to the crowds passing her by.

'You've done it before.' He didn't add *Many times* but the words hung in the air. 'At least this time you won't have to baste chickens or pipe icing while you're talking.'

Flora still couldn't joke about her childhood spots in front of the camera. To be honest she wasn't sure she ever would reach that state. 'Can you imagine what it was like going into school after Dad's shows aired? Me this tall and this...' She sketched an arc around her chest. She had been the tallest in her class from nursery onwards—and the most developed from the end of primary school. 'The last thing I want to do is talk about me, you know that. And if I chat to journalists they'll know who I am…'

'And they'll love it. Youngest daughter of food writer and TV chef, Ted Buckingham and TV doctor Jane Buckingham? They won't try and catch you out, Flora. We're talking travel sections, maybe some lifestyle blogs. I promise you. It'll be a lot less stressful than your dad's Internet videos of family get-togethers.'

'Horry says neurosurgery is less stressful than the Internet get-togethers.'

'All you have to do this week is have fun. Try to ski, chat to people, talk colours and materials and be enthusiastic. If Camilla offers you the commission then you can worry about the other side of it later, but if I were you I'd think about how a little publicity in the right places could send your stock sky-high. Come on, Flora. You never know, you might even enjoy it. Now, Christmas markets or ice skating? Your choice.'

Flora took in a deep shuddering breath. Alex was right, if he'd mentioned any of this before she would have hightailed it back to London before he could say *prost*. Minerva positively fed off their parents' fame, using it as a springboard when she opened her PR firm, and Horry was oblivious. Flora, on the other hand, had always found it mortifying, whether appearing on her dad's cookery programme or listening to her mother talk about Flora's first period on national TV. She wasn't sure the scars from that particular episode would ever fade.

Still, silver linings and all that—she hadn't thought

about the kiss or their sleeping arrangements once in the last half-hour. It turned out there were only so many things even she could stress about.

'I haven't been ice skating for years.'

'Indoors or outdoors?'

Flora looked around, at the blue sky, the sun warm despite the chill of the air. 'Oh, outside, please.'

'Come on, then, I challenge you to a backwards-skating race. Loser buys the mulled wine.'

CHAPTER FIVE

THIS WHOLE WEEK was doomed. Alex had known it from the minute he'd got Lola's email. Camilla Lusso liked to work with people she could show off. Extroverted, larger than life, Lola had fitted the bill perfectly. Flora? Not so much. But she did have the training, after all. It wasn't as if he had thrown her in unprepared; she'd been brought up with camera crews, journalists and interviewers traipsing through the house, had been expected to converse intelligently at dinner parties and receptions since she'd hit double figures.

Of course, that didn't mean she *enjoyed* any of it. Alex knew all too well that if he'd been completely honest with her at the start she'd have run a mile.

Maybe that would have been for the best. No Flora, no kiss, no sleepless night.

Because, try as he might, he just couldn't shake the memory of the warmth of her mouth, the sweetness of her lips, the way his hands had held her as if she were made just for him, every curve slotting so perfectly against him.

There had been far too many kisses from far more women than Alex cared to remember. Not one had stayed with him, not for a second. This one he could still taste. He had a feeling he would still feel it imprinted on his lips in fifty years' time.

And it was all he could do not to put his hands on her shoulders, turn her around and kiss her once again. And this time there would be no stepping back. Not ever.

But he couldn't. She deserved better than him. She needed someone who wasn't dead inside, someone who could match her sweetness and generous spirit. Sometimes Alex thought that Flora could be the saving of him—but he'd be the damning of her. His father's last words echoed around his brain yet again.

You taint everything you touch. You were born bad and grew up worse.

And his father was right.

But he wouldn't taint Flora, never Flora.

'I haven't been ice skating in years.' She worried away at her lower lip as they walked through the twisty streets. 'Not since we used to go to the ice discos on a Friday night. Not that you did much skating. You were usually in a corner snogging some random girl.'

He had been. A different girl each week. The worse he'd behaved, the more they'd seemed to find him irresistible. He had hated himself every single Friday night as he'd smiled across at yet another hopeful— but it hadn't stopped him moving in while last week's conquest had watched from a corner.

Had anything changed? He went in for relationships now, not kisses in a booth by an ice rink, but he didn't commit as much as a toothbrush to them—and Flora had a point when she said that each of his girlfriends was interchangeable. A warm body to lose himself in, a talisman against the dark.

Could he change that—did he even want to? Or would it be just as lonely with one woman by his side as it was with dozens?

He shook off the thought. 'It'll be just like riding a bike—the skating, not the snogging.' Why had he said that? He was pretty sure that the red in her cheeks had nothing to do with the cold and she ducked her head so that he couldn't see her expression.

It'll get easier, he told himself. But he hoped it was soon. He couldn't imagine being this awkward in front of her parents. He knew Flora thought they favoured him but there was no contest—she was their little girl and if he hurt her they'd take her side. As they should.

It made him aware just how alone he was in the world. Was there anyone who would be on his side no matter what?

There were lots of ice rinks in and around Innsbruck, the prettiest on naturally frozen lakes, but the one Alex had chosen had a charm all of its own. It was a temporary rink right in the centre of town, just a short walk from the bustling Christmas markets. The early afternoon sun was too bright for the Christmas lights hanging overhead and bedecking every tree to make any impact but Alex knew that once dusk fell the whole town would light up, a dazzling, golden winter wonderland of crystal and light.

The rink was busy and it took a while before they could pay and order their skates. The boots were tight and stiff, unfamiliar on his feet, a reminder as he awkwardly stood up just how long it was since he had last been skating. Judging by Flora's awkward gait, she felt the same way. Gingerly they walked, stiff-legged and heavy-footed, to the wide entrance and peered at the whirling crowd. Even the toddlers seemed to have a professional air as they flew round and round, their mittened hands clasped behind their backs.

Alex grimaced. 'I'm not sure about that backward race; right now just going forwards feels like it might be a struggle.'

Flora slid her foot forward, wobbling like a fawn who had only just found her feet, her arms windmilling madly as she found her balance. 'Come on, we just need to find our feet. It'll be fine. I used to be able to dance on the ice.'

'Synchronised moves to pop. It wasn't exactly figure skating,' he pointed out as he put a tentative toe on the white surface, his eyes following a slight figure who did seem to be practising figure skating as she looped elegant circles round and round. 'I don't think we ever got to Austrian standards.'

Flora slid out another cautious foot and then another, a smile playing around her mouth as she began to pick up speed. 'Speak for yourself! You should have spent more time skating, less time being the local Casanova,' she yelled over her shoulder as she struck out for the centre of the rectangular rink.

Alex took a quick look around. On the far side the tented café was open to the rink and filled with cheerful onlookers clutching hot drinks and waving at family members as they skated close. At both ends spectators paused in their shopping to watch the sport. Christmas music blared from speakers and a giant, lit-up Christmas tree occupied the very centre of the rink.

He could stay here, clinging to the handrail, or he could venture out. Come on, he used to spend every weekend doing this. His body must remember the moves. Grimly he let go and began to move.

That was it, knees bent, body weight forward, letting the blades cut at an angle and propel him forward. The air chilled on his face as he got up some speed, the rest of his body warming with the exertion. Where was Flora? Squinting through a gang of teens, arms locked as they swung round in matching step, he saw her, weaving nimbly in and out of the other skaters. He'd always liked to watch her on the ice. She lost all self-consciousness, graceful as she pirouetted around.

She saw him and skated an elegant figure of eight, the ice swishing under her skates as she pulled up alongside him.

'Hey.' She smiled at him, any trace of reserve gone in the wide beam. 'This is brilliant. Why don't we do this any more?'

'Because we're not sixteen?'

'That's a rubbish reason. Look, there are plenty of people here way older than us.'

'And way younger.' Alex nodded towards one of the toddler prodigies and Flora laughed.

'He must have been born with skates on. Come on, let's go faster…'

She grabbed his hand and struck out and with a shout of alarm mixed with exultation he joined her, their gloved hands entwined, their bodies moving in swift, perfect synchronicity as they whirled faster and faster and faster round and round and round. All he could hear was his blood pumping in his ears, the roar of the wind and the beat of the music; colours swirled together as they moved past, through and round other groups until someone's foot, he wasn't sure whose, slipped and they crashed together, a sliding, flailing, unbalancing. Somehow he managed to grab hold of Flora and steady her before she fell completely onto the ice and they backed carefully to the side, holding onto each other, laughing.

'That was brilliant.' Her eyes shone, her cheeks were pink with exertion and her breath came in pants. She had never looked more magnificent, like some winter naiad glorying in the ice.

'Yes.' He wanted to say more but all the words had gone. All he could see were her long lashes, tipped with snow, her wide laughing mouth, a mouth made for kissing. All he could feel was her softness, nestled in next to him.

He had held her before, stood this close to her before. If he was honest he had wanted her before. But he'd hidden it, even from himself, every single time before. It was as if yesterday's kiss had opened the gates, shown him the forbidden fruit concealed behind them and now that he had tasted he wasn't sure he could ever stop craving.

It was a bad idea. But God help him he'd forgotten why. And when she looked at him like that, tentative, hopeful, naked desire blazing from those dark, dark eyes, he was utterly undone.

It was a bad idea. But Alex pushed that thought away as the air stilled, as the beat of the music faded away replaced with the thrum of need beating its own time through his veins, through his blood. He stood, drinking her in like a dying man at an oasis. All he had to do was bend his head…

He paused, allowing the intoxicating possibility to fill him—and then he stood back. 'Come on.' His voice was rough, rasping like yesterday's beard. 'We need to get back.'

It was a bad idea. If only it didn't feel so wickedly, seductively good. If only doing the right thing didn't rip his heart right out of his chest.

He turned and skated away. And didn't look back once.

He'd nearly kissed her. She knew it completely. She'd seen it as his eyes had darkened to a stormy grey, as his breath had hitched and a muscle had pulsed on his cheek. She'd felt it as his arm had tightened around her shoulders, as her body had swayed into his. She hadn't thrown herself at him; she couldn't blame the schnapps, not this time.

No, Alex Fitzgerald had looked at her as if she were his last hope.

Of course, then he had turned and skated away as if all the Furies were chasing him down, but still. They had had a definite moment.

Which was pretty inconvenient because hadn't she vowed that this was it and she was going to Get Over Him no matter what? And then he had to go and look at her like that and all her good intentions were trampled into the ground like yesterday's snowfall.

Because that look went beyond mere lust. It *did*. It wasn't just wishful thinking. No, she had felt it penetrate right through to the core of her.

Flora sighed and nudged the hot tap with her foot and let another fall of steaming water into the tub. It felt decadently wrong to lie naked in the middle of such a big room, wearing just hot water and scented oils. The view from the bathtub might be incredible but it seemed, a little disconcertingly, as if she were bathing right outside in the middle of a mountain glade.

Still, it was pretty relaxing—as long as Alex stuck to his timetable and didn't walk back in.

What if he did? Would he look like that again or would he back away terrified again?

Something was going on. *I need answers,* she decided, allowing herself to slip deep into the hot, almost to the point of discomfort, luxuriantly smelling water. She couldn't go on like this.

It was one thing thinking he was indifferent; horrid to think he was repulsed. But now? She had no idea. It was as if she were sixteen again. His face had that same remote, shuttered look it had worn all that long, hot summer.

She couldn't let him slip back to that place, wherever it was. She had been too shy, too unsure to ask questions then, to demand answers.

But maybe he needed her to ask them? Maybe by letting whatever had happened lie festering all these years she had done him a disservice. It didn't mean he would end up declaring his undying love for her, she knew that. It might change things for ever. But if she loved him then she needed to be strong, for once in her life. No matter what the personal cost.

And she wouldn't get anywhere lying in this bath, tempting as it was to stay in here all night long.

Although she wanted to try out one of the dresses she had bought that day, the prospect of a potential sledge ride made her think again and in the end Flora opted for her smartest black skinny jeans and a long, soft grey jumper with a snowflake motif. She started to automatically twist her hair into a ponytail but instead she let it flow freely across her shoulders, thankful that the wave had held and it hadn't been too flattened by the hat.

She stood before the mirror and looked down at the last purchase of the day, an impulse buy urged upon her by the shop assistants in the vintage shop. There was no way, they told her, that she could team her formal dress with her usual, insipid shade of lipstick.

She untwisted the top and stared down at the deep, dark red. A colour like that would only draw attention to her mouth and Flora had done her best to disguise its width since the day she had bought her first make-up. It had been the first thing she had been teased about— the kids at school had called her the wide-mouthed frog until she'd started to develop. The names after that had been cruder and even less original.

A sigh escaped her. It was just a colour. And nobody here knew her, would think twice about what colour she chose to paint her mouth. That was it, no more thought. She raised the small stick and quickly dabbed it across her lips, blending in the deep, rich colour. Then before she could backtrack and wipe it off again she turned on her heel and walked away from the mirror. No more hiding.

'This one seems to be ours.' Alex reached out and helped Flora into the old-fashioned, wooden sleigh. She climbed up carefully and settled herself onto the padded bench, drawing the fleecy blankets closely round herself, her feet thankful for the hot bricks placed on the floor. 'Four horses? They must have heard about the six cakes you put away during *Kaffee* and *Kuchen*.'

'At least I stuck to single figures,' she countered as

he swung himself in beside her. Very close bedside her. Flora narrowed her eyes as she tried to make out the other sledges, already sliding away into the dark in a trample of hooves and a ringing of bells. Were they all so intimately small?

The driver shook the reins, causing a cascade of bells to ring out jauntily, and the sledge moved forward. She was all too aware of Alex's knee jammed tight against hers, his shoulders, his arm. The smell of him; like trees in spring and freshly cut grass, the scent incongruous in the dark of winter.

'Have you had a good time at the reception?' He was as formal as a blind date. It was the first time they had spoken this evening, the first interaction since she had taken a long deep breath and walked into the buzzing lounge. To her surprised relief the reception had been a lot less terrifying than she had anticipated. It was informal, although waitresses circled with glasses of mulled wine, spiced hot-chocolate rum and small, spicy canapés, and most people were more than happy to introduce themselves. The vibe was very much anticipatory and relaxed—the whole hotel felt very different, felt alive now that it was filled. It was no longer their private domain.

'You know, I actually have.' She turned and smiled at him. 'I had a lovely chat to Holly, she writes travel blogs and articles. Did you know her parents are journalists too? Her mum writes one of those family confessional weekly columns and Holly spent her whole childhood being mercilessly exposed in print as well!'

'That's great. I can see why you're so thrilled for her.'

'Obviously not great for *her*,' Flora conceded. 'But

it was so nice to meet someone who understands just how mortifying it is. Her mum still writes about her—only now it's all about how she wishes she would stop travelling, settle down and pop out grandkids. At least mine hasn't gone there—yet.'

'No, but leave it more than five years and she might do a whole show about women who leave it too late to have babies.' His mouth quirked into a wicked smile.

'If she does I'll get her to do a companion show about aging sperm count and use *you* as her patient,' Flora countered sweetly and was rewarded by an embarrassed cough.

Silence fell, a silence as dark and impenetrable as the night sky. They were both sitting as far apart as possible, almost clinging onto the side rails, but it was no good; every move of the sleigh slid them back along the narrow bench until they were touching again.

It was all too horribly, awkwardly, toe-curlingly romantic. From the sleigh bells tinkling as the proud-necked white horses trotted along the snowy tracks, to the lanterns the hotel had thoughtfully placed along the paths, the whole scenario was just begging for the lucky passengers to snuggle up under the thick blankets and indulge in some romance beneath the breathtakingly starry sky.

Or, alternatively, they could sit as far apart as possible and make the kind of stilted small talk that only two people who very much didn't want to be romantic could make. Remarks like, 'Look, aren't the stars bright?' and, 'The mountains are pretty.' Yep, Flora reflected after she had ventured a sentence about the height of the pine trees that stretched high up the mountainside, they were definitely reaching new depths of inanity.

If things were normal then they would be curled up laughing under the blankets. She would tease him about the women who had been clustered around him at the reception; he would try and cajole her to be a little more open-minded about her first ski lesson. They would probably refresh themselves from a hip flask. Completely at ease. But tonight the memory of that almost-kiss hung over them. It was in the clip clop of the horse's hooves, in the gasp of the sharp, cold mountain air, in the tall ghostly shadows cast by the lantern-lit trees.

'I feel like I should apologise,' she said after a while. 'And I *am* sorry for being drunk and silly, for putting you in a difficult position with Camilla. I am really sorry that you are having to sleep on the narrowest, most uncomfortable sofa I have ever had the misfortune to sit on in my life. And I'm sorry I kissed you.' She swallowed. 'I should have taken the hint when you stopped me all those years ago. But I've wanted to know what we'd be like most of my life. And when you told me I couldn't live in fear of rejection I just had to try, one more time…'

'And?' His voice was husky, as if it hurt him to speak. 'Was it worth it?'

'You tell me.' Flora shifted so she was sitting side on, so that she could see the inscrutable profile silhouetted against the dark night by the lantern light. 'Because I think actually that you wanted to as well. Maybe you have always wanted to. Even back then.'

He didn't answer for a long moment. Flora's heart speeded up with every second of silence until she felt as if it might explode open with a bang.

'You're right. I did. And it was…it was incredible.

But you and me, Flora. It would never work. You know that, right?'

Her heart had soared with the word incredible, only to plummet like an out-of-control ski jumper as he finished speaking.

She wasn't good enough for him. Just as she had always known. 'Because I don't have aspirations?' she whispered. 'Because I mess up?'

'No! It's not you at all.'

The denial only served to irritate her. Did he think she was stupid? 'Come on, Alex. I expected better from you of all people. You don't have to want me, it's okay, but please respect me enough not to fob me off with the whole "It's not you, it's me" line. Do you know how many times I've heard it? And I know *you* trot it out on a regular basis.'

'But this time I mean it. Dammit, Flora. Do you really think I'm good enough for you? That there's anything in my soulless, workaholic, shallow life that could make you happy?'

'I...' Was that really what he thought? 'You do make me happy. You're my best friend.'

'And you're mine and, believe me, Flora, I am more grateful for that than you will ever know. But you've been saving me since you were eight. Now it's my turn to save you. From me. Don't you think I haven't thought about it? How easy it would be? You're beautiful and funny and we fit. We fit so well. But you deserve someone whole. And I haven't been whole for a long, long time.'

How could she answer that? How could she press further when his voice was bleak and the look in his eyes, when the lamp highlighted them, was desolate?

She took in a deep breath, the cold air sharpening her focus, the icy breeze freezing the tears that threatened to fall.

'I break everything I touch, Flora,' Alex said after a while. 'I can't, I won't break you. I won't break us. Because if I didn't have you in my life I wouldn't have anything. And I'm just too selfish to risk that.'

What about me? she wanted to ask. Don't I get a say? But she didn't say anything. Instead she slipped her glove off and reached her hand across until she found his, looping her cold fingers through his, anchoring him tightly. 'I'm not going anywhere,' she whispered, her head on his shoulder, breathing him in. 'I promise, you don't get rid of me that easily.'

He didn't answer but she felt the rigid shoulder relax, just a little, and his fingers clasped hers as if he would never let her go. Maybe this would be enough. It would have to be enough because it was all he was offering her.

CHAPTER SIX

'YOU ARE NOT seriously expecting me to get down there?' Flora pushed up her goggles and glared at the ski instructor.

He shrugged. 'It's the only way down.'

'Yes, but I thought we would stay on the nursery slopes until I could actually ski! This is a proper mountain. With snow on it.'

'Flora, you were too good for those within an hour and you nailed that blue. You are more than ready for this. Come on, it's an easy red. End the day on a high note.'

'Red!' She stared down the icy slope. Easy? It was practically vertical. Her palms dampened at the thought of launching her body down there. She glared at a small group of schoolkids as they enthusiastically pushed off. They were smaller, more compact. Had a lot less further to fall...

A figure skied easily down the higher slopes towards them and pulled up with a stylish turn, which made Flora yearn to push them right over.

'Having trouble?' Alex. Of course. He was annoyingly at home on the slopes. Although, she reflected, he had an unfair disadvantage; after all he'd gone skiing with his school every year since he was eight. After he had left home and put himself through college and then university, his one extravagance was skiing holidays—although a host of rich school friends with their own chalets helped keep the costs down.

'She won't go,' her instructor explained. 'I tell her it's more than doable but she refuses.'

'So how are you planning to get down, Flora? Bottom first?'

She glared at the two of them, hating their identical, idiotic male grins. If only this particular slope had a nice cable car, like the one that had brought them up to the nursery slopes from the hotel. Then she could have just hopped back in and had a return ride. But no, it was a one way trip up in the lift and no way back down apart from on two plastic sticks.

Or she could wait here until spring and walk down in a nice sensible fashion.

The surprising thing was that she *had* been doing okay, that was very true. Surprisingly okay in fact. But not so okay that she wanted to take on such a big run. Not yet.

'The only way to improve is to test yourself,' Alex said, still annoyingly smug. 'And this looks far worse than it is. Really it's just a teeny step up from a blue.'

'Stop throwing colours at me. It's not helping.' The truth was she had barely slept again. An early start and an entire day of concentrating on a new sport had pushed her somewhere beyond tiredness to exhaustion. Muscles she hadn't even known she possessed ached, her feet hurt and all she wanted was a long, hot bath.

But she wouldn't be able to relax even once back in

the room. Because Alex would be there. Their conversation from last night had buzzed around and around and around in her head until she wanted to scream with frustration. It had told her so much—and yet it had told her nothing at all. Why did he think he was broken?

'Look, I'll take it from here,' Alex told her instructor. 'Why don't you get going and you can start again tomorrow? I promise to return her in one piece.'

The instructor regarded her inscrutably from behind his dark lenses. He was tall, tanned and had a lithe grace that at any other time she would have had some pleasure in appreciating but it had been absolutely wasted on her today—she had been far too tired to attempt to flirt back.

'Tomorrow morning,' he said finally. It didn't sound like a request. 'You will be begging to try a black slope by the end of the week.'

'Never,' but she muttered it under her breath, just holding up a hand in farewell as he launched himself down, as graceful as a swallow in flight.

'So, you know another way down?'

Alex shook his head. 'It's on your own two skis only. And we need to hurry up. It's getting late.'

Flora bit her lip. She shouldn't be such a wuss but staring down that great expanse made her stomach fall away in fear. It was the same reaction she'd had when Alex took her abseiling. She and mountains were not a good mixture. From now on she would stick to flat surfaces only. Like beaches; she was good with beaches.

'Okay.' She inhaled but the action didn't soothe her at all, her stomach still twisting and turning. Did people really do this for fun?

'I'll be right next to you,' he said, his voice low and comforting. 'I'll talk you through every turn.'

'Right.'

She pulled her goggles back down. Alex was right. It was just after four p.m. and the sun was beginning to disappear, the sky a gorgeous deep red. The slopes had been getting quieter so gradually she had barely noticed, but now it was obvious as she looked around that they were almost alone. Ahead of her the last few skiers were taking off, leaving the darkening slopes, ready to enjoy the huge variety of après-ski activities Innsbruck had to offer.

'It's a shame I didn't know you were here earlier.' Alex adjusted his own goggles. 'A couple of the hotel lodges are on this shelf. I'd have liked to show them to you.'

'It is a shame you didn't because I am never coming back here again.'

But he just laughed. 'You wait, when you've done it twice you'll wonder what all the fuss was about and be begging me to let you try something harder. Okay, count of three. One…two…three.'

Flora gritted her teeth and pushed off as he said three. The slope had been completely deserted as Alex began his countdown but as he reached the last number a group of snowboarders appeared from the slope above. Impossibly fast, impossibly spread out and impossibly out of control. Flora saw them out of the corner of her eyes and panicked, losing control of her own skis almost immediately as they swarmed by her, one of them catching her pole with his stick and spinning her as he sped by. She shouted out in fear and grappled for her balance, falling heavily, her ankle twisting beneath her.

'Oi!' But by the time Alex had caught her and yelled out a warning they were gone, their whoops and yells dissipating on the breeze. 'Are you okay?'

'I think so.' But Flora couldn't quite stop the little shivers of fear as Alex pulled her up. 'I thought they were going to run me right over.'

'I'll be putting in a complaint as soon as we get back down.' He retrieved her ski and handed it to her. 'Here you go, you're fine. I hate to hurry you, Flora, but it's getting pretty late. I don't want to guide you down in the dark. That *would* send you over the edge.'

'I know...' How long would it take? Her instructor had said that it was a ten-minute run but if Alex was going to talk her through it surely that would add on a few crucial minutes. She looked anxiously at the sky; the red was already turning the purple of twilight. Did they have fifteen minutes?

She put the ski down and slid her foot into the binding, wincing as a spasm of pain ran across her ankle. 'Ow!'

'What's wrong?'

'I must have twisted my ankle as I fell. It's not too bad. I should be able to walk it off...'

'But you can't ski on it.' His mouth tightened. 'Those damned idiots.'

'Can't we ask for help?'

'We could. But I hate to ask the rescue guys to come out in the dark for a twisted ankle—especially as we took so long to get started. We're going to look pretty silly.'

'But we can't stay here all night.' Or did he still

think she was going to make it down while they could still see? Flora swallowed. She was not going to cry.

Alex grinned. 'Panic not. I have a solution. Remember I said the ski lodges were on this shelf? This kind of situation is exactly what they're for. They should be completely kitted out because I know Camilla is hoping that some guests will try them out. It's hard to get permission to build anything up here so they're pretty special. Warm, comfortable and there should be food.'

'You built them for guests who got stranded on the slopes?' Now she thought she really might cry. Salvation! If the lodge only had running hot water then she would never ever complain about anything ever again. Her ankle was beginning to throb in earnest now and, standing still, Flora was all too aware of the chill bite of the wind.

'Really they're for people who want privacy or to spend time with nature. But this is as valid a reason as any. They're about half a mile this way. Can you manage?'

Half a mile? Through the snow? But if it was a choice between that and skiing down then Flora guessed it wasn't much choice at all. She nodded as convincingly as she could. 'Let's do it'

By the time they reached the first cabin the sun had disappeared completely and the twilight was moving rapidly from a hazy lilac grey to the thicker velvety purple that heralded night. Luckily both Flora and Alex had phones with torch apps on, which provided some illumination against the encroaching dark.

'Here we go,' Alex said with more than a hint of relief as they approached the pine grove. 'Good to know my memory hasn't forsaken me.'

The Alpine shelf was much narrower than the wide, buzzing nursery slopes and empty apart from the ski-lift way station. There wasn't even a *gasthaus* to serve up beer, hot chocolate and snacks, which meant that once the ski lifts had stopped running the guests would have total privacy.

'We built them in a pine grove, which means they have the advantage of shade in the much hotter summer months,' Alex explained as he guided her along the path. 'There are two in this grove and two even higher up. It makes them easier to service in pairs. But we've spaced them apart so guests should get the illusion of being all alone. In a fully catered, all-whims-pandered-to way.'

'I like the idea of being pandered to,' Flora said as Alex led her into the trees and down a little path. 'Oh, it's like a fairy tale cottage, hidden amongst the trees like that! A kind of sci-fi fairy tale anyway.'

It was a futuristic design, more of a pod than a traditional lodge with a low curving roof, built to blend into the landscape. 'They're so well insulated,' Alex said as Flora stopped still, trying to take it in fully, 'that they're warm in winter and cool in summer—although there's a stove in there to make it cosier.'

'It's gorgeous.'

It was, however, a little eerie arriving as darkness fell. Flora felt like a trespasser as they stamped their way through the snow to the door, discreetly situated at the side. 'It's as if we are the only two people in the world,' Flora whispered, not waiting to break the absolute silence with the sound of her voice. 'Like there's been some kind of apocalypse and we're all that's standing between the world and the zombies. Or the aliens.'

Alex shone his torch onto the keypad and punched at the buttons. 'Which would you rather?'

'Which would I rather what?'

'Zombies or aliens?'

This was so like their teen conversations that for one moment Flora forgot the cold, the ache in her ankle, the awkwardness of the last few days and was transported back to the roof of her house, accessed reasonably safely—although not with parental permission—from her attic window. She and Alex had spent many a summer night up there, staring up at the stars, discussing the Big Questions. Would you rather be eaten by a tiger or a shark? What would you do if you had twenty-four hours left to live? Were invisible? Could travel anywhere in time?

'Depends on what the aliens want, I suppose,' she said as she watched Alex swing the keypad open and extricate a key.

'If everyone's wiped out it can't be anything good.'

'No, but they might be allergic to something like salt water so we could do a mass extermination. With zombies you have to destroy their brains. That's quite a long process. Unless there were other pockets of survivors around. You?'

'Aliens would be cool. I always think zombies must reek.' He pushed the door open. 'Welcome, my lady.'

The door led into a spacious cloakroom with a flagstone floor. Hooks and shelves awaited, ready to dry out ski clothes or hiking jackets. Flora sank onto the nearest bench with a moan of bliss as she worked her boot off her sore ankle. It was a little swollen but not as bad as she'd feared and when she poked it nervously it didn't hurt too badly. She put her bare foot on the floor and squeaked in surprise. 'It's warm!'

'Underfloor heating. No expense spared here—and it means everything should dry out for tomorrow.' Alex was stripping off without any sense of embarrassment, his padded trousers and jackets neatly hung up, his boots put onto the bench provided, his socks stretched out ready to dry.

Flora's mouth dried. He was still decent—just—in his tight-fitting, thermal trousers and a T-shirt. But they fitted him so well it was almost more indecent than if he had been half naked, highlighting every muscle. Alex was so tall, so rangy he seemed deceptively slight when in a suit but the form-fitting material made it clear he was in perfect shape.

The last thing she wanted to do was parade around in leggings and her T-shirt, the wide straps of her sports bra visible beneath the neckline. But neither could she stay bundled up in her padded clothes any more. The pod was beautifully warm.

She reluctantly pulled down the zip and shrugged off her jacket. Alex had already taken her boots and socks and when he turned back she handed him the jacket as if it were fine, as if she were as comfortable as he seemed to be. But she couldn't help noticing how his eyes fastened onto the generous curve of her chest, made far more prominent by the light, tight material, or how they lingered there.

'I don't suppose there's anything I can change into?'

He looked away, a faint colour on the high cheekbones. 'As a matter of fact I think they are keeping some spare clothes here for guests. I'll…er…go and see.' He backed towards the door that led into the rest of the pod, opened it and backed out, looking anywhere but at her.

What had he been doing? Staring at Flora's chest like, well, as any red-blooded male would. She might and did bemoan her curves but they were pretty magnificent—and, showcased by the tight black stretchy material, had been even more magnificent than usual.

Or was it just that he was more aware of her than he usually was, than he allowed himself to be? Of the way her hair waved around her face, of the sweetness in her eyes, the humour in her mouth?

'Did you find anything yet? Oh, my goodness. Alex, this is sensational!' Flora appeared at the door and looked around the room, her mouth open in admiration. The main room *was* sensational. It was also pretty intimate. He had designed the pod for romance. To allow the guests complete privacy, to make them feel as if they were the only people in the world. The skylights were the only windows, allowing the occupants to look up and see the night sky as they slept, although summer guests could slide open the back wall and enjoy the outside from the wooden terrace attached to the back of the pod if they wished.

A small kitchen area curved around the front wall; just a hob, a microwave, and a sink, the large, well-stocked fridge was back in the drying room. On the opposite side a second door led into the bathroom and a wood-burning stove was cosily tucked into the corner, a love seat, rugs and cushions heaped before it. But the main focus of the pod was the huge bed. It dominated the room; covered in throws and fake furs, it was big enough to fit several people. Flora's eyes settled on the bed and she swallowed. 'Very discreet.'

'Let me just look for some clothes and I'll let the hotel know where we are. They'll need to organise a cleaning crew to come up tomorrow. I know that Camilla is making sure every couple gets a night up here. She's hoping these pods will be a big hit with honeymooners.'

'Yes.' Flora's gaze was still fixed on the bed. 'I'm sure they will be.'

Alex ducked out of the room and into the quiet of the bathroom. Not that it was much better, the huge oval bath, designed for two, taking up most of the central space and the walk-in shower dominating the wall opposite. What had he been thinking? If they had set off down the mountain straight away they could have got back okay. Now here they were. Together. In a place designed for seduction. It made their hotel suite seem positively chaste.

Normally they would have laughed about it—and goodness knew that bed was big enough for them both to sleep completely sprawled out and never touch.

But these weren't normal times.

The cupboards, built in around the sinks, held fluffy towels and, he was glad to see, a selection of warm clothes. He pulled out one of the hotel-branded tracksuits for himself and looked for something for Flora. There was another tracksuit, an extra-large that would swamp her, or a couple of white silky robes. Grabbing one of the robes, he handed it to her as he walked back into the main room. 'Why don't you…? There's a bath or a shower. I'll just get the stove lit and see what's in the fridge.'

She took the robe with a self-conscious smile of thanks and walked into the bathroom. Alex tried, he really did try, but he couldn't help watch her walk out of the room. The sway of her hips, her deliciously curved backside perfectly displayed in the tight leggings.

He stood there and inhaled. *Get a grip, Fitzgerald,* he told himself.

Ten minutes later the hotel had been contacted, the stove lit and Alex had raided the fridge for supplies. It wasn't hugely promising—unless he was bent on seduction. The fridge held several bottles of champagne, some grapes and cheeses. The freezer was stocked full of hotel-prepared meals ready to pop into the microwave: creamy risottos, rich beef casseroles, chicken in white wine sauce. All of it light and fragrant. He'd have given much for a decent curry or a couple of bloody steaks. Substantial, mates' food, full of carbs and chilli, beer and laughter.

'I'm all done if you want the bathroom…' Flora stood by the bathroom door, her eyes lowered self-consciously. She had washed her hair and it was still damp, already beginning to curl around her face. The robe was a little too big and she had tucked it securely around her and belted it tightly. But no matter how she swathed herself in it, no matter how she tied it, she couldn't hide how the silky material clung to her curves, how the ivory set off the dark of her hair, the cream of her skin, the deep red of her mouth. She looked like a bride on her wedding night. Purity and decadence wrapped in one enticing package.

'If I want…' he echoed. His pulse was racing, the beat so loud it echoed through the room. Twice in the last twenty-four hours he had walked away. Twice he had done the right thing.

He didn't think he could manage it a third time because when it came down to it he was only a man, only flesh and blood, and she was goddess incarnate.

He couldn't move. All he could do was stand and stare. She took a faltering step and then stopped, raising her eyes to meet his. 'Alex?'

'I want *you*.' There it was said. Words he had first thought at sixteen. Words he had never allowed himself to say, words he had made himself bury and forget. 'I want you, Flora.'

Her mouth parted and he couldn't take his eyes off it. Couldn't stop thinking about how it had felt under his, how she had tasted, how they fitted so perfectly he could have kissed her for ever.

'If I say yes…' Her voice was low, a slight tremble in it betraying her nerves. 'If I agree will you back out again? Because I'm not sure I can take another rejection, Alex.'

'I can't make you any promises beyond tonight,' he warned her. Warned himself.

She raised her eyebrows. 'I'm not asking for an eternity ring.'

'This will change everything.'

She nodded slowly. 'I think everything has already changed. We opened Pandora's box and now it's out there.'

He held her gaze. 'What is?'

'Knowledge.'

That was it. That was it exactly. Because now he knew. Knew how she felt, how she tasted, how she kissed, how her hands felt when they slid with intent.

He knew the beginning; he had no idea how it ended. And oh, how he wanted to know.

And now that they had started they couldn't just pretend. Maybe this was what they needed, one night. One night to really know each other in every way possible. What was it Flora had said just two nights ago? That they should have done this in their teenage years?

He begged to disagree. He knew a lot more now than he did then. No less eager, a lot more patient.

She still hadn't moved although her hands were twisting nervously and her eyelashes fluttered shut under the intensity of his gaze, shielding her expressive eyes as he watched her. 'You're so beautiful, Flora.'

Her eyes opened again, wide with surprise. 'Me? No, I'm too…' She gestured wildly. 'I'm too everything.'

'No, you're perfect.' He took a step nearer, his eyes trained on her, the small room narrowing until he could see nothing else, just damp, dark curls, ivory silk and long lashes over velvet dark eyes. Another step and another until he was standing right there. Within touching distance. 'Like a snow princess, hair as black as night…' He twisted a silky curl around his finger and heard her gasp. Just a little. 'Skin as white as snow.' He brushed her cheek lightly. 'Lips as red as rubies.' His finger trailed down her cheek and along the wide curve of her mouth.

She stared at him for one second more, her breath coming quick, fast and shallow, and he could hold back no longer. He held her gaze deliberately as his hands moved caressingly down her shoulders, her arms until he reached her waist. He held them there for one moment, the heat of her flesh burning through the cool silk and then, in one quick gesture, he pulled at the knot holding her robe together. The belt fell away and as it did so the delicate ivory silk slithered back off first one white shoulder and then the other.

Flora reached out automatically to pull it back and he put out a hand to stop her.

'No, let it go.'

Her face flushed a fierce rose but she stood still in response to his words and allowed the robe to fall away, allowed herself to be unveiled to the heat of his gaze. She stood like the goddess she was named for, fresh as the spring.

Alex sucked in a breath, his stomach, his chest tightening as he saw her, really saw her. She was all softness and curves, all hidden dips and valleys, ready for an explorer's touch. He reached out reverently, to follow the curve of one breast. 'Let me worship you, Flora.'

She nodded. Just the once but it was all he needed as he took her hand and led her over to the bed. They had all night. He hoped it would be enough.

CHAPTER SEVEN

'I AM ABSOLUTELY STARVING.' Flora sat up, wrapping the sheet around her breasts as she did so. How could Alex parade around stark naked so unconsciously? It must be that public-school upbringing.

Not that she was complaining. Her eyes travelled across his finely sculpted shoulders, down the firm chest, the flat stomach and, as he turned, dwelled appreciatively on a pair of buttocks Michelangelo would have been proud to carve. No, she wasn't complaining at all.

'It's all that exercise,' he said as he disappeared through the cloakroom door, reappearing with a bottle of champagne, so chilled she could see the frost beginning to melt on the bottle.

'Mmm, the skiing was hard work,' she replied as demurely as she could and laughed at the affronted look he gave her.

'Minx,' he muttered. 'It'll serve you right if I let you go hungry.'

'Did I say skiing? Slip of the tongue. Oh, thank you…' She took the glass handed her and sipped it appreciatively. 'This is delicious.'

Don't be too happy, she warned herself. *Don't be too comfortable. This isn't real.* But it was hard not to be. It just felt so…so right. She should be embarrassed. This was Alex. Her oldest and bestest friend. They had just done things that definitely went against any friendship code but it wasn't awkward. It was horribly perfect.

He touched her as if he knew her intimately, as if he knew instinctively just what she wanted, what she needed, and she had wanted to touch every inch of him, nibble her way across every square inch of skin. No inhibitions—just want and need and giving and taking and gasping and moaning until she hadn't known where he stopped and she started.

Flora took another hurried sip of the champagne as her body tingled with remembered pleasure.

And now she could sit there, her hair tumbling down, her lips swollen and tender, muscles aching in ways that she was pretty sure had nothing to do with her earlier exertions on the slopes, clad only in a sheet and, although she might not feel confident enough to wander around in the buff, she was comfortable. Usually she jumped straight back into her clothes after lovemaking but with Alex she didn't feel too tall or too curvy. He'd made her feel fragile, desirable.

'Look how tiny your waist is,' he'd breathed as his hands had roamed knowledgeably across her body. 'Perfect,' he'd whispered as he'd kissed his way down her stomach. And that was how she'd felt. Perfect.

He sat down on the edge of the bed with that lithe casual grace she envied so much. 'I could heat up one of the frozen meals or, if you don't want to wait, there's cheese, biscuits and grapes?'

'Oh, cheese, please. That sounds perfect. Are you sure you don't want me to help?'

His eyes flashed with wicked intent. 'Nope, I don't want you to get out of that bed. Ever.'

'Sounds good to me.' How she wished this could *be* for ever, this perfect moment. The fire blazing in the stove, the stars bright in the skylights, she blissfully sated, lying in bed sipping champagne watching her man prepare dinner.

But he wasn't her man. And she needed to remember that.

'Alex, are you awake?' They had dozed off some time after midnight, blissed out after an evening of champagne and lovemaking. Flora had no idea what time it was now; the cabin was completely dark except for a faint reddish-gold glow from the stove.

Alex rolled over, throwing his arm across her as he did so, and she lay there, enjoying his weight on her, the skin against skin, the smell of him. 'Mmm?'

'Nothing,' she said. 'Go back to sleep.'

'Are you okay?'

'Yes, more than okay.' But she wasn't. The reality of what they had done was bearing down upon her. 'Are we?'

'Are we what?'

'Okay?'

He moved, propping himself up on one arm so that he could look down at her, a dark shadow in the dim room. 'Second thoughts, Flora?'

'No. I mean, it's a little late for that.'

He smoothed her hair back from her face, a tender gesture that made her chest ache and her eyes swell. 'Good. I don't know what tomorrow will bring, but right now I don't want to change a thing. Except wonder why we didn't do this a long time ago.' His hand trailed a long, languorous line down her face, down her throat, down and down. It would be so easy to let it continue its slow tortuous journey.

But his words reminded her of her vow. Her vow to try and help him. To make things right, somehow. She caught his wrist as it moved to her ribcage and held it. 'What happened, Alex?'

He laughed low and soft. 'Do you need me to explain it to you?'

She couldn't help smiling in response but she clasped his wrist, her fingers stroking the tender skin on the inside. 'Not tonight. Then.'

He froze. 'Don't, Flora.'

But she knew. If she didn't ask him now he would never tell her. After all he had kept his secrets through the long, boozy university years, through long walks and bonfire heart-to-hearts. Through backpacking and narrow boats and noisy festivals. But tonight was different. Tonight there were no rules.

'You came home from school,' she remembered. 'I had finished my GCSEs and you had done your AS Levels. I thought we would have another long summer together. But you were different. Quieter, more intense. More buttoned up. I had the most ginormous crush on you, which I tried to hide, of course. But that summer there were times when you looked at me as if…' Her voice trailed off.

'As if I felt the same way?' he said softly.

'We would be somewhere, just the two of us. On the roof talking, or lying on the grass, and I would look at you and it was as if time would stop.' Their eyes would meet, her stomach would tighten in delicious anticipation and she would find it hard to get her breath. 'And then nothing...' She sighed. 'I tried to kiss *you* that time. When we were watching that ridiculous horror film where all the teenagers died. I thought you would kiss me back but you didn't. You looked so revolted...' Her voice trailed away as she relived the utter humiliation, the heartbreak all over again.

He pulled his hand away from her gentle grasp, pushing the hair out of his eyes. 'Sometimes I wonder what would have happened if we had got together then. Do you think we'd be the friends we are now, our past relationship something to look back on nostalgically? Or maybe we would have ended badly and not speak at all. Or maybe we would have made it. Do you think that likely? How many people get together in their teens and make it all the way through college and university?'

'Not many,' she conceded. But *they* might have. If he'd wanted it.

'You changed that year.' He was still propped up on one arm, still looking down at her. She could smell the champagne on his breath, feel each rustle as he moved. 'Boys watched you all the time—and I watched them watching you. But you didn't even notice. I nearly made a move that New Year but I was away at school and we both had exams. So I told myself to wait. Wait till the summer.'

'What changed?' She hadn't imagined it; he had felt it too.

'My dad blamed me for my mother's death.' He said it so matter-of-factly that she could only lie there, blinking at the sudden change in conversation. 'Did I ever tell you that?'

'No.' She moved away, just far enough to allow her to sit up, hugging her knees to her chest as she tried to make out his expression in the dim light from the fire. 'I don't understand. How? I mean, it was suicide, wasn't it? Awful and tragic but nobody's fault.'

'He didn't want children. All he wanted was her, just her. You know my father. He's not the caring, sharing type. But she wanted a baby so much he gave in. He said it was the biggest mistake he ever made. That I was the biggest mistake... He was never really explicit but I think she suffered from fairly severe postnatal depression.'

A stab of sorrow ran her straight through as she pictured the lonely motherless little boy alone with an indifferent father. Allowed to grow up believing he was the cause of his mother's death. 'Oh, Alex. I'm so sorry.'

He shifted, sitting up beside her on the bed, leaning back against the pillows. 'She hid it from him, from the doctors, from everyone. Until I was two. Then she just gave up. She left a note, saying what a terrible mother she was. That she couldn't love me the way she was supposed to. That I would be better off without her...'

Flora touched his face. 'That doesn't make it your fault. You know that, right?'

'My father thought so.' His voice was bleak. 'That's when he began to work all hours, leaving me with a series of nannies, packing me off to boarding school as soon as he could. He told me it was a shame he had to wait until I was eight, that he would have sent me at five if he could have.'

Flora hadn't thought it was possible to think any worse of Alex's father. She had been spectacularly wrong. 'He's a vicious, nasty man. No wonder you came to live with us.'

He carried on as if she hadn't interrupted. 'He married again. I didn't really see much of him then, or of that particular stepmother, but apparently she wanted kids, wanted me around more and so the marriage broke up. He blamed me for that as well. I guess it was easier than blaming himself. And then that year, when I was seventeen, he remarried again.'

'Christa.' Oh, Flora remembered Alex's second stepmother with her habit of flirting with every male within a five-mile radius. She had made Flora, already self-conscious, feel so gauche, so huge like an oversized giant. 'Horry had a real crush on her. Do you remember how she used to parade around in those teeny bikinis when we came over to swim?' She laughed but he didn't join in and her laughter trailed off awkwardly.

'It was so nice at first to have someone care. Someone to bring me drinks, and praise me and take notice, as if I were part of a real family. It didn't even occur to me that other people's mums didn't ask their teenaged sons to rub suntan oil onto their bare back or sunbathe topless in front of them.'

Flora's stomach churned and she pressed her hand to her mouth. 'Alex...'

'She started to drop by my room for a chat when I was in bed. She'd stroke my hair and rub my shoulders.' His voice cracked. 'I was this big hormonal wreck. This woman, this beautiful, desirable woman, was touching me and I wanted her. I wanted her to keep touching me. But at the same time she revolted me, she was married to my *father*. And there was you...'

'Me?' Flora didn't know at which point her eyes had filled with tears, hadn't felt them roll down her face, it wasn't until her voice broke on a sob that she realised she was crying. Crying for the little boy abandoned by his father, for the boy on the brink of adulthood betrayed by those he trusted to look after him.

'I was falling in love with you that summer. But how could I touch you when at night…when I didn't turn her away…when I lay there waiting and didn't say no.'

'You were a child!'

'I was seventeen,' he corrected her. 'I knew what I was doing. I knew it was wrong—on every level. But I didn't stop her. I let her in my room, I let her into my bed and in the end I didn't just lie there…'

Flora swallowed, clutching her stomach, nausea rolling through her. That woman with her tinkling laugh and soft voice and Alex? And yet it all made a hideous kind of sense. How withdrawn he had become, the way he would look at her as if something was tearing him apart but Flora couldn't reach him. The knowing smile Christa would wear, the possessive way she'd clasp his shoulders. How had she been so blind?

She made an effort to sound calm, to let him finally relieve himself of the burden he'd been carrying. 'What happened next?'

'By the end of the summer she had stopped being cautious. I didn't want… It was one thing at night, with the lights out—that was more like a dream, you know? As if it wasn't real. I would be back at school soon and the whole thing would just disappear. But Christa didn't want that. She started to try and kiss me in the house, run her hand over my shoulder in front of people. She wanted to make love in the pool, in the kitchen. The more I tried to pull away, the more determined she became. I was just a pet, her toy. She didn't want me to have any say in where or when or what. She was in control. And she was out of control. It was inevitable, I guess, that we'd be found out. My dad came home early one day and caught us.'

'He blamed you.' It wasn't a question. She'd seen the aftermath. Alex, white-faced, all his worldly possessions in one bag, determined to make his own way in the world.

'He told me I tainted everything I touched.'

'That's not true,' but he was shaking his head even as she protested.

'My mother died because she couldn't love me. My father hates me. My stepmother…there's something rotten at the heart of me, Flora.'

'No. No, there isn't.' She was on her knees and holding onto him. 'I love you, my parents adore you, for goodness' sake even Minerva loves you, in her own way. There *is* a darkness in your family but it's not you. It was never you.'

But she wasn't getting through; his voice was bleak, his face as blank as if it were carved out of marble. 'I saw you look at me, back then, so hopeful. As if you were expecting something more. But I had nothing to give. Christa took it all, like some succubus, taking another piece of my soul every time we had sex. All those girls at the ice rink, and the girls I date now. I felt nothing. I am incapable of feeling anything real. That's why I warned you to steer clear of me, Flora. There's nothing real inside me.'

She kissed him, his eyes, his cheeks, the strong line of his jaw, tasting the salt of her tears mingled with the salt on his skin. 'You are real,' she whispered as she pressed her mouth to his cold lips. 'I know you are.'

He didn't respond for a long moment and then, with an anguished cry, he kissed her back; hard, feverish kisses as if he were drowning and she the air. Flora held on and let him hold on in return. She didn't know who was saving who. And she wasn't sure that it mattered.

Alex knew the exact moment Flora woke up. She didn't move, didn't speak, but he knew. He had kept watch over her through the night. A lone knight guarding his lady. Her breathing, so slow and steady, quickened. Her body tensed. Was she wondering what would happen in the harsh light of day? What reality would mean after the passions, the confidences, the outpourings of the night before.

He wondered that too. He knew what had to be done but how he wished things were different. That he were different. 'Lukewarm left-over champagne or coffee?'

'Hmm?' She sat up unsteadily, brushing the long tangled curls from her face and scrubbing her eyes like a small girl, her eyes widening as she looked at him. Was she surprised that he was out of bed? That he was already dressed in jogging bottoms and his own top, showered, shaved and ready to go. 'You're not serious about the champagne?'

'It seems a shame to throw it away,' he teased, deliberately keeping his tone light. 'No. If it was chilled then that would be a whole different matter. There's eggs. We could make breakfast or would you rather have some back at the hotel? There's time. I texted your instructor to arrange a later meeting time.'

'A later time?' She sank back down onto her pillows dramatically. 'I was planning to spend all day in the spa today. I have barely slept…' She stopped, her cheeks pinkening in an interesting way. He wondered just how far down her blush crept—and then pulled his mind resolutely back to the matter at hand.

'Don't forget you have to get down the mountain first,' Alex said helpfully and was rewarded with a glare.

'Can't we just stay here for ever?' There was a plaintive note in her voice. He knew with utter certainty that it wasn't just the skiing she was thinking about. It was the aftermath. Of course she was.

His chest squeezed in sudden longing. *Stay here for ever.* Just Flora and Alex and a large bed and a supply of champagne. No facing the real world, no dealing with any situation. He inhaled long and deep, pushing the enticing vision away. 'What would we do when the food ran out? Hunt squirrels and roast them on the stove?'

'Not much meat on a squirrel.'

'Then we'd better return to real life. Sorry, Flora.'

She put out her hand. Part of him wanted to pretend he hadn't seen it, the other part was drawn to her, could no more walk away than he could stop breathing. He paced himself as he walked towards the bed, slow, unhurried steps, seating himself on the edge, deliberately not touching her.

'So, we pretend this hasn't happened.' She made it sound like a statement but he knew she needed an answer. Was she hoping he'd change his mind?

'That's best, isn't it? No need to complicate things further.' All he had to do was reach across, across just a few centimetres of rumpled white sheet. But it might as well have been metres, miles, oceans. Would she see a casual touch as encouragement? As a declaration?

Would he mean it as such?

He couldn't. He mustn't. If he allowed the slight torch she had always carried for him to blaze into brightness then all would be lost. He didn't know which would be worse—if it flickered and died when she discovered how hollow he really was for herself. Or if it continued to flame until he did something stupid, something unconscionable and broke her heart.

And he would.

His father's voice echoed through his mind. Mocking him. *You taint everything you touch. Nobody could care for you. You disgust me.*

He couldn't cope if he lost Flora.

She touched his arm, a small caress. 'What are you thinking?' Ah, the million-dollar question and one he had always hated. He never got the answer right.

But he was compelled to tell the truth. 'I don't want you to hate me.'

She rounded on him, eyes blazing. 'I could never hate you. Why? Because of last night? You were very clear it was a one-night deal and I understood that. Don't make this into some kind of melodrama. It was just sex.'

But her eyes fluttered as she said the words and she couldn't look him in the eye.

'Good sex,' she amended. 'But, you know, I'm not planning to join a nunnery because there won't be a repeat.'

Alex didn't feel quite as comforted by her words as he should have done. This was the result he wanted, wasn't it? There was a little part of him that had always wondered *what if* about Flora Buckingham and, sure, he had pointed out last night that a teen grand affair was bound to crash and burn, but still. He had wondered.

Now he knew. And even better she had no expectations beyond a cup of coffee and that he guide her safely to the bottom of the ski slope. By the time they got back to her parents' they would be their old selves. Only better. No more moments when he would look up and see a hopeful yearning in her face, no more watching her covertly as she walked across a room.

They had scratched that itch and it was satisfied. Let Flora move on to someone who deserved her. As for him? Well, maybe he would date a little less widely, date a little more wisely.

The thought made his chest feel as hollow as his heart.

Flora scrambled to her knees, the sheet held high against her chest, a thin barrier of cotton yet as effective as a cast-iron chastity belt. *You have no rights here.* 'We just need to get through the rest of this week. What do you want to do, tell Camilla that we quarrelled and get your room back? I mean…' as he raised an eyebrow at her '…you don't want to spend the next three nights on that sofa, do you? Unless…'

'Unless?' His pulse began to pound at the spark in her eye.

'We *are* meant to be dating, after all.'

'Flora…'

'Same rules,' she said hurriedly. 'No expectations, no protestations. What happens in Innsbruck stays in Innsbruck but, seriously. You can't stay on the sofa.

We don't want to make Camilla suspicious. As long as we're both clear about the rules, what's the harm?'

'We get back on Christmas Eve,' he reminded her. 'Straight to your parents'. Won't they guess?'

'How? We promised not to let anything change our friendship and it'll be finished by then. Finished the moment we get into the taxi to drive to the airport. Maybe you were right, we would have had a mad teen thing, all drama and lust, and it would have been glorious—and it might have ruined us for ever. But we're older now, we're far more sensible. It doesn't have to ruin anything. But I reckon we're owed just a few days of crazy fun. We owe it to our younger selves.'

It was a convincing argument—if he didn't examine it too closely. 'I suppose we do at some point. Guess it's either now or when we're in the nursing home.'

'We might be married to other people when we're in the nursing home,' she pointed out. 'Plus right now I'm still reasonably pert and have all my own teeth. You might not be so keen when we're finally retired.'

His mouth dried. Did she know what she was offering? The rest of the week as a no-strings, full-fun affair. He didn't deserve it; he didn't deserve her. But he wasn't strong enough to turn her down.

You've always been weak. He thrust the insidious thought aside. They were supposed to be dating, they were sharing a room and they had just spent the night very much together.

'May as well be hung for a sheep as a lamb.'

Her mouth curved into an irresistible smile. 'You do say the most romantic things. I can see why the girls love you. What's the very latest we have to be out of here?'

'We have about an hour if you want to eat, shower and change before your hot date with your dashing instructor. Why?'

'Well…' she let the sheet fall, just a little, not nearly enough '… I thought we might seal our deal with a kiss.'

CHAPTER EIGHT

'CAMILLA SEEMED IMPRESSED with your ideas.'

Flora put her hairbrush down and turned to look at Alex, admiring the lithe grace as he sprawled on the bed, completely at his ease as he looked through her sketchbook. 'It was like being summoned for an audience with the queen,' she said, her palms damp at just the memory. 'It's a good thing she can't actually raise those eyebrows of hers, she made me feel about six as it was.'

'That's just her way. I don't think she meant to question you quite so closely—she knew you would have no real idea of cost at this stage. We're still at the initial concepts.'

'How can I even think about putting costs in when she hasn't even decided which of your ideas she wants? Plus I have no idea of what I can actually source there—or what her actual budget is.' At least when she had worked in-house she hadn't had to worry about any of this part. She had been given a task, she'd completed it, easy—even if it had been dull and monotonous and about as creative as granola.

He turned another page, nodding as he looked at her carefully drawn plans. 'Relax. No one expects you to know any of this yet. Once Camilla gives us the go-ahead we can do a reconnaissance trip out there. We'll need to talk about money as well. The interior design is all subcontracted through my firm. Lola charged for each project as a whole but I could take you on as a contracted member of staff if that makes things easier.'

Flora froze. It would make things a *lot* easier. She had no idea about how much to charge if she free-lanced, nor how often she could invoice, when she would get paid—or how she'd live until she did. But working with Alex? Travelling to Bali with him? It wasn't going to be the kind of cold turkey she thought she might need...

Because four nights in and she was already getting a little addicted to his touch. To the way his eyes seemed to caress her. To the way his hands most definitely did. To his mouth and the long, lean lines of his body.

She was in way over her head, barely graduated off the nursery slopes and yet heading full tilt down a black run and she didn't even care. 'Do we have to go on this evening's jaunt?' She allowed her eyes to travel suggestively over his body. 'I've seen the Christmas markets.'

'Not at night, you haven't, and yes, you do. Three-line whip. But we don't have to hang around in the bar after we get back if you would rather get some rest.' He smiled like the big bad wolf eyeing up Red Riding Hood.

'I do need a lot of rest,' she agreed solemnly. 'All this mountain air is exhausting me. I may also need a really long hot bath.'

'I was thinking about a bath too,' he said softly and she shivered at the intent look in his eyes as he slowly glanced from the large tub to her. 'I do feel particularly dirty this evening.'

A jolt of pure lust shot through her and Flora gripped the top of the dressing table, her knuckles white. What was she doing? How on earth could they ever return to their old, easy camaraderie after this? How would she manage when his hand was no longer hers to hold, when she couldn't run her fingers over the soft skin on the inside of his wrists, when she couldn't kiss her way along the planes of his face and down his neck?

She had dreamt of this for so long that it all felt completely right, completely fitting. Stepping back again? That was going to hurt. But she had promised him that it would all be fine, that she would be fine, they would be fine and she couldn't let him down. She would just have to keep smiling and pretend her heart wasn't shattering into millions of little pieces.

'Okay.' She turned back to the mirror and outlined her mouth with the deep red lipstick. She'd almost got used to the striking colour over the last few days. It sent out a statement of confidence that she might not feel but that she could fake. She caught up a silk scarf, a midnight blue patterned with abstract snowflakes, and knotted it around her neck, the accessory adding some much-needed style to the cream jumper and blue velvet skinny jeans she'd chosen for their warmth. 'I'm ready.'

Alex caught her hand as they left the hotel room, an easy gesture. She fought to keep her hand loosely clasped in his, not to curl her fingers tightly around and hold on, never letting him go.

'You can help me choose Christmas presents,' he said as they made their way along the wide corridor to the stairs. 'I haven't managed to buy any yet. I expect yours were all done and dusted by September.'

'This year's fabric was designed and printed by then,' she agreed. Twice a year Flora got several of her designs printed up into silks and cottons, which she then used to make the cushions and scarves she sold online. She also combined her own designs with vintage fabrics to create quilts, which she made to order. 'I've made both Mum and Minerva clutch bags. I hope they like them. I don't think Minerva has ever worn last year's skirt.'

'Strawberries and cream isn't particularly Minerva,' he pointed out. 'But it was a beautiful design. I'm sure she really appreciates it. Apron for your dad?'

'Of course.' Every year she made her father a new apron and a selection of tea towels and he always made sure they were prominently displayed in every tutorial and photoshoot. 'I've bought dolls for the twins and made them entire wardrobes.' She had also made shirts for Horry, Greg her brother-in-law and Alex in the same pattern as the scarf she was wearing this evening. Flora always made her presents; she suspected Minerva at least would rather she stuck to scented candles and bath salts but Flora loved to create things, especially for the people she cared about.

'As we're in Austria I'm thinking glass all round, animals for the littlies, crystal glasses and bowls for the adults. Too obvious?'

'No, they'll love them. It's unfair how you always manage to pull the perfect present out of the bag last minute when some of us plan all year round.' She squeezed his hand in mock protest and he grinned.

'Not unfair, it's because I have good taste.'

And money to spare, she wanted to retort—but she didn't. After all, he'd always managed to find the right thing, even when he was at college and working three jobs in order to pay his way, refusing to allow the Buckinghams to house and feed him rent free. This man who didn't think he was worth loving.

'I was thinking,' she said hesitantly. They hadn't discussed anything personal since the night at the ski lodge, a tacit agreement to keep the week as carefree as they could.

'Careful…'

She elbowed him. 'Ha-ha. Don't you have any grandparents? Uncles, aunts?'

'Trying to get rid of me, Flora?'

'Never. It just seems odd, that's all. There must be someone.'

But he was shaking his head. 'As far as I know my father's parents died before I was born and he was an only child—not that he'd tell me if there were a hundred relatives out there, I suppose. As for my mother, I did see my grandmother when I was much younger but she gave up. Either my father frightened her off or I…'

Flora squeezed his hand. 'Don't even go there with the "or I". If she disappeared I would bet all my Christmas presents your father was behind it. You should try and track her down. She might have some answers.'

'Maybe.' But he didn't sound convinced and she didn't want to push any further.

Flora was surprised by how at ease she felt as they approached the hotel lounge. It was busy; the guests buzzing as they discussed their impending visit to Innsbruck's famous Christmas markets, sampling the food and drink on offer and purchasing some last-minute gifts. Normally she'd find such a noisy and full room intimidating, hang behind Alex as he strode confidently in, let him be the one to mingle, she following where he led. But over the last couple of days she had struck up a few acquaintances and greeted her new friends with pleasure when Alex disappeared over to the other side of the room to charm an influential broadsheet journalist who was considering a magazine feature on Alex's work.

'I hear you skied down several red runs today,' Holly, the travel journalist Flora had met on the first evening, teased her. Flora was the only learner in the entire hotel and many people were watching her progress with encouragement and interest. 'We'll have you out on the blacks before we leave.'

'Not this trip.' Flora shook her head emphatically. 'But, I have to say—and I am amazed I am about to admit this—I think I'll come back and ski again. It has been sort of fun. Although I still prefer the hot-chocolate, hot-tub part of the proceedings most!'

'If I was sharing a hot tub with your boyfriend I think that would be my favourite part of the evening too.' Holly looked over at Alex, a wistful expression on her face. He was casually dressed: jeans, a dark green cashmere jumper, hair characteristically tousled. There were more obviously handsome men in the room, more famous men—richer men—but somehow he stood out.

Or maybe it was just that Flora instinctively knew where he was at every moment. Her north star.

Flora stood back to let one of the other women pass by. Although she recognised her they hadn't spoken during the week; the celebrity guests, mostly socialites and gossip-magazine staples, tended to keep to their own tanned, designer-clad selves and only a few people like Alex passed from one group to the other with no hint of unease. Bella Summers was gossip-magazine gold—an ex-model, TV presenter and extremely keen skier, she had been invited to bring the launch week a sprinkle of glamour and help create a buzz around the hotel.

'Oh, my goodness.' To Flora's amazement Bella stopped dead in front of her, staring at her neck in undisguised envy. 'Your scarf! Isn't that the same one Lexy Chapman is wearing in this week's *Desired*?' Her eyes flickered to Flora's face, curiosity mingling with undisguised surprise. 'Where on earth did you get it?'

'This scarf.' Flora touched it self-consciously. 'No, it can't be the same. It must be a coincidence.'

'It is exactly the same. That abstract snowflake print is unmistakeable,' Bella Summers insisted. 'Mitzy, come here. Isn't this the same scarf Lexy wore on her date with Aaron? The one in *Desired*?'

Another tall, skinny, elegant girl loped across to join them. The two of them stood there gazing at Flora's neck like a couple of fashion-hungry vampires. 'Yes, that's the one,' she said. 'Hang on. I think I left the magazine on the shelves over there. It only came out yesterday. Luckily a shop in Innsbruck stocks it.'

It can't be the same. It's just a coincidence, Flora told herself. It was always happening, designers inspired by the same things coming up with similar designs. Or of course work got plagiarised; small solo outfits like hers were particularly vulnerable.

Unfortunately it was a much more likely scenario than the other—It girls and style icons just didn't buy from small solo nobodies like her. She didn't even have a brand name or a website of her own, using an Internet marketplace to sell the handful of items she produced each year.

'Yes, I knew it.' Mitzy and Bella came back waving the latest copy of *Desired* triumphantly. 'Here you go. Flora, isn't it? Look.'

Flora took the glossy magazine from them. *Desired* was an upmarket weekly combining fashion, gossip and lifestyle in easily digestible sound bites and pictures. It was already open at the page they wanted, the street-style section. Photos of fashion-forward celebrities out and about, their outfits and accessories critiqued. Girls like Lexy Chapman were staples on this page—as were girls like Bella and Mitzy, although neither had the cool kudos of Lexy Chapman.

Normal people didn't have a hope of appearing on the hallowed pages, no matter how stylishly they dressed. And Flora was too awkward for style.

But maybe, just maybe she had some influence after all.

She sucked in a deep breath as her eyes skimmed over the photo. Lexy Chapman was casually dressed for her date with her on-off rock-star boyfriend in tight-fitting skinny jeans and a cream, severely cut silk shirt visible underneath an oversized navy military coat. The starkness of the outfit was softened by the scarf, tied around her slender neck with a chicness Flora could only envy.

She skimmed the brief wording, her heart thumping.

How does she do it? Once again Lexy Chapman strips back this season's must-have styles

*to their bare essentials combining masculine tai-
loring with military chic.*

*A clever touch is the snowflake motif scarf,
which adds a feminine twist and is a clever nod
to the season.*

The article was followed by a list of the clothes
and accessories, with price, designer and website. Sure
enough, right at the bottom…

Scarf, Flora B, £45

It was followed by her website address.

'Hang on.' Mitzy snatched the magazine back off
Flora and read the article again. 'Flora B? Is that you?
Oh, my goodness, you have to let me have one of your
scarves. What other designs do you have? Do you have
any on you?'

'I…' Flora tried to think. What did she have in stock
and ready made up? 'Sure. When we get back from
Innsbruck I'll show you my web shop. I only make
up a couple of patterns a year so it does depend on
what's left.'

'Exclusive.' Mitzy nodded in satisfaction. 'Good.'

'If you could just excuse me…' Flora tore her eyes
away from the page, her head giddy. What if the photo
had generated more interest? She hadn't checked her
orders since she had arrived in Austria. It wasn't as
if they usually came flooding in—more than three a
week would be a rush—and she had designated the
Friday of last week the last day she could guarantee
Christmas delivery. 'I just need to check on something.'

Flora was glad to escape from the noisy room. The

mood had changed as the news flew through the room. People—especially the celebrity clique—were looking at her differently, actually seeing her. Or seeing her value to them. One scarf in one picture. Was that all it took to go from zero to person of interest?

With this lot it appeared so.

She hurried upstairs, back to their recently vacated suite. It looked different, smelt different with Alex's belongings casually strewn around. His laptop was set up on the desk in the corner, a pair of his shoes left by the door. His book on the side table—not that he'd been doing much reading. Or work. Neither of them had. She liked it. Liked the casual mingling of their belongings.

Flora's phone was in a drawer along with her charger. She hadn't wanted it on, hadn't wanted to be in contact with the outside world, to be reminded that this short idyll was temporary. She switched it on, her mind whirling while it powered up. Would this mean a run on her small amount of stock? If so would it be worth investing in more fabric? How would she fund it? How could she make and store decent amounts of stock in her small rented room? What if she did invest and demand dried up?

She shook her head. Talk about counting chickens! She might find that Mitzy and Bella were the only people who had even noticed the scarf—and only because she was wearing it.

Her phone sprang into life, pinging with a notification—and another and another like a much less musical one-note version of the sleigh bells. Social-media notifications, emails, voicemails. Flora stared at her buzzing screen and felt her head spin. She had only started the social-media accounts for her business to stop her sister, Minerva, nagging her but rarely used them. She didn't know what to say to her tiny handful of followers.

'Flora?' The door had opened while she watched the notifications multiply. 'We're heading off.' Alex paused, waiting for her to answer but she couldn't find the words. 'What is it?'

She handed him the phone and Alex stared at it incredulously.

'What? Have you just won a popularity contest?'

'I don't know. I think it's about a scarf but I don't know where to start.'

'A scarf? Is this the same scarf that has half the women downstairs frothing at the mouth?'

She nodded, the surrealism of the situation disorientating her. 'Either that or I've won the lottery, been photographed kissing a boyband member or I am a long-lost princess. There are over fifty voicemail messages and I don't know how many emails.'

The phone beeped again. 'More than fifty...' he peered at the phone '...although it looks as if at least half are from Minerva. Hold on.' He put the phone back down a little gingerly, as if it were an unexploded bomb. 'I am going to make our apologies to Camilla and I'll help you sort this out.'

'Your glass animals...'

'Can wait. I'll pop down tomorrow before the Christmas Ball. Wait here. Don't touch anything.'

Flora sank onto the sofa, almost too distracted to notice just how uncomfortable it was. Her phone beeped a few more times and then it was mercifully silent. She unlooped the scarf from around her neck and passed it from one hand to the other, the silk cool under her fingertips. A midnight-blue silk with her snowflake design on it. She had only printed one roll of fabric. It was destined for the central square and edging for a handful of quilts, as the cuff lining on the shirts she had made Alex, Greg and Horatio, the lining of a few bags, some cushions and twenty or thirty scarves.

Her fabric design and sewing were a hobby that barely paid for itself. It took up time she should be spending trying to get her talents noticed so she could work in-house again or at least pick up some freelance contracts in her own field and leave the world of temping far behind.

She didn't do it for money or fame. The truth was it just made her happy.

Just...

'Right.' Alex appeared back, the magazine in his hands and open at the fateful page. 'It looks like this *is* the cause of all the fuss. I've just been asked by at least ten people if I can get them one of these scarves and they are all prepared to pay a great deal more than forty-five pounds.' His brow wrinkled as he looked at the photo. 'Who is this woman?'

'You know who she is. That's Lexy Chapman.'

He looked blank. 'Nope. What does she do?'

That was a good question. What did she do apart from look cool and date famous people? 'Right now she's making my scarves sought after.'

He took the scarf from her loose grasp and held it up to the light, turning it this way and that. 'I didn't know you sold them. I just thought it was a hobby.'

'It is a hobby.' She turned away from his scrutiny, jumping to her feet and retrieving her phone from the side. 'I have a little online shop, to help fund my projects, that's all.'

'Is it?' But he didn't probe any further. 'Okay, this is how we're going to play it. You listen to your voicemails and make a note of all the names, messages and numbers and we'll see who you need to call back and when. I'll log onto your email and social-media accounts, put a holding message on them and see if there's anything really urgent. What do you think?'

Flora nodded. 'Thanks, Alex.' It was what she would have done but having some help would make it easier—and a lot faster. 'I really appreciate it.'

'Come on, what else are friends for?' But he didn't quite meet her eyes as he said it. Worry skittered along her skin, slow and sure as a cat on a fence. Had grabbing a few days' pleasure meant the end of everything? Like a gambler staking everything on one last spin and losing. Was the thrill of watching the wheel turn and the ball hover on first red and then black worth it? That moment when anything was possible worth the inevitable knowledge that nothing was?

He opened his laptop. 'I hope you can remember your passwords. Right, where shall I start?'

It didn't take too long for Flora to open up each of her accounts for Alex, averting her eyes from the dozens of messages and multitudes of new followers. She retreated to the bed with a notebook, a pen and her phone ready to start listening to her messages. Alex was right; Minerva had been calling consistently all day. Flora steeled herself and began to listen.

Minerva, a fashion buyer from Rafferty's, one of London's most exclusive department stores, a couple of magazines, Minerva, Minerva—Minerva again. By the time she got to her sister's seventh message Flora knew she'd better call her back.

'At last!' Her sister didn't bother with formalities like 'Hello' or 'How's Austria?'

'Evening, Merva,' Flora said pointedly. But the point, as always, was lost.

'I'm glad you've decided to emerge from hibernation. I couldn't get hold of you or Alex.'

'We've been working.' Minerva hadn't been able to get hold of Alex either? It was most unlike him not to have one phone in one hand and the other in front of him—although now Flora thought about it she had only seen him check his work phone and emails a few times—and she hadn't seen his personal phone at all. Not since the ski lodge. Maybe he was enjoying living off grid just as she was. She glanced over at him. He was tapping away, frowning with concentration. Her entire body ached at his nearness.

Minerva's tart tones recalled her to the matter at hand. 'Working? Whatever. So who is handling this for you? I've asked around but no one has admitted it. Not surprisingly, I would never let you disappear at such a crucial time in a campaign. Unless that's part of the plan, to drum up more interest? Too risky, I would have thought.'

Handling, campaign? It didn't take too long for a conversation with her sister to feel like a particularly nasty crossword where the clues were in one language and the answers another. 'Minerva,' she said patiently. 'I have no idea what you're talking about.'

'Of course it didn't take too long for people to work out who you were, thanks to Dad's aprons. Another serious misstep. You really need him in the latest designs in this crucial period while you're establishing yourself, although I do think the whole apron thing is a bit saccharine myself. Still, it establishes you as part of that quirky routine he has going on. But you should be here, not drinking schnapps and frolicking on mountains.'

Flora froze. How did her sister know? 'I haven't been frolicking,' she said, hating how unconvincing she sounded. Alex looked up at her words and his mouth curved wickedly.

'I beg to differ,' he said, too quietly for Minerva to hear, and Flora's whole body began to simmer in response.

'Look,' she said hurriedly, wanting to get Minerva off the phone, everything else replied to and Alex back here, on the bed, while she was still allowed to want that. 'You are going to have to speak in words of one syllable. What are you talking about?'

Her sister huffed. 'Who is handling your PR for the Lexy Chapman campaign? I hope you know how humiliating it is for me that you didn't even ask me to pitch.'

Her what? 'Merva, there isn't a campaign.'

Disbelieving silence. 'You expect me to believe that the most stylish woman in Britain was photographed in your scarf by a complete coincidence?'

'I know you too well to expect anything, but yes. That's what happened. Goodness, Merva, as if I would ever not ask you in the highly unlikely event I was going to run a campaign. My inbox is full, my social media is insane, I have voicemails from scary influential people I don't dare call back and I'm terrified even thinking about logging onto my shop because I don't have enough stock to fulfil half a dozen orders.' She could hear her voice rising and took a deep breath. 'Come on, even I know enough not to launch a campaign like that.'

Minerva was silent for a moment and Flora could picture her as if they were in the same room, the gleam of excitement in her eyes, the satisfaction on her cat-like face. Her sister loved a challenge—and she always won. 'I need you,' she added.

'I know you do,' but Minerva's voice wasn't smug. She sounded businesslike. 'Leave everything to me. I'll take care of it all. Right. I need to know who has left you a message and why, all your social-media account details and you need to forward me every email. Oh, and let me know your current stock list. You won't be able to supply everyone so let's make sure you only focus on the people who matter. When are you back?'

'The day after tomorrow.' *Too soon.*

'Christmas Eve? The timing is really off. We'll lose all momentum over the holidays.'

'Yes, well, next time I inadvertently sell a scarf to a style icon I'll make sure she only wears it at a more convenient time.'

'Luckily...' it was as if she hadn't spoken '...I am a genius and I can fix this. Right, I want all that information in the next half-hour. Do not speak to a single journalist without my say-so, do not promise as much as a scrap of fabric to anyone—and, Flora? Keep your phone on.' Minerva rang off.

'Goodbye, Flora. It was nice speaking to you. The kids send their love,' Flora muttered as she put the phone down, her head spinning. 'Alex, it's okay. Minerva is going to save the world armed with a few Tweets and her contact list.'

'Thank goodness.' He pushed the chair back. 'There are some hysterical women out there—and some even more hysterical men who think they will never have sex again if they don't produce one of your scarves on Christmas morning. No pressure.'

She flopped back onto the bed, her phone clutched in her hand. 'I just need to get all this information to Minerva and then we can head into Innsbruck—if you still want to go, that is?'

'We could.' His voice was silky; that particular tone was the one that always made her blood heat up, her body ache. 'Or we could use our time far more productively.'

Flora propped herself up on one arm and looked at him from under her lashes. 'Productive sounds good. What do you have in mind?'

He picked up the scarf and twisted it into a slim rope, pulling it taut between his hands before looking back at her, a gleam in his eye. 'Such a versatile material. I'm sure we'll think of something.'

CHAPTER NINE

'HERE YOU ARE. I was beginning to think you'd got yourself stranded in a ski lodge again.' Alex allowed the hotel door to swing closed behind him and leaned against the wall, watching her appreciatively. 'Room in there for a little one?'

'It's not that sort of bath,' Flora told him, slipping a little further into the bubbles so that all he could see was her hair piled into a messy knot on the top of her head. Little tendrils had escaped and were curling in the heat; his hands itched with the need to touch them.

'What other sort is there?' It was hard to make conversation knowing that she was naked and wet. Totally exposed and yet completely veiled. Whose idea was it to put a bath in the middle of the bedroom? Probably Lola's. If he weren't so angry with his ex-designer's lack of professionalism he would track her down and offer her a bonus. It was genius. That was it; every building he designed from now on would have a bath in the middle of a room. Even if it was supposed to be an office. Or a shopping centre.

Flora moved and the water lapped against the side of the bath, the sound another tantalising reminder of her undressed state. 'This is a ball-preparation bath.

It involves all kinds of depilation, exfoliating, filing and moisturising.'

'Sounds serious.' He took a step closer to her, then another. Each step unveiled a little bit more, the tilt of her face, rosy from the hot water, her long neck a delicate blush pink. Then bubbles, clothing the rest of her, although if he craned his neck and looked really hard there were a few intriguing gaps in the white suds revealing hints of interesting things.

'It is. Deadly serious. Did you find everything you wanted at the Christmas markets?'

'Yep. Eventually. I had a long hard morning on the slopes first. Gustav was desolated that you missed your last day's lessons. He had a particularly challenging slope ready for you. So what have you been doing while I was skiing and shopping?'

'Ugh.' The sigh was long and heartfelt. 'I have spent most of the day sat at my laptop video-calling Minerva. Although you'll never guess what she was wearing…'

Alex's mouth curved into a slow smile. He knew Minerva. 'Last Christmas's skirt.'

'*And* a scarf I gave her a couple of years ago in her hair. Nice to know my presents suddenly have value. Not that I should complain. She has sorted everything. Although she's set up a couple of interviews for next week.' She sounded apprehensive. 'Face to face and photos, which is not good news after all the *Kaffee* and *Kuchen* I've had—especially the *Kuchen*.'

'Don't forget your dad's five-course Christmas dinner,' Alex reminded her helpfully and laughed as she groaned.

'Don't—you know how upset he gets if we skip

anything—and he thinks that seconds is the only real way of gauging a dish's success. But I *am* really grateful. She's taken over the social media and created waiting lists, replied to all the emails and soothed every fashion editor's ruffled feathers. Her poor staff, two days before Christmas, and she pulled a three-line whip. I almost feel guilty that I'm luxuriating in this bath—and then I remember that this too is work.' She sank a little further into the steaming water with a small purr of pleasure.

'How much is she charging you?'

'That's the best bit. It's my Christmas present. She's keeping the exorbitantly expensive scented candles she *had* bought me, which are far more her bag anyway, and is giving me her staff's toil instead, nicely wrapped with a big bow on top.'

Alex bit back a smile. 'How very generous of her, although a cynical person would point out that it's not doing her any harm. You're the one in demand. She's handling the buzz, not creating it.'

'It's two days before Christmas and I'm about to go to a ball. No cynicism allowed.'

Alex perched on the edge of the bathtub and looked down at her. 'How are you feeling about your designs being out there?'

Her eyelashes fell. 'Half excited, half terrified. Naked—and not just because I am.'

'That's how it should be,' he told her. 'Even when you're working to a brief there should be a little something of you in there. You should be exposed, otherwise you haven't gone as far as you could have.'

She raised an eyebrow. 'Always? Even when I had to rebrand the Village Inns wine bar chain and they wanted pinks and lime greens and bits of fruit every-where?'

'Especially then. Otherwise what's the point? That's why I struck out on my own so early. I wanted to be able to pick and choose my own work—that doesn't mean I don't listen to my clients though. There has to be a balance. I wonder…' He paused, not wanting to push too much when she was still adjusting.

'Wonder what?'

Oh, well, in for a penny… 'At your degree show it was obvious your passion—and a huge amount of your talent—lay in textile design. It shows every Christmas, with every gift you make. But you've never tried to make it your career. You set your sights on interior design and took the first job you were offered even though you hated their whole brand.'

'Hate's a bit strong…' she protested. 'Wholeheart-edly disliked maybe. That's why it would never have worked with Finn. Even if he hadn't been a golf-obsessed workaholic, he really loved the branding.'

'It wouldn't have worked with Finn because he was an idiot.' Alex's teeth began to grind just at the thought of Flora's ex. How a girl with such good taste had such bad taste in men he would never know.

Not that he was any improvement. Actually that was untrue. A warthog was an improvement on Finn.

'Good point.'

'So why haven't you tried to sell your designs be-fore? Into shops or to fashion designers? It seems like the perfect path for you.'

'I guess because I don't design fabric to make money. I do it because I love it.'

'Exactly. Why shouldn't you do what you love? I do. Your whole family does. Don't you deserve to as well?'

She slithered further down into the water, as if she were hiding from the question. 'It's different for you. You know what you want. You don't let anything stand in your way. That thing you said, about having a piece of you in everything you do? I see that in your work. In this hotel, in your designs for Bali. And it's wonderful. But it's so exposing.'

'And that frightens you?'

'If people hate the neon limes, and they mostly will, then that's fine. It's not *my* creatives they hate. I'm just following the brief. But if they hate my scarves or my quilts or my bags, things I've poured love and attention into? That feels like I've failed—again. Like I've been rejected again. I don't want the things I love tainted.'

Alex reached out and twisted one of the piled-up tendrils of dark silky hair around his finger. 'Everything worthwhile comes with a price, Flora.'

She sighed. 'Sometimes the price is too high. I don't want to feel that exposed. I've spent my whole life being judged. Noticed because of my height, leered at because I was a teenager with big boobs, every teacher pointing out how unlike my siblings I was. My parents dragging me onto TV. I just want to be anonymous.'

His voice softened as he pulled at the curl. 'But you're out there now. You need to harden up, think about the next step.'

'It's not that easy though, is it? I need money to expand—to buy fabric, a better machine, a studio, somewhere to keep stock. Even if I stay small and exclusive I don't think keeping my stock in boxes under my bed is going to cut it—or make me enough to live on!'

'That's where I have good news. Camilla caught me on the way in. She very much wants you to work on the next three hotels and is prepared to pay for the privilege. Do you trust me to negotiate you a good deal?'

Flora sat up, the water sloshing as she did so. It was so deep she was still respectably covered, just her shoulders rising from the white foam like Aphrodite. As enticing and tempting as Aphrodite. 'A good deal? Does she know that my previous experience pretty much consisted of that awful pink fruit décor and the teapot theme for those cosy retro cafés? And let's not forget the chintzy bedding range. This is a massive step up. I should be paying her!'

He grinned. 'All she's heard for the last twenty-four hours are her guests desperate to get hold of your work. If she can announce right now, while the buzz is still big, that you're the designer for her next three hotels then that's quite a coup for Lusso Hotels. I told you she likes to work with people who have a marketable story and right now that's you. It's a great way to get publicity for both here and for her future plans.'

She bit her lip. 'I suppose. And she was already considering me so nothing much has changed.'

'Nothing much but the price tag. If you subcontract to me then I can pay you monthly—which will give you some stability while you step up your own designs as well. Like all projects there will be weeks when you don't need to do much for Lusso Hotels and other weeks when it will be frantic. But the subcontract could include studio space at my office for the length of the contract and if you use it for your other work then that's fine. It'll be yours.'

'That would be great. At least that's the space issue sorted.'

Alex had saved the best bit for last. 'And she would like to see a touch of your own style in your plans for the Bali hotel, so I guess I was wrong when I said to watch the whimsy.'

Her eyes sparkled. 'Really? You were wrong? Can I have that in writing?'

'Watch it.' He dipped a hand in the bath and scooped up a little bit of water.

'Don't you dare…this is a serious bath. I already told you.'

'Don't I dare what? Do this?' He trickled the water slowly onto the exposed part of her chest, his heart-beat quickening as he watched the silvery drops trace a trail down her skin until they disappeared into the deep vee between her breasts.

'Or this?' she countered sweetly and before he could move away she grabbed the front of his shirt and hauled him into the bath, laughing as he landed on top of her. 'Mind my hair. I don't want to get it wet!'

Alex raised himself onto his hands and knees. 'Now look what you've done. My clothes are all soaking.' He rocked back onto his heels, ignoring the splash of the water as it sloshed over the side of the bath. 'I'm going to have to take them off. You wanted a serious bath, Flora Buckingham? You've got one.'

Her eyes didn't leave his as he pulled the sopping-wet shirt over his head, or as he began to unbutton his trousers. 'Bring it on,' she said, her voice breaking huskily, belying the tough words. 'If you think you're man enough.'

'Oh, Flora,' he promised her as his trousers and boxers followed his shirt over the side of the bath. 'I'm more than man enough. Just wait and see.'

'Come on, what's taking so long?' Alex sounded impatient as he rapped on the bathroom door. Again.

Flora rolled her eyes at her reflection. 'It's not my fault I had to redo my hair,' she called back. 'I told you not to get it wet.'

He didn't answer for a moment, then: 'Regrets, Flora?'

'That my hair got wet? It might have been worth it.' That didn't mean she was entirely regret free but she wasn't going to admit that to him. Or to herself. Not tonight. It was their last night, they were going to a Christmas ball and she looked, even if she said so herself, pretty darn smoking.

The dress she had bought from the vintage shop in Innsbruck was deceptively demure. The chiffon cap sleeves revealed just a hint of her shoulder and the neckline hugged the tops of her breasts, the bodice narrowing at her waist before flaring out again, the full skirt finishing at her calves. She saw more revealing outfits every day in the offices she temped in.

Deceptively demure. It covered everything and yet…was it the bright red, a shocking contrast to the paleness of her skin? Was it the fit, the way it clung like a second skin? Or was it the way it defined and enhanced every curve so that, despite the modest neckline, Flora felt more exposed than if she was venturing out in just her bra?

Maybe it was because she was so obviously and evidently dolled up? Her hair tumbled free in carefully arranged curls, her lips were red and her eyes outlined in dark, dark kohl and, for once, she had slipped her feet into heels, which would make her taller than most of the men in the room.

But Alex would still top her.

'Flora...'

'Okay, okay, I'm coming.' She took one last look. Yes, she was definitely smoking—either that or she looked like a pin-up version of Mrs Claus but either way she had no choice. She had nothing else even remotely suitable for a Christmas ball. Inhaling deeply, Flora opened the bathroom door.

And stared. It was so unfair. Here she was. Two hours later. Hair washed, curled, sprayed and teased. Body plucked free of each and every stray hair, moisturised and buffed, face artfully painted, nails filed and polished, dress squeezed into, shoes forced on. And what had Alex done? Showered, shaved and shrugged himself into his tux.

She swallowed, her mouth dry. The stark black, relieved only by the crisp white of his shirt, suited him, brought out the auburn glints in his hair, made his eyes greener than grey. He looked like a stranger; a powerful, imposing and hot stranger.

A powerful, imposing and hot stranger who was staring straight back at her, mouth slightly open and a dazed expression on his face.

'Will I do?'

He didn't answer straight away, just nodded. 'Yes,' he said, clearing his throat. 'You look incredible.'

Heat flooded her cheeks at the expression in his

eyes. 'Fine feathers,' she said a little unsteadily. 'Put anyone into a dress like this and they'll scrub up okay.'

'No.' His eyes were so intent, heat smouldering in their depths, that she felt completely exposed, naked. 'The dress is…' His gaze travelled over her, burning a trail onto her, marking her, claiming her. 'The dress is sensational. But it's all you, Flora. You'd look just as amazing in a sheet.'

'Thank you.' She blinked, unexpected tears filling her eyes at the raw want in his voice. 'You don't look too bad yourself.'

They stood, caught in time just staring at each other, the pressure in the room intensifying until it was just the two of them, caught in a spotlight. Flora cleared her throat. 'Shall we go?' She didn't want to prolong the moment. Not tonight. Not when tomorrow meant moments such as this would be finished for ever.

Flora waited for him to open the door but he just stood there. 'I…er… I got you this. I know Christmas isn't for another couple of days but, well…' He held out a black velvet jewellery box.

Flora froze. He had never bought her jewellery before. Alex was usually a generous and perceptive gift buyer but jewellery buying was too intimate, a line he had never crossed before. Still, they were crossing all sorts of lines this week. Why not this one?

'For me?' She was aware how stupid the words were as she uttered them and he nodded, a faint smile playing on his lips as he did so.

'For you. Don't you want to open it?'

She reached out cautiously. 'I'm not sure,' she confessed. 'There's not a trick snake in there, is there?'

'One time, Flora, one time. And I was ten!'

'Okay, then.' The box was solid, heavier than she expected and she turned it around in her hands, the velvet soft against her skin. It wasn't new, she knew that at once; the hinges were tarnished and the velvet rubbed in places. She smiled over at Alex, her heart lifting with the discovery; she wasn't much of one for new, she preferred her possessions to have a history, a story.

She found the clasp and sprung it before carefully opening the lid and let out a little anticipatory breath she hadn't even been aware that she was holding. A necklace sparkled on the yellowing white satin cushion. Flora stole a quick look up at Alex. His face was impassive, as if he were waiting for her to comment on the weather or ask the time, but the strained set of his shoulders showed that he was waiting for her reaction. Slowly she hooked the necklace onto one newly manicured finger and drew it out of the box.

It was a two-tiered circlet of large, crystal beads designed to fall just below the neck, nestling on the collarbone. 'It's…' She shook her head, searching for the right words. 'It's perfect. How?' She couldn't complete the question.

'I knew where you bought the dress from so I popped in and said I wanted something to go with it. They remembered you quite clearly.' He took the necklace from her unresisting hand and moved behind her. She felt the cool heaviness of the beads settle around her neck, his fingers brush against the nape of her neck as he swept her hair aside, his breath on her skin as he leaned forward and clasped the necklace.

'It's nineteen fifties, like your dress, and made of the local Austrian crystal.' He let her hair fall back and stepped away. She instantly felt colder.

'It's absolutely gorgeous.' Flora put her hand up to her neck and fingered the chunky beads. 'Thank you, Alex. It's very thoughtful of you.' She turned around and ròse on her tiptoes, pressing a kiss onto his cheek, inhaling his freshly washed scent as she did so. It *was* thoughtful—and it finished her dress off perfectly— but part of her wished that he hadn't bought it. That he'd stuck to books, or tickets or any of the usual gifts. Because each time she saw it she would be reminded of this night, of this trip. Each time she saw it she would be reminded of him. Not of Alex Fitzgerald, best mate and partner in crime, but of *this* Alex. The one who made her stomach turn over, her legs tremble and who made all good sense go flying out of the window.

The one she would say goodbye to in the morning. She put a hand up to her necklace and touched the central bead, the truth hitting her with brutal force. It wasn't going to be easy because she didn't want it to end. She wanted him to look at her with that mingling of desire and need and appreciation and humour for ever. But she'd made him a promise and she was going to keep it. No fuss, no repercussions, nothing was going to change. But, oh, how she wished it would.

'Come on.' She stepped back and turned to the door, her voice as artificially bright as her lipstick. 'We don't want to be late. Camilla has invited some local dignitaries and that means that you, my friend architect, have some schmoozing to do.'

'Oh, my goodness.' Flora stopped dead at the entrance to the dining room and stared, open-mouthed, at the décor within. 'This is…'

'Like the ghost of Christmas kitsch just threw up in here?' Alex murmured in her ear.

'No!' She gave him a little shove. 'Well, only a little. It's very pretty though.'

Lights hung in the windows encircling the rooftop room; lit, dazzling, heavily bedecked Christmas trees stood to attention between each window like an army of greenery guarding the room. More lights were draped from a centre point in the ceiling, creating a marquee-like effect.

The lighting was all blues and whites, giving the illusion that they were standing in a particularly gaudy ice cave. The same colours were repeated on the tree decorations, on the tables that were dotted around the room, on the huge snowflakes and baubles that hung from the ceiling. A small band in the corner played a waltz, the music soaring over the glamorous guests as they stood chatting in small groups throughout the room.

'I hope the colour scheme isn't reflected in the drinks,' Flora whispered. 'I haven't drunk blue curaçao since university but I don't think it agrees with me.'

'It could be white drinks. What about advocaat?'

She shuddered. 'Now you're being mean. I thought we'd promised never to mention that New Year ever again.'

Luckily, before too many more embarrassing memories could be dredged up, a waitress stopped before them with a tray of kir royales, topped with raspberries. Flora took the glass Alex handed to her, thankful it was nothing more dangerous. 'Happy Christmas,' she said and raised her glass to him.

'Happy Christmas, Flora.' He toasted her back but

the expression in his eyes was completely unreadable; his face wore the shuttered look she hated. It made him seem so far away. They only had tonight; she couldn't say goodbye early. She wasn't ready…

'Dance with me?'

He looked up at that, surprised. 'What? No one's dancing. It's still early.'

'So? If I can ski a red run on my second day you can be the first person onto the dance floor.'

'First couple,' he corrected her. 'There is no way on earth I would face that alone.' But he didn't demur any longer, holding his hand out to her and leading her to the centre of the room. There was a sudden hush as the other guests saw them step out but it was brief; the chatter starting up again as quickly as it had stopped.

Alex pulled her closer, one arm settling around her waist, the other clasping her hand. 'If we must do an exhibition dance then I am, for the first time, thankful that Minerva insisted that the whole wedding party needed to learn to dance properly.' It was a few years since the mandatory dance lessons but as he adjusted to the beat of the music it all began to come back. He could hear the teacher marking out the time as he had attempted to steer a mutinous Flora around the floor.

It was all so different now. She was pliant in his arms, letting him lead, her feet following his, her body at one with his—even if she did keep looking down at their feet.

'I don't remember you saying thank goodness at the time,' she pointed out, pausing to count under her breath. '*One* two three, *one* two three. It's a good job Minerva didn't want us all to salsa though.' She raised her eyes to his. They were luminous in the low light. 'Can you imagine how we'd look trying to salsa to this? We'd have to just do that slightly awkward shuffle instead.'

He tightened his arm, enjoying the feel of her so close to him, knowing that she was completely compliant, allowing him to take control. 'Did you know that the waltz was once considered scandalous?'

'Was it? Why?'

He lowered his voice. 'Just two people, a man, a woman, moving so closely together there's barely any space between them. His arm holding her to him, her hand clasped in his. He can feel her breasts pressing against his chest, smell the shampoo in her hair. If he wanted to...' He paused and looked directly into her upturned face, her mouth parted. 'If he wanted to kiss her then all he has to do is bend his head.'

'What if she didn't want him to kiss her?'

'Doesn't she?'

'Well...' Her lips curved into an enticing smile. 'Not in the middle of the dance floor. That really would cause a scandal. He would have to marry her if that happened.'

Alex blinked and she squeezed his hand reassuringly. 'In olden times I mean, silly. Don't worry, that wasn't a proposal.'

'Of course not.' But the words echoed round and round in his head. *Then he would have to marry her.*

The evening passed by in a quick blur as if someone had pressed fast forward. Alex lost Flora soon after their dance. Camilla whisked him away to meet, greet and act merry with the local dignitaries and influential industry movers and shakers while Flora was absorbed into a laughing group of revellers. The band switched to covers of popular songs and the dance floor was full.

But he could always find Flora; she stood out. Not just because of her height and her vibrant dress, but because she glowed as she moved across the floor.

He envied her even though he knew she deserved a carefree evening. He, on the other hand, was on his best behaviour, projecting the right image as he chatted to the VIPs Camilla needed him to impress.

Tomorrow it would all be over. This dazzling throng would pack away their finery ready for their trips home. He would return to Kent with Flora ready to resume their old friendship. Would it be enhanced by this week or tarnished? Maybe now they had given way to that old thrill of attraction they could move on—properly. She deserved a good man, someone to worship her, love her properly.

Alex folded his hands into tight fists, jealousy burning through him at the thought. How would he be able to stand there and smile as she held hands with another man, laughed up at another man, kissed another man?

There was only one way to bear it—to start thinking of his own future. A future beyond work and the need for success and recognition that had driven him so far, so fast. Was it so unthinkable that he too could have a long-term relationship? Maybe even marriage? Plenty of people had satisfactory, even successful lives together based on mutual respect and shared goals rather than passion and romance. Why not him?

He took another glass of kir royale from a passing

waitress, mechanically nodding and smiling as the conversation around him turned to families and Christmas. His least favourite subject.

It wasn't that he didn't love spending the festive season with the Buckinghams. It wasn't as if they ever treated him as anything but one of the family. They didn't. He had been expected to muck in with the rest of them long before he'd started living there, peeling potatoes, setting the table, chopping logs for the fire—whatever was needed. Yes, they treated him like one of the family. But he *wasn't* family.

His own family had cast him out and one day the Buckinghams would too. Not on purpose but time wouldn't freeze. They wouldn't all return to the small Kentish village for the festive season for ever. One day Minerva would want to host Christmas, or Horry, if he ever looked up from his scalpel long enough to have a relationship. Or Flora would. Would there be a place for him in the family then? In ten years? In twenty?

He downed his drink. The solution was simple. It was time he thought about creating his own place. His own traditions and memories. Somewhere he built so he couldn't be cast out. The problem was he couldn't imagine anyone beside him but Flora.

And she deserved more…

He took another glass from a passing tray. And he watched her, trying to ignore the unwanted leap his heart gave when she smiled over at him. A secret smile of complicity.

Yes, she deserved more. But would she get it?

The thing was, he decided as he finished one glass and swapped it for another, that good things didn't always come to those who waited. After all, Flora hadn't

had much luck with her past boyfriends. Just because
he was prepared to do the right thing and stand aside
didn't mean she would end up with someone who deserved her. It was all such a lottery. *He* could offer
stability, space, affection. These were all good com-
modities in the trading place that was marriage. In return he would get a home. A place that was his.

It was a good trade.

Marriage.

Was he seriously thinking about it?

The room had darkened, the music quietening back
to the classical waltzes so typical of Austria and the
dance floor was now occupied by couples, the English
swaying together awkwardly, the Austrians waltzing
with the same grace he had admired on the ice rink
and on the slopes.

Flora stood on the opposite side of the room, leaning
against a chair and watching the dances, yearning on
her face. Alex put his glass down and weaved his way
over to her. He had drunk more than he usually allowed
himself to; everything felt fuzzier, softer. Sweeter.

'Hi, have you been released early?'

'Time off for good behaviour. Having fun?'

'You know what…' she blinked at him, owlish in
her solemn surprise '… I have. There are some really
lovely people here.'

'Dance with me.' It wasn't a request and she obediently took his proffered hand, allowing him to lead her
back onto the floor. She sank in close, her hand splayed
on his back, and he could feel where every part of her
touched him as if they weren't separated by layers of
material but as if they were back in the ski lodge, learning each other anew.

Her head was on his shoulder, nestled in trustingly. They had trust. They had friendship.

They had passion.

It was a lot.

Alex stopped. 'Flora?'

'Mmm…why aren't we dancing?' She looked up at him, her mouth curved invitingly, and that was all he needed. Alex dipped his head and kissed her, a sweet, gentle caress.

She smiled up at him. 'That was nice. What was that for?'

'I wanted to.' He began to move again, slowing the steps down so that they were out of time with the music, dancing to their own private beat, their lips finding each other again, a deeper, intoxicating kiss. He was dimly aware that they were still moving, that the violins were soaring, the lights were low, but none of it was real. Only they were real. Just the taste of her, the feel of her, the scent of her. He wanted to sink deeper and deeper, to be absorbed by her, into her.

Only she was real. She made him real.

'Not here.' Flora's breath was ragged as she broke away. 'Not like that.'

He stared at her uncomprehendingly, still lost in the memory of her warmth.

'I mean…' She squeezed his hand, running her thumb over his palm, trailing fire with her touch. Fire that threatened to consume him. 'We're in the middle of a dance floor. I think we should take this back to our room.'

Of course. How could he have forgotten? How could he have been so swept up in the moment that he had lost track of where they were, forgotten that they weren't alone?

He swallowed. 'I warned you that the waltz was a scandalous dance.'

'You did,' she agreed. 'Am I quite compromised?'

''I think so…' His earlier thoughts came back to haunt him. Peace, stability, a family of his own… 'Unless we marry. What about it, Flora? Will you marry me?'

CHAPTER TEN

THE WALK BACK to the room seemed to take for ever. Every few steps they bumped into a group of Flora's new friends wanting to drag her off to the bar, to after parties, for midnight walks out in the snow.

She turned each of them down with a laughing non-committal reply but the whole situation didn't seem real. Her voice was too bright, her smile too wild and there was a buzzing in her ears as if she were in a waking dream.

Alex didn't say anything at all. His hand clasped hers tight; his eyes burned with that same strange intensity she had seen on the dance floor.

And his words echoed round and round in her head. *Will you marry me?*

Of course he had been joking. Of course. There was no doubt. Just because his fingers were gripping hers tightly, just because she had daydreamed a similar scenario more times than she had imagined winning the lottery didn't make it real.

Only…he had sounded serious.

What if he was serious?

No. Of course he wasn't because dreams didn't simply just come true. A dance floor, a waltz, beautiful lighting, champagne; that was the stuff of fairy tales, not real life. Not Flora's life.

But he *looked* serious.

She had been so desperate to get him back to the room but as they approached the door an unexpected caution hit her. Whatever was done and said when they got inside couldn't be unsaid, couldn't be undone. And his face was so very set. The passion and laughter wiped clear as if they had never been.

Flora took a deep breath as they walked into the room. It was her imagination, that was all, working on his words and twisting them into something more serious than intended. She needed to lighten up, enjoy these last few hours before it all changed back and she was back in her rags clutching a pumpkin.

Okay. Lightening up. 'Alone at last.' She smiled provocatively at him but there was no answering smile on his face.

'I meant it, you know. Marry me.'

Flora reached up to unclasp her necklace but at his quiet words her hands dropped helplessly to her side. 'No bended knee, no flash mob, no ring in my ice cream?' She tried to tease but the joke was flatter than one of her father's failed soufflés, and Alex didn't acknowledge it with as much as a flicker of an eyelid.

She walked over to the window and stared out. Ahead was darkness but if she looked up then the stars shone with an astonishing intensity, unfamiliar to a girl used to London's never fully darkened skies. Below Innsbruck was lit up like a toy town. Not quite real.

Like this moment.

'Why?'

She held her breath, hope fluttering wildly in her

chest. Would he say it? *Because I love you. I have always loved you.*

He didn't answer, not straight away. She heard him pace back and forth, imagined him shrugging off the tuxedo jacket, undoing his bow tie, running his hands through his disordered curls.

'Does it matter why?' he asked at last.

She still couldn't turn to face him but at his words hope's flutters became feebler and nausea began to swirl in her stomach.

'I think so, yes.' *Tell me, tell me,* she silently begged him. *Tell me what I need to hear and I'll believe you.*

Even though she knew it wouldn't be true.

'No one knows me like you do. You know everything, all the darkness, and you're still here.'

'Of course I am.'

'We know we're compatible. I think we could lead very comfortable, happy lives together. The sex is good—more than good. And marriage would tick other boxes too.'

Flora swallowed. Hope finally gave up and withered away. Her stomach still twisted with nausea but most thought and feeling drained away to a much-needed numbness. 'Great,' she murmured. Marriage as a box-ticking exercise. Just what she had always dreamed of. Maybe they could make a list and follow it up with a presentation on the computer.

'It would make things a lot easier for you as you change focus. I know money has been tight. That wouldn't be an issue any longer, and there's plenty of space at my house for a studio and storage.'

'Money, storage...' she repeated as if in a dream,

the practical words not quite sinking in. 'And what about you? What's in it for you, apart from good sex?'

He didn't seem to hear the bitterness in her last words, just continuing as if this were a completely sane conversation. 'For me? No more dating, trying to be someone I'm not. Freedom to work—you wouldn't mind when work took me abroad, wouldn't expect me to check in every five minutes. There wouldn't be any misunderstandings, any expectations—you wouldn't want more than I can give.'

'No, I suppose I wouldn't.' Not now anyway. It wasn't as if he hadn't warned her, was it? She had chosen not to listen. Not to guard herself against this.

She wasn't numb now, she was cold. A biting chill working its way up from her toes, bone deep.

He hadn't noticed, was still listing soulless benefits as if it were next week's shopping list. 'And there would be no real adjustment. We know each other's bad habits, moods, and I get on with your family. Think about it, Flora. It makes perfect sense.'

'Yes, I can see that.' She turned at last. He had discarded his jacket and his tie, his shirt half untucked and unbuttoned, his hair falling over his forehead. He looked slightly dangerous, a little degenerate like the sort of regency rake who would kiss a girl on a dance floor and not care about the consequences.

And yet here he was offering a marriage of convenience. If she said no—*when* she said no—then everything really would change. They might be able to sweep a week of passion under the carpet. They wouldn't be able to sweep this away.

Especially when every traitorous fibre of her wanted to say yes.

'I can't…' she said before she allowed herself to weaken.

His eyes blazed for one heartbreaking moment and then the shutters came down. 'Right. I see. Fine. Silly of me to think you would. Let's not mention it again.'

'I need more from marriage.' The words were tumbling out. 'I want love.'

A muscle worked in his cheek. 'I do love you, you know that. As much as I can.'

'But are you *in* love with me?'

She couldn't believe she'd asked that. The last taboo, more powerful than the kisses they had shared, the whispered intimacies. This, *this* was the big one. But she had to know. She took a deep, shuddering breath and waited. Would he? Did he? All he had to do was tell her he loved her and she would be in.

He ran a hand through his hair. 'Do I care about you? Yes. Desire you? Absolutely. Like your company? You know I do. Isn't that enough?'

Flora shook her head. 'I wish it was,' she whispered. 'But I want more. I want the whole crazy, passionate, all-consuming love. I want to be the centre of someone's world and for my world to revolve around them.'

But he was shaking his head, a denial of her words, of her hopes and dreams. 'That's not real love, Flora. That's a crush at best, obsession at worst,' and with those calm words Flora felt something inside her crack clean in two.

'Oxytocin, serotonin. Hormones telling you lies. Love? It's unstable, it can't be trusted. But you're right. Marriage between us is a bad idea.' He stepped back and picked up his jacket, shrugging himself into it. 'I'm sorry I embarrassed you. If you'll excuse me, then I am going to get a drink. I'll see you later. Don't wait up.'

The plane was buzzing with festive spirit. Bags stuffed into the overhead lockers filled with brightly wrapped presents, people chatting eagerly to their seatmates— even strangers—about their plans for the next few days. Even the pilot made some flying reindeer jokes as he prepared them for take-off.

But the buzz didn't reach their two seats. They were ensconced in roomy first-class comfort. There were free drinks, legroom, food—but Alex and Flora sat stiffly as if they were crammed into the most cramped economy seat.

Flora was sleeping—or, Alex suspected, she was pretending to—and he was looking through documents as if the fate of Christmas depended on his memorising them by heart. If that had been the case then Christmas was in trouble; no matter how often he skimmed a sentence his brain could not make head or tail of it, his brain revolving round and round and round.

She'd said no. Even the person who knew him best, who he thought loved him best, didn't want to risk her happiness on him.

And now he'd done exactly what he had sworn he would never do. He'd broken Flora's heart, tainted their friendship, ruined his relationship with her family. Because how could he possibly turn up there tomorrow ready to bask in Christmas cheer when he couldn't even look at Flora?

Especially as she couldn't look at him either. Oh, she was trying. She made stilted conversation, her smile too bright, her voice too cheery, but her eyes slid away when they reached his face, her body leaning away from his whenever they were close. Luckily his monosyllabic replies hadn't seemed too out of character when other people were around—most of the departing guests were similarly afflicted, suffering the effects of overindulgence the night before.

It wasn't a hangover that affected him, although heaven only knew he'd tried his best. Sitting in the bar until three a.m., drinking alone at the end, trying to block out the voices from his head.

You taint everything.

I can't marry you.

I want love.

What could he answer to that when he didn't even know what love was? The twisted obsession his father had had for his mother, so jealous he didn't even want to share her affection with their child? The grateful desperation he had shown towards his stepmother for deigning to notice him and the dark turning that had taken?

He didn't want or need that selfish emotion. There was a time when that made him feel invincible, as if he had an invisible armour protecting him from the follies that befell so many of his friends.

Now he just felt lost. Stuck in a labyrinth he didn't have the key for—only there was no princess holding a ball of string ready to guide him out. And there was no monster. *He* was the monster.

How could he return to Kent with her now? It was her home, not his. The only place he belonged to was the house he had designed in Primrose Hill. But he didn't want to return there alone, to spend Christmas alone in a house without a heart.

Maybe it wasn't too late to grab a last-minute flight and head out again. He looked around the plane at the bland décor, the packed seats filled with strangers, the almost soothing signs telling him to sit back, switch his phone off, keep his seat belt on. He could spend Christmas Day on a flight. It almost didn't matter where to.

'Do you have to pick up presents and things before you head back home?' His throat scratched as he forced the words out, as if unaccustomed to speaking.

Flora's eyes opened a fraction. 'Yes, if that's okay.'

'I've ordered you a car. It'll run you back to yours and wait for you, as long as you need, then take you home to Kent.'

She sat up at that, any pretence at sleep forgotten. 'You're not coming back with me?'

'Not tonight, I have too much to do.'

'Too much to do on Christmas Eve? Everything's shut for the next few days. What on earth can't wait? But you are driving down tomorrow?'

He couldn't answer.

Her eyes flashed. 'We promised, Alex, we promised that we wouldn't let things change.'

Had she really believed they wouldn't? Had he? He closed his eyes, exhausted. 'We lied.'

There was no more to be said. Not for the last hour of the flight, not during the tedious business of disembarking, immigration and baggage collecting. Not as he saw the sign with his name on it and steered a mute Flora towards it.

'Can you drop my bags and skis off at my house on your way out?' he asked. 'You have your key?'

She turned to look at him, her face paler than usual, the white accented by the deep shadows under her eyes.

'You're not even travelling with me? How are you getting home?'

He shrugged. 'Train, Tube. My own two feet.'

'You're getting on the train? On Christmas Eve? It'll be packed!'

He couldn't explain it, the need to wander, to be anonymous in a vast sea of people where nobody knew him, judged him. 'I'll be fine. I just need some space.'

She stared at him sceptically and then turned away, the dismissive movement conveying everything. Hurting far more than he had expected. 'Suit yourself. You always do.'

He stood and watched her walk away. 'Merry Christmas, Flora.' But she was too far away and his words fell unheard.

The train was as unpleasant as Flora had forecast. Alex was unable to get a seat and so he stood for the fifteen-minute journey back into London, barricaded into his spot by other people's suitcases and bulging bags of presents. The carriage stank of sweat, alcohol, fried chicken and desperation, the air punctuated by a baby's increasingly desperate cries and the sounds of several computer games turned up to a decidedly anti-social volume.

No wonder he rarely travelled by public transport. Alex gritted his teeth and hung on; he deserved no better.

Not that anyone else seemed to be suffering. His fellow travellers seemed to be as full of Christmas Eve cheer as those on the plane, upbeat despite the conditions. But once he had finally got off the train and stood under the iconic glass curved roof of Paddington Station the last thing he wanted was to disappear underground and repeat the experience on a Tube train full of last-minute desperate shoppers, Christmas revellers and people freed from work and ready to celebrate. It was a couple of miles' walk to Primrose Hill but half of that was through Regent's Park and he could do with clearing his head.

Besides, he didn't want to risk bumping into Flora when she dropped his bags off. For the first time in his life he had no idea what to say to her.

It was hard not to contrast the grey, unseasonably warm day with the crisp air and snowy scenes he had left behind. Hard not to dwell on the fact that for the first time in a week he was alone.

Hard to face the reality that this was his future. He'd always thought of himself as so self-sufficient. Hardened.

He'd been lying to himself.

Alex bought a coffee from one of the kiosks, curtly refusing any festive flavourings, and set off, the last week replaying through his head on repeat, slowing down to dwell in agonising detail at every misstep. He shouldn't have kissed her. He shouldn't have allowed her to kiss him.

He shouldn't have proposed.

It shouldn't hurt so much that she said no...

He wandered aimlessly, not caring much where his feet took him. The back streets were an eclectic mix of tree-lined Georgian squares, post-war blocks and newer, shabbier-looking business premises. Like all of central London, the very wealthy rubbed shoulders with the poor; wine bars, delis and exclusive boutiques on one street, a twenty-four-hour supermarket and take-away on the next.

It wasn't until he hit Russell Square that Alex realised just how far he had walked—and how far out of his way he was. He stood for a moment in the middle of the old Bloomsbury square wondering what to do. Head into a pub and drink himself into oblivion? Keep walking until he was so exhausted the pain in his legs outweighed the weight in his chest? Just sit here in the busy square and gradually decompose?

Or run home, grab the car and head off to Kent. He'd be welcomed; he knew that. Flora would try her best to pretend everything was okay. But he didn't belong there, not really. He didn't belong anywhere or with anyone.

So what would it be? Pub, walk or wither away in the middle of Bloomsbury? He leaned against a bench, unsure for the first time in a really long time which way he should go, looking around at the leafless trees and railings for inspiration when a brown sign caught his eye. Of course! The British Museum was just around the corner. He could while away the rest of the afternoon in there. Hide amongst the mummies and the ancient sculptures and pretend that it wasn't Christmas Eve. Pretend he had somewhere to go, someone to care.

Pretend he was worth something.

His decision was made; only as he rounded the corner and hurried towards the huge gates shielding the classically inspired façade of the famous museum he was greeted, not by open gates and doors and a safe neutral place, but by iron bars and locks. The museum was closed.

Alex let out a deep breath, one he hadn't even

known he was holding, gripping the wrought-iron bars as if he could push them apart. No sanctuary for him. Maybe it was a judgement. He wasn't worthy, no rest for him.

He stared at the steps, the carved pillars, the very shut doors. It was strange he hadn't visited the museum in the eleven years he'd lived in London; after all, it was visiting this very building that had first triggered his interest in building design. The neoclassical façade built to house the ancient treasures within. He used to come here every summer with his grandmother.

With his grandmother…

When had that stopped? When had he stopped seeing her? Before he was ten, he was pretty sure. She took him out a couple of times his first year at prep school, had visited regularly before then, although he had never been allowed an overnight stay. And then? Nothing.

No cards, no Christmas presents. Nothing. He hadn't even thought to ask where she had gone—after all, his father had made it very clear that it was Alex who was the problem. Alex who was innately unlovable.

But it wasn't normal, was it? For a grandparent to disappear so completely from a child's life? If she had blamed Alex for her daughter's death then she wouldn't have been around at all. And surely even his father would have told him if she had died.

There was something missing, something rotten at the heart of him and he had to know what it was, had to fix it. Fix his friendship with Flora.

Be worthy of her…

He couldn't ask his mother why she couldn't love him, why she'd left him. He couldn't expect any meaningful dialogue with his father. But maybe his grand-mother had some answers. If he could find her.

He had to find her. He couldn't go on like this.

Christmas Eve was usually Flora's favourite day of the year. All the anticipation, the air of secrecy and suppressed excitement. The rituals, unchanging and sacred. They were usually all home and unpacked by late afternoon before gathering together in the large sitting room to admire the tree and watch Christmas films. The last couple of years they had pretended that the films were to amuse the children—but the children usually got bored and wandered off leaving the adults rapt, enthralled by stories they had watched a hundred times before.

Then a takeaway to spare Flora's dad cooking for this one evening, before stockings were hung. Milk and carrots would be put out for the reindeers, home-made gingerbread and a snifter of brandy for Father Christmas himself and then the children were bundled off to bed. The last few years Minerva and Flora's mother had stayed behind to babysit the children and put the last few touches to presents but the rest of the family would disappear off to the pub for a couple of hours, finishing off at Midnight Mass in the ancient village church.

She loved every unchanging moment of it.

But this year it would all be different.

What if she had said yes? Right now she and Alex could be walking into the house hand in hand to con-gratulations, tears, champagne.

But it would all have been a lie.

Flora took a deep breath, trying to steady her nerves

as the car Alex had ordered for her rolled smoothly through the village towards the cottage her parents had bought over thirty years before, but her hands were trembling and her stomach tumbling with nervous anticipation. They must never know. Alex thought they would blame him but she knew better; they would blame her for driving him away.

She needed some air, time to compose herself before the onslaught of her family. 'This will be fine, thanks,' she said to the driver as they reached the bottom of her lane. 'I can walk from here.'

Flora stood for a moment gulping in air before shrugging her weekend bag onto her back and picking up the shopping bags full of presents. The bags were heavy and her back was aching before she had got more than halfway down the lane but she welcomed the discomfort. It was her penance.

The cottage stood alone at the end of the lane, a low-roofed half-timber, half-redbrick house surrounded by a wild-looking garden and fruit trees. Her father grew most of his own vegetables and herbs and kept noisy chickens in the back, although he was too soft-hearted to do more than collect their eggs.

The house was lit up against the grey of a late December afternoon, smoke wafting from the chimney a welcome harbinger. All she wanted to do was curl up in front of the fire and mourn but instead Flora pinned a determined smile onto her face and pushed open the heavy oak front door.

Game face on. 'Merry Christmas,' she called as the door swung open.

'Flora!' 'Aunty Flora!' 'Darling.' She was almost instantly enveloped in hugs and kisses, her coat re-

moved, bags taken from her aching arms, drawn into
the sitting room, a mince pie put into one hand, a cup
of tea into the other as the chatter continued.

'How was Austria? Did you see snow?'

'Your scarf looked lovely in that picture. Congratulations, darling.'

'We need to talk strategy.' Minerva, of course. 'Boxing Day you are mine. No running off.'

'Nice journey back, darling?'

And the inevitable: 'Where's Alex?' 'Didn't Alex
travel with you?' 'Did you leave Alex in Austria?'

If she had come back to a quiet house. If it had just
been Flora and her dad, she sitting at the wide kitchen
counter while he bustled and tasted and stirred. Then
she might have cracked. But the tree was in the corner of the room, decorated to within an inch of its
life and blazing with light, her nieces were already at
fever-pitch point and for once nobody was asking when
she was going to get a real job/move out of that poky
room/get a boyfriend/grow up.

So she smiled and agreed that yes, the scarf looked
lovely; yes, Minerva could have all the time she
needed; yes, there was plenty of snow and guess what,
she'd even been on a horse-drawn sleigh. And no, Alex
wasn't with her, he had been delayed but he should be
with them tomorrow.

And if she crossed her fingers at that last statement
it wasn't because she was lying. It was because she
was hoping. Because now she was here she couldn't
imagine Christmas without him. She couldn't imagine
a life that didn't have him in it.

And even though she wished that he loved her the
way that she loved him. And even though she would

have given everything for his proposal to have come from his heart and not his head, she still wished he were here. Even if it was as friends. Because friends was still something special. Something to cherish.

She needed to tell him. Before he sealed himself away. Before he talked himself into utter isolation.

'I'm just going to take my bags upstairs. No, it's okay, thanks, Greg,' she assured her brother-in-law. 'I can manage. Besides…' she looked mock sternly at her giggling nieces '…I don't want any peeping.' She kissed her still-chattering mother on the cheek and went back into the hallway to retrieve her bags and hoist them up the wide carpeted staircase that led to the first floor and then up the winding, painted wooden stairs to the attic. There were just two bedrooms up here, sharing a small shower room. To the left was Flora's room, to the right a small box room they had converted into a room for Alex.

His bedroom door was ajar and Flora couldn't help peeking in as she turned. The bed had been made up with fresh linen and towels were piled onto the wicker chair in the corner. An old trunk lay at the foot of the bed—his old school trunk—a blanket laid across the top. A small bookshelf held some books but otherwise it was bare. Spartan. He had never allowed himself to be too at home here. Or anywhere. No wonder he was such an expert packer.

Flora's room was a stark contrast. It was more than twice the size of his with a wide dormer window as well as a skylight. Old toys, books and ornaments were still displayed on the shelves and on the white, scalloped dressing table and chest of drawers she had thought so sophisticated when she was twelve. Old posters of ponies and boy bands were stuck to her walls and a clutter of old scarves, old make-up and magazines gave the room a lived-in air.

She dropped her bags thankfully in a corner of the room and pulled her phone out of her pocket. The message light flashed and Flora's heart lurched with hope as she eagerly scanned it, but, although she had received at least a million emails urging her to buy her last-minute Christmas gifts Right Now, been promised the best rate to pay off her Christmas debts by several credit-card companies and a very good deal on sexual enhancement products, there was nothing at all from Alex.

Swallowing back her disappointment, she stared thoughtfully at her screen. Call or text? Texting would be easier, give her a chance to phrase her words carefully. But maybe this shouldn't be careful. It had to be from the heart. She pressed his number before she could talk herself out of it and listened to the dial tone, her heart hammering.

She was so keyed up it didn't register at first that the voice at the other end wasn't Alex but his voicemail message. 'Darn it,' she muttered while his slightly constrained voice informed her that he wasn't available right now but would get back to her as soon as he could.

'Alex,' she said quickly as soon as it beeped. 'It's me. Come home. Please? It's not the same without you. We all miss you. We'll be okay, I promise. Just come home. Come home for Christmas.'

She clicked the hang-up icon and let the phone drop onto her bed. She had done all she could. It was up to him now.

CHAPTER ELEVEN

HOW HE REMEMBERED the address, Alex had no idea. He must have written it on enough letters that somehow he had retained the information, lying dormant until his need unlocked it once again. It took less than an hour of research to ascertain that his grandmother was still alive and living in the same house. But as he drove along the leafy, prosperous-looking road it was all completely unfamiliar and doubts began to creep in.

What if he had got the name and address wrong?

Or worse, what if he had got them right and she didn't want to see him?

He pulled up outside a well-maintained-looking white house and killed the engine. What was he doing? It was Christmas Eve and he was about to drop in, unannounced, on a long-lost relative who probably didn't want to see him. He must be crazy. Alex gripped the steering wheel and swore softly. But then he remembered Flora's face as she walked away from him at the airport. Disappointed, defeated. If there was any way he could put things right, he would.

And this might help.

The house looked shut up. Every curtain was drawn and there was no sign of light or life anywhere. The driveway was so thickly gravelled that he couldn't step quietly no matter how lightly he trod, and the crunch from each step echoed loudly, disturbing the eerie twilight silence. Any minute he expected a neighbour to accost him but there was no movement anywhere. It was like being in an alternative universe where he was the last soul standing.

The door was a substantial wooden oval with an imposing brass door knocker. It was cold and heavy as he lifted it, making far more of a bang than he expected when he rapped it on the door. He stood listening to the echo disturb the absolute silence, shivering a little in the murky air.

Alex shifted from foot to foot as he waited, straining to hear any movement in the house. He was just debating whether to try again or give up, half turning to walk away, when the door swung open.

'Oh, you're not the carol singers.' He turned back, words of explanation ready on his tongue when he found himself staring into a pair of familiar green-grey eyes, eyes growing round, hope and shock mingled in their depths. 'Alex? Is it really you?'

'You're not watching the films?' Flora's dad looked up from the pastry he was expertly rolling out and smiled at her. 'It's *The Muppet Christmas Carol.*'

'I know.' Flora wandered over to the oak and marble counter where her father practised his recipes and slipped a finger into the bowl of fragrant home-made mincemeat, sucking the sweet, spicy mixture appreciatively. 'Mmm, this is gorgeous. What's the secret ingredient?'

'Earl Grey and lemon.' He nodded at her finger. 'Dip

that again and I'll chop it off. I thought the Muppets were your favourite?'

'They are.' Flora slid onto a high stool and leaned forward, propping her chin in her hands as she watched her father work. The pastry was a perfect smooth square as he began to cut out the rounds. 'Only I peeped in and Minerva, the twins and Greg are all curled up on the sofa. They looked so sweet I didn't want to disturb them.'

'They wouldn't have minded.'

'I know, but it's not often I see Minerva so relaxed. She might have wanted to start talking marketing strategy or buzz creation and then the film would have been ruined for everyone.'

'That's very thoughtful of you.' Her mother bustled into the kitchen, her phone in her hand. 'Great news, darling. Horry's colleague wants to work Christmas, bad break-up apparently, so she'd rather work. Awful for her but it means Horry can come home this evening after all. Now we just need Alex and the whole family is together again.'

Guilt punched Flora's chest and she resisted the urge to look at her phone to see if he'd responded. 'I'm sure he'll be here as soon as he can.'

'We're all very excited about your scarves.' Her mother filled the kettle and began to collect cups from the vast dresser that dominated the far wall. The kitchen used to be two rooms but they had been knocked into one and a glass-roofed extension added to make it a huge, airy, sun-filled space filled with gadgets, curios and the bits and bobs Flora's dad couldn't resist: painted bowls, salt and pepper pots, vintage jugs and a whole assortment of souvenirs. Saucepans hung from a rack on the ceiling, there were planted herbs on every window sill and the range cooker usually had something tasty baking, bubbling or roasting, filling the air with rich aromas.

'It doesn't seem quite real.' Flora grimaced. 'I'm sure Minerva will change that. She was hissing something about Gantt charts earlier.'

'She's right, you should take this seriously.' Her mother added three teaspoons of tea to the large pot and topped it with the boiled water. No teabags or shortcuts in the Buckingham kitchen. 'I don't know why it's taken you so long. It's obvious you should have been focusing on this, not wasting your talents on that awful pub chain. Those disgusting neon lemons…' She shuddered.

Flora stared at her mother. 'I thought you wanted me to have a steady job.' She couldn't keep the hurt out of her voice. 'You're always asking me when I'm going to settle down—in a job, a relationship, a place of my own.'

'No,' her mother contradicted as she passed Flora a cup of tea. Flora wrapped her hands around it, grateful for its warmth. 'I wanted you to have direction. To know where you *wanted* to go. You always seemed so lost, Flora. Vet school to compete with the twins, interior design to fit in with Alex. I just wanted you to follow your own heart.'

'It's not always that easy though, is it? I mean, sometimes your heart can lead you astray.' To Flora's horror she could feel tears bubbling up. She swallowed hard, trying to hold back the threatening sob, ducking her head to hide her eyes. She should have known better. Nothing ever escaped Dr Jane Buckingham's sharp eyes.

'Flora?' Her mother's voice was gentle and that, combined with the gentle hug, pushed Flora over the edge she had been teetering on. It was almost a relief to let the tears flow, to let the sobs burst out, easing the painful pressure in her chest just a little. Her mother didn't probe or ask any more, she just held Flora as she cried, rubbing her back and smoothing her hair off her wet cheeks.

It was like being a child again. If only her mother could fix this. If only it *were* fixable.

It took several minutes before the sobs quietened, the tears stopped and the hiccups subsided. Flora had been guided to the old but very comfortable chintzy sofa by the window, her tea handed to her along with yet another of her father's mince pies. She curled up onto the cushions and stared out of the window at the pot-filled patio and the lawn beyond.

'I won't ask any awkward questions,' her mother promised as she sat next to her. 'But if you do want to talk we're always here. You do know that, I hope, darling.'

Flora nodded, not quite trusting herself to speak. She didn't often confide in her parents, not wanting to see the disappointed looks on their faces, not to feel that yet again she was a let-down compared to her high-flying siblings.

But she wasn't sure she could carry this alone. Not any more.

'Alex asked me to marry him.'

She didn't miss the exchange of glances between her parents. They didn't look shocked, more saddened.

'I wondered if it was Alex. You've always loved him so.'

She had no secrets, it seemed, and there was no point in denying it. She nodded. 'But he doesn't love me. He thought marriage would be sensible. He said I would have financial stability and storage for my designs.'

'Oh.'

'I mean, I didn't expect sonnets but I didn't think anyone would ever suggest storage as a reason for marriage.' Flora was aware she sounded bitter. 'How could I say yes? It would have been so wrong for both of us. Only now he's not here and I miss him so much...'

Her mother patted her knee. 'Have I ever told you how your father and I met?'

Flora stifled a sigh. Here it came, the patented Dr Jane Buckingham anecdote filled with advice. 'You were flatmates,' she muttered.

'For a year,' her father said, standing back to survey the trays of finished mince pies.

'And then you went out for dinner and looked into each other's eyes and the rest is history.' Perfect couple with their perfect jobs and a perfect home and nearly perfect children. The story had been rehashed in a hundred interviews.

'I think I fell in love with your mother the moment I saw her,' her father said, a reminiscent tone in his voice. 'But I didn't think I was good enough for her. I was a hobby baker and trainee food journalist and there she was, a junior doctor. Brilliant, fierce, dedicated. I didn't know what to say to her. So I didn't really say anything at all.'

Flora's mother picked up the tale. 'But when I came off shift—exhausted after sixty hours on my feet, malnourished after grabbing something from the hospital canteen—I would walk in and there would be something ready for me. No matter what time. A filo pie and roasted vegetables at two in the morning, piles of fluffy pancakes heaped with fruit at seven a.m. Freshly made bread and delicious salads at noon.' A soft smile curved her mother's lips. 'Do you remember when I said I missed falafel and you made them? They weren't readily available then,' she told her daughter. 'It was just a passing comment but I got home two days later to find freshly made falafel and home-made hummus in the fridge.'

'You old romantic.' Flora smiled over at her dad.

'I still barely spoke to her,' he admitted. 'I didn't know what to say. But I listened.'

'And then on Valentine's Day I came in, so tired I could barely drag myself in through the door, and waiting for me was the most beautiful breakfast. Home-made granola, eggs Benedict, little pastries. And I understood what he'd been telling me for the last year. Not with words but with food, with his actions. So I slept and then I took *him* out for dinner to say thank you. We got married six months later.'

'If you want to be wooed with flowers and lovely words, then Alex is never going to be the man for you, Flora,' her father added. 'And maybe he really does think storage and stability is enough. But *maybe* those words mask something more. You need to dig a little deeper. See what's really in his heart. A pancake isn't always just a pancake.'

Flora bit into the mince pie. The pastry was perfect, firm yet melting with a lemony tang, the filling spicy yet subtle. When it came to food her dad was always spot on. Maybe he was right here as well.

'Thank you,' she said, but she couldn't help checking her phone as she did so. Nor could she deny the sharp stab of disappointment when she saw that Alex hadn't replied.

Was her father right? Was Alex's matter-of-fact proposal a cover for deeper feelings and if so would she be able to live with someone who would never be able to say what was in their heart? Live with the constant uncertainty? Flora sighed; maybe she was clutching at straws and there was no hidden meaning. Maybe storage was just that. The question was how willing was she to find out and what compromises was she willing to make?

And if a practical marriage was the only way to keep him, then could she settle for that when the alternative was losing him for ever?

'That's you and your mother. You must have been about eighteen months.'

Alex stared at the photo, lovingly mounted in a leather book. It was one of several charting his mother's brief life from a smiling baby to a wary-looking teen, a shy young bride to a proud mother.

'She looks…'

'Happy?' his grandmother supplied. 'She was, a lot of the time.'

Alex struggled to marry this side of his mother with the few pieces of information his father had begrudgingly fed him. He put the album back onto the low wooden coffee table and stared around the room in search of help.

Alex had never really known any of his grandparents but he had always imagined them in old, musty houses filled with cushions, lace tablecloths and hordes of silver-framed photos. The light, clean lines of his grandmother's sitting room were as far from the dark rooms of his dreams as the slim woman opposite with her trendy pixie cut and jeans and jacket was from the grey-haired granny of his imagination.

'My father said she cried all the time. That she hated being a mother, hated me. That's why...' he faltered. 'That's why she did what she did.'

His grandmother closed her eyes briefly. 'I should have tried harder, Alex. I should have fought for you. Your father made things so difficult. I was allowed a day here, a day there, no overnight stays or holidays and I was too scared to push in case he locked me out completely—but he did that anyway. In the end my letters were returned, my gifts sent back. He said it was too hard for you to be reminded of the past, that he wanted you to settle with your stepmother.'

Letters, gifts? His father hadn't just returned material items. He had made sure that Alex would never have a loving relationship with his family.

His grandmother twisted her hands. 'If I had tried harder then I could have made sure you knew about your mother. The colours she liked, her favourite books, the way she sang when she was happy. But most importantly I could have told you that she loved you. Because she did, very, very much. But she wasn't well. She didn't think she was a good enough mother, she worried about every little thing—every cry was a reminder that she was letting you down. Every tiny incident a reminder that she was failing you. In the end she convinced herself that you would be better off without her.'

Alex blinked, heat burning his eyes. 'She was wrong.'

'I know. I should have made her get help.' She closed her eyes and for a moment she looked much older, frailer, her face lined with grief. 'But she was good at hiding her feelings and she was completely under your father's control. He couldn't admit that she wasn't well; it didn't fit with his vision of the perfect family. And so she got more adept at denying she was struggling but all the time she was sinking deeper and deeper. I knew something was wrong but every time I tried to talk to her she would back away. So I stopped trying, afraid that I would lose her. But I lost her anyway. And I lost you.' Her voice faltered, still raw with grief all these years later.

Alex swallowed. 'Can you tell me about her now?'

His grandmother blinked, her eyes shiny with tears, and glanced up at the clock on the mantelpiece. 'Goodness, is that the time? My son—your uncle—will be collecting me soon. I always spend Christmas Eve at their house. You have three cousins, all younger than you, of course, but they will be so excited to meet you.'

Christmas Eve, how could he have forgotten? 'I'm sorry, I didn't think…'

His grandmother carried on as if he hadn't spoken. 'I'm just going to ask him to collect me in the morning instead. You will stay for dinner? There's a room if you want to spend the night. We have a lifetime of catching up to do. Unless, there must be somewhere you need to be. A handsome boy like you. A wife?' Her eyes flickered to his left hand. 'A girlfriend?'

Alex shook his head. 'No,' he said. 'There isn't anyone.' But as he spoke the words he knew they weren't entirely true.

Alex wasn't sure how long his grandmother was

gone. He was lost in the past, going through each album again, committing each photo to heart. His mother as a young girl on the beach, her graduation photos, her wedding pictures. There was a proud, proprietorial gleam in his father's eyes that sent a shiver snaking down Alex's spine. Love wasn't meant to be selfish and destructive; he might not know much but he knew that. Surely it was supposed to be about support, putting the other person first. Shared goals.

Pretty much what he had offered Flora.

And yet it hadn't been enough…

His brooding thoughts were interrupted as his grandmother backed into the room holding a tray and Alex jumped to his feet to take it from her. 'Thank you,' she said. 'There's not much, I'm afraid. I'm at your uncle's until after New Year so rations are rather sparse.' She directed him to the round table near the patio doors and Alex placed the tray onto it, carefully setting out the bowls of piping-hot soup and the plates heaped with crackers, cheese and apples.

'It looks perfect. Thank you for rearranging your plans. You really didn't have to.'

'I wanted to. Everything's arranged and your uncle has asked me to let you know that you are welcome to come too tomorrow—or at any point over the holidays. For an hour or a night or the whole week. Whatever you need. There's no need to call ahead, please. If you want to come just turn up, I'll make sure you have the address. Now sit down, do. I tend to eat in here—I don't like eating in the kitchen and sitting in sole state in the dining room would be far too lonely. I rarely use it now.' She sighed. 'This house is far too big but it's so crammed with memories—of my husband, of your mother—that I hate the idea of leaving.'

'When did my grandfather die?' Another family member he would never know.

'When your mother was eighteen. It hit her very hard. She was a real daddy's girl. I sometimes think that's why she fell for your father. He was so certain of everything and she was still so vulnerable. Your grandfather's death had ripped our family apart and we were all alone in our grief. I still miss him every day. He was my best friend. He made every day an adventure.'

The soup was excellent, thick, spicy and warming, but Alex was hardly aware of it. Best friends? So it *could* work.

'That's the nicest epitaph I ever heard. He must have been an amazing man.'

How would Alex be remembered after he died? Hopefully as a talented and successful architect. But was that enough?

No. It wasn't. He wanted someone to have that same wistful look in their eye. That same mingled grief, nostalgia, affection and humour. No. He didn't want just *someone* to remember him that way.

He wanted Flora to. He wanted every day to be an adventure with his best friend. Not because it was safe and made sense. No. Because he loved her.

CHAPTER TWELVE

FLORA WOKE WITH a start, rolling over to check her phone automatically. Five a.m. and still no answer from Alex.

She rolled onto her back and stared at the luminous green stars still stuck to her ceiling. It had been a typical Christmas Eve; Horry had turned up during dinner, ready to hoover up all the left-over rice, pakoras and dahl, and then Greg had insisted on babysitting so that Minerva and Flora's mother could join the rest of their family for a couple of drinks before they all trooped to the ancient Norman church for the short and moving celebration of Midnight Mass. It wasn't often they were all together like this, but it just made Alex's absence all the more achingly obvious. Flora had tried not to spend the whole evening checking her phone. She had failed miserably, barely taking part in the conversation and mouthing her way through the carols.

Still no word. She just needed to know he was okay.

No, she was kidding herself. She wasn't that altruistic. She wanted to *know*, to look deeper, to see if somewhere, deep inside, he cared for her the way she so desperately wanted him to.

And if not to ask herself if that was all right. If all

he was capable of offering was friendship mixed with passion, then should she agree to marry him anyway— because she would still be with him? Was it settling or being pragmatic? Selling herself short or grabbing the opportunity with both hands?

Although it was rather moot; having said no once, she wasn't sure how to let him know if she did change her mind. It wasn't exactly something you could drop into conversation.

Flora turned her pillow over, plumping it back up with a little more force than was strictly necessary, and attempted to snuggle back down; but it was no use. She was wide awake. Not the pleasurable anticipatory tingle of a Christmas morning but the creeping dread that nothing would ever be the same again.

Well, she could lie here and brood or she could get up, make coffee and make a plan. She reached for her phone again and the sudden light illuminated her room and the bags of presents still piled in the corner. It was an unwritten law that all presents had to be snuck under the Christmas tree without the knowledge of anyone else in the household. Flora and Alex usually spent most of the early hours trying to catch the other out—a heady few hours of ambush, traps and whispered giggles because it was also a sternly enforced law that nobody could get up before seven a.m., the edict a hangover from her childhood.

She swung her legs out of the bed, feeling for her slippers in the dark and shrugging on the old vintage velvet dressing gown Alex had bought her for her six-teenth birthday, before padding quietly across the room to retrieve the bags. The house was in darkness and, not wanting to wake anyone else up, she switched on the torch on her phone to help guide her down the windy stairs. Alex's door was still ajar, the empty room dark.

Her bags were bulky and it was all Flora could do to get them quietly along the landing and down the main stairs. Every rustle of paper, every muffled bang as the bag hit the bannister made her freeze in place, but finally she stepped over the creaky last step and into the hallway. Not for the first time she cursed her mother's decision to furnish the wide hall as a second sitting area. Not only did she have to dodge the hat stand, umbrella stand and the hall table, but she also had to weave around a bookcase and a couple of wing-backed chairs before she reached the safety of the sitting-room door.

Flora froze, her hand on the handle as she clocked the faint light seeping under the door? Another early riser? She could have sworn she had heard all her family make their stealthy present-laying trips soon after she had gone to bed, and it was far too quiet to be either of her nieces.

One of them had probably left the light on, that was all. She turned the handle and nudged the door open with her hip as she lugged the two bags into the room, turning to place them next to the tree...

Only to jump back when she saw a shadowy figure already kneeling under the tree. Grey with tiredness, hair rumpled and still in the clothes she had seen him in yesterday morning, on his knees as he added his own gifts to the pleasingly huge pile. 'Alex?'

He rocked back onto his heels. 'Merry Christmas, Flora.'

Her throat swelled and she swallowed hard, so many things to say and she had no idea which one to start with. 'You're here?' Great, start with the blindingly obvious. 'I tried calling…'

'I know. I got your message, thank you.'

'Where have you been?'

'That's a long story.' He nodded at the bags lying forgotten at her feet. 'Shall I pretend I haven't seen those and go and put some coffee on?'

She blinked, trying to clear her head, take in that he was actually here, that he had come home. 'Yes. Coffee. Thanks.'

The corners of his mouth quirked up in a brief smile. 'Good. I could kill for one of your dad's mince pies as well.'

Normally Flora took her time placing her gifts, making sure they were spread out, tucked away, but right now she didn't care, chucking them onto the pile haphazardly with no care for the aesthetic effect. She switched off the lamps and sidled out of the room, closing the door quietly behind her before turning into the kitchen.

The scent of coffee was as welcome as the sight of Alex. Really here, reassuringly here, leaning against the counter, a mince pie in one hand, a mug in the other. 'Nothing says Christmas like your dad's baking.'

'That was the title of his last interview.' Flora leaned over and stole a crumb off his plate. 'It's good to see you, Alex.' It didn't feel like less than twenty-four hours since they had parted; it felt like a lifetime.

'I'm sorry I just took off but I needed some time, some space. I took your advice. I looked up my mother's family.'

Whatever Flora had been expecting, it wasn't this. 'You did? I thought you didn't know where they were?'

'I didn't. Only since you mentioned them the idea was niggling away at the back of my mind. You were right, there had to be someone out there. And then I remembered, when I was a little boy I used to see my grandmother sometimes—and I wrote to her a lot. I remembered enough of her address to be able to track her down.'

'What it is to have a photographic memory.'

'Turns out it comes in useful.'

'So.' Flora felt unaccountably shy. 'What was she like? Did you meet her?'

To her surprise Alex laughed. 'Nothing like I expected, very chic, rather cool and very lovely. You'll like her, Flora. And it was as if all the missing pieces just slotted together. She had answers and photos and she knew.'

'Knew what?'

His voice broke. 'That my mother loved me. She didn't kill herself because she hated me. She killed herself because she thought she was letting me down. It was her illness that was to blame, not me.'

Tears burned the backs of her eyes, her throat. How could he have lived all these years believing it was his fault? How could his father have allowed him to? All awkwardness, all restraint disappeared as Flora reached over to grab his hand, her fingers enfolding his. 'Of course it was—and of course she loved you. How could she not have?'

'She hung on for two years after I was born, terrified and so unhappy, but she tried. She really tried. If she'd got help it would all have been so different but she was in denial and my father thought that she was weak. He didn't want her talking to anyone but him.'

'If anyone's to blame he is. For all of it. For your mother, for taking your stepmother's side, for allowing you to leave home.'

'I think I know that now. The stupid thing is I have spent my whole life wishing I had a family and a home and yet I had one all along.'

Flora looked down at the counter. 'With your grandmother.'

'No.' His voice softened. 'With you.'

She looked up, startled at his words. Her eyes locked onto his and her pulse began to thump at the look in his eyes. It was more than the desire she had enjoyed over the last week, more than the candid friendship of the last twenty years. It was new, unknown and so intense she could barely breathe. 'I'm glad you know that. No matter what happened with you and me your home is here…'

'I know that but that's not what I mean. I mean that wherever you are, Flora, that's where I belong. London, Kent, Bali, Austria. My house, your room or a tent in the pouring rain. I could lose everything tomorrow and as long as you were with me I wouldn't mind. You…' His voice cracked. 'You make every day an adventure, Flora, and I was too blind or too scared to see it before.'

The blood was rushing in her ears and she had to grip the counter tightly, afraid that she might fall without its solid support. 'Me?'

'I think I've always known it—from the very first day when you helped me make a den. Remember? I was running away but I wasn't scared because I'd found someone to be with. But I didn't want to face it. I didn't want to taint you. My father said I ruined everything and everyone I touched and, oh, Flora, I didn't want to ruin you.'

'You won't, you couldn't.'

'When I asked you to marry me I was a fool. I thought I meant those things, those sensible reasons, the list of positives, but really I was a coward. I was too afraid to tell you what I really meant. I wanted to tell you that you were the most beautiful woman in the ballroom, that I couldn't take my eyes off you all night, that you were my best friend and that I loved you and didn't want to spend a single second of my life away from you. That's what I should have said.'

Flora blinked hard, willing the tears not to fall. 'It's a little more convincing than storage.'

'If I'd told you all this then, would you have said yes?'

She nodded, unable to get the words out.

'And...' he stepped around the counter so that he was right next to her, turning her unresisting body so that she faced him, cupping her face in his hands and looking down at her, tenderness in his eyes '...if I ask you now?'

Flora smiled up at him, her voice scarcely more than a whisper. 'Why don't you ask me and see?'

Laughter flashed in his eyes as he took her hand in his. 'No flash mobs, no rings in ice cream, no sonnets. Just you and me, Flora. Just like it's always been.'

She nodded, her chest so swollen with happiness she thought she might drift away.

'Flora Prosperine Buckingham, would you do me the incredible honour of being my best friend, my companion, my lover, my confidante and my partner in adventure every day for the rest of my life?'

'I can't think of anyone I'd rather spend my life with.' Flora looked at him, at the ruddy, disordered curls, the freckles, the long-lashed eyes, and her heart turned over with love. 'Of course I'll marry you. I think I fell in love with you too, that day in the lane. You were so determined and so brave. I just wanted to make it all better.'

'You did, you do. It just took me far too long to notice.'

'Look.' She pointed upwards to the beam overhead. 'Mistletoe.'

'I don't need mistletoe to tell me to kiss you, not any more.' Alex leaned forward and brushed her mouth with his. 'Merry Christmas, Flora.'

'Merry Christmas, Alex.' She could finally say the words she had been holding in for so long. 'I love you.'

He looked over at the grandfather clock in the corner. 'We still have ninety minutes before the household's allowed to get up. Can you think of any way to spend it?'

Flora rose onto her tiptoes and allowed herself to kiss him properly, deeply, lovingly. Her fiancé, her man, her best friend. 'I'm sure we can think of something...'

* * * * *

GIFT-WRAPPED IN HER WEDDING DRESS

KANDY SHEPHERD

To all my Christmas magazine colleagues, in
particular Helen, Adriana and Jane—
the magic of the season lives on!

CHAPTER ONE

SO HE'D GOT on the wrong side of the media. Again. Dominic's words, twisted out of all recognition, were all over newspapers, television and social media.

Billionaire businessman Dominic Hunt refuses to sleep out with other CEOs in charity event for homeless.

Dominic slammed his fist on his desk so hard the pain juddered all the way up his arm. He hadn't *refused* to support the charity in their Christmas appeal, just refused the invitation to publicly bed down for the night in a cardboard box on the forecourt of the Sydney Opera House. His donation to the worthy cause had been significant—but anonymous. *Why wasn't that enough?*

He buried his head in his hands. For a harrowing time in his life there had been no choice for him but to sleep rough for real, a cardboard box his only bed. He couldn't go there again—not even for a charity stunt, no matter how worthy. There could be no explanation—he would not share the secrets of his past. *Ever.*

With a sick feeling of dread he continued to read on-screen the highlights of the recent flurry of negative press about him and his company, thoughtfully compiled in a report by his Director of Marketing.

Predictably, the reporters had then gone on to rehash his well-known aversion to Christmas. Again he'd been misquoted. It was true he loathed the whole idea of celebrating Christmas. But not for the reasons the media had so fancifully contrived. Not because he was a *Scrooge*. How he hated that label and the erroneous aspersions that he didn't ever give to charity. Despaired that he was included in a round-up of Australia's Multi-Million-Dollar Misers. *It couldn't be further from the truth.*

He strongly believed that giving money to worthy causes should be conducted in private—not for public acclaim. But this time he couldn't ignore the name-calling and innuendo. He was near to closing a game-changing deal on a joint venture with a family-owned American corporation run by a man with a strict moral code that included obvious displays of philanthropy.

Dominic could not be seen to be a Scrooge. He had to publicly prove that he was not a miser. But he did not want to reveal the extent of his charitable support because to do so would blow away the smokescreen he had carefully constructed over his past.

He'd been in a bind. Until his marketing director had suggested he would attract positive press if he opened his harbourside home for a lavish fund-raising event for charity. 'Get your name in the newspaper for the right reasons,' he had been advised.

Dominic hated the idea of his privacy being invaded but he had reluctantly agreed. He wanted the joint venture to happen. If a party was what it took, he was prepared to put his qualms aside and commit to it.

The party would be too big an event for it to be organised in-house. His marketing people had got outside companies involved. Trouble was the three so-called 'party planners' he'd been sent so far had been incompetent and he'd shown them the door within minutes of meeting. Now there was a fourth. He glanced down at the eye-catching card on the desk in front of him. Andrea Newman from a company called Party Queens—*No party too big or too small* the card boasted.

Party Queens. It was an interesting choice for a business name. Not nearly as stitched up as the other companies that had pitched for this business. But did it have the gravitas required? After all, this event could be the deciding factor in a deal that would extend his business interests internationally.

He glanced at his watch. This morning he was working from his home office. Ms Newman was due to meet with him right now, here at his house where the party was to take place. Despite the attention-grabbing name of the business, he had no reason to expect Party Planner Number Four to be any more impressive than the other three he'd sent packing. But he would give her twenty minutes—that was only fair and he made a point of always being fair.

On cue, the doorbell rang. Punctuality, at least, was a point in Andrea Newman's favour. He headed down the wide marble stairs to the front door.

His first impression of the woman who stood on his porch was that she was attractive, not in a conventionally pretty way but something rather more interesting—an angular face framed by a tangle of streaked blonde hair, a wide generous mouth, unusual green eyes. So attractive he found himself looking at her for a moment longer than was required to sum up a possible contractor. And the almost imperceptible curve of her mouth let him know she'd noticed.

'Good morning, Mr Hunt—Andie Newman from Party Queens,' she said. 'Thank you for the pass code that got me through the gate. Your security is formidable, like an eastern suburbs fortress.' Was that a hint of challenge underscoring her warm, husky voice? If so, he wasn't going to bite.

'The pass code expires after one use, Ms Newman,' he said, not attempting to hide a note of warning. The three party planners before her were never going to get a new pass code. But none of them had been remotely like her—in looks or manner.

She was tall and wore a boldly patterned skirt of some silky fine fabric that fell below her knees in uneven layers, topped by a snug-fitting rust-coloured jacket and high heeled shoes that laced all the way up her calf. A soft leather satchel was slung casually across her shoulder. She presented as smart but more unconventional than the corporate dark suits and rigid briefcases of the other three—whose ideas had been as pedestrian as their appearances.

'Andie,' she replied and started to say something else about his security system. But, as she did, a sudden gust of balmy spring breeze whipped up her skirt, revealing long slender legs and a tantalising hint of red underwear. Dominic tried to do the gentlemanly thing and look elsewhere—difficult when she was standing so near to him and her legs were so attention-worthy.

'Oh,' she gasped, and fought with the skirt to hold it down, but no sooner did she get the front of the skirt in place, the back whipped upwards and she had to twist around to hold it down. The back view of her legs was equally as impressive as the front. He balled his hands into fists by his sides so he did not give into the temptation to help her with the flyaway fabric.

She flushed high on elegant cheekbones, blonde hair tousled around her face, and laughed a husky, uninhibited laugh as she battled to preserve her modesty. The breeze died down as quickly as it had sprung up and her skirt floated back into place. Still, he noticed she continued to keep it in check with a hand on her thigh.

'That's made a wonderful first impression, hasn't it?' she said, looking up at him with a rueful smile. For a long moment their eyes connected and he was the first to look away. *She was beautiful.*

As she spoke, the breeze gave a final last sigh that ruffled her hair across her face. Dominic wasn't a fanciful man, but it seemed as though the wind was ushering her into his house.

'There are worse ways of making an impression,' he said gruffly. 'I'm interested to see what you follow up with.'

Andie wasn't sure what to reply. She stood at the threshold of Dominic Hunt's multi-million-dollar mansion and knew for the first time in her career she was in serious danger of losing the professional cool in which she took such pride.

Not because of the incident with the wind and her skirt. Or because she was awestruck by the magnificence of the house and the postcard-worthy panorama of Sydney Harbour that stretched out in front of it. No. It was the man who towered above her who was making her feel so inordinately flustered. Too tongue-tied to come back with a quick quip or clever retort.

'Th…thank you,' she managed to stutter as she pushed the breeze-swept hair back from across her face.

During her career as a stylist for both magazines and advertising agencies, and now as a party planner, she had acquired the reputation of being able to manage difficult people. Which was why her two partners in their fledgling business had voted for her to be the one to deal with Dominic Hunt. Party Queens desperately needed a high-profile booking like this to help them get established. Winning it was now on her shoulders.

She had come to his mansion forewarned that he could be a demanding client. The gossip was that he had been scathing to three other planners from other companies much bigger than theirs before giving them the boot. Then there was his wider reputation as a Scrooge—a man who did not share his multitude of money with others less fortunate. He was everything she did not admire in a person.

Despite that, she been blithely confident Dominic Hunt wouldn't be more than she could handle. Until he had answered that door. Her reaction to him had her stupefied.

She had seen the photos, watched the interviews of the billionaire businessman, had recognised he was good-looking in a dark, brooding way. But no amount of research had prepared her for the pulse-raising reality of this man—tall, broad-shouldered, powerful muscles apparent even in his sleek tailored grey suit. He wasn't pretty-boy handsome. Not with that strong jaw, the crooked nose that looked as though it had been broken by a viciously aimed punch, the full, sensual mouth with the faded white scar on the corner, the spiky black hair. And then there was the almost palpable emanation of power.

She had to call on every bit of her professional savvy to ignore the warm flush that rose up her neck and onto her cheeks, the way her heart thudded into unwilling awareness of Dominic Hunt, not as a client but as a man.

She could not allow that to happen. This job was too important to her and her friends in their new business. *Anyway, dark and brooding wasn't her type.* Her ideal man was sensitive and sunny-natured, like her first lost love, for whom she felt she would always grieve.

She extended her hand, willing it to stay steady, and forced a smile. 'Mr Hunt, let's start again. Andie Newman from Party Queens.'

His grip in return was firm and warm and he nodded acknowledgement of her greeting. If a mere handshake could send shivers of awareness through her, she could be in trouble here.

Keep it businesslike. She took a deep breath, tilted back her head to meet his gaze full-on. 'I believe I'm the fourth party planner you've seen and I don't want there to be a fifth. I should be the person to plan your event.'

If he was surprised at her boldness, it didn't show in his scrutiny; his grey eyes remained cool and assessing.

'You'd better come inside and convince me why that should be the case,' he said. Even his voice was attractive—deep and measured and utterly masculine.

'I welcome the opportunity,' she said in the most confident voice she could muster.

She followed him into the entrance hall of the restored nineteen-twenties house, all dark stained wood floors and cream marble. A grand central marble staircase with wrought-iron balustrades split into two sides to climb to the next floor. This wasn't the first grand home she'd been in during the course of her work but it was so impressive she had to suppress an impulse to gawk.

'Wow,' she said, looking around her, forgetting all about how disconcerted Dominic Hunt made her feel. 'The staircase. It's amazing. I can just see a choir there, with a chorister on each step greeting your guests with Christmas carols as they step into the house.' Her thoughts raced ahead of her. Choristers' robes in red and white? Each chorister holding a scrolled parchment printed with the words to the carol? What about the music? A string quartet? A harpsichord?

'What do you mean?' he said, breaking into her reverie.

Andie blinked to bring herself back to earth and turned to look up at him. She smiled. 'Sorry. I'm getting ahead of myself. It was just an idea. Of course I realise I still need to convince you I'm the right person for your job.'

'I meant about the Christmas carols.'

So he would be that kind of pernickety client, pressing her for details before they'd even decided on the bigger picture. Did she need to spell out the message of 'Deck the Halls with Boughs of Holly'?

She shook her head in a don't-worry-about-it way. 'It was just a top-of-mind thought. But a choir would be an amazing use of the staircase. Maybe a children's choir. Get your guests into the Christmas spirit straight away, without being too cheesy about it.'

'It isn't going to be a Christmas party.' He virtually spat the word *Christmas*.

'But a party in December? I thought—'

He frowned and she could see where his reputation came from as his thick brows drew together and his eyes darkened. 'Truth be told, I don't want a party here at all. But it's a necessary evil—necessary to my business, that is.'

'Really?' she said, struggling not to jump in and say the wrong thing. A client who didn't actually want a party? This she hadn't anticipated. Her certainty that she knew how to handle this situation—this man—started to seep away.

She gritted her teeth, forced her voice to sound as conciliatory as possible. 'I understood from your brief that you wanted a big event benefiting a charity in the weeks leading up to Christmas on a date that will give you maximum publicity.'

'All that,' he said. 'Except it's not to be a Christmas party. Just a party that happens to be held around that time.'

Difficult and demanding didn't begin to describe this. But had she been guilty of assuming December translated into Christmas? Had it actually stated that in the brief? She didn't think she'd misread it.

She drew in a calming breath. 'There seems to have been a misunderstanding and I apologise for that,' she said. 'I have the official briefing from your marketing department here.' She patted her satchel. 'But I'd rather hear your thoughts, your ideas for the event in your own words.

A successful party plan comes from the heart. Can we sit down and discuss this?'

He looked pointedly at his watch. Her heart sank to the level of the first lacing on her shoes. She did not want to be the fourth party planner he fired before she'd even started her pitch. 'I'll give you ten minutes,' he said.

He led her into a living room that ran across the entire front of the house and looked out to the blue waters of the harbour and its icons of the Sydney Harbour Bridge and the Opera House. Glass doors opened out to a large terrace. *A perfect summer party terrace.*

Immediately she recognised the work of one of Sydney's most fashionable high-end interior designers—a guy who only worked with budgets that started with six zeros after them. The room worked neutral tones and metallics in a nod to the art deco era of the original house. The result was masculine but very, very stylish.

What an awesome space for a party. But she forced thoughts of the party out of her head. She had ten minutes to win this business. Ten minutes to convince Dominic Hunt she was the one he needed.

CHAPTER TWO

DOMINIC SAT ANDIE NEWMAN down on the higher of the two sofas that faced each other over the marble coffee table—the sofa he usually chose to give himself the advantage. He had no need to impress her with his greater height and bulk—she was tall, but he was so much taller than her even as he sat on the lower seat. Besides, the way she positioned herself with shoulders back and spine straight made him think she wouldn't let herself be intimidated by him or by anyone else. *Think again.* The way she crossed and uncrossed those long legs revealed she was more nervous than she cared to let on.

He leaned back in his sofa, pulled out her business card from the inside breast pocket of his suit jacket and held it between finger and thumb. 'Tell me about Party Queens. This seems like a very new, shiny card.'

'Brand new. We've only been in business for three months.'

'We?'

'My two business partners, Eliza Dunne and Gemma Harper. We all worked on a magazine together before we started our own business.'

He narrowed his eyes. 'Now you're "party queens"?' He used his fingers to enclose the two words with quote marks. 'I don't see the connection.'

'We always were party queens—even when we were working on the magazine.' He quirked an eyebrow and she

paused. He noticed she quirked an eyebrow too, in unconscious imitation of his action. 'Not in that way.' She tried
to backtrack, then smiled. 'Well, maybe somewhat in that
way. Between us we've certainly done our share of party-
ing. But then you have to actually enjoy a party to organise one; don't you agree?'

'It's not something I've given thought to,' he said. Busi-
ness-wise, it could be a point either for her or against her.

Parties had never been high on his agenda—even after
his money had opened so many doors for him. Whether
he'd been sleeping rough in an abandoned building project in the most dangerous part of Brisbane or hobnobbing
with decision makers in Sydney, he'd felt he'd never quite
fitted in. So he did the minimum socialising required for
his business. 'You were a journalist?' he asked, more than
a little intrigued by her.

She shook her head. 'My background is in interior design but when a glitch in the economy meant the company
I worked for went bust, I ended up as an interiors editor
on a lifestyle magazine. I put together shoots for interiors
and products and I loved it. Eliza and Gemma worked on
the same magazine, Gemma as the food editor and Eliza
on the publishing side. Six months ago we were told out
of the blue that the magazine was closing and we had all
lost our jobs.'

'That must have been a shock,' he said.

When he'd first started selling real estate at the age of
eighteen he'd lived in terror he'd lose his job. Underlying all his success was always still that fear—which was
why he was so driven to keep his business growing and
thriving. Without money, without a home, he could slide
back into being Nick Hunt of 'no fixed abode' rather than
Dominic Hunt of Vaucluse, one of the most exclusive ad-
dresses in Australia.

'It shouldn't have come as a shock,' she said. 'Magazines close all the time in publishing—it's an occupational hazard. But when it actually happened, when *again* one minute I had a job and the next I didn't, it was…soul-destroying.'

'I'm sorry,' he said.

She shrugged. 'I soon picked myself up.'

He narrowed his eyes. 'It's quite a jump from a magazine job to a party planning business.' Her lack of relevant experience could mean Party Planner Number Four would go the way of the other three. He was surprised at how disappointed that made him feel.

'It might seem that way, but hear me out,' she said, a determined glint in her eye. If one of the other planners had said that, he would have looked pointedly at his watch. This one, he was prepared to listen to—he was actually interested in her story.

'We had to clear our desks immediately and were marched out of the offices by security guards. Shell-shocked, we all retired to a café and thought about what we'd do. The magazine's deputy editor asked could we organise her sister's eighteenth birthday party. At first we said no, thinking she was joking. But then we thought about it. A big magazine shoot that involves themes and food and props is quite a production. We'd also sometimes organise magazine functions for advertisers. We realised that between us we knew a heck of a lot about planning parties.'

'As opposed to enjoying them,' he said.

'That's right,' she said with a smile that seemed reminiscent of past parties enjoyed. 'Between the three of us we had so many skills we could utilise.'

'Can you elaborate on that?'

She held up a slender index finger, her nails tipped with orange polish. 'One, I'm the ideas and visuals person—creative, great with themes and props and highly organised with follow-through.' A second finger went up.

'Two, Gemma trained as a chef and is an amazing food person—food is one of the most important aspects of a good party, whether cooking it yourself or knowing which chefs to engage.'

She had a little trouble getting the third finger to stay straight and swapped it to her pinkie. 'Then, three, Eliza has her head completely around finances and contracts and sales and is also quite the wine buff.'

'So you decided to go into business together?' Her entrepreneurial spirit appealed to him.

She shook her head so her large multi-hoop gold earrings clinked. 'Not then. Not yet. We agreed to do the eighteenth party while we looked for other jobs and freelanced for magazines and ad agencies.'

'How did it work out?' He thought about his eighteenth birthday. It had gone totally unmarked by any celebration —except his own jubilation that he was legally an adult and could never now be recalled to the hell his home had become. It had also marked the age he could be tried as an adult if he had skated too close to the law—though by that time his street-fighting days were behind him.

'There were a few glitches, of course, but overall it was a great success. The girl went to a posh private school and both girls and parents loved the girly shoe theme we organised. One eighteenth led to another and soon we had other parents clamouring for us to do their kids' parties.'

'Is there much money in parties for kids?' He didn't have to ask all these questions but he was curious. Curious about her as much as anything.

Her eyebrows rose. 'You're kidding, right? We're talking wealthy families on the eastern suburbs and north shore. We're talking one-upmanship.' He enjoyed the play of expressions across her face, the way she gesticulated with her hands as she spoke. 'Heck, we've done a four-year-old's party on a budget of thousands.'

'All that money for a four-year-old?' He didn't have anything to do with kids except through his anonymous charity work. Had given up on his dream he would ever have children of his own. In fact, he was totally out of touch with family life.

'You'd better believe it,' she said.

He was warming to Andie Newman—how could any red-blooded male not?—but he wanted to ensure she was experienced enough to make his event work. All eyes would be on it as up until now he'd been notoriously private. If he threw a party, it had better be a good party. Better than good.

'So when did you actually go into business?'

'We were asked to do more and more parties. Grown-up parties too. Thirtieths and fortieths, even a ninetieth. It snowballed. Yet we still saw it as a stopgap thing although people suggested we make it a full-time business.'

'A very high percentage of small businesses go bust in the first year,' he couldn't help but warn.

She pulled a face that told him she didn't take offence. 'We were very aware of that. Eliza is the profit and loss spreadsheet maven. But then a public relations company I worked freelance for asked us to do corporate parties and product launches. The work was rolling in. We began to think we should make it official and form our own company.'

'A brave move.' He'd made brave moves in his time—and most of them had paid off. He gave her credit for initiative.

She leaned forward towards him. This close he could appreciate how lovely her eyes were. He didn't think he had ever before met anyone with genuine green eyes. 'We've leased premises in the industrial area of Alexandria and we're firing. But I have to be honest with you—we haven't done anything with potentially such a profile as your party.

We want it. We need it. And because we want it to so much we'll pull out every stop to make it a success.'

Party Planner Number Four clocked up more credit for her honesty. He tapped the card on the edge of his hand. 'You've got the enthusiasm; do you have the expertise? Can you assure me you can do my job and do it superlatively well?'

Those remarkable green eyes were unblinking. 'Yes. Absolutely. Undoubtedly. There might only be three of us, but between us we have a zillion contacts in Sydney—chefs, decorators, florists, musicians, waiting staff. If we can't do it ourselves we can pull in the right people who can. And none of us is afraid of the hard work a party this size would entail. We would welcome the challenge.'

He realised she was now sitting on the edge of the sofa, her hands clasped together and her foot crossed over her ankle was jiggling. She really did want this job—wanted it badly.

Dominic hadn't got where he was without a fine-tuned instinct for people. Instincts honed first on the streets where trusting the wrong person could have been fatal and then in the cut-throat business of high-end real estate and property development. His antennae were telling him Andie Newman would be able to deliver—and that he would enjoy working with her.

Trouble was, while he thought she might be the right person for the job, he found her very attractive and would like to ask her out. And he couldn't do both. He *never* dated staff or suppliers. He'd made that mistake with his ex-wife—he would not make it again. Hire Andie Newman and he was more than halfway convinced he would get a good party planner. Not hire her and he could ask her on a date. But he needed this event to work—and for that the planning had to be in the best possible hands. He was torn.

'I like your enthusiasm,' he said. 'But I'd be taking

a risk by working with a company that is in many ways still…unproven.'

Her voice rose marginally—she probably didn't notice but to him it betrayed her anxiety to impress. 'We have a file overflowing with references from happy clients. But before you come to any decisions let's talk about what you're expecting from us. The worst thing that can happen is for a client to get an unhappy surprise because we've got the brief wrong.'

She pulled out a folder from her satchel. He liked that it echoed the design of her business card. That showed an attention to detail. The chaos of his early life had made him appreciate planning and order. He recognised his company logo on the printout page she took from the folder and quickly perused.

'So tell me,' she said, when she'd finished reading it. 'I'm puzzled. Despite this briefing document stating the party is to be "A high-profile Christmas event to attract favourable publicity for Dominic Hunt" you still insist it's not to reference Christmas in any way. Which is correct?'

Andie regretted the words almost as soon as they'd escaped from her mouth. She hadn't meant to confront Dominic Hunt or put him on the spot. Certainly she hadn't wanted to get him offside. But the briefing had been ambiguous and she felt she had to clarify it if she was to secure this job for Party Queens.

She needed their business to succeed—never again did she want to be at the mercy of the whims of a corporate employer. To have a job one day and then suddenly not the next day was too traumatising after that huge personal change of direction she'd had forced upon her five years ago. But she could have put her question with more subtlety.

He didn't reply. The silence that hung between them became more uncomfortable by the second. His face tightened with an emotion she couldn't read. Anger? Sorrow? Regret? Whatever it was, the effect was so powerful she had to force herself not to reach over and put her hand on his arm to comfort him, maybe even hug him. And that would be a mistake. Even more of a mistake than her ill-advised question had been.

She cringed that she had somehow prompted the unleashing of thoughts that were so obviously painful for him. Then braced herself to be booted out on to the same scrapheap as the three party planners who had preceded her.

Finally he spoke, as if the words were being dragged out of him. 'The brief was incorrect. Christmas has some… difficult memories attached to it for me. I don't celebrate the season. Please just leave it at that.' For a long moment his gaze held hers and she saw the anguish recede.

Andie realised she had been holding her breath and she let it out with a slow sigh of relief, amazed he hadn't shown her the door.

'Of…of course,' she murmured, almost gagging with gratitude that she was to be given a second chance. And she couldn't deny that she wanted that chance. Not just for the job but—she could not deny it—the opportunity to see more of this undoubtedly interesting man.

There was something deeper here, some private pain, that she did not understand. But it would be bad-mannered prying to ask any further questions.

She didn't know much about his personal life. Just that he was considered a catch—rich, handsome, successful. *Though not her type, of course.* He lived here alone, she understood, in this street in Vaucluse where house prices started in the double digit millions. Wasn't there a bitter divorce in his background—an aggrieved ex-wife, a public battle for ownership of the house? She'd have to look it up. If she were to win this job—and she understood that it was still a big *if*—she needed to get a grasp on how this man ticked.

'Okay, so that's sorted—no Christmas,' she said, aiming to sound briskly efficient without any nod to the anguish she had read at the back of his eyes. 'Now I know what you *don't* want for your party, let's talk about what you *do* want. I'd like to hear in your words what you expect from this party. Then I can give you my ideas based on your thoughts.'

The party proposals she had hoped to discuss had been based on Christmas; she would have to do some rapid thinking.

Dominic Hunt got up from the sofa and started to pace. He was so tall, his shoulders so broad, he dominated even the large, high-ceilinged room. Andie found herself wondering about his obviously once broken nose—who had thrown the first punch? She got up, not to pace alongside him but to be closer to his level. She did not feel intimidated by him but she could see how he could be intimidating.

'The other planners babbled on about how important it was to invite A-list and B-list celebrities to get publicity. I don't give a damn about celebrities and I can't see how that's the right kind of publicity.'

Andie paused, not sure what to say, only knowing she had to be careful not to *babble on*. 'I can organise the party, but the guest list is up to you and your people.'

He stopped his pacing, stepped closer. 'But do you agree with me?'

Was this a test question? Answer incorrectly and that scrapheap beckoned? As always, she could only be honest. 'I do agree with you. It's my understanding that this party is aimed at...at image repair.'

'You mean repair to my image as a miserly Scrooge who hoards all his money for himself?'

She swallowed a gasp at the bitterness of his words, then looked up at him to see not the anger she expected but a kind of manly bewilderment that surprised her.

'I mightn't have put it quite like that, but yes,' she said. 'You do have that reputation and I understand you want to demonstrate it's not so. And yes, I think the presence of a whole lot of freeloading so-called celebrities who run the gamut from the A to the Z list and have nothing to do with the charities you want to be seen to be supporting might not help. But you *are* more likely to get coverage in the social pages if they attend.'

He frowned. 'Is there such a thing as a Z-list celebrity?'

She laughed. 'If there isn't, there should be. Maybe I made it up.'

'You did say you were creative,' he said. He smiled— the first real smile she'd seen from him. It transformed his face, like the sun coming out from behind a dark storm cloud, unleashing an unexpected charm. Her heartbeat tripped into double time like it had the first moment she'd seen him. Why? Why this inexplicable reaction to a man she should dislike for his meanness and greed?

She made a show of looking around her to disguise her consternation. Tamed the sudden shakiness in her voice into a businesslike tone. 'How many magazines or lifestyle programmes have featured this house?' she asked.

'None. They never will,' he said.

'Good,' she said. 'The house is both magnificent and unknown. I reckon even your neighbours would be willing to cough up a sizeable donation just to see inside.' In her mind's eye she could see the house transformed into a glittering party paradise. 'The era of the house is nineteen-twenties, right?'

'Yes,' he said. 'It was originally built for a wealthy wool merchant.'

She thought some more. 'Why not an extravagant

Great Gatsby twenties-style party with a silver and white theme—that gives a nod to the festive season—and a strictly curated guest list? Guests would have to dress in silver or white. Or both. Make it very exclusive, an invitation to be sought after. The phones of Sydney's social set would be set humming to see who got one or not.' Her eyes half shut as her mind bombarded her with images. 'Maybe a masked party. Yes. Amazing silver and white masks. Bejewelled and befeathered. Fabulous masks that could be auctioned off at some stage for your chosen charity.'

'Auctioned?'

Her eyes flew open and she had to orientate herself back into the reality of the empty room that she had just been envisioning filled with elegant partygoers. Sometimes when her creativity was firing she felt almost in a trance. Then it was her turn to frown. How could a Sydney billionaire be such a party innocent?

Even she, who didn't move in the circles of society that attended lavish fund-raising functions, knew about the auctions. The competitive bidding could probably be seen as the same kind of one-upmanship as the spending of thousands on a toddler's party. 'I believe it's usual to have a fund-raising auction at these occasions. Not just the masks, of course. Other donated items. Something really big to up the amount of dollars for your charity.' She paused. 'You're a property developer, aren't you?'

He nodded. 'Among other interests.'

'Maybe you could donate an apartment? There'd be some frenzied bidding for that from people hoping for a bargain. And you would look generous.'

His mouth turned down in an expression of distaste. 'I'm not sure that's in keeping with the image I want to… to reinvent.'

Privately she agreed with him—why couldn't people just donate without expecting a lavish party in return? But she kept her views to herself. Creating those lavish parties was her job now.

'That's up to you and your people. The guest list and the auction, I mean. But the party? That's my domain. Do you like the idea of the twenties theme to suit the house?' In her heart she still longed for the choristers on the staircase. Maybe it would have to be a jazz band on the steps. That could work. Not quite the same romanticism and spirit as Christmas, but it would be a spectacular way to greet guests.

'I like it,' he said slowly.

She forced herself not to panic, not to bombard him with a multitude of alternatives. 'If not that idea, I have lots of others. I would welcome the opportunity to present them to you.'

He glanced at his watch and she realised she had been there for much longer than the ten-minute pitch he'd allowed. Surely that was a good sign.

'I'll schedule in another meeting with you tomorrow afternoon,' he said.

'You mean a second interview?' she asked, fingers crossed behind her back.

'No. A brainstorming session. You've got the job, Ms Newman.'

It was only as, jubilant, she made her way to the door—conscious of his eyes on her back—that she wondered at the presence of a note of regret in Dominic Hunt's voice.

CHAPTER THREE

TRY AS SHE MIGHT, Andie couldn't get excited about the nineteen-twenties theme she had envisaged for Dominic Hunt's party. It would be lavish and glamorous and she would enjoy every moment of planning such a visually splendid event. Such a party would be a spangled feather in Party Queens' cap. But it seemed somehow *wrong*.

The feeling niggled at her. How could something so extravagant, so limited to those who could afford the substantial donation that would be the cost of entrance make Dominic Hunt look less miserly? Even if he offered an apartment for auction—and there was no such thing as a cheap apartment in Sydney—and raised a lot of money, wouldn't it be a wealthy person who benefited? Might he appear to be a Scrooge hanging out with other rich people who might or might not also be Scrooges? Somehow, it reeked of...well, there was no other word but hypocrisy.

It wasn't her place to be critical—the media-attention-grabbing party was his marketing people's idea. Her job was to plan the party and make it as memorable and spectacular as possible. But she resolved to bring up her reservations in the brainstorming meeting with him. *If she dared.*

She knew it would be a fine line to tread—she did not want to risk losing the job for Party Queens—but she felt she had to give her opinion. After that she would just keep her mouth shut and concentrate on making his event the most memorable on the December social calendar.

She dressed with care for the meeting, which was again at his Vaucluse mansion. *An outfit that posed no danger of showing off her underwear.* Slim white trousers, a white top, a string of outsize turquoise beads, silver sandals that strapped around her ankles. At the magazine she'd made friends with the fashion editor and still had access to sample sales and special deals. She felt her wardrobe could hold its own in whatever company she found herself in— even on millionaire row.

'I didn't risk wearing that skirt,' she blurted out to Dominic Hunt as he let her into the house. 'Even though there doesn't appear to be any wind about.'

Mentally she slammed her hand against her forehead. What a dumb top-of-mind remark to make to a client. But he still made her nervous. Try as she might, she couldn't shake that ever-present awareness of how attractive he was.

His eyes flickered momentarily to her legs. 'Shame,' he said in that deep, testosterone-edged voice that thrilled through her.

Was he flirting with her?

'It…it was a lovely skirt,' she said. 'Just…just rather badly behaved.' How much had he seen when her skirt had flown up over her thighs?

'I liked it very much,' he said.

'The prettiness of its fabric or my skirt's bad behaviour?'

She held his cool grey gaze for a second longer than she should.

'Both,' he said.

She took a deep breath and tilted her chin upward. 'I'll take that as a compliment,' she said with a smile she hoped radiated aplomb. 'Thank you, Mr Hunt.'

'Dominic,' he said.

'Dominic,' she repeated, liking the sound of his name on her lips. 'And thank you again for this opportunity to plan your party.' *Bring it back to business.*

In truth, she would have liked to tell him how good he looked in his superbly tailored dark suit and dark shirt but she knew her voice would come out all choked up. Because it wasn't the Italian elegance of his suit that she found herself admiring. It was the powerful, perfectly proportioned male body that inhabited it. And she didn't want to reveal even a hint of that. *He was a client.*

He nodded in acknowledgement of her words. 'Come through to the back,' he said. 'You can see how the rooms might work for the party.'

She followed him through where the grand staircase split—a choir really would be amazing ranged on the steps—over pristine marble floors to a high-ceilinged room so large their footsteps echoed as they walked into the centre of it. Furnished minimally in shades of white, it looked ready for a high-end photo shoot. Arched windows and a wall of folding doors opened through to an elegant art deco style swimming pool and then to a formal garden planted with palm trees and rows of budding blue agapanthus.

For a long moment Andie simply absorbed the splendour of the room. 'What a magnificent space,' she said finally. 'Was it originally a ballroom?'

'Yes. Apparently the wool merchant liked to entertain in grand style. But it wasn't suited for modern living, which is why I opened it up through to the terrace when I remodelled the house.'

'You did an awesome job,' she said. In her mind's eye she could see flappers in glittering dresses trimmed with feathers and fringing, and men in dapper suits doing the Charleston. Then had to blink, not sure if she was imagining what the room had once been or how she'd like it to be for Dominic's party.

'The people who work for me did an excellent job,' he said.

'As an interior designer I give them full marks,' she said. She had gone to university with Dominic's designer. She just might get in touch with him, seeking inside gossip into what made Dominic Hunt tick.

She looked around her. 'Where's the kitchen? Gemma will shoot me if I go back without reporting to her on the cooking facilities.'

'Through here.'

Andie followed him through to an adjoining vast state-of-the-art kitchen, gleaming in white marble and stainless steel. The style was sleek and modern but paid homage to the vintage of the house. She breathed out a sigh of relief and pleasure. A kitchen like this would make catering for hundreds of guests so much easier. Not that the food was her department. Gemma kept that under her control. 'It's a superb kitchen. Do you cook?'

Was Dominic the kind of guy who ate out every night and whose refrigerator contained only cartons of beer? Or the kind who excelled at cooking and liked to show off his skills to a breathlessly admiring female audience?

'I can look after myself,' he said shortly. 'That includes cooking.'

That figured. After yesterday's meeting she had done some research into Dominic Hunt—though there wasn't much information dating back further than a few years. Along with his comments about celebrating Christmas being a waste of space, he'd also been quoted as saying he would never marry again. From the media accounts, his marriage in his mid-twenties had been short, tumultuous and public, thanks to his ex-wife's penchant for spilling the details to the gossip columns.

'The kitchen and its position will be perfect for the caterers,' she said. 'Gemma will be delighted.'

'Good,' he said.

'You must love this house.' She could not help a wistful note from edging her voice. As an interior designer she knew only too well how much the remodelling would have cost. Never in a million years would she live in a house like this. He was only a few years older than her—thirty-two to her twenty-eight—yet it was as if they came from different planets.

He shrugged those impressively broad shoulders. 'It's a spectacular house. But it's just a house. I never get attached to places.'

Or people?

Her online research had showed him snapped by paparazzi with a number of long-legged beauties—but no woman more than once or twice. *What did it matter to her?*

She patted her satchel. *Back to business.* 'I've come prepared for brainstorming,' she said. 'Have you had any thoughts about the nineteen-twenties theme I suggested?'

'I've thought,' he said. He paused. 'I've thought about it a lot.'

His tone of voice didn't give her cause for confidence. 'You…like it? You don't like it? Because if you don't I have lots of other ideas that would work as well. I—'

He put up his right hand to halt her—large, well sculpted, with knuckles that looked as if they'd sustained scrapes over the years. His well-spoken accent and obvious wealth suggested injuries sustained from boxing or rugby at a private school; the tightly leashed power in those muscles, that strong jaw, gave thought to injuries sustained in something perhaps more visceral.

'It's a wonderful idea for a party,' he said. 'Perfect for this house. Kudos to you, Ms Party Queen.'

'Thank you.' She made a mock curtsy and was pleased when he smiled. *How handsome he was without that scowl.* 'However, is that a "but" I hear coming on?'

He pivoted on his heel so he faced out to the pool, gleaming blue and pristine in the afternoon sun of a late-spring day in mid-November. His back view was impressive, broad shoulders tapering to a tight, muscular rear end. Then he turned back to face her. 'It's more than one "but",' he said. 'The party, the guest list, the—'

'The pointlessness of it all?' she ventured.

He furrowed his brow. 'What makes you say that?'

She found herself twisting the turquoise beads on her necklace between her finger and thumb. Her business partners would be furious with her if she lost Party Queens this high-profile job because she said what she *wanted* to say rather than what she *should* say.

'This party is all about improving your image, right? To make a statement that you're not the…the Scrooge people think you are.'

The fierce scowl was back. 'I'd rather you didn't use the word Scrooge.'

'Okay,' she said immediately. But she would find it difficult to stop *thinking* it. 'I'll try again: that you're not a…a person lacking in the spirit of giving.'

'That doesn't sound much better.' She couldn't have imagined his scowl could have got any darker but it did. 'The party is meant to be a public display of something I would rather be kept private.'

'So…you give privately to charity?'

'Of course I do but it's not your or anyone else's business.'

Personally, she would be glad if he wasn't as tight-fisted as his reputation decreed. But this was about more than what she felt. She could not back down. 'If that's how you feel, tell me again why you're doing this.'

He paused. 'If I share with you the reason why I agreed to holding this party, it's not to leave this room.'

'Of course,' she said. A party planner had to be dis-

creet. It was astounding what family secrets got aired in
the planning of a party. She leaned closer, close enough
to notice that he must be a twice-a-day-shave guy. *Lots of
testosterone, all right.*

'I've got a big joint venture in the United States on
the point of being signed. My potential business partner,
Walter Burton, is the head of a family company and he is
committed to public displays of philanthropy. It would go
better with me if I was seen to be the same.'

Andie made a motion with her fingers of zipping her
lips shut. 'I…I understand,' she said. Disappointment
shafted through her. *So he really was a Scrooge.*

She'd found herself wanting Dominic to be someone
better than he was reputed to be. But the party, while pur-
porting to be a charity event, was simply a smart business
ploy. More about greed than good-heartedness.

'Now you can see why it's so important,' he said.

Should she say what she thought? The scrapheap of discarded party planners beckoned again. She could imagine
her silver-sandal-clad foot kicking feebly from the top of
it and hoped it would be a soft landing.

She took a deep steadying breath. 'Cynical journalists
might have a field-day with the hypocrisy of a Scrooge—
sorry!—trying to turn over a new gilded leaf in such an
obvious and staged way.'

To her surprise, something like relief relaxed the tense
lines of his face. 'That's what I thought too.'

'You…you did?'

'I could see the whole thing backfiring and me no better off in terms of reputation. Possibly worse.'

If she didn't stop twisting her necklace it would break
and scatter her beads all over the marble floor. 'So—help
me out here. We're back to you not wanting a party?'

*She'd talked him out of the big, glitzy event Party
Queens really needed.* Andie cringed at the prospect of

the combined wrath of Gemma and Eliza when she went back to their headquarters with the contract that was sitting in her satchel waiting for his signature still unsigned.

'You know I don't.' *Thank heaven.* 'But maybe a different kind of event,' he said.

'Like…handing over a giant facsimile cheque to a charity?' Which would be doing her right out of a job.

'Where's the good PR in that?'

'In fact it could look even more cynical than the party.'

'Correct.'

He paced a few long strides away from her and then back. 'I'm good at turning one dollar into lots of dollars. That's my skill. Not planning parties. But surely I can get the kind of publicity my marketing department wants, impress my prospective business partner and actually help some less advantaged people along the way?'

She resisted the urge to high-five him. 'To tell you the truth, I couldn't sleep last night for thinking that exact same thing.' *Was it wise to have admitted that?*

'Me too,' he said. 'I tossed and turned all night.'

A sudden vision of him in a huge billionaire's bed, all tangled in the sheets wearing nothing but…well nothing but a billionaire's birthday suit, flashed through her mind and sizzled through her body. *Not my type. Not my type.* She had to repeat it like a mantra.

She willed her heartbeat to slow and hoped he took the flush on her cheekbones for enthusiasm. 'So we're singing from the same hymn sheet. Did you have any thoughts on solving your dilemma?'

'That's where you come in; you're the party expert.'

She hesitated. 'During my sleepless night, I did think of something. But you might not like it.'

'Try me,' he said, eyes narrowed.

'It's out of the ball park,' she warned.

'I'm all for that,' he said.

She flung up her hands in front of her face to act as a shield. 'It…it involves Christmas.'

He blanched under the smooth olive of his tan. 'I told you—'

His mouth set in a grim line, his hands balled into fists by his sides. Should she leave well enough alone? After all, he had said the festive season had difficult associations for him. 'What is it that you hate so much about Christmas?' she asked. She'd always been one to dive straight into the deep end.

'I don't *hate* Christmas.' He cursed under his breath. 'I'm misquoted once and the media repeat it over and over.'

'But—'

He put up his hand to halt her. 'I don't have to justify anything to you. But let me give you three good reasons why I don't choose to celebrate Christmas and all the razzmatazz that goes with it.'

'Fire away,' she said, thinking it wasn't appropriate for her to counter with three things she adored about the festive season. This wasn't a debate. It was a business brainstorming.

'First—the weather is all wrong,' he said. 'It's hot when it should be cold. A *proper* Christmas is a northern hemisphere Christmas—snow, not sand.'

Not true, she thought. For a born-and-bred Australian like her, Christmas was all about the long, hot sticky days of summer. Cicadas chirruping in the warm air as the family walked to a midnight church service. Lunch outdoors, preferably around a pool or at the beach. Then it struck her—Dominic had a distinct trace of an English accent. That might explain his aversion to festivities Down Under style. But something still didn't seem quite right. His words sounded…too practised, as if he'd recited them a hundred times before.

He continued, warming to his point as she wondered

about the subtext to his spiel. 'Then there's the fact that the whole thing is over-commercialised to the point of being ludicrous. I saw Christmas stuff festooning the shops in September.'

She almost expected him to snarl a Scrooge-like *Bah! Humbug!* but he obviously restrained himself.

'You have a point,' she said. 'And carols piped through shopping malls in October? So annoying.'

'Quite right,' he said. 'This whole obsession with extended Christmas celebrations, it…it…makes people who don't celebrate it—for one reason or another—feel…feel excluded.'

His words faltered and he looked away in the direction of the pool but not before she'd seen the bleakness in his eyes. She realised those last words hadn't been rehearsed. That he might be regretting them. Again she had that inane urge to comfort him—without knowing why he needed comforting.

She knew she had to take this carefully. 'Yes,' she said slowly. 'I know what you mean.' That first Christmas without Anthony had been the bleakest imaginable. And each year after she had thought about him and the emptiness in her heart he had left behind him. But she would not share that with this man; it was far too personal. And nothing to do with the general discussion about Christmas.

His mouth twisted. 'Do you?'

She forced her voice to sound cheerful and impersonal. Her ongoing sadness over Anthony was deeply private. 'Not me personally. I love Christmas. I'm lucky enough to come from a big family—one of five kids. I have two older brothers and a sister and a younger sister. Christmas with our extended family was always—still is—a special time of the year. But my parents knew that wasn't the case for everyone. Every year we shared our celebration with children who weren't as fortunate as we were.'

'Charity cases, you mean,' he said, his voice hard-edged with something she couldn't identify.

'In the truest sense of the word,' she said. 'We didn't query them being there. It meant more kids to play with on Christmas Day. It didn't even enter our heads that there would be fewer presents for us so they could have presents too. Two of them moved in with us as long-term foster kids. When I say I'm from five, I really mean from seven. Only that's too confusing to explain.'

He gave a sound that seemed a cross between a grunt and a cynical snort.

She shrugged, inexplicably hurt by his reaction. 'You might think it goody-two-shoes-ish but that's the way my family are, and I love them for it,' she said, her voice stiff and more than a touch defensive.

'Not at all,' he said. 'I think it…it sounds wonderful. You were very lucky to grow up in a family like that.' With the implication being he hadn't?

'I know, and I'm thankful. And my parents' strong sense of community didn't do us any harm. In fact those Christmas Days my family shared with others got me thinking. It was what kept me up last night. I had an idea.'

'Fire away,' he said.

She channelled all her optimism and enthusiasm to make her voice sound convincing to Sydney's most notorious Scrooge. 'Wouldn't it be wonderful if you opened this beautiful home on Christmas Day for a big lunch party for children and families who do it hard on Christmas Day? Not as a gimmick. Not as a stunt. As a genuine act of hospitality and sharing the true spirit of Christmas.'

CHAPTER FOUR

DOMINIC STARED AT Andie in disbelief. Hadn't she heard a word he'd said about his views on Christmas? She looked up at him, her eyes bright with enthusiasm but backlit by wariness. 'Please, just consider my proposal,' she said. 'That's all I ask.' He could easily fire her for straying so far from the brief and she must know it—yet that didn't stop her. Her tenacity was to be admired.

Maybe she had a point. No matter what she or anyone else thought, he was not a Scrooge or a hypocrite. To make a holiday that could never be happy for him happy for others had genuine appeal. He was aware Christmas *was* a special time for a huge percentage of the population. It was just too painful for him to want to do anything but lock himself away with a bottle of bourbon from Christmas Eve to Boxing Day.

Deep from within, he dredged memories of his first Christmas away from home. Aged seventeen, he'd been living in an underground car park beneath an abandoned shopping centre project. His companions had been a ragtag collection of other runaways, addicts, criminals and people who'd lost all hope of a better life. Someone had stolen a branch of a pine tree from somewhere and decorated it with scavenged scraps of glittery paper. They'd all stood around it and sung carols with varying degrees of sobriety. Only he had stood aloof.

Now, he reached out to where Andie was twisting her

necklace so tightly it was in danger of snapping. Gently, he disengaged her hand and freed the string of beads. Fought the temptation to hold her hand for any longer than was necessary—slender and warm in his own much bigger hand. Today her nails were painted turquoise. And, as he'd noticed the day before, her fingers were free of any rings.

'Your idea could have merit,' he said, stepping back from her. Back from her beautiful interesting face, her intelligent eyes, the subtle spicy-sweet scent of her. 'Come and sit outside by the pool and we can talk it over.'

Her face flushed with relief at his response and he realised again what spunk it had taken for her to propose something so radical. He was grateful to whoever had sent Party Planner Number Four his way. Andie was gorgeous, smart and not the slightest in awe of him and his money, which was refreshing. His only regret was that he could not both employ her and date her.

He hadn't told the complete truth about why he'd been unable to sleep the night before. Thoughts of her had been churning through his head as much as concerns about the party. He had never felt so instantly attracted to a woman. Ever. If they had met under other circumstances he would have asked her out by now.

'I really think it could work,' she said as she walked with him through the doors and out to the pool area.

For a heart-halting second he thought Andie had tuned into his private thoughts—that she thought dating her could work. *Never.* He'd met his ex-wife, Tara, when she'd worked for his company, with disastrous consequences. The whole marriage had, in fact, been disastrous—based on lies and deception. He wouldn't make that mistake again—even for this intriguing woman.

But of course Andie was talking about her party proposal in businesslike tones. 'You could generate the right kind of publicity—both for your potential business partner and in general,' she said as he settled her into one of the white outdoor armchairs that had cost a small fortune because of its vintage styling.

'While at the same time directly benefiting people who do it tough on the so-called Big Day,' he said as he took the chair next to her.

'Exactly,' she said with her wide, generous smile. When she smiled like that it made him want to make her do it again, just for the pleasure of seeing her face light up. *Not a good idea.*

Her chair was in the shade of one of the mature palm trees he'd had helicoptered in for the landscaping but the sun was dancing off the aqua surface of the pool. He was disappointed when she reached into her satchel, pulled out a pair of tortoiseshell-rimmed sunglasses and donned them against the glare. They looked 'vintage' too. In fact, in her white clothes and turquoise necklace, she looked as if she belonged here.

'In principal, I don't mind your idea,' he said. 'In fact I find it more acceptable than the other.'

Her smile was edged with relief. 'I can't tell you how pleased that makes me.'

'Would the lunch have to be on actual Christmas Day?' he said.

'You could hold it on Christmas Eve or the week leading up to Christmas. In terms of organisation, that would be easier. But none of those peripheral days is as lonely and miserable as Christmas Day can be if you're one…one of the excluded ones,' she said. 'My foster sister told me that.'

The way she was looking at him, even with those too-perceptive green eyes shaded from his view, made him think she was beginning to suspect he had a deeply personal reason for his anti-Christmas stance.

He'd only ever shared that reason with one woman—Melody, the girl who'd first captivated, then shredded, his teenage heart back in that car park squat. By the time Christmas had loomed in the first year of his marriage to Tara, he'd known he'd never be sharing secrets with her. But there was something disarming about Andie that seemed to invite confidences—something he had to stand guard against. She might not be what she seemed—and he had learned the painful lesson not to trust his first impressions when it came to beautiful women.

'I guess any other day doesn't have the same impact,' he reluctantly agreed, not sure he would be able to face the festivities. Did he actually have to be present on the day? Might it not be enough to provide the house and the meal? No. To achieve his goal, he knew his presence would be necessary. Much as he would hate every minute of it.

'Maybe your marketing people will have other ideas,' she said. 'But I think opening your home on the actual December twenty-five to give people who really need it a slap-up feast would be a marvellous antidote to your Scrooge…sorry, *miser*…I mean *cheap* reputation.' She pulled a face. 'Sorry. I didn't actually mean any of those things.'

Why did it sting so much more coming from her? 'Of course you did. So does everyone else. People who have no idea of what and where I might give without wanting any fanfare.' The main reason he wanted to secure the joint venture was to ensure his big project in Brisbane would continue to be funded long after his lifetime.

She looked shamefaced. 'I'm sorry.'

He hated that people like Andie thought he was stingy. Any remaining reservations he might hold about the party had to go. He needed to take action before this unfair reputation become so deeply entrenched he'd never free himself from it. 'Let's hope the seasonal name-calling eases if I go ahead with the lunch.'

She held up a finger in warning. 'It wouldn't appease everyone. Those cynical journalists might not be easily swayed.'

He scowled. 'I can't please everyone.' But he found himself, irrationally, wanting to please *her*.

'It might help if you followed through with a visible, ongoing relationship with a charity. If the media could see…could see…'

Her eyes narrowed in concentration. He waited for the end of her sentence but it wasn't forthcoming. 'See what?'

'Sorry,' she said, shaking her head as if bringing herself back to earth. 'My thoughts tend to run faster than my words sometimes when I'm deep in the creative zone.'

'I get it,' he said, though he wasn't sure what the hell being in the creative zone meant.

'I meant your critics might relent if they could see your gesture was genuine.'

He scowled. 'But it *will* be genuine.'

'You know it and I know it but they might see it as just another publicity gimmick.' Her eyes narrowed again and he gave her time to think. 'What if you didn't actually seek publicity for this day? You know—no invitations or press releases. Let the details leak. Tantalise the media.'

'For a designer, you seem to know a lot about publicity,' he said.

She shrugged. 'When you work in magazines you pick up a lot about both seeking and giving publicity. But your marketing people would have their own ideas, I'm sure.'

'I should talk it over with them,' he said.

'As it's only six weeks until Christmas, and this would be a big event to pull together, may I suggest there's not a lot of discussion time left?'

'You're right. I know. But it's a big deal.' So much bigger for him personally than she realised.

'You're seriously considering going ahead with it?'

He so much preferred it to the Z-list celebrity party. 'Yes. Let's do it.'

She clapped her hands together. 'I'm so glad. We can make it a real dream-come-true for your guests.'

'What about you and your business partners? You'd have to work on Christmas Day.'

'Speaking for me, I'd be fine with working. True spirit of Christmas and all that. I'll have to speak to Gemma and Eliza, but I think they'd be behind it too.' Securing Dominic Hunt's business for Party Queens was too important for them to refuse.

'What about caterers and so on?' he asked.

'The hospitality industry works three hundred and sixty-five days a year. It shouldn't be a problem. There are also people who don't celebrate Christmas as part of their culture who are very happy to work—especially for holiday pay rates. You don't have to worry about all that— that's our job.'

'And the guests? How would we recruit them?' He was about to say he could talk to people in Brisbane, where he was heavily involved in a homeless charity, but stopped himself. That was too connected to the secret part of his life he had no desire to share.

'I know the perfect person to help—my older sister, Hannah, is a social worker. She would know exactly which charities to liaise with. I think she would be excited to be involved.'

It was her. *Andie.* He would not be considering this direction if it wasn't for her. The big glitzy party had seemed so wrong. She made him see what could be right.

'Could we set up a meeting with your sister?' he asked.

'I can do better than that,' she said with a triumphant toss of her head that set her oversized earrings swaying. 'Every Wednesday night is open house dinner at my parents' house. Whoever of my siblings can make it comes.

Sometimes grandparents and cousins too. I know Hannah will be there tonight and I'm planning to go too. Why don't you come along?'

'To your family dinner?' His first thought was to say no. Nothing much intimidated him—but meeting people's families was near the top of the list.

'Family is an elastic term for the Newmans. Friends, waifs and strays are always welcome at the table.'

What category would he be placed under? His memory of being a real-life stray made him wince. Friend? Strictly speaking, if circumstances were different, he'd want to be more than friends with Andie. Would connecting with her family create an intimacy he might later come to regret?

He looked down at his watch. Thought about his plan to return to the office.

'We need to get things moving,' she prompted.

'I would like to meet your sister tonight.'

Her wide smile lit her eyes. 'I have a really good feeling about this.'

'Do you always go on your feelings?' he asked.

She took off her sunglasses so he was treated to the directness of her gaze. 'All the time. Don't you?'

If he acted on his feelings he would be insisting they go to dinner, just the two of them. He would be taking her in his arms. Tasting her lovely mouth. Touching. Exploring. *But that wouldn't happen.*

He trusted his instincts when it came to business. But trusting his feelings when it came to women had only led to bitterness, betrayal and the kind of pain he never wanted to expose himself to again.

No to feeling. *Yes* to pleasant relationships that mutually fulfilled desires and were efficiently terminated before emotions ever became part of it. And with none of the complications that came with still having to work with that person. Besides, he suspected the short-term liaison that was all he had to offer would not be acceptable to Andie. She had *for ever* written all over her.

Now it was her turn to look at her watch. 'I'll call my mother to confirm you'll be joining us for dinner. How about I swing by and pick you up at around six?'

He thought about his four o'clock meeting. 'That's early for dinner.'

'Not when there are kids involved.'

'Kids?'

'I have a niece and two nephews. One of the nephews belongs to Hannah. He will almost certainly be there, along with his cousins.'

Dominic wasn't sure exactly what he was letting himself in for. One thing was for certain—he couldn't have seen himself going to a family dinner with any of Party Planners Numbers One to Three. And he suspected he might be in for more than one surprise from gorgeous Party Planner Number Four.

Andie got up from the chair. Smoothed down her white trousers. They were nothing as revealing as her flyaway skirt but made no secret of her slender shape.

'By the way, I'm apologising in advance for my car.'

He frowned. 'Why apologise?'

'I glimpsed your awesome sports car in the garage as I came in yesterday. You might find my hand-me-down hatchback a bit of a comedown.'

He frowned. 'I didn't come into this world behind the wheel of an expensive European sports car. I'm sure your hatchback will be perfectly fine.'

Just how did she see him? His public image—Scrooge, miser, rich guy—was so at odds with the person he knew himself to be. That he wanted her to know. But he could not reveal himself to her without uncovering secrets he would rather leave buried deep in his past.

CHAPTER FIVE

DOMINIC HAD FACED down some fears in his time. But the prospect of being paraded before Andie's large family ranked as one of the most fearsome. As Andie pulled up her hatchback—old but in good condition and nothing to be ashamed of—in front of her parents' home in the northern suburb of Willoughby, sweat prickled on his forehead and his hands felt clammy. How the hell had he got himself into this?

She turned off the engine, took out the keys, unclipped her seat belt and smoothed down the legs of her sleek, very sexy leather trousers. But she made no effort to get out of the car. She turned her head towards him. 'Before we go inside to meet my family I... I need to tell you something first. Something...something about me.'

Why did she look so serious, sombre even? 'Sure, fire away,' he said.

'I've told them you're a client. That there is absolutely nothing personal between us.'

'Of course,' he said.

Strange how at the same time he could be relieved and yet offended by her categorical denial that there ever could be anything *personal* between them.

Now a hint of a smile crept to the corners of her mouth. 'The thing is...they won't believe me. You're good-looking, you're smart and you're personable.'

'That's nice of you to say that,' he said. He noticed she hadn't added that he was rich to his list of attributes.

'You know it's true,' she said. 'My family are determined I should have a man in my life and have become the most inveterate of matchmakers. I expect they'll pounce on you. It could get embarrassing.'

'You're single?' He welcomed the excuse to ask.

'Yes. I…I've been single for a long time. Oh, I date. But I haven't found anyone special since…since…' She twisted right around in the car seat to fully face him. She clasped her hands together on her lap, then started to twist them without seeming to realise she was doing it. 'You need to know this before we go inside.' The hint of a smile had completely dissipated.

'If you think so,' he said. She was twenty-eight and single. What was the big deal here?

'I met Anthony on my first day of university. We were inseparable from the word go. There was no doubt we would spend our lives together.'

Dominic braced himself for the story of a nasty break-up. Infidelity? Betrayal? A jerk in disguise as a nice guy? He was prepared to make polite noises in response. He knew all about betrayal. But a *quid pro quo* exchange over relationships gone wrong was not something he ever wanted to waste time on with Andie or anyone else.

'It ended?' he said, making a terse contribution only because it was expected.

'He died.'

Two words stated so baldly but with such a wealth of pain behind them. Dominic felt as if he'd been punched in the chest. Nothing he said could be an adequate response. 'Andie, I'm sorry,' was all he could manage.

'It was five years ago. He was twenty-three. He…he went out for an early-morning surf and didn't come back.' He could hear the effort it took for her to keep her tone even.

He knew about people who didn't come back. Good-byes left unsaid. Personal tragedy. That particular kind of pain. 'Did he...? Did you—?'

'He...he washed up two days later.' She closed her eyes as if against an unbearable image.

'What happened?' He didn't want her to think he was interrogating her on something so sensitive, but he wanted to find out.

'Head injury. An accident. The doctors couldn't be sure exactly how it happened. A rock? His board? A sandbank? We'll never know.'

'Thank you for telling me.' He felt unable to say anything else.

'Better for you to know than not to know when you're about to meet the family. Just in case someone says something that might put you on the spot.'

She heaved a sigh that seemed to signal she had said what she felt she had to say and that there would be no further confidences. Why should there be? *He was just a client.* Something prompted him to want to ask—was she over the loss? Had she moved on? But it was not his place. Client and contractor—that was all they could be to each other. Besides, could anyone *ever* get over loss like that?

'You needed to be in the picture.' She went to open her door. 'Now, let's go in—Hannah is looking forward to meeting you. As I predicted, she's very excited about getting involved.'

Her family's home was a comfortable older-style house set in a chaotic garden in a suburb where values had rocketed in recent years. In the car on the way over, Andie had told him she had lived in this house since she was a baby. All her siblings had. He envied her that certainty, that security.

'Hellooo!' she called ahead of her. 'We're here.'

He followed her down a wide hallway, the walls crammed with framed photographs. They ranged from old-fashioned sepia wedding photos, dating from pre-Second World War, to posed studio shots of cherubic babies. Again he found himself envying her—he had only a handful of family photos to cherish.

At a quick glance he found two of Andie—one in a green checked school uniform with her hair in plaits and that familiar grin showing off a gap in her front teeth; another as a teenager in a flowing pink formal dress. A third caught his eye—an older Andie in a bikini, arm in arm with a tall blond guy in board shorts who was looking down at her with open adoration. The same guy was with her in the next photo, only this time they were playing guitars and singing together. Dominic couldn't bear to do more than glance at them, aware of the tragedy that had followed.

Just before they reached the end of the corridor, Andie stopped and took a step towards him. She stood so close he breathed in her scent—something vaguely oriental, warm and sensual. She leaned up to whisper into his ear and her hair tickled his neck. He had to close his eyes to force himself from reacting to her closeness.

'The clan can be a bit overwhelming *en masse*,' she said. 'I won't introduce you to everyone by name; it would be unfair to expect you to remember all of them. My mother is Jennifer, my father is Ray. Hannah's husband is Paul.'

'I appreciate that,' he said, tugging at his collar that suddenly seemed too tight. As an only child, he'd always found meeting other people's families intimidating.

Andie gave him a reassuring smile. 'With the Newman family, what you see is what you get. They're all good people who will take you as they find you. We might even get some volunteers to help on Christmas Day out of this.'

The corridor opened out into a spacious open-plan family room. At some time in the last twenty years the parents had obviously added a new extension. It looked dated now but solid—warm and comfortable and welcoming. Delicious aromas emanated from the farmhouse-style kitchen in the northern corner. He sniffed and Andie smiled. 'My mother's lasagne—wait until you taste it.'

She announced him with an encompassing wave of her arm. 'Everyone, this is Dominic. He's a very important new client so please make him welcome. And yes, I know he's gorgeous but it's strictly business between us.'

That was met with laughter and a chorus of 'Hi, Dominic!' and 'Welcome!' Andie then briefly explained to them about the party and Hannah's likely role in it.

There were so many of them. Andie's introduction had guaranteed all eyes were on him. About ten people, including kids, were ranged around the room, sitting in comfortable-looking sofas or around a large trestle table.

Each face came into focus as the adults greeted him with warm smiles. It wasn't difficult to tell who was related—Andie's smile was a strong family marker that originated with her father, a tall, thin man with a vigorous handshake. Her mother's smile was different but equally welcoming as she headed his way from the kitchen, wiping her hands on her apron before she greeted him. Three young children playing on the floor looked up, then kept on playing with their toys. A big black dog with a greying muzzle, lying stretched out near the kids, lifted his head, then thumped his tail in greeting.

Andie's sister Hannah and her husband, Paul, paused in their job of setting the large trestle table to say hello. His experience with social workers in his past had been good—a social worker had pretty much saved his life—and he was not disappointed by Hannah's kind eyes in a gentle face.

'I straight away know of several families who are facing a very grim Christmas indeed,' she said. 'Your generous gesture would make an immense difference to them.'

Andie caught his eye and smiled. Instinctively, he knew she had steered him in the right direction towards her sister. If all Andie's ideas for his party were as good as this one, he could face the Christmas Day he dreaded with more confidence than he might have expected.

Andie's policy of glaring down any family member who dared to even hint at dating possibilities with Dominic was working. Except for her younger sister, Bea, who could not resist hissing, 'He's hot,' at any opportunity, from passing the salad to refilling her water glass. Then, when Andie didn't bite, Bea added, 'If you don't want him, hand him over to me.' Thankfully, Dominic remained oblivious to the whispered exchanges.

Her family had, unwittingly or not, sat Dominic in the same place at the table where Anthony had sat at these gatherings. *Andie and Ant—always together.* She doubted it was on purpose. Dominic needed to sit between Hannah and her and so it had just happened.

In the years since he'd died, no man had come anywhere near to replacing Anthony in her heart. How could they? Anthony and she had been two halves of the same soul, she sometimes thought. Maybe she would never be able to love anyone else. *But she was lonely.* The kind of loneliness that work, friends, family could not displace.

In the months after Anthony's death her parents had left Anthony's customary seat empty out of respect. Unable to bear the emptiness that emphasised his absence, she had stopped coming to the family dinners until her mother had realised the pain it was causing. From then on, one of her brothers always occupied Anthony's chair.

Now she told herself she was okay with Dominic sitting there. He was only a client, with no claim to any place in her heart. Bringing him along tonight had worked out well—one of those spur-of-the-moment decisions she mightn't have made if she'd given it more thought.

Dominic and Hannah had spent a lot of time talking—but he'd managed to chat with everyone else there too. They were obviously charmed by him. That was okay too. *She* was charmed by him. Tonight she was seeing a side of him, as he interacted with her family, that she might never have seen in everyday business dealings.

Her sister was right. *Dominic was hot.* And Andie was only too aware of it. She was surprised at the fierce urge of possessiveness that swept over her at the thought of 'handing over' Dominic to anyone else. Her sister could find her own hot guy.

Even at the dinner table, when her back was angled away from him to talk to her brother on her other side, she was aware of Dominic. His scent had already become familiar—citrus-sharp yet warm and very masculine. Her ears were tuned into the sound of his voice—no matter where he was in the room. Her body was on constant alert to that attraction, which had been instant and only continued to grow with further contact. On their way in, in the corridor, when she'd drawn close to whisper so her family would not overhear, she'd felt light-headed from the proximity to him.

It had been five years now since Anthony had gone—the same length of time they'd been together. She would never forget him but that terrible grief and anguish she had felt at first had eventually mellowed to a grudging acceptance. She realised she had stopped dreaming about him.

People talked about once-in-a-lifetime love. She'd thought she'd found it at the age of eighteen—and a cruel fate had snatched him away from her. Was there to be only one great love for her?

Deep in her heart, she didn't want to believe that. Surely there would be someone for her again? She didn't want to be alone. One day she wanted marriage, a family. She'd been looking for someone like Anthony—and had been constantly disappointed in the men she'd gone out with. But was it a mistake to keep on looking for a man like her teenage soulmate?

Thoughts of Dominic were constantly invading her mind. He was so different from Anthony there could be no comparison. Anthony had been blond and lean, laidback and funny, always quick with a joke, creative and musical. From what she knew of Dominic, he was quite the opposite. She'd dismissed him as not for her. But her body's reaction kept contradicting her mind's stonewalling. How could she be so certain he was Mr Wrong?

Dessert was being served—spring berries and homemade vanilla bean ice cream—and she turned to Dominic at the precise moment he turned to her. Their eyes connected and held and she knew without the need for words that he was happy with her decision to bring him here.

'Your family is wonderful,' he said in a low undertone.

'I think so,' she said, pleased. 'What about you? Do you come from a large family?'

A shadow darkened his eyes. He shook his head. 'Only child.'

She smiled. 'We must seem overwhelming.'

'In a good way,' he said. 'You're very lucky.'

'I know.' Of course she and her siblings had had the usual squabbles and disagreements throughout their childhood and adolescence. She, as number four, had had to fight for her place. But as adults they all got on as friends as well as brothers and sisters. She couldn't have got through the loss of Anthony without her family's support.

'The kids are cute,' he said. 'So well behaved.'

Her nephews, Timothy and Will, and her niece, Caitlin,

were together down the other end of the table under the watchful eye of their grandmother. 'They're really good kids,' she agreed. 'I adore them.'

'Little Timothy seems quite…delicate,' Dominic said, obviously choosing his words carefully. 'But I notice his older cousin looks after him.'

A wave of sadness for Hannah and Paul's little son overwhelmed her. 'They're actually the same age,' she said. 'Both five years old. Timothy just looks as though he's three.'

'I guess I don't know much about kids,' Dominic said, shifting uncomfortably in his chair.

She lowered her voice. 'Sadly, little Timothy has some kind of rare growth disorder, an endocrine imbalance. That's why he's so small.'

Dominic answered in a lowered voice. 'Can it be treated?'

'Only with a new treatment that isn't yet subsidised by the public health system. Even for private treatment, he's on a waiting list.' It was the reason why she drove an old car, why Bea had moved back home to save on rent, why the whole family was pulling together to raise the exorbitant amount of money required for tiny Timothy's private treatment.

But she would not tell Dominic that. While she might be wildly attracted to him, she still had no reason to think he was other than the Scrooge of his reputation. A man who had to be forced into a public display of charity to broker a multi-million-dollar business deal. Not for one moment did she want him to think she might be angling for financial help for Timothy.

'It's all under control,' she said as she passed him a bowl of raspberries.

'I'm glad to hear that,' he said, helping himself to the berries and then the ice cream. 'Thank you for inviting

me tonight and for introducing me to Hannah. The next
step is for you and your business partners to come in to
my headquarters for a meeting with my marketing people.
Can the three of you make it on Friday?'

CHAPTER SIX

ANDIE AND HER two business partners, Gemma and Eliza, settled themselves in a small waiting room off the main reception area of Dominic's very plush offices in Circular Quay. She and her fellow Party Queens had just come out of the Friday meeting with Dominic, his marketing people and senior executives in the boardroom and were waiting for Dominic to hear his feedback.

Situated on Sydney Cove, at the northern end of the CBD, the area was not just one of the most popular harbourside tourist precincts in Sydney—it was also home to the most prestigious office buildings. Even in this small room, floor-to-ceiling glass walls gave a magnificent close view of the Sydney Harbour Bridge and a luxury cruise liner in dock.

Andie couldn't help thinking the office was an ideal habitat for a billionaire Scrooge. Then she backtracked on the thought. That might not be fair. He hated the term and she felt vaguely disloyal even thinking it. Dominic was now totally committed to the Christmas Day feast for underprivileged families and had just approved a more than generous budget. She was beginning to wonder if his protestation that he was *not* a Scrooge had some truth in it. And then there was his gift to her mother to consider.

As she pondered the significance of that, she realised her thoughts had been filled with nothing much but Dominic since the day she'd met him. Last night he had even invaded her dreams—in a very passionate encounter that made her blush at the hazy dream memory of it. *Did he kiss like that in real life?*

It was with an effort that she forced her thoughts back to business.

'How do you guys think it went?' she asked the other two. 'My vote is for really well.' She felt jubilant and buoyant—Dominic's team had embraced her idea with more enthusiasm than she could ever have anticipated.

'Considering the meeting was meant to go from ten to eleven and here it is, nearly midday, yes, I think you could say that,' said Eliza with a big smile splitting her face.

'Of course that could have had something to do with Gemma's superb macadamia shortbread and those delectable fruit mince pies,' said Andie.

'Yes,' said Gemma with a pleased smile. 'I thought I could describe until I was blue in the face what I wanted to serve for the lunch, but they'd only know by tasting it.'

Party Queens' foodie partner had not only come up with a detailed menu for Dominic's Christmas Day lunch, but she'd also brought along freshly baked samples of items from her proposed menus. At the end of the meeting only a few crumbs had remained on the boardroom's fine china plates. Andie had caught Dominic's eye as he finished his second pastry and knew it had been an inspired idea. The Christmas star shaped serviettes she had brought along had also worked to keep the meeting focused on the theme of traditional with a twist.

'I think they were all-round impressed,' said Eliza. 'We three worked our collective socks off to get our presentations so detailed and professional in such a short time. Andie, all the images and samples you prepared to show the decorations and table settings looked amazing—I got excited at how fabulous it's going to look.'

'I loved the idea of the goody bags for all the guests too,' said Gemma. 'You really thought of everything.'

'While we're doing some mutual backslapping I'm giving yours a hearty slap, Eliza,' said Andie. 'Their finance guy couldn't fault your detailed costings and timelines.'

Eliza rubbed her hands together in exaggerated glee. 'And I'm sure we're going to get more party bookings from them. One of the senior marketing people mentioned her daughter was getting married next year and asked me did we do weddings.'

'Well done, Party Queens,' said Andie. 'Now that the contract is signed and the basic plan approved I feel I can relax.' Her partners had no idea of how tight it had been to get Dominic across the line for the change from glitz and glamour to more humble with heart.

She and her two friends discreetly high-fived each other. The room was somewhat of a goldfish bowl and none of them wanted to look less than professional to any of Dominic's staff who might be walking by.

Eliza leaned in to within whispering distance of Andie and Gemma. 'Dominic Hunt was a surprise,' she said in an undertone. 'I thought he'd be arrogant and overbearing. Instead, I found myself actually liking him.'

'Me too,' said Gemma. 'Not to mention he's so handsome. I could hardly keep my eyes off him. And that voice.' She mimed a shiver of delight.

'But *he* couldn't keep his eyes off Andie,' said Eliza. 'You'd be wasting your time there, Gemma.'

Had he? Been unable to keep his eyes off her? Andie's Dominic radar had been on full alert all through the meeting. Again she'd that uncanny experience of knowing exactly where he was in the room even when her back was turned. Of hearing his voice through the chatter of others. She'd caught his eye one too many times to feel comfortable. Especially with the remnants of that dream lingering in her mind. She'd had to force herself not to let her gaze linger on his mouth.

'Really, Andie?' said Gemma. 'Has he asked you out?'

'Nothing like that,' Andie said.

Eliza nodded thoughtfully. 'But you like him. Not in the way I liked him. I mean you *really* like him.'

Andie had no intention of admitting anything to anyone. She forced her voice to sound cool, impartial—though she doubted she would fool shrewd Eliza. 'Like you, I was surprised at how easy he is to get on with and how professional he is—even earlier this week when I switched the whole concept of his party into something he had never envisaged.' That overwhelming attraction was just physical—nothing more.

'And you totally didn't get how hot he was?' said Gemma. 'Don't expect me to believe that for one moment.'

Eliza rolled her eyes at Andie. 'I know what's coming next. *He's not your type.* How many times have I heard you say that when you either refuse a date or dump a guy before you've even had a chance to get to know him?'

Andie paused. 'Maybe that's true. Maybe that's why I'm still single. I'm beginning to wonder if I really know what *is* my type now.'

Her friendships with Gemma and Eliza dated from after she'd lost Anthony. They'd been sympathetic, but never really got why she had been so determined to try and find another man cast in the same mould as her first love. That her first love had been so perfect she'd felt her best chance of happiness would be with someone like Anthony.

Trouble was, they'd broken the mould when they'd made Anthony. Maybe she just hadn't been ready. Maybe she'd been subconsciously avoiding any man who might challenge her. Or might force her to look at why she'd put her heart on hold for so long. *Dominic would be a challenge in every way.* The thought both excited and scared her.

Eliza shook her head. 'It's irrelevant anyway,' she said. 'It would be most unwise for you to start anything with Dominic Hunt. His party is a big, important job for us and we don't have much time to organise it. It could get very messy if you started dating the client. Especially when I've never known you to stay with anyone for more than two weeks.'

'In my eagerness to get you fixed up with a handsome rich guy, I hadn't thought of that,' said Gemma. 'Imagine if you broke up with the billionaire client right in the middle of the countdown to the event. Could get awkward.'

'It's not going to happen, girls,' Andie said. 'I won't lie and say I don't think he's really attractive. But that's as far as it goes.' Thinking of last night's very intimate dream, she crossed her fingers behind her back.

'This is a huge party for us to pull together so quickly. We've got other jobs to get sorted as well. I can't afford to get...distracted.' How she actually stopped herself from getting distracted by Dominic was another matter altogether.

'I agree,' said Eliza. 'Eyes off the client. Okay?'

Andie smiled. 'I'll try,' she said. 'Seriously, though, it's really important for Dominic that this party works. He's got a lot riding on it. And it's really important for us. As you say, Eliza, more work could come from this. Not just weddings and private parties. But why not his company's business functions too? We have to think big.'

Gemma giggled. 'Big? Mr Hunt is way too big for me anyway. He's so tall. And all those muscles. His face is handsome but kind of tough too, don't you think?'

'Shh,' hissed Eliza, putting her finger to her lips. 'He's coming.'

Andie screwed up her eyes for a moment. How mortifying if he'd caught them gossiping about him. She'd been just about to say he wasn't too big for her to handle.

Along with the other two, she looked up and straightened her shoulders as Dominic strode towards them. In his dark charcoal suit he looked every inch the billionaire businessman. And, yes, very big.

She caught her breath at how handsome he looked. At the same time she caught his eye. And got the distinct impression that, of the three women in the room, she was the only one he really saw.

Did Andie get more and more beautiful every time he saw her? Dominic wondered. Or was it just the more he got to know her, the more he liked and admired her?

He had been impressed by her engaging and professional manner in the boardroom—the more so because he was aware she'd had such a short time to prepare her presentation. Her two business partners had been impressive too. It took a lot to win over his hard-nosed marketing people but, as a team, Party Queens had bowled them over.

The three women got up from their seats as he approached. Andie, tall and elegant in a deceptively simple caramel-coloured short dress—businesslike but with a snug fit that showed off her curves. Her sensational legs seemed to go on for ever to end in sky-high leopard-skin-print stilettos. He got it. She wanted to look businesslike but also let it be known who was the creative mind behind Party Queens. It worked.

Gemma—shorter, curvier, with auburn hair—and sophisticated, dark-haired Eliza were strikingly attractive too. They had a glint in their eyes and humour in their smiles that made him believe they could enjoy a party as well as plan them. But, in his eyes, Andie outshone them. Would any other woman ever be able to beat her? It was disturbing that a woman who he had known for such a short time could have made such an impression on him.

He addressed all three, while being hyper aware of

Andie as he did so. Her hair pulled back in a loose knot that fell in soft tendrils around her face, her mouth slicked with coral gloss, those remarkable green eyes. 'As I'm sure you're aware,' he began, 'my marketing team is delighted at both the concept for the party and the way you plan to implement the concept to the timeline. They're confident the event will meet and exceed the target we've set for reputation management and positive media engagement.'

It sounded like jargon and he knew it. But how else could he translate the only real aim of the party: to make him look less the penny-pincher and more the philanthropist?

'We're very pleased to be working with such a professional team,' said Eliza, the business brains of the partnership. But all three were business savvy in their own way, he'd realised through the meeting.

'Thank you,' he said. He glanced at his watch. 'The meeting ran so late it's almost lunchtime. I'm extending an invitation to lunch for all of you,' he said. 'Not that restaurants around here, excellent as they are, could match the standard of your cooking, Gemma.'

'Thank you,' said Gemma, looking pleased. 'But I'm afraid I have an appointment elsewhere.'

'Me too, and I'm running late,' said Eliza. 'But we couldn't possibly let you lunch alone, Mr Hunt, could we, Andie?'

Andie flushed high on those elegant cheekbones. 'Of course not. I'd be delighted to join Dominic for lunch.'

Her chin tilted upwards and he imagined her friends might later be berated for landing her in this on her own. Not that he minded. The other women were delightful, but lunch one-on-one with Andie was his preferred option.

'There are a few details of the plan I need to finalise with Dominic anyway,' she said to her friends.

Dominic shook hands with Gemma and Eliza and they

headed towards the elevators. He turned to Andie. 'Thank you for coming to lunch with me,' he said.

She smiled. 'Be warned, I'm starving. I was up at the crack of dawn finalising those mood boards for the presentation.'

'They were brilliant. There's only one thing I'd like to see changed. I didn't want to mention it in the meeting as it's my personal opinion and I didn't want to have to debate it.'

She frowned, puzzled rather than worried, he thought. 'Yes?'

He put his full authority behind his voice—he would not explain his reasons. Ever. 'The Christmas tree. The big one you have planned for next to the staircase. I don't want it.'

'Sure,' she said, obviously still puzzled. 'I thought it would be wonderful to have the tree where it's the first thing the guests see, but I totally understand if you don't want it there. We can put the Christmas tree elsewhere. The living room. Even in the area near where we'll be eating. Wherever you suggest.'

He hadn't expected this to be easy—he knew everyone would expect to see a decorated tree on Christmas Day. 'You misunderstood me. I mean I don't want a Christmas tree anywhere. No tree at all in my house.'

She paused. He could almost see her internal debate reflected in the slight crease between her eyebrows, the barely visible pursing of her lips. But then she obviously thought it was not worth the battle. 'Okay,' she said with a shrug of her slender shoulders. 'No tree.'

'Thank you,' he said, relieved he wasn't going to have to further assert his authority. At this time of year, Christmas trees were appearing all over the place. He avoided them when he could. But he would never have a tree in his home—a constant reminder of the pain and loss and guilt associated with the festive season.

They walked together to the elevator. When it arrived, there were two other people in it. They got out two floors below. Then Dominic was alone in the confined space of the elevator, aware of Andie's closeness, her warm scent. What was it? Sandalwood? Something exotic and sensual. He had the craziest impulse to hold her closer so he could nuzzle into the softness of her throat, the better to breathe it in.

He clenched his fists beside him and moved as far as he could away from her so his shoulder hit the wall of the elevator. That would be insanity. And probably not the best timing when he'd just quashed her Christmas tree display.

But she wouldn't be Andie if she didn't persevere. 'Not even miniature trees on the lunch table?' she asked.

'No trees,' he said.

She sighed. 'Okay, the client has spoken. No Christmas tree.'

The elevator came to the ground floor. He lightly placed his hand at the small of her back to steer her in the direction of the best exit for the restaurant. Bad idea. Touching Andie even in this casual manner just made him want to touch her more.

'But you're happy with the rest of the plan?' she said as they walked side by side towards the restaurant, dodging the busy Sydney lunchtime crush as they did.

'Very happy. Except you can totally discard the marketing director's suggestion I dress up as Santa Claus.'

She laughed. 'Did you notice I wrote it down but didn't take the suggestion any further?' Her eyes narrowed as she looked him up and down in mock inspection. 'Though it's actually a nice idea. If you change your mind—'

'No,' he said.

'That's what I thought,' she said, that delightful smile dancing around the corners of her mouth.

'You know it's been a stretch for me to agree to a Christmas party at all. You won't ever see me as Santa.'

'What if the marketing director himself could be convinced to play Santa Claus?' she said thoughtfully. 'He volunteered to help out on the day.'

'This whole party thing was Rob Cratchit's idea so that might be most appropriate. Take it as an order from his boss.'

'I'll send him an email and say it's your suggestion,' she said with a wicked grin. 'He's quite well padded and would make a wonderful Santa—no pillow down the front of his jacket required.'

'Don't mention that in the email or all hell will break loose,' he said.

'Don't worry; I can be subtle when I want to,' she said, that grin still dancing in her eyes as they neared the restaurant.

In Dominic's experience, some restaurants were sited well and had a good fit-out; others had excellent food. In this case, his favourite place to eat near the office had both—a spectacular site on the top of a heritage listed building right near the water and a superlative menu.

There had been no need to book—a table was always there for him when he wanted one, no matter how long the waiting list for bookings.

An attentive waiter settled Andie into a seat facing the view of Sydney Harbour. 'I've always wanted to eat at this restaurant,' she said, looking around her.

'Maybe we should have our meetings here in future?'

'Good idea,' she said. 'Though I'll have to do a detailed site inspection of your house very soon. We could fit in a meeting then, perhaps?'

'I might not be able to be there,' he said. 'I have a series of appointments in other states over the next two weeks. Any meetings with you might have to be via the Internet.'

Was that disappointment he saw cloud her eyes. 'That's a shame. I—'

'My assistant will help you with access and the security code,' he said. He wished he could cancel some of the meetings, but that was not possible. Perhaps it was for the best. The more time he spent with Andie, the more he wanted to break his rules and ask her on a date. But those rules were there for good reason.

'As you know, we have a tight timeline to work to,' she said. 'The more we get done early the better, to allow for the inevitable last-minute dramas.'

'I have every confidence in you that it will go to plan.'

'Me too,' she said with another of those endearing grins. 'I've organised so many Christmas room sets and table settings for magazine and advertising clients. You have to get creative to come up with something different each year. This is easier in a way.'

'But surely there must be a continuity?' he asked, curious even though Christmas was his least favourite topic of conversation.

'Some people don't want to go past traditional red and green and that's okay,' she said. 'I've done an entire room themed purple and the client was delighted. Silver and gold is always popular in Australia, when Christmas is likely to be sweltering—it seems to feel cooler somehow. But—'

The waiter came to take their orders. They'd been too busy talking to look at the menu. Quickly they discussed their favourites before they ordered: barramundi with prawns and asparagus for him; tandoori roasted ocean trout with cucumber salsa for her and an heirloom tomato salad to share. They each passed on wine and chose mineral water. 'Because it's a working day,' they both said at the exact time and laughed. *It felt like a date.* He could not let his thoughts stray that way. Because he liked the idea too much.

'You haven't explained the continuity of Christmas,' he said, bringing the conversation back to the party.

'It's nothing to do with the baubles and the tinsel and everything to do with the feeling,' she said with obvious enthusiasm. 'Anticipation, delight, joy. For some it's about religious observance, spirituality and new life; others about sharing and generosity. If you can get people feeling the emotion, then it doesn't really matter if the tree is decorated in pink and purple or red and green.'

How about misery and fear and pain? Those were his memories of Christmas. 'I see your point,' he said.

'I intend to make sure your party is richly imbued with that kind of Christmas spirit. Hannah told me some of the kids who will be coming would be unlikely to have a celebration meal or a present and certainly not both if it wasn't for your generosity.'

'I met with Hannah yesterday; she mentioned how important it will be for the families we're inviting. She seems to think the party will do a powerful lot of good. Your sister told me how special Christmas is in your family.' It was an effort for him to speak about Christmas in a normal tone of voice. But he seemed to be succeeding.

'Oh, yes,' said Andie. 'Heaven help anyone who might want to celebrate it with their in-laws or anywhere else but my parents' house.'

'Your mother's a marvellous cook.'

'True, but Christmas is well and truly my dad's day. My mother is allowed to do the baking and she does that months in advance. On the day, he cooks a traditional meal—turkey, ham, roast beef, the lot. He's got favourite recipes he's refined over the years and no one would dare suggest anything different.'

Did she realise how lucky she was? How envious he felt when he thought about how empty his life had been of the kind of family love she'd been gifted with. He'd used to think he could start his own family, his own traditions, but his ex-wife had disabused him of that particular dream. It involved trust and trust was not a thing that came easily to him. Not when it came to women. 'I can't imagine you would want to change a tradition.'

'If truth be told, we'd be furious if he wanted to change one little thing,' she said, her voice warm with affection for her father. *She knew.*

He could see where she got her confidence from—that rock-solid security of a loving, supportive family. But now he knew she'd been tempered by tragedy too. He wanted to know more about how she had dealt with the loss of her boyfriend. But not until it was appropriate to ask.

'What about you, Dominic—did you celebrate Christmas with your family?' she asked.

This never got easier—which was why he chose not to revisit it too often. 'My parents died when I was eleven,' he said.

'Oh, I'm so sorry,' she said with warm compassion in her eyes. 'What a tragedy.' She paused. 'You were so young, an only child…who looked after you?'

'We lived in England, in a village in Norfolk. My father was English, my mother Australian. My mother's sister was staying with us at the time my parents died. She took me straight back with her to Australia.' It was difficult to keep his voice matter of fact, not to betray the pain the memories evoked, even after all this time.

'What? Just wrenched you away from your home?' She paused. 'I'm sorry. That wasn't my call to say that. You were lucky you had family. Did your aunt have children?'

'No, it was just the two of us,' he said and left it at that. There was so much more he could say about the toxic relationship with his aunt but that was part of his past he'd rather was left buried.

Wrenched. That was how it had been. Away from everything familiar. Away from his grandparents, whom he didn't see again until he had the wherewithal to get himself back to the UK as an adult. Away from the dog he'd adored. Desperately lonely and not allowed to grieve, thrust back down in Brisbane, in the intense heat, straight into the strategic battleground that was high school in a foreign country. To a woman who had no idea how to love a child, though she had tried in her own warped way.

'I'd prefer not to talk about it,' he said. 'I'm all grown up now and don't angst about the past.' Except when it was dark and lonely and he couldn't sleep and he wondered if he was fated to live alone without love.

'I understand,' she said. But how could she?

She paused to leave a silence he did not feel able to fill.

'Talking about my family,' she finally said, 'you're my mother's new number one favourite person.'

Touched by not only her words but her effort to draw him in some way into her family circle, he smiled. 'And why is that?'

'Seriously, she really liked you at dinner on Wednesday night. But then, when you had flowers delivered the next day, she was over the moon. Especially at the note that said she cooked the best lasagne you'd ever tasted.'

'I'm glad she liked them. And it was true about the lasagne.' Home-made anything was rarely on the menu for him so he had appreciated it.

'How did you know pink was her favourite colour in flowers?'

'I noticed the flowers she'd planted in her garden.'

'But you only saw the garden so briefly.'

'I'm observant,' he said.

'But the icing on the cake was the voucher for dinner for two at their local bistro.'

'She mentioned she liked their food when we were talking,' he said.

'You're a thoughtful guy, aren't you?' she said, tilting her head to the side.

'Some don't think so,' he said, unable to keep the bitterness from his voice.

She lowered her voice to barely a whisper so he had to lean across the table to hear her, so close their heads were touching. Anyone who was watching would think they *were* on a date.

She placed her hand on his arm in a gesture of comfort which touched him. 'Don't worry. The party should change all that. I really liked Rob's idea that no media would be invited to the party. That journalists would have to volunteer to help on the day if they wanted to see what it was all about.'

'And no photographers allowed, to preserve our guests' privacy. I liked that too.'

'I really have a good feeling about it,' she said. She lifted her hand off his arm and he felt bereft of her touch.

He nodded. If it were up to him, if he didn't *have* to go ahead with the party, he'd cancel it at a moment's notice. Maybe there was a touch of Scrooge in him after all.

But he didn't want Andie to think that of him. Not for a moment.

He hadn't proved to be a good judge of women. His errors in judgement went right back to his aunt—he'd loved her when she was his fun auntie from Australia. She'd turned out to be a very different person. Then there'd been Melody—sweet, doomed Melody. At seventeen he'd been a man in body but a boy still in heart. He'd been gutted at her betrayal, too damn wet behind the ears to realise a teenage boy's love could never be enough for an addict. Then how could he have been sucked in by Tara? His ex-wife was a redhead like Melody, tiny and delicate. But her frail exterior hid an avaricious, dishonest heart and she had lied to him about something so fundamental to their marriage that he could never forgive her.

Now there was Andie. He didn't trust his feelings when he'd made such disastrous calls before. *'What you see is what you get,'* she'd said about her family.

Could he trust himself to judge that Andie was what she appeared to be?

He reined in his errant thoughts—he only needed to trust Andie to deliver him the party he needed to improve his public image. Anything personal was not going to happen.

CHAPTER SEVEN

'ANDIE, I NEED to see you.' Dominic's voice on her smart-phone was harsh in its urgency. It was eight a.m. and Andie had not been expecting a call from him. He'd been away more than a week on business and she'd mainly communicated with him by text and email—and only then if it was something that needed his approval for the party. The last time she'd seen him was the Friday they'd had lunch together. The strictly business lunch that had somehow felt more like a date. But she couldn't let herself think like that.

'Sure,' she said. 'I just have to—'

'Now. Please. Where do you live?'

Startled at his tone, she gave him the address of the apartment in a converted warehouse in the inner western suburb of Newtown she shared with two old schoolfriends. Her friends had both already left for work. Andie had planned on a day finalising prop hire and purchase for Dominic's party before she started work for a tuxedo-and-tiara-themed twenty-first birthday party.

She quickly changed into skinny denim jeans and a simple loose-knit cream top that laced with leather ties at the neckline. Decided on her favourite leopard-print stilettos over flats. And make-up. And her favourite sandalwood and jasmine perfume. What the heck—her heart was racing at the thought of seeing him. She didn't want to seem as though she were trying too hard—but then again she didn't want to be caught out in sweats.

When Dominic arrived she was shocked to see he didn't look *his* sartorial best. In fact he looked downright dishevelled. His black hair seemed as if he'd used his fingers for a comb and his dark stubble was one step away from a beard. He was wearing black jeans, a dark grey T-shirt and had a black leather jacket slung over his shoulders. Immediately he owned the high-ceilinged room, a space that overwhelmed men of lesser stature, with the casual athleticism of his stance, the power of his body with its air of tightly coiled energy.

'Are you alone?' he asked.

'Yes,' she said. *Yes!*

Her first thought was that he looked hotter than ever—so hot she had to catch her breath. This Dominic set her pulse racing even more than executive Dominic in his made-to-measure Italian suits.

Her second thought was that he seemed stressed—his mouth set in a grim line, his eyes red-rimmed and darkly shadowed. 'Are you okay?' she asked.

'I've come straight from the airport. I just flew in from Perth.' Perth was on the other side of Australia—a six-hour flight. 'I cut short my trip.'

'But are you okay?' She forced her voice to sound calm and measured, not wanting him to realise how she was reacting to his untamed good looks. Her heart thudded with awareness that they were alone in the apartment.

With the kind of friendly working relationship they had now established, it would be quite in order to greet him with a light kiss on his beard-roughened cheek. But she wouldn't dare. She might not be able to resist sliding her mouth across his cheek to his mouth and turning it into a very different kind of kiss. And that wouldn't do.

'I'm fine. I've just…been presented with…with a dilemma,' Dominic said.

'Coffee might help,' she said.

'Please.'

'Breakfast? I have—'

'Just coffee.'

But Andie knew that sometimes men who said they didn't want anything to eat needed food. And that their mood could improve immeasurably when they ate something. Not that she'd been in the habit of sharing breakfast with a man. Not since... She forced her mind back to the present and away from memories of breakfasts with Anthony on a sun-soaked veranda. Her memories of him were lit with sunshine and happiness.

Dominic dragged out a chair and slumped down at her kitchen table while she prepared him coffee. *Why was he here?* She turned to see him with his elbows on the tabletop, resting his head on his hands. Tired? Defeated? Something seemed to have put a massive dent in his usual self-assured confidence.

She slid a mug of coffee in front of him. 'I assumed black but here's frothed milk and sugar if you want.'

'Black is what I need,' he said. He put both hands around the mug and took it to his mouth.

Without a word, she put a thick chunk of fresh fruit bread, studded with figs and apricots, from her favourite baker in King Street in front of him. Then a dish of cream cheese and a knife. 'Food might help,' she said.

He put down his coffee, gave her a weary imitation of his usual glower and went to pick up the bread. 'Let me,' she said and spread it with cream cheese.

What was it about this man that made her want to comfort and care for him? He was a thirty-two-year-old billionaire, for heaven's sake. Tough, self-sufficient. Wealthier than she could even begin to imagine. And yet she sometimes detected an air of vulnerability about him that wrenched at her. A sense of something broken. But it was not up to her to try and fix him. He ate the fruit bread in two bites. 'More?' she asked.

He nodded. 'It's good,' he said.

Andie had to be honest with herself. She wanted to comfort him, yes. She enjoyed his company. But it was more than that. She couldn't deny that compelling physical attraction. He sat at her kitchen table, his leather jacket slung on the back of the chair. His tanned arms were sculpted with muscle, his T-shirt moulded ripped pecs and abs. With his rough-hewn face, he looked so utterly *male.*

Desire, so long unfamiliar, thrilled through her. She wanted to kiss him and feel those strong arms around her, his hands on her body. *She wanted more than kisses.* What was it about this not-my-type man who had aroused her interest from the moment she'd first met him?

When he'd eaten two more slices of fruit bread, he pushed his plate away and leaned back in his seat. His sigh was weary and heartfelt. 'Thank you,' he said. 'I didn't realise I was hungry.'

She slipped into the chair opposite him and nursed her own cooling cup of coffee to stop the impulse to reach over and take his hand. 'Are you able to tell me about your dilemma?' she asked, genuinely concerned.

He raked his hands through his hair. 'My ex-wife is causing trouble. Again.'

In her research into Dominic, Andie had seen photos of Tara Hunt—she still went by his name—a petite, pale-skinned redhead in designer clothes and an over-abundance of jewellery.

'I'm sorry,' she said, deciding on caution in her reaction. 'Do you want to tell me about it?' Was that why he wanted to see her? To cry on her shoulder about his ex-wife? Dominic didn't seem like a crying-on-shoulders kind of guy.

He went to drink more coffee, to find his mug was

nearly empty. He drained the last drops. 'You make good coffee,' he said appreciatively.

'I worked as a barista when I was a student,' she said.

She and Anthony had both worked in hospitality, saving for vacation backpacker trips to Indonesia and Thailand. It seemed so long ago now, those days when she took it for granted they had a long, happy future stretched out ahead of them. They'd been saving for a trip to Eastern Europe when he'd died.

She took Dominic's mug from him, got up, refilled it, brought it back to the table and sat down again. He drank from it and put it down.

Dominic leaned across the table to bring him closer to her. 'Can I trust you, Andie?' he asked in that deep, resonant voice. His intense grey gaze met hers and held it.

'Of course,' she said without hesitation.

He sat back in his chair. 'I know you're friends with journalists, so I have to be sure what I might talk to you about today won't go any further.' The way he said it didn't sound offensive; in fact it made her feel privileged that he would consider her trustworthy. Not to mention curious about what he might reveal.

'I assure you, you can trust me,' she said.

'Thank you,' he said. 'Tara found out about my impending deal with Walter Burton and is doing her best to derail it.'

Andie frowned. 'How can she do that?'

'Before I married Tara, she worked for my company in the accounts department. She made it her business to find out everything she could about the way I ran things. I didn't know, but once I started dating her she used that knowledge to make trouble, hiding behind the shield of our relationship. None of my staff dared tell me.'

'Not good,' Andie said, wanting to express in no uncertain terms what she thought of his ex, yet not wanting to get into a bitching session about her.

'You're right about that,' he said. 'It's why I now never date employees.'

His gaze met hers again and held it for a long moment. Was there a message in there for her? If she wasn't a contractor, would he ask her out? If she hadn't promised her partners to stay away from him, would she suggest a date?

'That policy makes…sense,' she said. What about after Christmas, when she and Dominic would no longer be connected by business? Could they date then? A sudden yearning for that to happen surprised her with its intensity. *She wanted him.*

'It gets worse,' he continued. 'A former employee started his own business in competition with me—' Andie went to protest but Dominic put up his hand. 'It happens; that's legit,' he said. 'But what happened afterwards wasn't. After our marriage broke up, Tara used her knowledge of how my company worked to help him.'

Andie couldn't help her gasp of outrage. 'Did her…her betrayal work?'

'She gave him the information. That didn't mean he knew how to use it. But now I've just discovered she's working with him in a last-minute rival bid for the joint venture with Walter Burton.'

Andie shook her head in disbelief. 'Why?' Her research had shown her Tara Hunt had ended up with a massive divorce settlement from Dominic. Per day of their short marriage, she had walked away with an incredible number of dollars.

Dominic shrugged. 'Revenge. Spite. Who knows what else?'

'Surely Walter Burton won't be swayed by that kind of underhand behaviour?'

'Traditional values are important to Walter Burton. We

know that. That's why we're holding the party to negate the popular opinion of me as a Scrooge.'

'So what does your ex-wife have to do with the deal?'

Dominic sighed, a great weary sigh that made Andie want to put comforting arms around him. She'd sensed from the get-go he was a private person. He obviously hated talking about this. Once more, she wondered why he had chosen to.

He drew those dark brows together in a scowl. 'Again she's raked over the coals of our disastrous marriage and talked to her media buddies. Now she's claiming I was unfaithful—which is a big fat lie. According to her, I'm a womaniser, a player and a complete and utter bastard. She dragged out my old quote that I will never marry again and claims it's because I'm incapable of settling with one woman. It's on one of the big Internet gossip sites and will be all over the weekend newspapers.' He cursed under his breath.

Andie could see the shadow of old hurts on his face. He had once loved his ex enough to marry her. A betrayal like this must be painful, no matter how much time had elapsed. She had no such angst behind her. She knew Anthony had been loyal to her, as she had been to him. *First love.* Sometimes she wondered if they might have grown apart if he'd lived. Some of their friends who had dated as teenagers had split when they got older. But she dismissed those thoughts as disloyal to his memory.

Andie shook her head at Dominic's revelations about his ex—it got worse and worse. 'That's horrible—but can't you just ignore it?'

'I would ignore it, but she's made sure Walter Burton has seen all her spurious allegations set out as truth.'

Andie frowned. 'Surely your personal life is none of Mr Burton's business? Especially when it's not true.' She believed Dominic implicitly—why, she wasn't completely sure. Trust went both ways.

'He might think it's true. The *"bed-hopping billionaire"*,' the article calls me.' Dominic growled with wounded outrage. 'That might be enough for Burton to reconsider doing business with me.'

Andie had to put her hand over her mouth to hide her smile at the description.

But Dominic noticed and scowled. 'I know it sounds ludicrous, but to a moralistic family man like Walter Burton it makes me sound immoral and not the kind of guy he wants to do business with.'

'Why do you care so much about the deal with Mr Burton? If you have to pretend to be someone you're not, how can it be worth it?'

'You mean I should pretend *not* to be a bed-hopping billionaire?'

'You must admit the headline has a certain ring to it,' Andie said, losing her battle to keep a straight face.

That forced a reluctant grin from him. 'A tag like that might be very difficult to live down.'

'Is…is it true? Are you a bed-hopping guy?' She held her breath for his reply.

'No. Of course I've had girlfriends since my divorce. Serial monogamy, I think they call it. But nothing like what this scurrilous interview with my ex claims.'

Andie let out her breath on a sigh of relief. 'But do you actually need to pursue this deal if it's becoming so difficult? You're already very wealthy.'

Dominic's mouth set in a grim line. 'I'm not going to bore you with my personal history. But home life with my aunt was less than ideal. I finished high school and got out. I'd tried to run away before and she'd dragged me back. This time she let me go. I ended up homeless, living in a squat. At seventeen I saw inexplicably awful things a boy that age should never see. I never again want to be without money and have nowhere to live. That's all I intend to say about that.' He nodded to her. 'And I trust you not to repeat it.'

'Of course,' she said, rocked by his revelations, aching to know more. *Dominic Hunt was a street kid?* Not boring. There was so much more about his life than he was saying. She thought again about his scarred knuckles and broken nose. There had been nothing about his past in her online trawling. She hoped he might tell her more. It seemed he was far more complex than he appeared. Which only made him more attractive.

'My best friend and first business partner, Jake Marlow, is also in with me on this,' he said. 'He wants it as much as I do, for his own reasons I'm not at liberty to share.'

'Okay,' she said slowly. 'So we're working on the party to negate the Scr…uh…the other reputation, to get Mr Burton on board. What do you intend to do about the bed-hopper one?'

'When Burton contacted me I told him that it was all scuttlebutt and I was engaged to be married.'

She couldn't help a gasp. 'You're engaged?' She felt suddenly stricken. 'Engaged to who?'

'I'm not engaged. I'm not even dating anyone.'

'Then why…?' she said.

He groaned. 'Panic. Fear. Survival. A gut reaction like I used to have back in that squat. When you woke up, terrified, in your cardboard box to find some older guy burrowing through your backpack and you told him you had nothing worth stealing even though there was five dollars folded tiny between your toes in your sock. If that money was stolen, you didn't eat.'

'So you lied to Mr Burton?'

'As I said, a panic reaction. But it gets worse.' Again he raked his fingers through his hair. 'Burton said he was flying in to Sydney in two weeks' time to meet with both me and the other guy. He wants to be introduced to my fiancée.'

Andie paused, stunned at what Dominic had done, appalled that he had lied. 'What will you do?'

Again he leaned towards her over the table. 'I want you to be my fiancée, Andie.'

CHAPTER EIGHT

DOMINIC WATCHED ANDIE'S reactions flit across her face—shock and indignation followed by disappointment. In him? He braced himself—certain she was going to say *no*.

'Are you serious?' she finally said, her hands flat down on the table in front of her.

'Very,' he said, gritting his teeth. He'd been an idiot to get himself into a mess like this. *Panic.* He shouldn't have given in to panic in that phone call with Walter Burton. He hadn't let panic or fear rule him for a long time.

Andie tilted her head to one side and frowned. 'You want me to *marry* you? We hardly know each other.'

Marriage? Who was talking about marriage? 'No. Just to *pretend*—' Whatever he said wasn't going to sound good. 'Pretend to be my fiancée. Until after the Christmas party.'

Andie shook her head in disbelief. 'To pretend to be engaged to you? To lie? No! I can't believe you asked me to…to even think of such a thing. I'm a party planner, not a…a…the type of person who would agree to that.'

She looked at him as though she'd never seen him before. And that maybe she didn't like what she saw. Dominic swallowed hard—he didn't like the feeling her expression gave him. She pushed herself up from the chair and walked away from the table, her body rigid with disapproval. He was very aware she wanted to distance herself from him. He didn't like that either. It had seemed so intimate, drinking coffee and eating breakfast at her table. And he *had* liked that.

He swivelled in his chair to face her. 'It was a stupid thing to do, I know that,' he said. He had spent the entire flight back from Perth regretting his impulsive action. 'But it's done.'

She turned around, glared at him. 'Then I suggest you undo it.'

'By admitting I lied?'

She shrugged. 'Tell Mr Burton your fiancée dumped you.'

'As if that would fly.'

'You think it's beyond belief that a woman would ever dump you?'

'I didn't say that.' Though it was true. Since it had ended with Melody, he had always been the one to end a relationship. 'It would seem too…sudden.'

'Just like the sudden engagement?'

'It wouldn't denote…stability.'

'You're right about that.' She crossed her arms in front of her chest—totally unaware that the action pushed up her breasts into an enticing cleavage in the V-necked top she wore. 'It's a crazy idea.'

'I'm not denying that,' he growled. He didn't need to have his mistake pointed out to him. 'But I'm asking you to help me out.'

'Why me? Find someone else. I'm sure there would be no shortage of candidates.'

'But it makes sense for my fiancée to be you.' He could be doggedly persistent when he wanted to be.

He unfolded himself from the too-small chair at the kitchen table. Most chairs were too small for him. He took a step towards her, only for her to take a step back from him. 'Andie. Please.'

Her hair had fallen across her face and she tossed it back. 'Why? We're just client and contractor.'

'Is that all it is between us?'

'Of course it is.' But she wouldn't meet his gaze and he felt triumphant. *So she felt it too.* That attraction that had flashed between them from the get-go.

'When I opened the door to the beautiful woman with the misbehaving skirt—' that got a grudging smile from her '—I thought it could be more than just a business arrangement. But you know now why I don't date anyone hired by the company.'

'And Party Queens has a policy of not mixing business with...with pleasure.' Her voice got huskier on the last words.

He looked her direct in the face, pinning her with his gaze. 'If it ever happened, it would be pleasure all the way, Andie, I think we both know that.' She hadn't quite cleared her face of a wisp of flyaway hair. He reached down and gently smoothed it back behind her ear.

She trembled under his touch. A blush travelled up her throat to stain her cheeks. 'I've never even thought about it, the...the *pleasure,* I mean,' she said.

She wouldn't blush like that if she hadn't. Or flutter her hands to the leather laces of her neckline. *Now who was lying?*

She took a deep breath and he tried to keep his gaze from the resulting further exposure of her cleavage. 'I don't want to be involved in this mad scheme in any way,' she said. 'Except to add your pretend fiancée—when you find one—to the Christmas party guest list.'

'I'm afraid you're already involved.'

She frowned. 'What do you mean?'

Dominic took the few steps necessary back to his chair and took out his smartphone from the inside pocket of his leather jacket. He scrolled through, then handed it to Andie.

She stared at the screen. 'But this is me. *Us.*'

The photo she was staring at was of him and her at a restaurant table. They were leaning towards each other, looking into each other's faces, Andie's hand on his arm.

'At the restaurant in Circular Quay, the day of the Friday meeting,' she said.

'Yes,' he said. The business lunch that had felt like a date. In this photo, it *looked* like a date.

She shook her head, bewildered. 'Who took it?'

'Some opportunistic person with a smartphone, I expect. Maybe a trouble-making friend of Tara's. Who knows?'

She looked back down at the screen, did some scrolling of her own. He waited for her to notice the words that accompanied the image on the gossip site.

Her eyes widened in horror. 'Did you see this?' She read out the heading. '*"Is This the Bed-Hopping Billionaire's New Conquest?"*' She swore under her breath—the first time he had heard her do so.

'I'm sorry. Of course I had no idea this was happening. But, in light of it, you can see why it makes sense that my fake fiancée should be you.'

She shook her head. 'No. It doesn't make any sense. That was a business lunch. Not the…the romantic rendezvous it appears to be in the picture.'

'You know that. I know that. But the way they've cropped the photo, that's exactly what it seems. Announce an engagement and suddenly the picture would make a whole lot of sense. Good sense.'

Her green eyes narrowed. 'This photo doesn't bother me. It will blow over. We're both single. Who even cares?' He'd been stunned to see the expression in his eyes as he'd looked into her face in the photo. It had looked as if he wanted to have her for dessert. Had she noticed? No wonder the gossip site had drawn a conclusion of romantic intrigue.

'If you're so indifferent, why not help me out?' he said. 'Be my fake fiancée, just until after Christmas.'

'Christmas is nearly a month away. Twenty-five days, to be precise. For twenty-five days I'd have to pretend to be your fiancée?'

'So you're considering it? Because we've already been "outed", so to speak, it wouldn't come out of the blue. It would be believable.'

'Huh! We've only known each other for two weeks. Who would believe it?'

'People get married on less acquaintance,' he said.

'Not people like me,' she said.

'You don't think anyone would believe you could be smitten by me in that time? I think I'm offended.'

'Of course not,' she said. 'I...I believe many women would be smitten by you. You're handsome, intelligent—'

'And personable, yes, you said. Though I bet you don't think I'm so personable right now.'

She glared at him, though there was a lilt to the corners of her mouth that made it seem like she might want to smile. 'You could be right about that.'

'Now to you—gorgeous, sexy, smart Andie Newman.' Her blush deepened as he sounded each adjective. 'People would certainly believe I could be instantly smitten with such a woman,' he said. 'In fact they'd think I was clever getting a ring on your finger so quickly.'

That flustered her. 'Th...thank you. I...I'm flattered. But it wouldn't seem authentic. We'd have to pretend so much. It would be such deception.'

With any other woman, he'd be waiting for her to ask: *What's in it for me?* Not Andie. He doubted the thought of a reward for her participation had even entered her head. He would have to entice her with an offer she couldn't refuse. And save the big gun to sway her from her final refusal.

'So you're going to say "yes"?'

She shook her head vehemently. 'No. I'm not. It wouldn't be right.'

'What's the harm? You'd be helping me out.'

She spun on her heel away from him and he faced her back view, her tensely hunched shoulders, for a long moment before she turned back to confront him. 'Can't you see it makes a mockery of…of a man and a woman committing to each other? To spending their lives together in a loving union? That's what getting engaged is all about. Not sealing a business deal.'

He closed his eyes at the emotion in her voice, the blurring of her words with choking pain. Under his breath he cursed fluently. Because, from any moral point of view, she was absolutely right.

'Were you engaged to…to Anthony?' he asked.

Her eyes when she lifted them to him glistened with the sheen of unshed tears. 'Not officially. But we had our future planned, even the names of our kids chosen. That's why I know promising to marry someone isn't something you do lightly. And not…not for a scam. Do you understand?'

Of course he did. He'd once been idealistic about love and marriage and sharing his life with that one special woman. But he couldn't admit it. Or that he'd become cynical that that kind of love would ever exist for him. Too much rode on this deal. Including his integrity.

'But this isn't really getting engaged,' he said. 'It's just …a limited agreement.'

Slowly she shook her head. 'I can't help you,' she said. 'Sorry.'

Dominic braced himself. He'd had to be ruthless at times to get where he'd got. To overcome the disadvantages of his youth. *To win.*

'What if by agreeing to be my fake fiancée you were helping someone else?' he said.

She frowned. 'Like who? Helping Walter Burton to make even more billions? I honestly can't say I like the sound of that guy, linking business to people's private lives. He sounds like a hypocrite, for one thing—you know, rich men and eyes of needles and all that. I'm not lying for him.'

'Not Walter Burton. I mean your nephew Timothy.' The little boy was his big gun.

'What do you mean, Timothy?'

Dominic fired his shot. 'Agree to be my fake fiancée and I will pay for all of Timothy's medical treatment—both immediate and ongoing. No limits. Hannah tells me there's a clinic in the United States that's at the forefront of research into treatment for his condition.'

Andie stared at him. 'You've spoken to Hannah? You've told Hannah about this? That you'll pay for Timothy if I agree to—'

He put up his hand. 'Not true.'

'But you—'

'I met with Hannah the day after the dinner with your family to talk about her helping me recruit the families for the party. At that meeting—out of interest—I asked her to tell me more about Timothy. She told me about the American treatment. I offered *then* to pay all the treatment—airfares and accommodation included.'

The colour rushed back into Andie's cheeks. 'That... that was extraordinarily generous of you. What did Hannah say?'

'She refused.'

'Of course she would. She hardly knows you. A Newman wouldn't accept charity. Although I might have tried to convince her.'

'Maybe you could convince her now. If Hannah thought

I was going to be part of the family—her brother-in-law, in fact—she could hardly refuse to accept, could she? And isn't it the sooner the better for Timothy's treatment?'

Andie stared at Dominic for a very long moment, too shocked to speak. 'Th…that's coercion. Coercion of the most insidious kind,' she finally managed to choke out.

A whole lot more words she couldn't express also tumbled around in her brain. Ruthless. Conniving. Heartless. And yet…he'd offered to help Timothy well before the fake fiancée thing. *Not a Scrooge after all.* She'd thought she'd been getting to know him—but Dominic Hunt was more of a mystery to her than ever.

He drew his dark brows together. 'Coercion? I wouldn't go that far. But I did offer to help Timothy without any strings attached. Hannah refused. This way, she might accept. And your nephew will get the help he needs. I see it as a win-win scenario.'

Andie realised she was twisting the leather thronging that laced together the front of her top and stopped it. Nothing in her life had equipped her to make this kind of decision. 'You're really putting me on the spot here. Asking me to lie and be someone I'm not—'

'Someone you're not? How does that work? You'd still be Andie.'

She found it difficult to meet his direct, confronting gaze. Those observant grey eyes seemed to see more than she wanted him to. 'You're asking me to pretend to be… to pretend to be a woman in love. When…when I'm not.' She'd only ever been in love once—and she didn't want to trawl back in her memories to try and relive that feeling—love lost hurt way too much. She did have feelings for Dominic beyond the employer/contractor relationship—but they were more of the other 'l' word—lust rather than love.

His eyes seemed to darken. 'I suppose I am.'

'And you too,' she said. 'You would have to pretend to be in love with…with me. And it would have to look darn authentic to be convincing.'

This was why she was prevaricating. As soon as he'd mentioned Timothy, she knew she would have little choice but to agree. If it had been any other blackmailing billionaire she would probably have said "yes" straight away—living a lie for a month would be worth it for Timothy to get the treatment her family's combined resources couldn't afford.

But not *this* man. How could she blithely *pretend* to be in love with a man she wanted as much as she wanted him? It would be some kind of torture.

'I see,' he said. Had he seriously not thought this through?

'We would be playing with big emotions, here, Dominic. And other people would be affected too. My family thinks you hung the moon. They'd be delighted if we dated—a sudden engagement would both shock and worry them. At some stage I would have to introduce you to Anthony's parents—they would be happy for me and want to meet you.'

'I see where you're going,' he said, raking his hand through his hair once more in a gesture that was becoming familiar.

She narrowed her eyes. 'And yet…would it all be worth it for Hannah to accept your help for Timothy?' She put up her hand to stop him from replying. 'I'm thinking out loud here.'

'And helping me achieve something I really want.'

There must be something more behind his drive to get this American deal. She hoped she'd discover it one day, sooner rather than later. It might help her understand him.

'You've backed me into a corner here, Dominic, and I can't say I appreciate it. How can I say "no" to such an incredible opportunity for Timothy?'

'Does that mean your answer is "yes"?'

She tilted her chin upwards—determined not to capitulate too readily to something about which she still had serious doubts. 'That's an unusual way to put it, Dominic—rather like you've made me a genuine proposal.'

Dominic pulled a face but it didn't dull the glint of triumph in his eyes. He thought he'd won. But she was determined to get something out of this deal for herself too.

Andie had no doubt if she asked for recompense—money, gifts—he'd give it to her. Dominic was getting what he wanted. Timothy would be getting what he so desperately needed. But what about *her*?

She wasn't interested in jewellery or fancy shopping. What she wanted was *him*. She wanted to kiss him, she wanted to hold him and she very much wanted to make love with him. Not for fake—for real.

There was a very good chance this arrangement would end in tears—her tears. But if she agreed to a fake engagement with this man, who attracted her like no other, she wanted what a fiancée might be expected to have—*him*. She thought, with a little shiver of desire, about what he'd said: *pleasure all the way.* She would be fine with that.

'Would it help if I made it sound like a genuine proposal?' he said, obviously bemused.

That hurt. Because the way he spoke made it sound as if there was no way he would ever make a genuine proposal to her. Not that she wanted that—heck, she hardly knew the guy. But it put her on warning. *Let's be honest,* she thought. She wanted him in her bed. But she also wanted to make darn sure she didn't get hurt. This was just a business deal to him—nothing personal involved.

'Do it,' she said, pointing to the floor. 'The full down-on-bended-knee thing.'

'Seriously?' he said, dark brows raised.

'Yes,' she said imperiously.

He grinned. 'Okay.'

The tall, black denim-clad hunk obediently knelt down on one knee, took her left hand in both of his and looked up into her face. 'Andie, will you do me the honour of becoming my fake fiancée?' he intoned in that deep, so-sexy voice.

Looking down at his roughly handsome face, Andie didn't know whether to laugh or cry. 'Yes, I accept your proposal,' she said in a voice that wasn't quite steady.

Dominic squeezed her hand hard as relief flooded his face. He got up from bended knee and for a moment she thought he might kiss her.

'But there are conditions,' she said, pulling away and letting go of his hand.

CHAPTER NINE

ANDIE ALMOST LAUGHED out loud at Dominic's perplexed expression. He was most likely used to calling the shots—in both business and his relationships. 'Conditions?' he asked.

'Yes, conditions,' she said firmly. 'Come on over to the sofa and I'll run through the list with you. I need to sit down; these heels aren't good for pacing in.' The polished concrete floor was all about looks rather than comfort.

'Do I have any choice about these "conditions"?' he grumbled.

'I think you'll see the sense in them,' she said. This was not going to go all his way. There was danger in this game she'd been coerced into playing and she wanted to make sure she and her loved ones were not going to get hurt by it.

She led him over to the red leather modular sofa in the living area. The apartment in an old converted factory warehouse was owned by one of her roommates and had been furnished stylishly with Andie's help. She flopped down on the sofa, kicked off the leopard stilettos that landed in an animal print clash on the zebra-patterned floor rug, and patted the seat next to her.

As Dominic sat down, his muscular thighs brushed against hers and she caught her breath until he settled at a not-quite-touching distance from her, his arm resting on the back of the sofa behind her. She had to close her eyes momentarily to deal with the rush of awareness from his already familiar scent, the sheer maleness of him in such close proximity.

'I'm interested to hear what you say,' he said, angling his powerful body towards her. He must work out a lot to have a chest like that. She couldn't help but wonder what it would feel like to splay her hands against those hard muscles, to press her body against his.

But it appeared he was having no such sensual thoughts about *her*. She noticed he gave a surreptitious glance to his watch.

'Hey, no continually checking on the clock,' she said. 'You have to give time to an engagement. Especially a make-believe one, if we're to make it believable. Not to mention your fake fiancée just might feel a tad insulted.'

She made her voice light but she meant every word of it. She had agreed to play her role in this charade and was now committed to making it work.

'Fair enough,' he said with a lazy half-smile. 'Is that one of your conditions?'

'Not one on its own as such, but it will fit into the others.'

'Okay, hit me with the conditions.' He feinted a boxer's defence that made her smile.

'Condition Number One,' she said, holding up the index finger of her left hand. 'Hannah never knows the truth—not now, not ever—that our engagement is a sham,' she said. 'In fact, none of my family is *ever* to know the truth.'

'Good strategy,' said Dominic. 'In fact, I'd extend that. *No one* should ever know. Both business partners and friends.'

'Agreed,' she said. It would be difficult to go through with this without confiding in a friend but it had to be that way. *No one must know how deeply attracted she was to him.* She didn't want anyone's pity when she and Dominic went their separate ways.

'Otherwise, the fallout from people discovering they'd been deceived could be considerable,' he said. 'What's next?'

She held up her middle finger. 'Condition Number Two—a plausible story. We need to explain why we got engaged so quickly. So start thinking...'

'Couldn't we just have fallen for each other straight away?'

Andie was taken aback. She hadn't expected anything that romantic from Dominic Hunt. 'You mean like "love at first sight"?'

'Exactly.'

'Would that be believable?'

He shook his head in mock indignation. 'Again you continue to insult me...'

'I didn't mean...' She'd certainly felt *something* for him at first sight. Sitting next to him on this sofa, she was feeling it all over again. But it wasn't *love*—she knew only too well what it was like to love. To love and to lose the man she loved in such a cruel way. Truth be told, she wasn't sure she wanted to love again. It hurt too much to lose that love.

'I don't like the lying aspect of this any more than you do,' he said. He removed his arm from the back of the sofa so he could lean closer to her, both hands resting on his knees. 'Why not stick to the truth as much as possible? You came to organise my party. I was instantly smitten, wooed you and won you.'

'And I was a complete walkover,' she said dryly.

'So we change it—you made me work very hard to win you.'

'In two weeks—and you away for one of them?' she said. 'Good in principle. But we might have to fudge the timeline a little.'

'It can happen,' he said. 'Love at first sight, I mean. My

parents…apparently they fell for each other on day one and were married within mere months of meeting. Or so my aunt told me.'

His eyes darkened and she remembered he'd only been eleven years old when left an orphan. If she'd lost her parents at that age, her world would have collapsed around her—as no doubt his had. But he was obviously trying to revive a happy memory of his parents.

'How lovely—a real-life romance. Did they meet in Australia or England?'

'London. They were both schoolteachers; my mother was living in England. She came to his school as a temporary mathematics teacher; he taught chemistry.'

Andie decided not to risk a feeble joke about their meeting being explosive. Not when the parents' love story had ended in tragedy. 'No wonder you're clever then, with such smart parents.'

'Yes,' he said, making the word sound like an end-of-story punctuation mark. She knew only too well what it was like not to want to pursue a conversation about a lost loved one.

'So we have a precedent for love at first sight in your family,' she said. 'I…I fell for Anthony straight away too. So for both of us an…an instant attraction—if not *love*—could be feasible.' Instant and ongoing for her—but he was not to know that.

That Dominic had talked about his parents surprised her. For her, thinking about Anthony—as always—brought a tug of pain to her heart but this time also a reminder of the insincerity of this venture with Dominic. She knew what real commitment should feel like. But for Timothy to get that vital treatment she was prepared to compromise on her principles.

'Love at first sight it is,' he said.

'*Attraction* at first sight,' she corrected him.

'Surely it would had to have led to love for us to get engaged,' he said.

'True,' she conceded. He tossed around concepts of love and commitment as if they were concepts with which to barter, not deep, abiding emotions between two people who cared enough about each other to pledge a lifetime together. *Till death us do part.* She could never think of that part of a marriage ceremony without breaking down. She shouldn't be thinking of it now.

'Next condition?' he said.

She skipped her ring finger, which she had trouble keeping upright, and went straight for her pinkie. 'Condition Number Three: no dating other people—for the duration of the engagement, that is.'

'I'm on board with that one,' he said without hesitation.

'Me too,' she said. She hadn't even thought about any man but Dominic since the moment she'd met him, so that was not likely to be a hardship.

He sat here next to her in jeans and T-shirt like a regular thirty-two-year-old guy—not a secretive billionaire who had involved her in a scheme to deceive family and friends to help him make even more money. If he were just your everyday handsome hunk she would make her interest in him known. But her attraction went beyond his good looks and muscles to the complex man she sensed below his confident exterior. She had seen only intriguing hints of those hidden depths—she wanted to discover more.

Andie's thumb went up next. 'Resolution Number Four: I dump you, not the other way around. When this comes to an end, that is.'

'Agreed—and I'll be a gentleman about it. But I ask you not to sell your story. I don't want to wake up one morning to the headline *"My Six Weeks with Scrooge"*.'

He could actually *joke* about being a Scrooge—Dominic had come a long way.

'Of course,' she said. 'I promise not to say *"I Hopped Out of the Billionaire's Bed"* either. Seriously, I would never talk to the media. You can be reassured of that.'

'No tacky headlines, just a simple civilised break-up to be handled by you,' he said.

They both fell silent for a moment. Did he feel stricken by the same melancholy she did at the thought of the imagined break-up of a fake engagement? And she couldn't help thinking she'd like a chance to hop *into* his bed before she hopped *out* of it.

'On to Condition Number Five,' she said, holding up all five fingers as she could not make her ring finger stand on its own. 'We have to get to know each other. So we don't get caught out on stuff we would be expected to know about each other if we were truly…committing to a life together.'

How different this fake relationship would be to a real relationship—getting to know each other over shared experiences, shared laughter, shared tears, long lazy mornings in bed…

Dominic sank down further into the sofa, his broad shoulders hunched inward. 'Yup.' It was more a grunt than a word.

'You don't sound keen to converse?'

'What sort of things?' he said with obvious reluctance. Not for the first time, she had a sense of secrets deeply held.

'For one thing, I need to know more about your marriage and how it ended.' And more about his time on the streets. And about that broken nose and scarred knuckles. And why he had let people believe he was a Scrooge when he so obviously wasn't. Strictly speaking, she probably didn't *need* to know all that about him for a fake engagement. Fact was, she *wanted* to know it.

'I guess I can talk to you about my marriage,' he said,

still not sounding convinced. 'But there are things about my life that I would rather remain private.'

What things? 'Just so long as I'm not made a fool of at some stage down the track by not knowing something a real fiancée would have known.'

'Fine,' he grunted in a response that didn't give her much confidence. She ached to know more about him. And yet there was that shadow she sensed. She wouldn't push for simple curiosity's sake.

'As far as I'm concerned, my life's pretty much an open book,' she said, in an effort to encourage him to open up about his life—or past, to be more specific. 'Just ask what you need to know about me and I'll do my best to answer honestly.'

Was any person's life truly an open book? Like anyone else, she had doubts and anxieties and dumb things she'd done that she'd regretted, but nothing lurked that she thought could hinder an engagement. No one would criticise her for finding love again after five years. In truth, she knew they would be glad for her. So would Anthony.

She remembered one day, lying together on the beach. *'I would die if I lost you,'* she'd said to Anthony.

'Don't say that,' he'd said. *'If anything happened to me, I'd want you to find another guy. But why are we talking like this? We're both going to live until we're a hundred.'*

'Why not schedule in a question-and-answer session?' Dominic said.

She pulled her thoughts back to the present. 'Good idea,' she said. 'Excellent idea, in fact.'

Dominic rolled his eyes in response.

'Oh,' she said. 'You weren't serious. I…I was.'

'No, you're right. I guess there's no room for spontaneity in a fake engagement.' It was a wonder he could get the words out when his tongue was so firmly in his cheek. 'A question-and-answer session it is. At a time to be determined.'

'Good idea,' she said, feeling disconcerted. Was all this just a game to him?

'Are there any more conditions to come?' he asked. 'You're all out of fingers on one hand, by the way.'

'There is one more very important condition to come— and may I remind you I do have ten fingers—but first I want to hear if there's anything you want to add.'

She actually had two more conditions, but the final condition she could not share with him: *that she could not fall for him.* She couldn't deal with the fallout in terms of pain if she were foolish enough to let down the guard on her heart.

Andie's beautiful green eyes had sparkled with good humour in spite of the awkward position he had put her into. *Coerced* her into. But now her eyes seemed to dim and Dominic wondered if she was being completely honest about being an 'open book'.

Ironically, he already knew more about Andie, the fake fiancée, than he'd known about Tara when he'd got engaged to her for real. His ex-wife had kept her true nature under wraps until well after she'd got the wedding band on her finger. *What you see is what you get.* He so wanted to believe that about Andie.

'My condition? You have to wear a ring,' he said. 'I want to get you an engagement ring straight away. Today. Once Tara sees that she'll know it's serious. And the press will too. Not to mention a symbol for when we meet with Walter Burton.'

She shrugged. 'Okay, you get me a ring.'

'You don't want to choose it yourself?' He was taken aback. Tara had been so avaricious about jewellery.

'No. I would find it…sad. Distressing. The day I choose

my engagement ring is the day I get engaged for real. To me, the ring should be a symbol of a true commitment, not a…a prop for a charade. But I agree—I should wear one as a visible sign of commitment.'

'I'll organise it then,' he said. He had no idea why he should be disappointed at her lack of enthusiasm. She was absolutely right—the ring would be a prop. But it would also play a role in keeping it believable. 'What size ring do you wear?'

'I haven't a clue,' she said. She held up her right hand to show the collection of tiny fine silver rings on her slender fingers. Her nails were painted cream today. 'I bought these at a market and just tried them on until I found rings that fitted.' She slid off the ring from the third finger of her right hand. 'This should do the trick.' She handed it to him. It was still warm with her body heat and he held it on his palm for a moment before pocketing it.

'What style of engagement ring would you like?' he asked.

Again she shrugged. 'You choose. It's honestly not important to me.'

A hefty carat solitaire diamond would be appropriate— one that would give her a good resale value when she went to sell it after this was all over.

'Did you choose your ex-wife's engagement ring?' Andie asked.

He scowled at the reminder that he had once got engaged for real.

Andie pulled one of her endearing faces. 'Sorry. I guess that's a sensitive issue. I know we'll come to all that in our question-and-answer session. I'm just curious.'

'She chose it herself. All I had to do was pay for it.' That alone should have alerted him to what the marriage was all about—giving her access to his money and the lifestyle it bought.

'That wasn't very…romantic,' Andie said.

'There was nothing romantic about my marriage. Shall I tell you about it now and get all that out of the way?'

'If you feel comfortable with it,' she said.

'Comfortable is never a word I would relate to that time of my life,' he said. 'It was a series of mistakes.'

'If you're ready to tell me, I'm ready to listen.' He thought about how Andie had read his mood so accurately earlier this morning—giving him breakfast when he hadn't even been aware himself that he was hungry. She was thoughtful. And kind. Kindness wasn't an attribute he had much encountered in the women he had met.

'The first mistake I made with Tara was that she reminded me of someone else—a girl I'd met when I was living in the squat. Someone frail and sweet with similar colouring—someone I'd wanted to care for and look after.' It still hurt to think of Melody. Andie didn't need to know about her.

'And the second mistake?' Andie asked, seeming to understand he didn't want to speak further about Melody. She leaned forward as if she didn't want to miss a word.

'I believed her when she said she wanted children.'

'You wanted children?'

'As soon as possible. Tara said she did too.'

Andie frowned. 'But she didn't?'

Even now, bitterness rose in his throat. 'After we'd been married a year and nothing had happened, I suggested we see a doctor. Tara put it off and put it off. I thought it was because she didn't want to admit to failure. It was quite by accident that I discovered all the time I thought we'd been trying to conceive, she'd been on the contraceptive pill.'

Andie screwed up her face in an expression of disbelief and distaste. 'That's unbelievable.'

'When I confronted her, she laughed.' He relived the horror of discovering his ex-wife's treachery and the realisation she didn't have it in her to love. Not him. Certainly not a child. Fortunately, she hadn't been clever enough to understand the sub-clauses in the pre-nuptial agreement and divorce had been relatively straightforward.

'You had a lucky escape,' Andie said.

'That's why I never want to marry again. How could I ever trust another woman after that?'

'I understand you would feel that way,' she said. 'But not every woman would be like her. Me…my sisters, my friends. I don't know anyone who would behave with such dishonesty. Don't write off all women because of one.'

Trouble was, his wealth attracted women like Tara.

He was about to try and explain that to Andie when her phone started to sound out a bar of classical music.

She got up from the sofa and headed for the kitchen countertop to pick it up. 'Gemma,' she mouthed to him. 'I'd better take it.'

He nodded, grateful for the reprieve. Tara's treachery had got him into this fake engagement scenario with Andie, who was being such a good sport about the whole thing. He did not want to waste another word, or indeed thought, on his ex. Again, he thanked whatever providence had sent Andie into his life—Andie who was the opposite of Tara in every way.

He couldn't help but overhear Andie as she chatted to Gemma. 'Yes, yes, I saw it. We were having lunch after the meeting that Friday. Yes, it does look romantic. No, I didn't know anyone took a photo.'

Andie waved him over to her. 'Shall I tell her?' she mouthed.

He gave her the thumbs-up. 'Yes,' he mouthed back as he got up. There was no intention of keeping this 'engagement' secret. He walked over closer to Andie, who was standing there in bare feet, looking more beautiful in jeans than any other woman would look in a ball gown.

'Actually, Gemma, I…haven't been completely honest with you. I…uh…we…well, Dominic and I hit it off from the moment we first saw each other.'

Andie looked to Dominic and he nodded—she was doing well.

She listened to Gemma, then spoke again. 'Yes. We are…romantically involved. In fact…well…we're engaged.' She held the phone out from her ear and even Dominic could hear the excited squeals coming from Gemma.

When the squeals had subsided, Andie spoke again. 'Yes. It is sudden. I know that. But…well…you see I've learned that you have to grab your chance at happiness when you can. I…I've had it snatched away from me before.' She paused as she listened. 'Yes, that's it. I didn't want to wait. Neither did he. Gemma, I'd appreciate it if you didn't tell anyone just yet. Eliza? Well, okay, you can tell Eliza. I'd just like to tell my family first. What was that? Yes, I'll tell him.' She shut down her phone.

'So it's out,' he said.

'Yes,' she said. 'No denying it now.'

'What did Gemma ask you to tell me?'

She looked up at him. 'That she hoped you knew what a lucky guy you are to…to catch me.'

He looked down at her. 'I know very well how lucky I am. You're wonderful in every way and I appreciate what you're doing to help me.'

For a long moment he looked down into her face—still, serious, even sombre without her usual animated expression. Her eyes were full of something he couldn't put a name to. But not, he hoped, regret.

'Thank you, Andie.'

He stepped closer. For a long moment her gaze met his and held it. He saw wariness but he also saw the stirrings of what he could only read as invitation. To kiss his pretend fiancée would probably be a mistake. But it was a mistake he badly wanted to make.

He lifted his hand to her face, brushed first the smooth skin of her cheek and then the warm softness of her lips with the back of his knuckles. She stilled. Her lips parted under his touch and he could feel the tremor that ran through her body. He dropped his hand to her shoulder, then dipped his head and claimed her mouth in a firm gentle kiss. She murmured her surprise and pleasure as she kissed him back.

CHAPTER TEN

DOMINIC WAS KISSING her and it was more wonderful than
Andie ever could have imagined. His firm, sensuous mouth
was sure and certain on hers and she welcomed the intimate caress, the nudging of his tongue against the seam of
her lips as she opened her mouth to his. His beard growth
scratched her face but it was a pleasurable kind of pain.
The man knew how to kiss.

But as he kissed her and she kissed him back she was
shocked by the sudden explosion of chemistry between
them that turned something gentle into something urgent
and demanding. She wound her arms around his neck to
bring him closer in a wild tangle of tongues and lips as she
pressed herself against his hard muscular chest. He tasted
of coffee and hot male and desire. Passion this instant, this
insistent was a surprise.

But it was too soon.

She knew she wanted him. But she hadn't realised until
now just how *much* she wanted him. And how careful she
would have to be to guard her heart. Because these thrilling kisses told her that intimate contact with Dominic
Hunt might just become an addiction she would find very
difficult to live without. To him, this pretend engagement
was a business ploy that might also develop into an en-
tertaining game on the side. *She did not want to be a fake
fiancée with benefits.*

When it came down to it, while she had dated over the

last few years, her only serious relationship had been with a boy who had adored her, and whom she had loved with all her heart. Not a man like Dominic, who had sworn off marriage and viewed commitment so lightly he could pretend to be engaged. Her common sense urged her to stop but her body wanted more, more, more of him.

With a great effort she broke away from the kiss. Her heart was pounding in triple time, her breath coming in painful gasps. She took a deep steadying breath. And then another.

'That…that was a great start on Condition Number Six,' she managed to choke out.

Dominic towered over her; his breath came in ragged gasps. He looked so darkly sensual, her heart seemed to flip right over in her chest. 'What?' he demanded. 'Stopping when we'd just started?'

'No. I…I mean the actual kiss.'

He put his hand on her shoulder, lightly stroking her in a caress that ignited shivers of delight all through her.

'So tell me about your sixth condition,' he said, his deep voice with a broken edge to it as he struggled to control his breathing.

'Condition Number Six is that we…we have to look the part.'

He frowned. 'And that means…?'

'I mean we have to act like a genuine couple. To seem to other people as if we're…we're crazy about each other. Because it would have to be…something very powerful between us for us to get engaged so quickly. In…real life, I mean.'

She found it difficult to meet his eyes. 'I was going to say we needed to get physical. And we just did…get physical. So we…uh…know that there's chemistry between us. And that…that it works.'

He dropped his hand from her shoulder to tilt her chin

upwards with his finger so she was forced to meet his gaze. 'There was never any doubt about that.'

His words thrummed through her body. That sexual attraction had been there for her the first time she'd met him. *Had he felt it too?*

'So the sixth condition is somewhat superfluous,' she said, her voice racing as she tried to ignore the hunger for him his kiss had ignited. 'I think we might be okay, there. You know, holding hands, arms around each other. Appropriate Public Displays of Affection.' It was an effort to force herself to sound matter of fact.

'This just got to be my favourite of all your conditions,' he said slowly, his eyes narrowing in a way she found incredibly sexy. 'Shall we practise some more?'

Her traitorous body wrestled down her hopelessly outmatched common sense. 'Why not?' she murmured, desperate to be in his arms again. He pulled her close and their body contact made her aware he wanted her as much as she wanted him. She sighed as she pressed her mouth to his.

Then her phone sang out its ringtone of a piano sonata.

'Leave it,' growled Dominic.

She ignored the musical tone until it stopped. But it had brought her back to reality. There was nothing she wanted more than to take Dominic by the hand and lead him up the stairs to her bedroom. She intended to have him before this contract between them came to an end.

But that intuition she usually trusted screamed at her that to make love with him on the first day of their fake engagement would be a mistake. It would change the dynamic of their relationship to something she did not feel confident of being able to handle.

No sooner had the ringtone stopped than it started again.

Andie untangled herself from Dominic's embrace and

stepped right back from him, back from the seductive reach of his muscular arms.

'I…I have to take this,' she said.

She answered the phone but had to rest against the kitchen countertop to support knees that had gone shaky and weak. Dominic leaned back against the wall opposite her and crossed his arms against his powerful chest. His muscles flexed as he did so and she had to force herself to concentrate on the phone call.

'Yes, Eliza, it's true. I know—it must have been a surprise to you. A party?' Andie looked up to Dominic and shook her head. He nodded. She spoke to Eliza. 'No. We don't want an engagement party. Yes, I know we're party queens and it's what we do.' She rolled her eyes at Dominic and, to her relief, he smiled. 'The Christmas party is more than enough to handle at the moment,' she said to Eliza.

We. She and Dominic were a couple now. A fake couple. It would take some getting used to. So would handling the physical attraction between them.

'The wedding?' Eliza's question about the timing of the wedding flustered her. 'We…we…uh…next year some time. Yes, I know next year is only next month. The wedding won't be next month, that's for sure.' *The* wedding—wouldn't a loved-up fiancée have said *our* wedding?

She finished the call to Eliza and realised her hands were clammy. 'This is not going to be easy,' she said to Dominic.

'I never thought it would be,' he said. Was there a double meaning there?

'I have no experience in this kind of deception. The first thing Eliza asked me was when are we getting married. She put me on the spot. I…I struggled to find an answer.'

He nodded slowly. 'I suggest we say we've decided on a long engagement. That we're committed but want to use the engagement time to get to know each other better.'

'That sounds good,' she said.

The deceptive words came so easily to him while she was so flustered she could scarcely think. She realised how hopelessly mismatched they were: he was more experienced, wealthier, from a completely different background. And so willing to lie.

And yet... That kiss had only confirmed how much she wanted him.

Her phone rang out again. 'Why do I get the feeling this phone will go all day long?' she said, a note of irritation underscoring her voice. She looked on the caller ID. 'It's my fashion editor friend, Karen. I knew Gemma wouldn't be able to stop at Eliza,' she told Dominic as she answered it.

The first part of the conversation was pretty much a repeat of the conversation she'd had with Gemma. But then Karen asked should she start scouting around for her wedding dress. Karen hunted down bargain-priced clothes for her; of course she'd want to help her with a wedding. 'My wedding dress? We...uh...haven't set a date for the wedding yet. Yes, I suppose it's never too early to think about the dress. Simple? Vintage inspired? Gorgeous shoes?' She laughed and hoped Karen didn't pick up on the shrill edge to her laughter. 'You know my taste only too well, Karen. A veil? A modest lace veil? Okay. Yes. I'll leave it to you. Thank you.'

'Your friends move fast,' Dominic said when she'd disconnected the call.

'They're so thrilled for me. After...after...well, you know. My past.' Her past of genuine love, unsullied by lies and deception.

'Of course,' he said.

She couldn't bring herself to say anything about the kisses they'd shared. It wasn't the kind of thing she found easy to talk about. Neither, it appeared, did he.

He glanced down at his watch. The action drew her attention to his hands. She noticed again how attractive they were, with long strong fingers. And thought how she would like to feel them on her body. Stroking. Caressing. Exploring. *She had to stop this.*

'I know I'm breaking the terms of one of your conditions,' he said. 'But I do have to get to the office. There are cancelled meetings in other states to reschedule and staff who need to talk to me.'

'And I've got to finalise the furniture hire for the Christmas party. With two hundred people for lunch, we need more tables and chairs. It's sobering, to have all those families in need on Christmas Day.'

'Hannah assures me it's the tip of a tragic iceberg,' said Dominic.

They both paused for a long moment before she spoke. 'I also have to work on a tiaras-and-tuxedos-themed twenty-first party. Ironic, isn't it, after what we've just been saying?' But organising parties was her job and brought not only employment to her and her partners but also the caterers, the waiting staff and everyone else involved.

'I didn't think twenty-first parties were important any more, with eighteen the legal age of adulthood,' Dominic said.

'They're still very popular. This lovely girl turning twenty-one still lives at home with her parents and has three more years of university still ahead of her to become a veterinarian. I have to organise tiaras for her dogs.'

'Wh...what?' he spluttered. 'Did you say you're putting a tiara on a *dog*?'

'Her dogs are very important to her; they'll be honoured guests at the party.'

He scowled. 'I like dogs but that's ridiculous.'

'We're getting more and more bookings for dog parties.

A doggy birthday boy or girl invites their doggy friends. They're quite a thing. And getting as competitive as the kids' parties. Of course it's a learning curve for a party planner—considering doggy bathroom habits, for one thing.'

'That is the stupidest—'

Andie put up her hand. 'Don't be too quick to judge. The doggy parties are really about making the humans happy—I doubt the dogs could care less. Frivolity can be fun. Eliza and I have laid bets on how many boys will arrive wearing tiaras to the vet student's twenty-first.'

She had to smile at his bah-humbug expression.

'By the time I was twenty-one, I had established a career in real estate and had my first million in sight.'

That interested her. 'I'd love to know about—'

He cut her off. 'Let's save that for the question-and-answer session, shall we?'

'Which will start…?'

'This afternoon. Can you come to my place?'

'Sure. It doesn't hurt to visit the party site as many times as I can.'

'Only this time you'll be coming to collect your engagement ring.'

'Of…of course.' She had forgotten about that. In a way, she dreaded it. 'And to find out more about you, fake fiancé. We have to be really well briefed to face my family tomorrow evening.'

She and Anthony had joked that by the time they'd paid off their student loans all they'd be able to afford for an engagement ring would be a ring pull from a can of soft drink. The ring pull would have had so much more meaning than this cynical exercise.

She felt suddenly subdued at the thought of deceiving her family. Her friends were used to the ups and downs of dating. A few weeks down the track, they'd take a broken engagement in their stride. If those kisses were anything to go by, she might be more than a tad upset when her time with Dominic came to an end. She pummelled back down to somewhere deep inside her the shred of hope that perhaps something real could happen between them after the engagement charade was done.

'When will you tell your parents?' Dominic asked.

'Today. They'd be hurt beyond belief if they found out from someone else.'

'And you'll talk to Hannah about Timothy?'

'At the family dinner. We should speak to her and Paul together.'

'I hope she won't be too difficult to convince. I really want to help that little boy.'

'I know,' she said, thinking of how grateful her family would be to him. How glad she was she'd agreed to all this for her tiny nephew's sake. But what about Dominic's family? This shouldn't be all about hers. 'What about your aunt? Do we need to tell her?'

The shutters came slamming down. 'No. She's out of the picture.'

The way he said it let her know not to ask more. Not now anyway.

Dominic shrugged on his leather jacket in preparation to go. She stared, dumbstruck, feasting her eyes on him. *He was so hot.* She still felt awkward after their passionate kissing session. Should she reach up and kiss him on the cheek?

While she was making up her mind, he pulled her close for a brief, exciting kiss on her mouth. She doubted there could be any other type of kiss but exciting from Dominic. 'Happy to fulfil Condition Number Six at any time,' he said, very seriously.

She smiled, the tension between them immediately dissipated. But she wasn't ready to say goodbye just yet.

'Before you go…' She picked up her smartphone again. 'The first thing my friends who don't know you will want to see is a photo of my surprise new fiancé.'

He ran his hand over his unshaven chin. 'Like this? Can't it wait?'

'I like your face like that. It's hot. No need to shave on my behalf.' Without thinking, she put her fingers up to her cheek, where there was probably stubble rash. *His kiss had felt so good.*

'If you say so,' he said, looking pleased.

'Just lean against the door there,' she said. 'Look cool.'

He slouched against the door and sent her a smouldering look. The wave of want that crashed through her made her nearly drop the phone. 'Do I look *cool*?' he said in a self-mocking tone. 'I thought you liked *hot*?'

'You know exactly what I mean.' She was discovering a light-hearted side to Dominic she liked very much.

Their gazes met and they both burst into laughter. He looked even more gorgeous when he laughed, perfect teeth white in his tanned face, and she immediately captured a few more images of him. Who would recognise this good-humoured hunk in jeans and leather jacket as the billionaire Scrooge of legend?

'What about a selfie of us together?' she asked. 'In the interests of authenticity,' she hastily added.

Bad idea. She stood next to him, aware of every centimetre of body contact, and held her phone out in front of them. She felt more self-conscious than she could ever remember feeling. He pulled her in so their faces were close together. She smiled and clicked, and as she clicked again he kissed her on the cheek.

'That will be cute,' she said.

'Another?' he asked. This time he kissed her on the mouth. *Click. Click. Click.* And then she forgot to click.

After he had left, Andie spent more minutes than she should scrolling through the photos on her phone. *No one would know they were faking it.*

CHAPTER ELEVEN

DOMINIC NOW KNEW more about diamond engagement rings than even a guy who was genuinely engaged to be married needed to know. He'd thought he could just march into Sydney's most exclusive jewellery store and hand over an investment-sized price for a big chunk of diamond. Not so.

The sales guy—rather, *executive consultant*—who had greeted him and ushered him into a private room had taken the purchase very seriously. He'd hit Dominic with a barrage of questions. It was unfortunate that the lady was unable to be there because it was very important the ring would suit her personality. What were the lady's favourite colours? What style of clothes did she favour? Her colouring?

'Were you able to answer the questions?' Andie asked, her lips curving into her delightful smile.

She had just arrived at his house. After she'd taken some measurements in the old ballroom, he had taken her out to sit in the white Hollywood-style chairs by the pool. Again, she looked as if she belonged. She wore a natural-coloured linen dress with her hair piled up and a scarf twisted and tied right from the base of her neck to the top of her head. It could have looked drab and old-fashioned but, on her, with her vintage sunglasses and orange lipstick, it looked just right.

Last time she'd been there he'd been so caught up with her he hadn't thought to ask her would she like a drink.

He didn't want a live-in housekeeper—he valued his privacy too much—but his daily housekeeper had been this morning and the refrigerator was well stocked. He'd carried a selection of cool drinks out to the poolside table between their two chairs.

'You're finding this story amusing, aren't you?' he said, picking up his iced tea.

She took off her sunglasses. 'Absolutely. I had no idea the rigmarole involved in buying an engagement ring.'

'Me neither. I thought I'd just march in, point out a diamond ring and pay for it.' This was a first for him.

'Me too,' said Andie. 'I thought that's what guys did when they bought a ring.'

'Oh, no. First of all, I'd done completely the wrong thing in not having you with me. He was too discreet to ask where you were, so I didn't have to come up with a creative story to explain your absence.'

'One less lie required anyway,' she said with a twist of her lovely mouth. 'Go on with the story—I'm fascinated.'

'Apparently, the done thing is to have a bespoke ring—like the business suits I have made to measure.'

'A bespoke ring? Who knew?' she said, her eyes dancing.

'Instead, I had to choose from their ready-to-wear couture pieces.'

'I had no idea such a thing existed,' she said with obvious delight. *Her smile*. It made him feel what he'd thought he'd never feel again, made him want what he'd thought he'd never want.

'You should have been there,' he said. 'You would have had fun.' He'd spent the entire time in the jewellery store wishing she'd been by his side. He could imagine her suppressing giggles as the consultant had run through his over-the-top sales pitch.

'Perhaps,' she said, but her eyes dimmed. 'You know

my reasons for not wanting to get involved in the purchase. Anyway, what did you tell them about my—' she made quote marks in the air with her fingers '—"personal style"? That must have put you on the spot?'

'I told the consultant about your misbehaving skirt— only I didn't call it that, of course. I told him about your shoes that laced up your calves. I told him about your turquoise necklace and your outsized earrings. I told him about your leopard-print shoes and your white trousers.'

Andie's eyes widened. 'You remember all that about what I wear?'

'I did say I was observant,' he said.

Ask him to remember what Party Planners Numbers One to Three had been wearing for their interviews and he would scarcely recall it. But he remembered every detail about her since that errant breeze at his front door had blown Andie into his life.

At the jewellery store, once he'd relaxed into the conversation with the consultant, Dominic had also told him how Andie was smart and creative and a touch unconventional and had the most beautiful smile and a husky, engaging laugh. 'This is a lucky lady,' the guy had said. 'You must love her very much.'

That had thrown Dominic. 'Yes,' he'd muttered. *Love* could not enter into this. He did not want Andie to get hurt. And hurt wasn't on his personal agenda either. He didn't think he had it in him to love. To give love you had to be loved—and genuine love was not something that had been part of his life.

'So… I'm curious,' said Andie. What kind of ring did you—did I—end up with?'

'Not the classic solitaire I would have chosen. The guy said you'd find it boring.'

'Of course I wouldn't have found it boring,' she said not very convincingly.

'Why do I not believe you?' he said.

'Stop teasing me and show me the darn ring,' she said.

Dominic took out the small, leather, case from his inside suit jacket pocket. 'I hope you like it,' he said. *He wanted her to like it.* He didn't know why it was suddenly so important that she did.

He opened the case and held it out for Andie to see. Her eyes widened and she caught her breath. 'It...it's exquisite,' she said.

'Is it something you think you could wear?' he asked.

'Oh, yes,' she said. 'I love it.'

'It's called a halo set ring,' he said. 'The ring of little diamonds that surround the big central diamond is the halo. And the very narrow split band—again set with small diamonds—is apparently very fashionable.'

'That diamond is enormous,' she said, drawing back. 'I'd be nervous to wear it.'

'I got it well insured,' he said.

'Good,' she said. 'If I lost it, I'd be paying you back for the rest of my life and probably still be in debt.'

'The ring is yours, Andie.'

'I know, for the duration,' she said. 'I promise to look after it.' She crossed her heart.

'You misunderstand. The ring is yours to keep after... after all this has come to an end.'

She frowned and shook her head vehemently. 'No. That wasn't part of the deal. Timothy's treatment was the deal. I give this ring back to you when...when I dump you.'

'We'll see about that,' he said, not wanting to get into an argument with her. As far as he was concerned, this ring was *hers*. She could keep it or sell it or give it away— he never wanted it back. 'Now, shouldn't I be getting that diamond on your finger?'

He was surprised to find his hand wasn't steady as he took the ring out of its hinged case. It glittered and sparkled as the afternoon sunlight danced off the multi-cut facets of the diamonds. 'Hold out your hand,' he said.

'No', she said, again shaking her head. 'Give it to me and I'll put it on myself. This isn't a real engagement and I don't want to jinx myself. When I get engaged for real, my real fiancé will put my ring on my wedding finger.'

Again, Dominic felt disappointed. Against all reason. He wanted to put the ring on her finger. But he understood why he shouldn't. He felt a pang of regret that he most likely would never again be anyone's 'real fiancé'—and a pang of what he recognised as envy for the man who would win Andie's heart for real.

He put the ring back in its case. 'You do want to get married one day?'

He wasn't sure if she was still in love with the memory of her first boyfriend—and that no man would be able to live up to that frozen-in-time ideal. Melody had been his first love—but he certainly held no romanticised memories of her.

'Of course I do. I want to get married and have a family. I…I… It took me a long time to get over the loss of my dreams of a life with Anthony. I couldn't see myself with anyone but him. But that was five years ago. Now… I think I'm ready to move on.'

Dominic had to clear his throat to speak. 'Okay, I see your point. Better put on the ring yourself,' he said.

Tentatively, she lifted the ring from where it nestled in the velvet lining of its case. 'I'm terrified I'll drop it and it will fall into the pool.' She laughed nervously as she slid it on to the third finger of her left hand. 'There—it's on.' She held out her hand, fingers splayed to better display the ring. 'It's a perfect fit,' she said. 'You did well.'

'It looks good on you,' he said.

'That sales guy knew his stuff,' she said. 'I can't stop looking at it. It's the most beautiful ring I've ever seen.'

She looked up at him. 'I still have my doubts about the wisdom of this charade. But I will enjoy wearing this magnificent piece of jewellery. Thank you for choosing something so perfect.'

'Thank you for helping me out with this crazy scheme,' he said. The scheme that had seemed crazy the moment he'd proposed it and which got crazier and crazier as it went along. But it was important he sealed that deal with Walter Burton. And was it such a bad thing to have to spend so much time with Andie?

Andie took a deep breath to try and clear her head of the conflicting emotions aroused by wearing the exquisite ring that sat so perfectly on her finger. *The ring pull would have been so much more valuable.* This enormous diamond with its many surrounding tiny diamonds symbolised not love and commitment but the you-scratch-my-back-and-I'll-scratch-yours deal between her and Dominic.

Still, she couldn't help wondering how he could have chosen a ring so absolutely *her.*

'I've been thinking about our getting-to-know-each-other session,' she said. 'Why don't we each ask the other three questions?'

'Short and to the point,' he said with obvious relief.

'Or longer, as needs might be. I want to be the best fake fiancée I can. No way do I want to be caught out on something important I should know about you. I didn't like the feeling this morning when I froze as Karen questioned me about our wedding plans.'

Dominic drank from his iced tea. To give himself time to think? Or plan evasive action? 'I see where you're going. Let's see if we can make it work.'

Andie settled back in the chair. She didn't know whether to be disappointed or relieved there was a small table between her and Dominic. She would not be averse to his thigh nudged against hers—at the same time, it would undoubtedly be distracting. 'Okay. I'll start. My Question Number One is: How did you get from street kid to billionaire?'

Dominic took his time to put his glass back down on the table. 'Before I reply, let's get one thing straight.' His gaze was direct. 'My answers are for you and you alone. What I tell you is to go no further.'

'Agreed,' she said, meeting his gaze full-on. 'Can we get another thing straight? You can trust me.'

'Just so long as we know where we stand.'

'I'm surprised you're not making me sign a contract.' She said the words half in jest but the expression that flashed across his face in response made her pause. She sat forward in her seat. 'You thought about a contract, didn't you?'

With Dominic back in his immaculate dark business suit, clean-shaven, hair perfectly groomed, she didn't feel as confident with him as she had this morning.

'I did think of a contract and quickly dismissed it,' he said. 'I do trust you, Andie.'

Surely he must be aware that she would not jeopardise Timothy's treatment in any way? 'I'm glad to hear that, Dominic, because this won't work if we don't trust each other—it goes both ways. Let's start. C'mon—answer my question.'

He still didn't answer. She waited, aware of the palm leaves above rustling in the same slight breeze that ruffled the aquamarine surface of the pool, the distant barking of a neighbour's dog.

'You know I hate this?' he said finally.

'I kind of get that,' she said. 'But I couldn't "marry" a man whose past remained a dark secret to me.'

Even after the question-and-answer session, she suspected big chunks of his past might remain a secret from her. Maybe from anyone.

He dragged in a deep breath as if to prepare himself for something unpleasant. 'As I have already mentioned, at age seventeen, I was homeless. I was living in an underground car park on the site of an abandoned shopping centre project in one of the roughest areas of Brisbane. The buildings had only got to the foundation stage. The car park was…well, you can imagine what an underground car park that had never been completed was like. It was a labyrinth of unfinished service areas and elevator shafts. No lights, pools of water whenever it rained, riddled with rats and cockroaches.'

'And human vermin too, I'll bet.' Andie shuddered. 'What a scary place for a teenager to be living—and dangerous.'

He had come from such a dark place. She could gush with sympathy and pity. But she knew instinctively that was not what he wanted to hear. Show how deeply moved she was at the thought of seventeen-year-old Dominic living such a perilous life and he would clam up. And she wanted to hear more.

Dominic's eyes assumed a dark, faraway look as though he was going back somewhere in his mind he had no desire to revisit. 'It was dangerous and smelly and seemed like hell. But it was also somewhere safer to sleep than on the actual streets. Darkness meant shadows you could hide in, and feel safe even if it was only an illusion of safety.'

She reached out and took the glass from his hand; he seemed unaware he was gripping it so tightly he might break it. 'Your home life must have been kind of hellish too for you to have preferred that over living with your aunt.'

'Hell? You could say that.' The grim set of his mouth let her know that no more would be forthcoming on that subject.

'Your life on the streets must have been…terrifying.'

'I toughened up pretty quick. One thing I had in my favour was I was big—the same height I am now and strong from playing football at school. It was a rough-around-the-edges kind of school, and I'd had my share of sorting out bullies there.' He raised his fists into a fighting position in a gesture she thought was unconscious.

So scratch the elite private school. She realised now that Dominic was a self-made man. And his story of triumph over adversity fascinated her. 'So you could defend yourself against thugs and…and predators.'

Her heart went out to him. At seventeen she'd had all the security of a loving family and comfortable home. But she knew first-hand from her foster sisters that not all young people were that fortunate. It seemed that the young Dominic had started off with loving parents and a secure life but had spiralled downwards from then on. What the heck was wrong with the aunt to have let that happen?

She reached over the table and trailed her fingers across his scarred knuckles. 'That's how you got these?' It was amazing the familiarity a fake engagement allowed.

'I got in a lot of fights,' he said.

'And this?' She traced the fine scar at the side of his mouth.

'Another fight,' he said.

She dropped her hands to her sides, again overwhelmed by that urge to comfort him. 'You were angry and frightened.'

He shifted uncomfortably in his seat. 'All that.'

'But then you ended up with this.' She waved her hand to encompass the immaculate art deco pool, the expensively landscaped gardens, the superb house. It was an oasis of beauty and luxury.

'My fighting brought me to the attention of the police. I was charged with assault,' he said bluntly.

She'd thought his tough exterior was for real—had sensed the undercurrents of suppressed rage.

'Believe me, the other guy deserved it,' he said with an expression of grim satisfaction. 'He was drug-dealing scum.'

'What happened? With the police, I mean.' He'd been seventeen—still a kid. All she'd been fighting at that age was schoolgirl drama.

'I got lucky. The first piece of luck was that I was under eighteen and not charged as an adult. The second piece of luck was I was referred to a government social worker—Jim, his name was. Poor man, having to deal with the sullen, unhappy kid I was then couldn't have been easy. Jim was truly one of the good guys—still is. He won my confidence and got me away from that squat, to the guidance of another social worker friend of his down the Queensland Gold Coast.'

'Sun, surf and sand,' she said. She knew it sounded flippant but Dominic would not want her to pity his young self.

'And a booming real estate market. The social worker down there was a good guy too. He got me a job as a gofer in a real estate agency. I was paid a pittance but it was a start and I liked it there. To cut a long story short, I was soon promoted to the sales team. I discovered I was good at selling the lifestyle dream, not just the number of bedrooms and bathrooms. I became adept at gauging what was important to the client.'

'Because you were observant,' she said. And tough and resilient and utterly admirable.

'That's important. Especially when I realised the role the woman played in a residential sale. Win her over and you more than likely closed the sale.'

Andie could see how those good looks, along with intuition and charm and the toughness to back it up, could have accelerated him ahead. 'Fascinating. And incredible how you've kept all the details away from the public. Surely people must have tried to research you, would have wanted to know your story?'

'As a juvenile, my record is sealed. I've never spoken about it. It's a time of my life I want well behind me. Without Jim the social worker, I might have gone the other way.'

'You mean you could have ended up as a violent thug or a drug dealer? I don't believe that for a second.'

He shrugged those broad street-fighter shoulders. 'I appreciate your faith in me. But, like so many of my fellow runaways, I could so easily have ended up…broken.'

Andie struggled to find an answer to that. 'It…it's a testament to your strength of character that you didn't.'

'If you say,' he said. But he looked pleased. 'Once I'd made enough money to have my own place and a car—nowhere as good as your hatchback, I might add—I started university part-time. I got lucky again.'

'You passed with honours?' She hadn't seen a university degree anywhere in her research on him but there was no harm in asking.

'No. I soon realised I knew more about making money and how business operated than some of the teachers in my commerce degree. I dropped out after eighteen months. But in a statistics class I met Jake Marlow. He was a brilliant, misunderstood geek. Socially, I still considered myself an outcast. We became friends.'

'And business partners, you said.' He was four years older than she was, and yet had lived a lifetime more. And had overcome terrible odds to get where he had.

'He was playing with the concept of ground-breaking online business software tools but no bank would loan him the money to develop them. I was riding high on commissions. We set up a partnership. I put in the money he needed. I could smell my first million.'

'Let me guess—it was an amazing success?'

'That software is used by thousands of businesses around the world to manage their digital workflow. We made a lot of money very quickly. Jake is still developing successful new software.' His obvious pride in his friend warmed his words.

'And you're still business partners.'

He nodded. 'The success of our venture gave me the investment dollars I needed to also spin off into my own separate business developing undervalued homemaker centres. We call them bulky goods centres—furnishing, white goods, electricals.'

'I guess the Gold Coast got too small for you.' That part she'd been able to research.

'I moved to Sydney. You know the rest.'

In silence she drank her mineral water with lime, he finished his iced tea. He'd given her a lot to think about. Was that anger that had driven him resolved? Or could it still be bubbling under the surface, ready to erupt?

He angled himself to look more directly at her. 'Now it's your turn to answer my question, Andie,' he said. 'How did you get over the death of your...of Anthony?'

She hadn't been expecting that and it hit her hard. But he'd dug deep. She had to too. 'I... I don't know that I will ever be able to forget the shock of it. One minute he was there, the next minute gone. I... I was as good as a widow, before I'd had the chance to be a bride.'

Dominic nodded, as if he understood. Of course he'd lost his parents.

'We were staying the weekend at his parents' beach house at Whale Beach. Ant got up very early, left a note to say he'd gone surfing, kissed me—I was asleep but awake enough to know he was going out—and then he was gone. Of course I blamed myself for not going with him. Then I was angry he'd gone out by himself.'

'Understandably,' he said and she thought again how he

seemed to see more than other people. She had no deep, dark secrets. But, if she did, she felt he'd burrow down to them without her even realising it.

'After Anthony died, I became terrified of the sea. I hated the waves—blamed them for taking him from me, which I know was all kinds of irrational. Then one day I went to the beach by myself and sat on the sand. I remember hugging my knees as I watched a teenage boy, tall and blond like Anthony, ride a wave all the way into the shore, saw the exultation on his face, the sheer joy he felt at being one with the wave.'

'If this is bringing back hurtful memories, you don't have to go any further.'

'I'm okay… When someone close dies, you look for a sign from them—I learned I wasn't alone in that when I had counselling. That boy on his board was like a message from Anthony. He died doing something he truly loved. I ran into the surf and felt somehow connected to him. It was a healing experience, a turning point in my recovery from grief.'

'That's a powerful story,' Dominic said.

'The point of it is, it's five years since he died and of course I've moved on. Anyone who might wonder if my past could affect our fake future can be assured of that. Anthony was part of my youth; we grew up together. In some ways I'm the person I am because of those happy years behind me. But I want happy years ahead of me too. I've dated. I just haven't met the right person.'

For the first time she wondered if she could feel more for Dominic than physical attraction. For a boy who had been through what he had and yet come through as the kind of man who offered to pay for a little boy's medical treatment? Who was more willing to open his house to disadvantaged people than celebrities? There was so much more to Dominic than she ever could have imagined—and the more she found out about him the more she liked about him.

And then there were those kisses she had not been able to stop thinking about—and yearning for more.

'I appreciate you telling me,' he said.

She poured herself another long, cool mineral water. Offered to pour one for Dominic, but he declined.

'On to my next question,' she said. 'It's about your family. Do you have family other than your aunt? My mother will certainly want to know because she's already writing the guest list for the wedding.'

'You told your mother about the engagement?'

'She couldn't be more delighted. In fact…well…she got quite tearful.' Andie had never felt more hypocritical than the moment she realised her mother was crying tears of joy for her.

'That's a relief,' he said.

'You could put it that way. I didn't realise quite how concerned they were about me being…lonely. Not that I am lonely, by the way—I have really good friends.' But it was not the same as having a special someone.

'I'm beginning to see that,' he said. 'I'm surprised we've been able to have this long a conversation without your phone going off.'

'That's because I switched it off,' she said. 'There'll probably be a million messages when I switch it back on.'

'So your mother didn't question our…haste?'

'No. And any guilt I felt about pulling the wool over her eyes I forced firmly to the back of my mind. Timothy getting the treatment he needs is way more important to my family than me finding a man.' She looked at him. 'So now—the guest list, your family?'

'My aunt and my mother were the only family each other had. So there is no Australian family.'

'Your aunt has…has passed away?' There was something awkward here that she didn't feel comfortable prob-ing. But they were—supposedly—planning to get married. It made sense for her to know something of his family.

'She's in the best of residential care, paid for by me. That's all I want to say about her.'

'Okay,' she said, shaken by the closed look on his face.

'I have family in the UK but no one close since my grandparents died.'

'So no guests from your side of the family for our imag-inary wedding?'

'That's right. And I consider the subject closed. In fact, I've had a gutful of talking about this stuff.'

'Me too,' she said. Hearing about his difficult youth, remembering her early loss was making her feel down. 'I reckon we know enough about each other now to be able to field any questions that are thrown at us. After all, we're not pretending to have known each other for long.'

She got up from her chair, walked to the edge of the pool, knelt at the edge and swished her hand through the water. 'This is such a nice pool. Do you use it much?'

'Most days I swim,' he said, standing behind her. 'There's a gym at the back of the cabana too.'

She imagined him working out in his gym, then plung-ing into the pool, muscles pumped, spearing through the water in not many clothes, maybe in *no* clothes.

Stop it!

She got up, wishing she could dive in right now to cool herself down. 'Do you like my idea to hire some lifeguards so the guests can swim on Christmas Day?'

'It's a good one.'

'And you're okay with putting a new swimsuit and towel in each of the children's goody bags? Hannah pointed out that some of the kids might not have a swimsuit.'

'I meant to talk to you about that,' he said. Surely he wasn't going to query the cost of the kids' gifts? She would be intensely disappointed if he did. 'I want to buy each of the adults a new swimsuit too; they might not have one either,' he said. 'I don't want anyone feeling excluded for any reason we can avoid.'

She looked up at him. 'You're not really a Scrooge, are you?'

'No,' he said.

'I don't think people are going to be calling you that for much longer. Certainly not if I've got anything to do with it.'

'But not a word about my past.'

'That's understood,' she said, making a my-lips-are-sealed zipping motion over her mouth. 'Though I think you might find people would admire you for having over-come it.'

The alarm on her watch buzzed. 'I'm running late,' she said. 'I didn't realise we'd been talking for so long.'

'You have an appointment? I was going to suggest din-ner.'

'No can do, I'm afraid.' Her first impulse was to can-cel her plans, to jump at the opportunity to be with Dom-inic. But she would not put her life on hold for the fake engagement.

'I have a hot date with a group of girlfriends. It's our first Tuesday of the month movie club. We see a movie and then go to dinner. We're supposed to discuss the movie but we mainly catch up on the gossip.' She held out her hand, where the diamond flashed on the third finger of her left hand. 'I suspect this baby is going to be the main topic of conversation.'

She made to go but, before she could, Dominic had pulled her close for a kiss that left not a scrap of lipstick on her mouth and her hair falling out of its knot.

It was the kind of kiss she could get used to.

CHAPTER TWELVE

ANDIE SAT AT her desk in the Party Queens' headquarters. 'Headquarters' was rather a grand term for their premises. It comprised an industrial kitchen where Gemma could do her thing; a workroom used for making props; a storage area; and an area loosely termed an office, where she and her two partners squeezed in their desks.

To say they were frantically busy would be an understatement. The weeks leading up to Christmas and New Year were the busiest time of the year for established party planners. For a new company like Party Queens to be so busy was gratifying. But it was the months after the end of the long Aussie summer vacation they had to worry about for advance bookings. Business brain, Eliza, was very good at reminding them of that.

Andie's top priority was Dominic's Christmas party. Actually, it was no longer just his party. As his fiancée, she had officially become co-host. But that didn't mean she wasn't flat-out with other bookings, including a Christmas Eve party for the parents of their first eighteenth party girl. Andie wanted to pull out all the stops for the people who'd given Party Queens their very first job. And then there was the business of being Dominic's fake fiancée—almost a job on its own.

Andie had been 'engaged' to Dominic for ten days and so far so good. She'd been amazed that no one had seriously queried the speed at which she had met, fallen in love with and agreed to marry a man she had known for less than a month.

The swooning sighs of 'love at first sight' and 'how romantic' from her girlfriends she understood, not so much the delight from her pragmatic father and the tears of joy from her mother. She hardly knew Dominic and yet they were prepared to believe she would commit her life to him?

Of course it was because her family and friends had been worried about her, wanted her to be happy, had been concerned she had grieved for Anthony for too long.

'Your dad and I are pleased for you, sweetheart, we really are,' her mother had said. 'We were worried you were so fearful about loving someone again in case you lost them, that you wouldn't let yourself fall in love again,' she'd continued. 'But Dominic is so strong, so right for you; I guess he just broke through those barriers you'd spent so long putting up. And I understand you didn't want to waste time when you knew what it was like to have a future snatched away from you.'

Really? She'd put up *barriers*? She'd just been trying to find someone worthy of stepping into Anthony's shoes. Now she'd found a man who had big boots of his own and would never walk in another man's shadow. *But he wasn't really hers.*

'You put us off the scent by telling us Dominic wasn't your type,' Gemma had said accusingly. Gemma, who was already showing her ideas for a fabulous wedding cake she planned to bake and decorate for her when the time came. Andie felt bad going through images of multi-tiered pastel creations with Gemma, knowing the cake was never going to happen.

Condition Number One, that she and Dominic didn't *ever* tell *anyone* about the deception, seemed now like a very good idea. To hear that their engagement had been a cold-blooded business arrangement was never going to go down well with all these people wishing them well.

At last Wednesday's family dinner, Dominic had been joyfully welcomed into the Newman family. 'I'm glad you saw sense about how hot he was,' her sister Bea had said, hugging her. 'And as for that amazing rock on your finger... Does Dominic have a brother? No? Well, can you find me someone just like him, please?'

But every bit of deception was all worth it for Timothy. After the family dinner, Andie and Dominic had drawn Hannah and Paul aside. Now that Dominic was to be part of the family—or so they thought—her sister and her husband didn't take much convincing to accept Dominic's offer of paying all Timothy's medical expenses.

Dominic's only condition was that they kept him posted on their tiny son's progress. 'Of course we will,' Hannah had said, 'but Andie will keep you updated and you'll see Timothy at family functions. You'll always be an important part of his life.' And the little boy had more chance of a better life, thanks to Dominic's generosity.

Later, Hannah had hugged her sister tight. 'You've got yourself a good man, Andie, a very, very good man.'

'I know,' said Andie, choked up and cringing inside. She was going to have to come up with an excellent reason to explain why she 'dumped' Dominic when his need for the fake engagement was over.

There had only been one awkward moment at the dinner. Her parents wanted to put an announcement of the engagement in the newspaper. 'Old-fashioned, I know, but it's the right thing to do,' her mother had said.

She'd then wanted to know what Dominic's middle name was for the announcement. Apparently full names were required, Andrea Jane Newman was engaged to Dominic *who*?

She had looked at Dominic, eyes widened by panic.

She should have known that detail about the man she was supposedly going to marry.

Dominic had quickly stepped in. 'I've kept quiet about my middle name because I don't like it very much,' he'd said. 'It's Hugo. Dominic Hugo Hunt.'

Of course everyone had greeted that announcement with cries of how much they loved the name Hugo. 'You could call your first son Hugo,' Bea had suggested.

That was when Andie had decided it was time to go home. She felt so low at deceiving everyone, she felt she could slink out of the house at ankle level. If it wasn't for Timothy, she would slide that outsize diamond off her finger and put an end to this whole deception.

Dominic had laughed the baby comment off—and made no further mention of it. He'd wanted a baby with his first wife—how did he feel about children now?

Her family was now expecting babies from her and Dominic. She had not anticipated having to handle that expectation. But of course, since then, the image of a dear little boy with black spiky hair and grey eyes kept popping into her mind. A little boy who would be fiercely loved and never have to face the hardships his father had endured.

She banished the bordering on insane thoughts to the area of her brain reserved for impossible dreams. Instead, she concentrated on confirming the delivery date of two hundred and ten—the ten for contingencies—small red-and-white-striped hand-knitted Christmas stockings for Dominic's party. They would sit in the centre of each place setting and contain all the cutlery required by that person for the meal.

She had decided on a simple red-and-white theme, aimed squarely at pleasing children as well as the inner child of the adults. Tables would be set up in the ballroom for a sit-down meal served from a buffet. She wanted it to be as magical and memorable as a Christmas lunch in the home of a billionaire should be—but without being intimidating.

Gemma had planned fabulous cakes, shaped and frosted like an outsize white candle and actually containing a tea light, to be the centrepiece of each table. Whimsical Santa-themed cupcakes would sit at each place with the name of the guest piped on the top. There would be glass bowls of candy canes and masses of Australian Christmas bush with its tiny red flowers as well as bowls of fat red cherries.

Andie would have loved to handle all the decorations herself but it was too big a job. She'd hired one of her favourite stylists to coordinate all the decorations. Jeremy was highly creative and she trusted his skills implicitly. And, importantly, he'd been happy to work on Christmas Day.

She'd been careful not to discuss anything too 'Christmassy' with Dominic, aware of his feelings about the festive season. He still hadn't shared with her just why he hated it so much; she wondered if he ever would. There was some deep pain there, going right back to his childhood, she suspected.

The alarm on her computer flashed a warning at her the same time the alarm on her watch buzzed. Not that she needed any prompts to alert her that she was seeing Dominic this evening.

He had been in meetings with Walter Burton all afternoon. Andie was to join them for dinner. At her suggestion, the meal was to be at Dominic's house. Andie felt that a man like Walter might prefer to experience home-style hospitality; he must be sick of hotels and restaurants. Not that Dominic's house was exactly the epitome of cosy, but it was elegant and beautiful and completely lacking in any brash, vulgar display of wealth.

A table set on the terrace at the front of the house facing the harbour. A chef to prepare the meal. A skilled waiter to serve them. All organised by Party Queens with a menu devised by Gemma. Eliza had, as a matter of course, checked with Walter's personal assistant as to the tycoon's personal dietary requirements.

Then there would be Andie, on her best fiancée behaviour. After all, Mr Burton's preference for doing business with a married man was the reason behind the fake engagement.

Not that she had any problem pretending to be an attentive fiancée. That part of the role came only too easily. Her heartbeat accelerated just at the thought of seeing Dominic this evening. He'd been away in different states on business and she'd only seen him a few times since the family dinner. She checked her watch again. There was plenty of time to get home to Newtown and then over to Vaucluse before the guest of honour arrived.

Dominic had been in Queensland on business and only flown back into Sydney last night. He'd met Walter Burton from a very early flight from the US this morning. After an afternoon of satisfactory meetings, Dominic had taken him back to his hotel. The American businessman would then make his own way to Vaucluse for the crucial dinner with Dominic and Andie.

As soon as he let himself in through the front door of the house Dominic sensed a difference. There was a subtle air of expectation, of warmth. The chef and his assistant were in the kitchen and, if enticing aromas had anything to do with it, dinner was under way. Arrangements of exotic orchids were discreetly arranged throughout the house. That was thanks to Andie.

It was all thanks to Andie. He would have felt uncomfortable hosting Walter Burton in his house if it weren't for her. He would have taken him to an upscale restaurant, which would have been nice but not the same. The older man had been very pleased at the thought of being invited to Dominic's home.

And now here she was, heading towards him from the terrace at the eastern end of the house where they would dine. He caught his breath at how beautiful she looked in a body-hugging cream top and matching long skirt that wrapped across the front and revealed, as she walked, tantalising glimpses of long slender legs and high heeled ankle-strap sandals. Her hair was up, but tousled strands fell around her face. Her only jewellery was her engagement ring. With her simple elegance, again she looked as if she belonged in this house.

'You're home,' she said in that husky voice, already so familiar.

Home. That was the difference in his house this evening. *Andie's presence made it a home.* And he had not felt he'd had a real home for a long time.

But Andie and her team were temporary hired help—she the lead actress in a play put on for the benefit of a visiting businessman. *This was all just for show.*

Because of Walter Burton, because there were strangers in the house, they had to play their roles—he the doting fiancé and she his betrothed.

Andie came close, smiling, raised her face for his kiss. Was that too for show? Or because she was genuinely glad to see him? At the touch of her lips, hunger for her instantly ignited. He closed his eyes as he breathed in her sweet, spicy scent, not wanting to let her go.

A waiter passed by on his way to the outdoor terrace, with a tray of wine glasses.

'I've missed you,' Andie murmured. For the waiter's benefit or for Dominic's? She sounded convincing but he couldn't be sure.

'Me too—missed you, I mean,' he said stiffly, self-consciously.

That was the trouble with this deception he had initiated. It was only too easy to get caught between a false intimacy and an intimacy that could possibly be real. Or could it? He broke away from her, stepped back.

'Is this another misbehaving skirt?' he asked.

He resisted the urge to run his hand over the curve of her hip. It would be an appropriate action for a fiancé but stepping over the boundaries of his agreement with Andie. Kisses were okay—their public displays of affection had to look authentic. Caresses of a more intimate nature, on the other hand, were *not* okay.

She laughed. 'No breeze tonight so we'll never know.' She lowered her voice. 'Is there anything else you need to brief me about before Mr Burton arrives? I've read through the background information you gave me. I think I'm up to speed on what a fiancée interested in her future husband's work would most likely know.'

'Good,' he said. 'I have every faith you won't let me down. If you're not sure of anything, just keep quiet and I'll cover for you. Not that I think I'll have to do that.'

'Fingers crossed I do you proud,' she said.

Walter Burton arrived punctually—Dominic would have been surprised if he hadn't. The more time he spent with his prospective joint venture partner, the more impressed he was by his acumen and professionalism. *He really wanted this deal.*

Andie greeted the older man with warmth and charm. Straight away he could see Walter was impressed.

She led him to the front terrace where the elegantly set round table—the right size for a friendly yet business orientated meal—had been placed against a backdrop of Sydney Harbour, sparkling blue in the light of the long summer evening. As they edged towards the longest day on December the twenty-second, it did not get dark until after nine p.m.

Christmas should be cold and dark and frosty. He pushed the painful thought away. Dwelling on the past was not appropriate here, not when an important deal hung in the balance.

Andie was immediately taken with Walter Burton. In his mid-sixties and of chunky build, his silver hair and close-trimmed silver beard gave him an avuncular appearance. His pale blue eyes actually sparkled and she had to keep reminding herself that he could not be as genial as he appeared and be such a successful tycoon.

But his attitude to philanthropy was the reason she was here, organising the party, pretending to be Dominic's betrothed. He espoused the view that making as much money as you could was a fine aim—so long as you remembered to share it with those who had less. 'It's a social responsibility,' he said.

Dominic had done nothing but agree with him. There was not a trace of Scrooge in anything he said. Andie had begun to believe the tag was purely a media invention.

Walter—he insisted she drop the 'Mr Burton'—seemed genuinely keen to hear all the details of the Christmas party. He was particularly interested when she told him Dominic had actively sought to dampen press interest. That had, as intended, flamed media interest. They already had two journalists volunteer to help out on that day—quite an achievement considering most people wanted to spend it with their families or close friends.

Several times during the meal, Andie squeezed Dominic's hand under the table—as a private signal that she thought the evening was going well. His smile in return let her know he thought so too. The fiancée fraud appeared to be doing the trick.

The waiter had just cleared the main course when Walter sat back in his chair, relaxed, well fed and praising the excellent food. Andie felt she and Dominic could also finally relax from the knife-edge of tension required to impress the American without revealing the truth of their relationship.

So Walter's next conversational gambit seemed to come from out of the blue. 'Of course you understand the plight of your Christmas Day guests, Dominic, as you've come from Struggle Street yourself,' he said. 'Yet you do your utmost to hide it.'

Dominic seemed shocked into silence. Andie watched in alarm as he blanched under his tan and gripped the edge of the table so his knuckles showed white. 'I'm not sure what you mean,' he said at last.

Walter's shrewd eyes narrowed. 'You've covered your tracks well, but I have a policy of never doing business with someone I haven't fully researched. I know about young Nick Hunt and the trouble he got into.'

Dominic seemed to go even paler. 'You mean the assault charge? Even though it never went to court. Even though I was a juvenile and there should be no record of it. How did you—?'

'Never mind how I found out. But I also discovered how much Dominic Hunt has given back to the world in which he had to fight to survive.' Walter looked to Andie. 'I guess you don't know about this, my dear.'

'Dominic has told me about his past,' she said cautiously. She sat at the edge of her seat, feeling trapped by uncertainty, terrified of saying the wrong thing, not wanting to reveal her ignorance of anything important. 'I also know how very generous he is.'

'Generous to the point that he funds a centre to help troubled young people in Brisbane.' Andie couldn't help a gasp of surprise that revealed her total lack of knowledge. 'He hasn't told you about his Underground Help Centre?' Walter didn't wait for her to answer. 'It provides safe emergency accommodation, health care, counselling, rehab—all funded by your fiancé. Altogether a most admirable venture.'

Why had Dominic let everyone think he was a Scrooge?

'You've done your research well, Walter,' Dominic said. 'Yes, I haven't yet told Andie about the centre. I wanted to take her to Brisbane and show her the work we do there.'

'I'll look forward to that, darling,' she said, not having to fake her admiration for him.

Dominic addressed both her and Walter. 'When I started to make serious money, I bought the abandoned shopping centre site where I'd sought refuge as a troubled runaway and redeveloped it. But part of the site was always going to be for the Underground Help Centre that I founded. I recruited Jim, the social worker who had helped me, to head it up for me.'

Andie felt she would burst with pride in him. Pride and something even more heartfelt. He must hate having to reveal himself like this.

Walter leaned towards Dominic. 'You're a self-made man and I admire that,' he said. 'You're sharing the wealth you acquired by your own hard work and initiative and I admire that too. What I don't understand, Dominic, is why you keep all this such a big secret. There's nothing to be ashamed of in having pulled yourself up by your bootstraps.'

'I'm not ashamed of anything I've done,' Dominic said. 'But I didn't want my past to affect my future success. Especially, I didn't want it to rub off on my business partner, Jake Marlow.'

Andie felt as if she was floundering. Dominic had briefed her on business aspects she might be expected to know about tonight, but nothing about this. She could only do what she felt was right. Without hesitation, she reached out and took his hand so they stood united.

'People can be very judgemental,' she said to Walter. 'And the media seem to be particularly unfair to Dominic. I'm incredibly proud of him and support his reasons for wanting to keep what he does in Brisbane private. To talk about that terrible time is to relive it, over and over again. From what Dominic has told me, living it once would be more than enough for anyone.'

Dominic squeezed her hand back, hard, and his eyes were warm with gratitude. Gratitude and perhaps—just perhaps—something more? 'I can't stop the nightmares of being back there,' he said. 'But I can avoid talking about it and bringing those times back to life.'

Andie angled herself to face Walter full-on. She was finding it difficult to keep her voice steady. 'If people knew about the centre they'd find out about his living rough and the assault charge. People who don't know him might judge him unfairly. At the same time, I'd love more people to know how generous and kind he actually is and—' She'd probably said enough.

Walter chuckled. 'Another thing he's done right is his choice of fiancée.'

Dominic reached over to kiss her lightly on the lips. 'I concur, Walter,' he said. Was it part of the act or did he really mean it?

'Th…thank you,' stuttered Andie. She added Walter to the list of people who would be disappointed when she dumped Dominic.

'I'm afraid I can't say the same for your choice of first wife,' Walter said.

Dominic visibly tensed. 'What do you mean?'

'I met with her and your former employee this morning. He's an impressive guy, though not someone I feel I want to do business with. But your ex-wife made it clear

she would do anything—and I stress *anything*—to seal
the deal. She suggested that to me—happily married for
more than forty years and who has never even looked at
another woman.'

Dominic made a sound of utter disgust but nothing
more. Andie thought more of him that he didn't say anything to disparage Tara, appalling though her behaviour
had been. Dominic had more dignity.

'The upshot of this is, Dominic, that you are exactly
the kind of guy I want to do business with. You and your
delightful wife-to-be. You make a great team.'

Dominic reached over to take Andie's hand again.
'Thank you, Walter. Thank you from us both.'

Andie smiled with lips that were aching from all her
false smiles and nodded her thanks. The fake engagement
had done exactly what it was intended to. She should be jubilant for Dominic's sake. But that also meant there would
soon be no need to carry on with it. And that made her
feel miserable. *She wasn't doing a very good job of guarding her heart.*

When Andie said goodnight to Dominic, she clung
to him for a moment longer than was necessary. Playing
wife-to-be for the evening had made her start to wish a
real relationship with Dominic could perhaps one day be
on the cards.

Perhaps it was a good thing she wouldn't see Dominic
again until Christmas Eve. He had to fly out to Minneapolis to finalise details with Walter, leaving her to handle
the countdown to the Christmas party. And trying not to
think too much about what had to happen after Christmas,
when her 'engagement' would come to an end.

CHAPTER THIRTEEN

IT WAS MIDDAY on Christmas Eve and as Andie pushed open the door into Dominic's house she felt as if she was stepping into a nightmare. The staircase railings were decorated as elegantly as she'd hoped, with tiny lights and white silk cord. The wreath on the door was superb. But dominating the marble entrance hall was an enormous Christmas tree, beautifully decorated with baubles and ornaments and winking with tiny lights. She stared at it in shocked disbelief. *What the heck was that doing there?*

When she said it out loud she didn't say *heck* and she didn't say it quietly.

Her stylist Jeremy's assistant had been rearranging baubles on the lower branches of the tree. She jumped at Andie's outburst and a silver bauble smashed on to the marble floor. Calmly, very calmly, Andie asked the girl where Jeremy was. The girl scuttled out to get him.

Throughout all the Christmas party arrangements, through all the fake fiancée dramas, Andie had kept her cool. Now she was in serious danger of losing it. She had planned this party in meticulous detail. Of all the things that could go wrong, it would have to be this—Dominic would think she had deliberately defied his specific demand. And she didn't want him thinking badly of her.

Jeremy came into the room with a swathe of wide red ribbons draped over his outstretched arm. Andie recognised them as the ones to be looped and tied into extravagant bows on the back of the two hundred chairs in the ballroom.

She had to grit her teeth to stop herself from exploding. 'Why is there a Christmas tree in here?' Her heart was racing with such panic she had to put her hand on her chest to try and slow it.

'Because this entrance space cried out for one. How can you have a Christmas party without a tree?' Jeremy said. 'I thought you'd made a mistake and left it off the brief. Doesn't it look fabulous?'

'It does indeed look fabulous. Except the client specifically said *no tree*.' She could hear her voice rising and took a deep breath to calm herself.

How had she let this happen? Maybe she should have written *NO CHRISTMAS TREE* in bold capitals on every page of the briefing document. She'd arrived here very early this morning to let the decorating crew in and to receive final deliveries of the extra furniture. Jeremy had assured her that all was on track. And it was—except for this darn tree.

'But why?' asked Jeremy. 'It seems crazy not to have a tree.'

Crazy? Maybe. She had no idea why—because Dominic, for all his talk with Walter Burton over dinner that night that had seemed so genuine, still refused to let her in on the events in his past he held so tightly to himself. He'd drip-fed some of the details but she felt there was something major linked to Christmas he would not share. It made her feel excluded—put firmly in her place as no one important in his life. And she wanted to be important to him. She swallowed hard. *Had she really just admitted that to herself?*

'The client actually has a thing against Christmas trees,' she said. 'You might even call it a phobia. For heaven's sake, Jeremy, why didn't you call me before you put this up?' Her mouth was dry and her hands felt clammy at the thought of Dominic's reaction if he saw the tree.

'I'm sorry,' said Jeremy, crestfallen. 'You didn't specify not to include a tree in the decorations. I was just using my initiative.'

On other jobs she'd worked with Jeremy she'd told him to think for himself and not bother her with constant calls, so she couldn't be *too* cranky with him. Creative people could be tricky to manage—and Jeremy's work was superb. The tree was, in fact, perfect for the spot where he'd placed it.

She took a step back to fully appraise its impact. The tree looked spectacular, dressed in silver with highlights of red, in keeping with her overall colour scheme. She sighed her pleasure at its magnificence. This perfect tree would make a breathtaking first impression for the guests tomorrow. To the children it would seem to be the entrance to a magical world. It spoke of tradition, of hope, of generosity. Everything they were trying to achieve with this party. It would make Dominic look good.

The beautiful tree was beginning to work its magic on her. Surely it would on Dominic too? He'd come such a long way since that first day, when he'd been so vehemently anti everything Christmas. *Christmas was not Christmas without a tree.*

She took a series of deep, calming breaths. Dominic should at least have the chance to see the tree in place. To see how wonderful it looked there. Maybe the sight of this tree would go some way towards healing those hidden deep wounds he refused to acknowledge.

She turned to Jeremy, the decision firm in her mind. 'We'll leave it. You've done such a good job on the tree, it would be a real shame to have to take it down.'

'What about the client?'

'He's a client but he's also my fiancé.' The lie threatened to choke her but she was getting more adept at spinning falsehoods. 'Leave him to me. In the meantime, let me give you a hand with placing the final few ornaments on the lower branches,' she said. She was wearing work clothes—jeans, sneakers and a loose white shirt. She rolled up her sleeves and picked up an exquisite glass angel. Her hand wasn't quite steady—if only she was as confident as she had tried to appear.

Dominic was due back in to Sydney early this evening. *What if he hated the tree?* Surely he wouldn't. He seemed so happy with everything else she'd done for the party; surely he would fall in love with the tree.

But it would take a Christmas miracle for him to fall in love with *her*.

She longed for that miracle. Because she couldn't deny it to herself any longer—she had developed feelings for him.

Dominic had managed to get an earlier flight out of Minneapolis to connect with a non-stop flight to Sydney from Los Angeles. Nonetheless, it was a total flight of more than twenty hours. Despite the comfort of first class, he was tired and anxious to get away from the snow and ice of Minnesota and home to sunny Sydney. A bitterly cold Christmas wasn't quite as he'd remembered it to be.

Overriding everything else, he wanted to get home to Andie. He had thought about her non-stop the whole trip, wished she'd been with him. Next time, he'd promised Walter, he'd bring Andie with him.

As the car he'd taken from the airport pulled up in front of his house, his spirits lifted at the thought of seeing her. He hadn't been able to get through to her phone, so he'd called Party Queens. Eliza had told him she was actually at his house in Vaucluse, working on the decorations for the party.

On the spur of the moment, he'd decided not to let her know he'd got in early. It might be better to surprise her. He reckoned if she didn't know he was coming, she wouldn't have time to put on her fake fiancée front. Her first reaction to him would give him more of a clue of her real feelings towards him.

Because while he was away he had missed her so intensely, he'd been forced to face *his* real feelings towards *her*. He was falling in love with her. Not only was he falling in love with her; he realised he had never had feelings of such intensity about a woman.

Melody had been his first love—and sweet, damaged Melody had loved him back to the extent she was capable of love. But it hadn't been enough. That assault charge had happened because he had been protecting her. Protecting her from a guy assaulting her in an alley not far from the takeaway food shop where he'd worked in the kitchen in return for food and a few dollars cash in hand.

But the guy had been her dealer—and possibly her pimp. Melody had squealed at Dominic to leave the guy alone. She'd shrieked at him that she knew what she was doing; she didn't need protecting. Dominic had ignored her, had pulled the creep off her, smashed his fist into the guy's face. Then the dealer's mates had shown up and Dominic had copped a beating too. But, although younger than the low-lifes, he'd been bigger, stronger and inflicted more damage. The cops had taken him in, while the others had disappeared into the dark corners that were their natural habitat. And Melody had gone with them without a backward glance, leaving him with a shattered heart as well as a broken nose. He'd never seen her again.

Of course Melody hadn't been her real name. He'd been too naïve to realise that at the time. Later, when he'd set up the Underground Help Centre, he'd tried to find her but without any luck. He liked to think she was living a safe happy life somewhere but the reality was likely to be less cosy than that.

Then there'd been Tara—the next woman to have betrayed him. The least thought he gave to his ex-wife the better.

But Andie. Andie was different. He felt his heart, frosted over for so long, warm when he thought about her. *What you saw was what you got.* Not only smart and beautiful, but loyal and loving. He'd told her more about his past than he'd ever told anyone. He could be himself with her, not have to pretend, be Nick as well as Dominic. Be not the billionaire but the man. Their relationship could be real. *He could spend his life with Andie.*

And he wanted to tell her just that.

The scent of pine needles assaulted his senses even before he put his key in his front door. The sharp resin smell instantly revived memories of that Christmas Eve when he'd been eleven years old and the happy part of his childhood had come to its terrible end. Christmas trees were the thing he most hated about Christmas.

The smell made him nauseous, started a headache throbbing in his temples. Andie must be using pine in some of the decorations. It would have to go. He couldn't have it in the house.

He pushed the door silently open—only to recoil at what he saw.

There was a Christmas tree in his house. A whopping great Christmas tree, taking up half his entrance hallway and rising high above the banisters of the staircase.

What the hell? He had told Andie in no uncertain terms there was to be no Christmas tree—anywhere. He gritted his teeth and fisted his hands by his sides. *How could she be so insensitive?*

There was a team of people working on the tree and its myriad glitzy ornaments. Including Andie. He'd never thought she could be complicit in this defiance of his wishes. He felt let down. *Betrayed.*

She turned. Froze. Her eyes widened with shock and alarm when she saw him. A glass ornament slid from her hands and smashed on the floor but she scarcely seemed to notice.

'What part of "no Christmas tree" did you not get, Andie?'

She got up from her kneeling position and took a step towards him, put up her hands as if to ward off his anger. The people she was with scuttled out of the room, leaving them alone. But he bet they were eavesdropping somewhere nearby. The thought made him even more livid.

'Dominic, I'm sorry. I know you said no tree.'

'You're damn right I did.'

'It was a mistake. The tree was never meant to be here. There were some…some crossed lines. I wasn't expecting it either. But then I saw it and it's so beautiful and looks so right here. I thought you might…appreciate it, might see how right it is and want to keep it.'

He could feel the veins standing out on his neck, his hands clenched so tight they hurt. 'I don't see it as beautiful.'

Her face flushed. She would read that as an insult to her skills. He was beyond caring. 'Why? Why do you hate Christmas trees?' she said. 'Why this…this irrational dislike of Christmas?'

Irrational? He gritted his teeth. 'That's none of your concern.'

'But I want it to be. I thought I could help you. I—'

'You thought wrong.'

Now her hands were clenched and she was glaring at him. 'Why won't you share it with me—what makes you hurt so much at this time of year? Why do I have to guess? Why do I have to tiptoe around you?' Her voice rose with each question as it seemed her every frustration and doubt rushed to the surface.

Dominic was furious. How dared she put him through this…this humiliation?

'Don't forget your place,' he said coldly. 'I employ you.' With each word he made a stabbing motion with his finger to emphasise the words. 'Get rid of the tree. Now.'

He hated the stricken look on Andie's face, knowing he had put it there. But if she cared about him at all she never would have allowed that tree to enter his house. He could barely stand to look at her.

For a long moment she didn't say anything. 'Yes,' she said finally, her voice a dull echo of its usual husky charm. 'Yes, sir,' she added.

In a way he appreciated the defiance of the hissed 'sir'. But he was tired and jet-lagged and grumpy and burning with all the pain and loss he associated with Christmas— and Christmas trees in particular. Above all, he was disappointed in her that she thought so little of his wishes that she would defy him.

His house was festooned with festive paraphernalia. Everywhere he looked, it glittered and shone, mocking him. He'd been talked into this damn party against his wishes. *He hated Christmas.* He uttered a long string of curses worthy of Scrooge.

'I'm going upstairs. Make sure this tree is gone when I come back down. And all your people as well.' He glared in the general direction of the door through which her team had fled.

She met his glare, chin tilted upwards. 'It will take some time to dismantle the tree,' she said. 'But I assure you I will get rid of every last stray needle so you will never know it was there.' She sounded as though she spoke through gritted teeth. 'However, I will need all my crew to help me. We have to be here for at least a few more hours. We still have to finish filling the goody bags and setting the tables.' She glared at him. 'This is *your* party. And you know as well as I do that it must go on. To prove you're not the Scrooge people think you are.'

Some part of him wanted to cross the expanse of floor between them and hug her close. To tell her that of course he understood. That he found it almost impossible to talk about the damage of his childhood. To knuckle down and help her adorn his house for the party tomorrow. But the habits of Christmases past were hard to break.

So was the habit of closing himself off from love. Letting himself love Andie would only end in disappointment and pain, like it had with every other relationship. For her as well as himself. *It seemed he was incapable of love.*

'Text me when you're done,' he said.

He stomped up the stairs to his study. And the bottle of bourbon that waited there.

Andie felt humiliated, angry and upset. How dared Dominic speak to her like that? *'Don't forget your place.'* His harsh words had stabbed into her heart.

Jeremy poked his head around the door that connected through to the living room. She beckoned him to come in. She forced her voice to sound businesslike, refused to let even a hint of a tear burr her tone. 'I told you he wouldn't be happy with the tree.' Her effort at a joke fell very flat.

'Don't worry about it,' Jeremy said, putting a comforting hand on her shoulder. 'We'll get rid of this tree quick-smart. No matter your man is in a mood. The show has to go on. You've got two hundred people here for lunch tomorrow.'

'Thanks, Jeremy,' she said. 'Dominic has just got off a long flight. He's not himself.' But her excuses for him sounded lame even to her own ears.

Was that angry man glaring at her with his fists clenched at his sides the true Dominic? She'd known the anger was there bubbling below the surface, was beginning to understand the reasons for it. But she'd thought that anger that had driven him to violence was in his past. How could she possibly have thought she'd fallen in love with him? She didn't even know the man.

'What do you suggest we do with the tree?' Jeremy asked. 'There are no returns on cut trees.'

Andie's thoughts raced. 'We've got a Christmas Eve party happening elsewhere tonight. The clients have put up a scrappy old artificial tree that looks dreadful. We'll get this delivered to them with the compliments of Party Queens. Keep whatever ornaments you can use here; the rest we'll send with the tree. Let's call a courier truck now.'

Seething, she set to work dismantling the beautiful tree. As she did so, she felt as if she were dismantling all her hopes and dreams for love with Dominic. The diamond ring felt like a heavy burden on her finger, weighted by its duplicity and hypocrisy. While he'd stood there insulting her, she'd felt like taking the ring off and hurling it at him. If it had hit him and drawn blood she would have been glad. His words had been so harsh they felt like they'd drawn blood from her heart.

But of course she couldn't have thrown her ring at him while there were other people in the house. She would be professional right to the end. After all, wasn't she known for her skill at dealing with difficult people?

In spite of that, she'd had her fill of this particular difficult man. He'd got what he wanted from her in terms of his American deal. She'd got what her family needed for Timothy. Both sides of the bargain fulfilled. He'd been her employer, her fake fiancé—she'd liked to think they'd become friends of a sort. She'd wanted more—but that was obviously not to be. She'd stick it out for the Christmas lunch. Then she'd be out of here and out of his life.

The crew worked efficiently and well. When they were done and the tree was gone she waved them goodbye and wished them a Merry Christmas. But not before asking them to please not repeat what they might have heard today. Talk of Dominic's outburst could do serious damage to the rehabilitation of his Scrooge image.

By the time they had all gone it was early evening. She stood and massaged the small of her back where it ached. She would let Dominic know she was done and going home. But she had no intention of texting him as he'd asked. Not asked. *Demanded.* She had things to say that had to be said in person.

CHAPTER FOURTEEN

WITH A HEAVY HEART—wounded hearts *hurt*—Andie made
her way up the stylishly decorated staircase, its tiny lights
discreetly winking. She hadn't been up here before, as
this part of the house was off-limits for the party. When
she thought of it, she actually had no idea where Dominic could be.

The first two doors opened to two fashionably furnished
empty bedrooms. The third bedroom was obviously his—a
vast bed with immaculate stone-coloured linens, arched
windows that opened to a sweeping view of the harbour.
But he wasn't there.

Then she noticed a door ajar to what seemed like a
study.

There was no response to her knock, so she pushed
it open. The blinds were drawn. Dominic lay sprawled
asleep on a large chesterfield sofa. The dull light of a tall,
arching floor lamp pooled on him and seemed to put him
in the spotlight.

His black lace-up business shoes lay haphazardly at the
end of the sofa. He had taken off his jacket and removed
his tie. The top buttons of his shirt were undone to reveal
an expanse of bare, well-muscled chest her traitorous libido
could not help but appreciate as it rose and fell in his sleep.

His right arm fell to the floor near a bottle of bourbon.
Andie picked it up. The bottle was nearly full, with probably no more than a glassful gone. Not enough for him to

be drunk—more likely collapsed into the sleep of utter exhaustion. She put the bottle on the desk.

There was a swivel-footed captain's chair near the sofa with a padded leather seat. She sat on the edge of it and watched Dominic as he slept. Darn it, but that wounded heart of hers beat faster as she feasted her eyes on his face, which had become so familiar. So…so—she nearly let herself think *so beloved*. But that couldn't be.

She swallowed hard at the lump that rose in her throat. Why on earth had she let herself fall for a man who was so difficult, so damaged, so completely opposite to the man who had made her so happy in the past?

Dominic's hair stood up in spikes. He obviously hadn't shaved since he'd left Minneapolis and his beard was in that stubble stage she found so incredibly sexy. She hadn't realised how long and thick his eyelashes were. His mouth was slightly parted. She longed to lean over and kiss it. She sighed. There would be no more kissing of this man.

He moaned in his sleep and she could see rapid eye movement behind his lids as if he were being tortured by bad dreams. She could not help but reach out to stroke his furrowed forehead. He returned to more restful sleep. Then his eyes flickered open. Suddenly he sat up, startling her. He looked around, disorientated, eyes glazed with sleep. He focused on her.

'Andie,' he breathed. 'You're here.' He gave a huge sigh, took her hand and kissed it. 'I didn't think I'd ever see you again.'

He didn't deserve to, she thought. But her resolve was weakening.

'Are you okay?' she said, trying to ignore the shivers of pleasure that ran up her arm from his kiss. He had been rude and hurtful to her.

'I've just had a horrible dream,' he said.

'What kind of dream?'

'A nightmare. I was in a cemetery and saw my own headstone.'

She shook her head. 'No, Dominic—I don't want to hear this.' The day of Anthony's funeral had been the worst day of her life. When she'd had to accept she'd never see him again. She couldn't bear to think of Dominic buried under a headstone.

But he continued in a dramatic tone she didn't think was appropriate for such a gruesome topic. 'It said: 'Here lies Dominic—they called him Scrooge'. And I think it was Christmas Day.'

Not so gruesome after all. She couldn't help a smile.

'You think my nightmare was funny?' he said, affronted.

'I'm sure it was scary at the time. But you'll never be called Scrooge again. Not after tomorrow. I…I'm sorry about what I said earlier. About your…your Scroogeness, I mean.'

He slammed the hand that wasn't holding hers against his forehead. 'The Christmas tree. I'm sorry, Andie. That was unforgivable. Pay your crew a bonus to make up for it, will you, and bill it to me.'

Did he think everything could be solved by throwing money at it?

'I'm also sorry about the tree, Dominic. It was an honest mistake. It's all gone now.'

Maybe she'd been in the wrong too, to imagine he might like the tree when he'd been so vehement about not having one in the house. But she hadn't been wrong about expecting better behaviour from him.

He shuddered. 'It was a shock. The smell of it. The sight of it. Brought back bad memories.'

She shifted in her seat but did not let go of his hand. 'Do you think it might be time to tell me why Christmas trees upset you so much? Because I didn't like seeing that anger. Especially not directed at me. How can I understand you when I don't know what I'm dealing with?'

He grimaced as if stabbed by an unpleasant memory. 'I suppose I have to tell you if I want you to ever talk to me again.'

'I'm talking to you now.'

She remembered what she'd said about recalling unpleasant memories being like reliving them. But this had to come out—one way or another. Better it was with words than fists.

'Christmas Eve is the anniversary of my parents' deaths.'

She squeezed his hand. 'Dominic, I'm so sorry.' That explained a lot. 'Why didn't you say so before?'

'I...I didn't want people feeling sorry for me,' he said gruffly.

'People wouldn't have... Yes, they would have felt sorry for you. But in a good way.' Could all this Scrooge business have been solved by him simply explaining that? 'Can you tell me about it now?'

'There...there's more. It was cold and frosty. My parents went out to pick up the Christmas tree. A deer crossed the road and they braked to avoid it. The road was icy and the car swerved out of control and crashed into a barrier. That's how they died. Getting the damn Christmas tree.'

She couldn't find the words to say anything other than she was sorry again.

'It was...it was my fault they died.'

Andie frowned. 'How could it be your fault? You were eleven years old.'

'My aunt told me repeatedly for the next six years it was my fault.'

'I think you'd better tell me some more about this aunt.'

'The thing is, it really *was* my fault. I'd begged my parents for a real tree. We had a plastic one. My best friend had a real one; I wanted a real one. If they hadn't gone out to get the tree I wanted they wouldn't have died.'

'You've been blaming yourself all these years? It was an accident. How any competent adult could let you blame yourself, I can't imagine.'

'Competent adult and my aunt aren't compatible terms,' he said, the bitterness underlying his words shocking her.

'I keep asking you about her; it's time you gave me some answers.' Though she was beginning to dread what she might hear.

'She used alcohol and prescription meds to mask her serious psychological problems. I know that now as an adult. As a kid, I lived with a bitter woman who swung between abuse and smothering affection.'

'And, as a kid, you put up with a lot in the hope of love,' Andie said softly, not sure if Dominic actually heard her. She could see the vulnerability in that strong-jawed hand-some face, wondered how many people he had ever let be aware of it. She thought again of that little boy with the dark hair. Her vision of Dominic's son merged with that of the young, grieving, abused Dominic. And her heart went out to him.

The words spilled out of him now, words that expressed emotions dammed for years. 'She was particularly bad at Christmas because that's when she'd lost her sister—which was, in her eyes, my fault. When she got fed up with me, she locked me in a cupboard. The physical abuse stopped when I got bigger than her. The mental abuse went on until the day I ran away. Yet all that time she held down a job and presented a reasonable face to the world. I talked to a teacher at school and he didn't believe me. Told me to man up.'

'I honestly don't know what to say…' But she hated his aunt, even though she was aware she'd been a deeply trou-bled person. No child should be treated like that.

'Say nothing. I don't want to talk about it any more. I'm thirty-two years old. That was all a long time ago.'

'But, deep down, you're still hurting,' she whispered. 'Dominic, I'm so sorry you had to go through all that. And I admire you so much for what you became after such a difficult start.'

Words could only communicate so much. Again, she felt that urge to comfort him. This time, she acted on it. She leaned over to him and kissed him, tasted bourbon on his lips, welcomed the scrape of his stubble on her skin. Immediately, he took the kiss deeper.

The kiss went on and on, passion building, thrilling her. But it was more than sensual pleasure; it was a new sense of connection, of shared emotion as well as sensation.

He broke the kiss to pull her shirt up and over her head. His shirt was already half unbuttoned. It didn't take much to have it completely undone and to slide it off his broad shoulders and muscular arms. She caught her breath in awe at the male perfection of his body.

She wanted him. Dominic had got what he wanted from Walter. Timothy was booked for the treatment he needed. She had promised herself to go after what she wanted—him—and now was her time. It might never be more than this. She knew it and was prepared to take that risk. But she hoped for so much more.

She hadn't known him for long but she had the same kind of certainty—that it could be for ever—as she'd felt for Anthony. A certainty she'd thought she'd never feel again. *For ever love.* Had she been given a chance for that special connection again? She thought *yes*, but could she convince Dominic she could bring him the kind of happiness that had seemed to evade him—that he deserved?

He threw his head back and moaned his pleasure as she planted urgent kisses down the firm column of his throat, then back up to claim his mouth again. He tasted so good, felt so good.

He caught her hands. 'Andie, is this what you want? Because we have to stop it now if you don't,' he said, his voice husky with need.

'Don't you dare stop,' she murmured.

He smiled a slow, seductive smile that sent her heart rate rocketing. 'In that case…' He unfastened the catch on her jeans. 'Let's see if we can get these jeans to misbehave…'

Satisfied, replete, her body aching in the most pleasurable of ways, Andie drowsed in his arms as Dominic slept. But she couldn't let herself sleep.

If she'd been a different kind of person she would have stayed there. Perhaps convinced Dominic to shower with her when they woke. She would enjoy soaping down that powerful body. Heaven knew what kind of fun they could have with the powerful jets of water in his spacious double shower. Then they could retire to spend the rest of the evening in that enormous bed of his.

But Andie was not that person. There was the Christmas Eve party she had committed to this evening. As the party planner, she was obliged to call in to see all was well. She also had to check the big tree had made its way there safely—though the eighteen-year-old daughter had texted Andie to thank her, thrilled with the 'real tree'.

There was nothing like the smell of pine resin and the beauty of a natural tree. As eleven-year-old Dominic had known. Her heart went out to that little boy who lived in the damaged soul of the big male, sleeping naked next to her, his arm thrown possessively over her. She was also naked, except for her engagement ring, shining with false promise under the lamplight.

She had agreed to see her family tonight. Tomorrow, Christmas Day, would be the first Christmas lunch she had not spent with them. She was surprised her father had taken it so lightly. 'You have to stand by Dominic, love. That party is not just a job for you now. You're his future wife.'

If only.

Reluctantly, she slid away from Dominic, then quietly got dressed. She would see him in the morning. Tomorrow was Christmas Day, a holiday she loved and he hated. Now she could see why. She ached to turn things around for him—if he would let her.

She looked at his face, more relaxed than she had seen it, and smiled a smile that was bittersweet. They had made love and it had been magnificent. But nothing had changed between them. Tomorrow she was facing the biggest party of her career so far. She would be by the side of the man she had fallen in love with, not knowing for how much longer he would be a part of her life.

When the truth was, she wanted Dominic for Christmas. Not just his body—his heart as well.

Somehow, tomorrow she would have to confess to Dominic the truth of how she felt about him. That she wanted to try a relationship for real. She hoped he felt the same. If so, this would be the best Christmas she had ever had. If not... Well, she couldn't bear to think about *if not.*

CHAPTER FIFTEEN

DOMINIC AWOKE ON Christmas morning as he was accustomed to waking on December the twenty-fifth—alone. It was very early, pale sunlight filtering through the blinds. He reached out his hand to the sofa beside him in the vain hope that Andie might still be there, only to find the leather on that side disappointingly cool to the touch. He closed his eyes again and breathed in the scent of her that lingered in the room, on his skin. Then was overtaken by an anguished rush of longing for her that made him double over with gut-wrenching pain.

He remembered her leaving his side, her quiet footsteps around the room, the rustling as she slid on her clothes. Then her leaning towards him, murmuring that she had to go. She had duties, obligations. He'd pulled her back close to him, tried to convince her with his hands, with his mouth why she should stay. But she'd murmured her regret, kissed him with a quick fierce passion, told him he had jet lag to get over. Then she'd gone.

All he'd wanted to say to her still remained unsaid.

Of course she'd gone to the other people in her life who needed her and loved her. The only commitment she'd made to him was based on the falsehoods he'd engendered and coerced her into. She'd played her role to perfection. So well he was uncertain what might be fact and what might be fiction. But surely making love to him with such passion and tenderness had not been play-acting?

He noticed the bourbon bottle on the desk, lid on, barely touched. This would be the first Christmas he could remember that he hadn't tried to obliterate. The first Christmas that he woke to the knowledge that while Andie might not be here now, she soon would be. And that his perfect, empty house would be filled with people. People who had known hardship like he had and whom he was in the position to help by making their Christmas Day memorable.

Not for the first time, he thought of the possibility of opening a branch of the Underground Help Centre here in Sydney, where it was so obviously needed. Profits from the joint venture with Walter could help fund it. He had much to learn from Walter—he could see it was going to end up a friendship as well as a business partnership.

For the first Christmas in a long time he had something to look forward to—and it was all thanks to Andie.

He hauled himself off the sofa and stretched out the cricks in his back. The sofa was not the best place to sleep—though it had proved perfectly fine for energetic lovemaking. He paused, overwhelmed by memories of the night before. *Andie.* Hunger for her threatened to overwhelm him again—and not just for her beautiful, generous body. He prayed to whatever power that had brought her to him to let him keep her in his life. He hoped she would forgive the way he'd behaved—understand why. And know that it would never happen again.

He headed down the stairs and stood in the entrance hall. Not a trace of the tree remained, thank heaven. He breathed in. And none of that awful smell. Andie had been well meaning but misguided about the tree—now she understood.

The ballroom was all set up, with tables and chairs adorned in various combinations of red and white. A large buffet table area stretched along the wall closest to the kitchen. He'd approved the menu with Gemma and knew within hours it would be groaning with a lavish festive feast. The dishes had been chosen with the diverse backgrounds of the guests in mind—some were refugees experiencing their first Christmas in Australia.

He still couldn't have tolerated a tree in the house but he had to admit to a stirring of interest in the celebrations—more interest than he'd had in Christmas since he'd been a child. Andie was clever—children would love all this and adults should also respond to the nostalgia and hope it evoked. Hadn't she said Christmas was about evoking emotion?

Thanks to the tragedy on Christmas Eve all those years ago, thanks to the way his aunt had treated him in the years that followed, the emotions the season had evoked for him had been unhappy in the extreme. Was there a chance now for him to forge new, happy memories with a kind, loving woman who seemed to understand his struggles?

Andie had said he could trust her, but after his display of anger over the Christmas tree last night would she let herself trust *him*?

There was a large Santa Claus figurine in the corner with rows of canvas, sunshine-themed goody bags stacked around it. Of course it should have been a tree—but the Santa worked okay too as a compromise. The sturdy bags could double as beach bags, the ever-practical Andie had pointed out to him. She had thought of everything. There were gifts there for the volunteers too.

The house seemed to hum with a quiet anticipation and he could feel his spirits rise. Christmas Day with Andie in his house must surely be a step up on the ones he'd been forced to endure up until now.

He swung open the doors and headed to his gym for a workout.

* * *

An hour later Andie arrived with the chef and his crew. Dominic had long given her a pass code to get in and out of fortress Vaucluse.

She was wearing working gear of shorts, T-shirt and sneakers. Later she would change into her beautiful new red lace dress and gorgeous shoes—strappy and red with tassels—in time to greet their guests. She took her dress on its hanger and her bag into the downstairs bathroom. As she did, she noticed the doors to the garden were open and someone was in the pool. She went out to investigate.

Of course it was Dominic, his powerful body spearing through the water. No wonder he had such well-developed muscles with vigorous swimming like this. She watched, mesmerised at his rhythmic strokes, the force of his arms and powerful kick propelling him with athletic grace.

She didn't say anything but maybe her shadow cast on the water alerted him to her presence. Maybe he caught sight of her when he turned his head to breathe. He swam to the edge of the pool and effortlessly pulled himself out of the water, muscles rippling. He wasn't even out of breath.

She almost swooned at the sight of him—could a man be more handsome? Memories of the ecstasy they had given each other the night before flashed through her, tightening her nipples and flooding her body with desire.

His wet hair was slick to his head, the morning sunlight refracted off droplets of water that clung to his powerfully developed shoulders and cut chest, his veins stood out on his biceps, pumped from exertion. And then there were the classic six-pack, the long, strong legs. He didn't have a lot of body hair for such a dark man, but what there was seemed to flag his outrageous masculinity.

She wanted him more than ever. Not just for a night. For many nights. Maybe every night for the rest of her life. There was so much she wanted to say to him but, for all the connection and closeness and *certainty* she had felt last night, she didn't know how to say it.

Her engagement ring glinted on her left hand. The deal with Walter was done. Dominic's Scrooge reputation was likely to be squashed after the party today. How much longer would this ring stay on her finger? What, if anything, would be her role in Dominic's life? She wanted to say something about last night, bring up the subject of the future, but she just couldn't. 'Happy Christmas,' she said instead, forcing every bit of enthusiasm she could muster into her voice.

He grabbed a towel from the back of the chair and slung it around his shoulders, towelling off the excess water. 'H... Happy Christmas to you too,' he said, his voice rusty in the way of someone unused to uttering those particular words. She wondered how long since he had actually wished anyone the Season's greetings.

He looked down into her face and she realised by the expression in his eyes that he might be as uncertain as she was.

Hope flared in her heart. 'Dominic, I—'

'Andie, I—'

They both spoke at the same time. They laughed. Tried again.

'About last night,' he said.

'Yes?' she said.

'I wanted to—'

But she didn't hear what he had to say, didn't get a chance to answer because at that moment the chef called from the doors that opened from the ballroom that Gemma and Eliza were there and needed to be buzzed in.

Dominic groaned his frustration at the terminated conversation. Andie echoed his groan.

'Later,' she said as she turned away, knowing that it

would be highly unlikely for them to get another private moment together for the next few hours.

Dominic found the amount of noise two hundred people could generate—especially when so many of them were children—quite astounding. He stood on the edge of the party, still at the meet-and-greet stage, with appetisers and drinks being passed around by waiters dressed as Christmas elves.

Santa Claus, otherwise known as Rob Cratchit, his Director of Marketing, sidled up next to him. 'It's going even better than I expected,' he said through his fake white beard. 'See that woman over there wiping tomato sauce off the little boy's shirt? She's a journalist, volunteering for the day, and one of your most strident Scrooge critics. She actually called you a multi-million-dollar miser. But I think she's already convinced that today is not some kind of cynical publicity stunt.'

'Good,' said Dominic. Strange that the original aim of this party—to curry favour with Walter Burton—seemed to have become lost. Now it was all about giving people who had it tough a heart-warming experience and a good meal. And enjoying it with Andie by his side.

'Good on you for dressing up as Santa Claus,' he said to Rob. Andie had been right—Rob made the perfect Santa and he had the outgoing personality to carry it off.

'Actually, *you're* the Santa Claus. I talked to one nice lady, a single mum, who said her kids would not have got Christmas lunch or a Christmas present this year, unless a charity had helped out. She said this was so much better than charity. You should mingle—a lot of people want to thank you.'

'I'm not the mingling type,' Dominic said. 'I don't need to be thanked. I just signed the cheques. It should be Andie they're thanking; this was all her idea.'

'She's brilliant,' said Rob. 'Smart of you to snap her up so quickly. You're a lucky man.'

'Yes,' said Dominic, not encouraging further conversation. He'd never been happy discussing his personal life with anyone. The thought that—unless he said something to her—this might be the last day he had with Andie in his life was enough to sink him into a decidedly unfestive gloom.

He hadn't been able to keep his eyes off Andie as she flitted around the room, looking her most beautiful in a very stylish dress of form-fitting lace in a dusky shade of Christmas red. It was modest but hugged every curve and showed off her long, gorgeous legs. He tried not to think of how it had felt to have those legs wrapped around him last night...

'Well, mustn't linger,' said Rob. 'I have to be off and do the *ho-ho-ho* thing.'

As Rob made his way back into the throng, Andie rang a bell for attention and asked everyone to move towards the entrance hall. 'Some of the children and their parents are singing carols for us today.' She'd told Dominic a few of the adults were involved in street choirs and had been happy to run through the carols with the kids.

There was a collective gasp from the 'audience' as they saw the children lined up on the stairs, starting from the tiniest to the teenagers with the adults behind. Again Andie had been right—the stairs made the most amazing showcase for a choir. Each of the choir members wore a plain red T-shirt with the word *'choir'* printed in white lowercase letters. It was perfect, gave them an identity without being ostentatious.

Andie met his gaze from across the room and she smiled. He gave her a discreet thumbs-up. Professional pride? Or something more personal?

The choir started off with the Australian Christmas

carol 'Six White Boomers' where Santa's reindeer were replaced by big white kangaroos for the Australian toy delivery. It was a good icebreaker, and had everyone laughing and clapping and singing along with the chorus.

As Dominic watched, he was surprised to see Andie playing guitar up on the balcony with two other guitarists. She was singing too, in a lovely warm soprano. He remembered that photo of her playing guitar in the hallway of her parents' home and realised how much there was he still didn't know about her—and how much he wanted to know.

When the choir switched to classics like 'Silent Night' and 'Away in a Manger', Dominic found himself transported back to the happy last Christmas when his parents were alive and they'd gone carol singing in their village. *How could he have forgotten?*

The music and the pure young voices resonated and seemed to unlock a well of feeling he'd suppressed—unable perhaps to deal with the pain of it during those years of abuse by his aunt. He'd thought himself incapable of love—because he had been without love. But he *had* been loved back then, by his parents and his grandparents—loved deeply and unconditionally.

He'd yearned for that love again but had never found it. His aunt had done her best to destroy him emotionally but the love that had nurtured him as a young child must have protected him. The realisation struck him—he had loved women incapable of loving him back, and all this time had thought the fault was his when those relationships had failed.

Andie's voice soared above the rest of the choir. Andie, who he sensed had a vast reserve of love locked away since she'd lost her boyfriend. He wanted that love for himself and he wanted to give her the love she needed. How could he tell her that?

He tried to join in with the words of the carol but his throat closed over. He pretended to cough. Before he made an idiot of himself by breaking down, he pushed his way politely through the crowd and made his way out to the cabana, the only place where he could be alone and gather his thoughts.

But he wasn't alone for long. Andie, her eyes warm with concern, was soon with him. 'Dominic, are you okay?' she said, her hand on his arm. 'I know how you feel about Christmas and I was worried—'

'I'm absolutely fine—better than I've been for a long time,' he said.

He picked up her left hand. 'Take off your ring and give it to me, please.'

Andie froze. She stared at him for a long moment, trying to conceal the pain from the shaft of hurt that had stabbed her heart. So it had come to this so soon. Her use was over. Fake fiancée no longer required. Party planner no longer required. Friend, lover, confidante and whatever else she'd been to him no longer required. *She was surplus to requirements.*

Dominic had proved himself to be generous and thoughtful way beyond her initial expectations of Scrooge. But she must not forget the cold, hard fact—people who got to be billionaires in their twenties must have a ruthless streak. And he'd reneged on his offer that she could keep the ring—not that she'd had any intention of doing so. To say she was disappointed would be the world's biggest understatement.

She felt as though all the energy and joy was flowing out of her to leave just a husk. The colour drained from her face—she must look like a ghost.

With trembling fingers, she slid off the magnificent ring and gave it back to him, pressing it firmly into the palm of his hand. Her finger felt immediately empty, her hand unbalanced.

'It's yours,' she said and turned on her heel, trying not to stagger. She would not cry. She would not say anything snarky to him. She would just walk out of here with dignity. *This was her worst Christmas Day ever.*

'Wait! Andie! Where are you going?'

She turned back to see Dominic with a look of bewilderment on his handsome, tough face. 'You're not going to leave me here with your ring?'

Now it was her turn to feel bewildered. '*My* ring? Then why—?' she managed to choke out.

He took her hand again and held it in a tight grip. 'I'm not doing a good job of this, am I?'

He drew her closer, cleared his throat. 'Andie, I... I love you, and I'm attempting to ask you to marry me. I'm hoping you'll say "yes", so I can put your ring back on your wedding finger where it belongs, as your *real* fiancé, as a *real* engagement ring. Just like you told me you wanted.'

She was stunned speechless. The colour rushed back into her face.

'Well?' he prompted. 'Andrea Jane Newman, will you do me the honour of becoming my wife?'

Finally she found her words. Although she only needed the one. 'Yes,' she said. 'I say "yes".'

With no further ado, he slid the beautiful ring back into its rightful place. To her happy eyes it seemed to flash even more brilliantly.

'Dominic, I love you too. I think maybe it *was* love at first sight the day I met you. I never really had to lie about that.'

She wound her arms around his neck and kissed him. They kissed for a long time. Until they were interrupted by a loud knock on the door of the pool house. Gemma.

'Hey, you two, I don't know what's going on in there

and I don't particularly want to know, but we're about to serve lunch and your presence is required.'

'Oh, yes, of course—we're coming straight away,' Andie called, flustered.

Dominic held her by the arm. 'Not so fast. There's something else I want to ask you. What would you like for Christmas?'

His question threw her. She had to think very hard. But then it came to her. 'All I want for Christmas is for us to get married as soon as possible. I... I don't want to wait. You...you know why.'

Anthony would have wanted this for her—to grab her second chance of happiness. She knew that as certainly as if he'd been there to give her his blessing.

'That suits me fine,' Dominic said. 'The sooner you're my wife the better.'

'Of course it takes a while to organise a wedding. Next month. The month after. I don't want anything too fussy anyway, just simple and private.'

'We'll have to talk to the Party Queens,' he said.

She laughed. 'Great idea. I have a feeling we'll be the best people for the job.'

She could hardly believe this was true, but the look in his eyes told her she could believe it. She wound her arms around his neck again. 'Dominic Hugo Hunt, you've just made this the very best Christmas of my life.'

He heaved a great sigh and she could see it was as if the weight of all those miserable Christmases he'd endured in the past had been thrown off. 'Me too,' he said. 'And all because of you, my wonderful wife-to-be.'

CHAPTER SIXTEEN

ANDIE FOUND HERSELF singing 'Rudolph the Red-Nosed Reindeer' as she drove to Dominic's house five days later. She couldn't remember when she'd last sung in the car—and certainly not such a cheesy carol as 'Rudolph'. No, wait. 'Six White Boomers' was even cheesier. But the choir had been so wonderful at Dominic's Christmas party she'd felt it had become the heart of the very successful party. The carols had stayed in her head.

It had only been significant to her, but it was the first time she'd played her guitar and sung in public since Anthony had died. She'd healed in every way from the trauma of his loss, although she would never forget him. Her future was with Dominic. How could she ever have thought he was not her type?

She didn't think Dominic would be burdened with the Scrooge label for too much longer. One of his most relentless critics had served as a volunteer at the party—and had completely changed her tune. Andie had committed to heart the journalist's article in one of the major newspapers.

Dominic Hunt appears more Santa Claus than Scrooge, having hosted a lavish Christmas party, not for celebrities and wealthy silvertails but for ordinary folk down on their luck. A publicity stunt? No way.

She suspected Dominic's other private philanthropic work would eventually be discovered—probably by the digging of this same journalist. But, with the support of her love and the encouragement of Walter Burton, she thought he was in a better place to handle the revelations of his past if and when they came to light.

Dominic had invited her for a special dinner at his house this evening, though they'd had dinner together every evening since Christmas—and breakfast. She hadn't been here for the last few days; rather, he'd stayed at her place. She didn't want to move in with him until they were married.

But he'd said they had to do something special this evening as they wouldn't be able to spend New Year's Eve together—December the thirty-first would be the Party Queens' busiest night yet.

She was looking forward to dinner together, just the two of them. It was a warm evening and she wore a simple aqua dress that was both cool and elegant. Even though they were now engaged for real, they were still getting to know each other—there was a new discovery each time they got the chance to truly talk.

As she climbed the stairs to his house, she heard the sounds of a classical string quartet playing through the sound system he had piped through the house. Dominic had good taste in music, thank heaven. But when she pushed open the door, she was astounded to see a live quartet playing in the same space where the ill-fated Christmas tree had stood. She smiled her delight. It took some getting used to the extravagant gestures of a billionaire.

Dominic was there to greet her, looking darkly handsome in a tuxedo. She looked down at her simple dress in dismay. 'I didn't realise it was such an occasion or I would have worn something dressier,' she said.

Dominic smiled. 'You look absolutely beautiful. Anyway, if all goes well, you'll be changing into something quite different.'

She tilted her head to the side. 'This is all very intriguing,' she said. 'I'm not quite sure where you're going with it.'

'First of all, I want to say that everything can be cancelled if you don't want to go ahead with it. No pressure.'

For the first time she saw Dominic look like he must have looked as a little boy. He seethed with suppressed excitement and the agony of holding on to a secret he was desperate to share.

'Do tell,' she said, tucking her arm through the crook of his elbow, loving him more in that moment than she had ever loved him.

A big grin split his face. 'I'm going to put my hands over your eyes and lead you into the ballroom.'

'Okay,' she said, bemused. Then she guessed it. The family had been determined to give her an engagement party. Now that she and Dominic actually were genuinely engaged she would happily go along with it. She would act suitably surprised. And be very happy. Getting engaged to this wonderful man was worth celebrating.

She could tell she was at the entrance to the ballroom. 'You can open your eyes now,' said Dominic, removing his hands.

There was a huge cry of 'Surprise!' Andie was astounded to see the happy, smiling faces of all her family and friends as well as a bunch of people she didn't recognise but who were also smiling.

What was more, the ballroom had been transformed. It was exquisitely decorated in shades of white with hints of pale blue. Round tables were set up, dressed with white ruffled cloths and the backs of the chairs looped with antique lace and white roses. It was as if she'd walked into a dream. She blinked. But it was all still there when she opened her eyes.

Dominic held her close. 'We—your family, your friends, me—have organised a surprise wedding for you.'

Andie had to put her hand to her heart to stop it from pounding out of her chest. 'A wedding!'

She looked further through the open glass doors to see a bridal arch draped with filmy white fabric and white flowers set up among the rows of blue agapanthus blooming in the garden. Again she blinked. Again it was still there when she opened her eyes.

'Your wedding,' said Dominic. '*Our* wedding. You asked to be married as soon as possible. I organised it. With some help from the Party Queens. Actually, a *lot* of help from the Party Queens. Jake Marlow and some other friends of mine are also here.'

'It…it's unbelievable.'

'Only if it's what you want, Andie,' Dominic said, turning to her so just she could hear. 'If it's too much, if you'd rather organise your own wedding in your own time, this can just turn into a celebration of our engagement.'

'No! I want it. It's perfect.' She turned to the expectant people who seemed to have all held their breath in anticipation of her response and gone silent. 'Thank you. I say I do—well, I'm *soon* going to say I do!'

There was an eruption of cheers and happy relieved laughter. 'Here comes the bride,' called out one of her brothers.

Andie felt a swell of joy and happy disbelief. It was usually her organising all the surprise parties. To have Dominic do this for her—well, she felt as if she was falling in love with him all over again.

But the party planner in her couldn't resist checking on the details. 'The rings?' she asked Dominic. He patted his breast pocket. 'Both ready-to-wear couture pieces,' he said.

'And this is all legal?'

'Strictly speaking, you need a month's notice of intent to be married—and we filled out our form less than a month ago. But I got a magistrate to approve a shorter notice period. It's legal all right.'

Her eyes smarted with tears of joy. This was really happening. She was getting married today to the man she adored and in front of the people she loved most in the world.

Her fashion editor friend, Karen, dashed out from the guests and took her by the arm. 'Hey! No tears. I've got my favourite hair and make-up artist on hand and we don't want red eyes and blotchy cheeks. Let's get your make-up done. She's already done your bridesmaids.'

'My bridesmaids?'

'Your sisters, Hannah and Bea, Gemma, Eliza and your little niece, Caitlin. The little nephews are ring-bearers.'

'You guys have thought of everything.'

Turning around to survey the room again, she noticed a fabulous four-tiered wedding cake, covered in creamy frosting and blue sugar forget-me-nots. It was exactly the cake she'd talked about with Gemma. She'd bet it was chocolate cake on the bottom layers and vanilla on the top—Gemma knew she disliked the heavy fruitcake of traditional wedding cakes.

'Wait until you see your wedding dresses,' said Karen.

'Dresses?'

'I've got you a choice of three. You'll love them all but there's one I think you'll choose. It's heavy ivory lace over silk, vintage inspired, covered at the front but swooping to the back.'

'And a veil? I always wanted to wear a veil on my wedding day.' This all felt surreal.

'I've got the most beautiful wisp of silk tulle edged with antique lace. You attach it at the back of a simple halo band twisted with lace and trimmed with pearls. A touch vintage, a touch boho—very Andie. Oh, and your mother's pearl necklace for your "something borrowed".'

'It sounds divine.' She hugged Karen and thanked her. 'I think you know my taste better than I do myself.'

It *was* divine. The dress, the veil, the silk-covered shoes that tied with ribbons around her ankles, the posy of white old-fashioned roses tied with mingled white and blue ribbon. The bridesmaids in their pale blue vintage style dresses with white rosebuds twisted through their hair. The little boys in adorable mini white tuxedos.

As she walked down the magnificent staircase on her father's arm, Andie didn't need the guests' *oohs* and *aahs* to know she looked her best and the bridal party was breathtaking. She felt surrounded by the people she cared for most—and who cared for her. She wouldn't wish anything to be different.

Dominic was waiting for her at the wedding arch, flanked by his best man, Jake Marlow—tall, broad-shouldered, blond and not at all the geek she'd imagined him to be—with her brothers and Rob Cratchit as groomsmen.

She knew she had to walk a stately, graceful bride's walk towards her husband-to-be. But she had to resist the temptation to pick up her skirts and run to him and the start of their new life as husband and wife.

Dominic knew the bridesmaids looked lovely and the little attendants adorable. But he only had eyes for Andie as she walked towards him, her love for him shining from her eyes.

As she neared where he waited for her with the celebrant, a stray breeze picked up the fine layers of her gown's skirts and whirled them up and over her knees. She laughed and made no attempt to pin them down.

As her skirts settled back into place, their glances met

and her lips curved in an intimate exchange of a private joke that had meaning only for two. It was just one of many private connections he knew they would share, bonding and strengthening their life as partners in the years of happy marriage that stretched out ahead of them.

Finally she reached him and looked up to him with her dazzling smile. He enfolded her hand in his as he waited with her by his side to give his wholehearted assent to the celebrant's question. 'Do you, Dominic Hugo Hunt, take this woman, Andrea Jane Newman, to be your lawful wedded wife?'

CHAPTER SEVENTEEN

Christmas Day the following year.

ANDIE STOOD WITHIN the protective curve of her husband's arm as she admired the fabulous Christmas tree that stood in the entrance of their Vaucluse home. It soared almost to the ceiling and was covered in exquisite ornaments that were set to be the start of their family collection, to be brought out year after year. Brightly wrapped gifts were piled around its base.

Christmas lunch was again being held here today, but this time it was a party for just Andie's family and a few other waifs and strays who appreciated being invited to share their family's celebration.

The big Scrooge-busting party had been such a success that Dominic had committed to holding it every year. But not here this time. This year he'd hired a bigger house with a bigger pool and invited more people. He'd be calling in to greet his guests later in the day.

Andie hadn't had to do a thing for either party. She'd had her input—how could a Party Queen not? But for this private party the decorating, table settings and gift-wrapping had all been done by Dominic and her family.

After much cajoling, Andie had convinced her father to transfer his centre of cooking operations to Dominic's gourmet kitchen—just for this year. Although Dad had

grumbled and complained about being away from familiar territory, Andie knew he was secretly delighted at the
top-of-the-range equipment in the kitchen. The aromas that
were wafting to her from the kitchen certainly smelled like
the familiar traditional family favourites her father cooked
each year. She couldn't imagine they would taste any less
delicious than they would cooked in her parents' kitchen.

It was people who made the joy of Christmas and all
the people she cherished the most were here to celebrate
with her.

And one more.

The reason for all the disruption lay cradled in her arms.
Hugo Andrew Hunt had been born in the early hours of
Christmas Eve.

The birth had been straightforward and he was a
healthy, strong baby. Andie had insisted on leaving the
hospital today to be home for Christmas. Dominic had
driven her and Hugo home so slowly and carefully they'd
had a line of impatient cars honking their horns behind
them by the time they'd got back to Vaucluse. He was over
the moon about becoming a father. This was going to be
one very loved little boy.

'Weren't you clever, to have our son born on Christmas Eve?' he said.

'I'm good at planning, but not *that* good,' she said. 'He
came when he was ready. Maybe…maybe your parents
sent him.' She turned her head so she could look up into
Dominic's eyes. 'Now Christmas Eve will be a cause for
celebration, not mourning, for you.'

'Yes,' he said. 'It will—because of you.'

Andie looked down at the perfect little face of her slum-
bering son and felt again the rush of fierce love for this
precious being she'd felt when the midwife had first laid
him on her tummy. He had his father's black hair but it was
too soon to tell what colour his eyes would be.

Her husband, he-who-would-never-be-called-Scrooge-again, gently traced the line of little Hugo's cheek with his finger. 'Do you remember how I said last year was the very best Christmas of my life? Scratch that. This one is even better.'

'And they will get better and better,' she promised, turning her head for his kiss.

As they kissed, she heard footsteps on the marble floor and then an excited cry from her sister Bea. 'They're home! Andie, Dominic and baby Hugo are home!'

* * * * *

WEDDING DATE WITH MR WRONG

NICOLA MARSH

CHAPTER ONE

'If you mention weddings or tinsel or Secret Santa one more time I'm going to ram this wax down your throat.'

Archer Flett brandished his number-one-selling surfboard wax at his younger brother, Travis, who grinned and snatched the wax out of his hand.

'Resist all you like, bro, you know you're fighting a losing battle.' Trav smirked and rubbed a spot he'd missed on his prized board.

When it came to his family it always felt as if Archer was fighting a losing battle.

Despite making inroads with his brothers Tom and Trav, nothing had changed with his parents over the years—his dad in particular. That was why coming home for his yearly obligatory Christmas visit set him on edge. And why he rarely stuck around more than a few days.

This year would be no exception, despite Travis turning into a romantic schmuck.

'What were you thinking?' Archer stuck his board vertically in the sand and leaned on it. 'A Christmas wedding? Could you get any cheesier?'

His brother's eyes glazed over and Archer braced for some more claptrap involving his fiancée. 'Shelly wanted to be a Christmas bride and we saw no point in waiting.'

Archer placed his thumb in the middle of Trav's forehead and pushed. 'You're under this already. You know that, right?'

'We're in love.'

As if that excused his brother's sappy behaviour.

The Fletts were third-generation Torquay inhabitants, so he could just imagine the shindig his parents would throw for the wedding. The entire town would turn up.

Christmas and a wedding at home. A combination guaranteed to make him run as soon as the cake had been cut.

'You're too young to get married.' Archer glared at the sibling who'd tagged after him for years, pestering him to surf.

He'd spent the bulk of the last eight years away from home and in that time Travis had morphed from gangly kid to lean and mean.

Heavy on the lean, light on the mean. Trav didn't have a nasty bone in his body, and the fact he was marrying at twenty-two didn't surprise Archer.

Trav was a marshmallow, and while Shelly seemed like a nice girl he couldn't imagine anything worse than being shackled to one person at such a young age.

Hell, at twenty-two *he'd* been travelling the world, surfing the hotspots, dating extensively and trying to put his folks' deception out of his mind.

A memory he'd long suppressed shimmered into his subconscious. South coast of Italy. Capri. Long hot nights filled with laughter and passion and heat.

Annoyingly, whenever anyone he knew was loco enough to tie the knot his mind drifted to Callie.

'So who're you bringing to the wedding?' Travis wrinkled his nose. 'Another of those high-maintenance city chicks you always bring home at Christmas?'

Archer chose those dates for a reason: women who demanded all his attention, so he didn't have time left over to spend one-on-one with his folks.

He'd honed avoidance to an art, ensuring he didn't say things he might regret. Like why the hell they hadn't trusted him to rally around all those years ago.

He wasn't the flighty, carefree surfer dude they'd assumed him to be and he'd prove it this trip. He hoped the surf school he'd developed would show them the type of guy he was—the type of guy he wanted to be.

'Leave my date to me.' He wriggled his board out of the sand and tucked it under his arm. 'Planning on standing here all day, gossiping like an old woman? Or are you going to back up some of your big talk by showing me a few moves out there?'

Trav cocked his thumb and forefinger and fired at him. 'I'm going to surf your show-pony ass into oblivion.'

'Like to see you try, pretty boy.'

Archer took off at a run, enjoying the hot sand beneath his feet, the wind buffeting his face, before he hit the water's edge. He lay prone on his board, the icy chill of Bell's Beach washing over him as the lure of the waves took hold. He'd never felt so alive. When he was in the ocean he came home.

The ocean was reliable and constant—two things he valued. Two things his parents didn't credit him as being.

He paddled harder, wishing he could leave

the demons of his past behind, knowing he should confront them over the next few days.

He'd made amends with his brothers four years ago, at a time when Tom had needed his support. His relationship with his mum had thawed too, considering he didn't blame her for what happened; she'd do anything for Frank.

But things were still rough with his dad. He'd wanted to make peace many times but a healthy dose of pride, an enforced physical distance and the passing of time had put paid to that fantasy.

He'd tried making small efforts to broach the distance between them, but the residual awkwardness lingered, reinforcing his choice to stay away.

Maybe, if he was lucky, this visit home would be different.

Callie went into overdrive as an Argentinian tango blared from her surround sound.

She bounced around her lounge room, swivelling her hips and striding across the floor with arm extended and head tilted, a fake rose between her teeth.

She'd cleaned her apartment for the last two hours, increasing the volume of the music as her scrubbing, polishing and vacuuming frenzy did little to obliterate what she'd confront this afternoon.

A face-to-face meeting with her number one client.

The client her beloved CJU Designs couldn't afford to lose.

The client who might well fire her lying butt when he discovered her identity.

Archer Flett didn't do commitment. He'd made that perfectly clear in Capri eight years ago. So how would he feel when he learned he'd committed his new mega campaign to a woman he'd deliberately walked away from because they'd been getting too close.

She stubbed her toe on a wrought-iron table and swore, kicking the ornate leg again for good measure.

She was furious with herself for not confronting this issue sooner. What had she expected? Never to cross paths with Archer physically again?

Yep, that was exactly what she'd expected.

It had been three years since she'd tendered for the lucrative Torquay Tan account, completely unaware the company was owned and run by the surf world's golden boy.

It had come as a double surprise discovering the laid-back charmer she'd met eight years ago had the business nous to own a mega corporation, let alone run it. It looked as if the guy she'd once been foolish enough to fall for was full of surprises.

Now she had a chance to take on her biggest account yet: the launch of Archer's surf school in Torquay, his home town. To do it she had to meet with the man himself.

She should have bowed out gracefully, been content to be his online marketing manager for lesser accounts.

But she needed the money. Desperately.

Her mum depended on her.

The music swelled, filling her head with memories and her heart with longing. She loved the passion of Latin American music—the distinct rhythms, the sultry songs.

They reminded her of a time gone by. A time when she'd danced all night with the stars overhead and the sand under her feet. A time when she'd existed on rich pasta and cheap Chianti and whispered words of her first love.

Archer.

The music faded, along with the sentimental rubbish infiltrating her long-established common sense.

These days she didn't waste time reminiscing. She'd given up on great loves and foolish dreams.

Watching her mum go through hell had seen to that.

She was like her hot-blooded Italian father, apparently: they shared starry-eyed optimism, their impulsiveness, their passion for food and fashion and flirting. She'd considered those admirable qualities until she'd witnessed first-hand what happened when impulsive passions turned sour—her dad's selfishness knew no bounds.

And just like that she'd given up on being like her dad. She didn't give in to grand passion or fall foolhardily in love. Not any more.

Sure, she dated. She liked it. Just not enough to let anyone get too close.

As close as Archer had once been.

'Damn Archer Flett,' she muttered, kicking the table a third time for good measure.

Housework might not have worked off steam but she'd do the next best thing to prepare for this meeting.

Choose a killer business suit, blow-dry her hair and apply immaculate make-up.

Time to show Mr Hot Surfer Dude he didn't affect her after all these years.

Not much anyway.

The tiny hole-in-the-wall office of CJU Designs didn't surprise Archer. Tech geeks didn't need much space.

What did surprise him were the profuse

splashes of colour adorning the walls. Slashes of magenta and crimson and turquoise against white block canvases drew his eye and brightened an otherwise nondescript space.

Small glass-topped desk, ergonomic chair, hardbacked wooden guest chair opposite. Exceedingly dull—except for that startling colour.

Almost as if the computer geek was trying to break out of a mould, trying to prove something to herself and her clients.

Well, all CJ had to prove to him was that she could handle the mega-launch he had planned for his pet project and she could hang the moon on her wall for all he cared.

He glanced around for a picture. Not for the first time he was curious about his online marketing manager.

He'd internet-searched CJU Designs extensively before hiring their services and had come up with nothing but positive PR and high praise from clients, including many sportspeople.

So he'd hired CJ, beyond impressed with her work. Crisp, clear, punctual, she always delivered on time, creating the perfect slogans, pitches and launches for any product he'd put his name to.

Trailing a finger along the dust-free desk, he wondered how she'd cope with a campaign of this size. Launching the first Flett Surf School for teens had to succeed. It was a prototype for what he planned in the surf hotspots around the world.

He'd seen too many kids in trouble—kids who hung around the beaches drinking, smoking dope, catching the occasional wave. They were aimless, trying to look cool, when in fact he'd seen the lost look in their eyes.

This was his chance to make a difference. And hopefully prove to his family just how wrong they'd been to misjudge him.

He'd never understood it—had done a lot of soul-searching to come up with one valid reason why they hadn't trusted him enough.

Had he been too blasé? Too carefree? Too narcissistic? Too wrapped up in his career to pick up the signs there'd been a major problem?

Tom and Trav hadn't helped when they'd discussed it a few years ago. He'd asked, and they'd hedged, reiterating that they'd been sworn to secrecy by Frank, embarrassed that their complicity had contributed to the ongoing gap between them.

So Archer had made a decision right then to forget his damn pride and re-bond with his brothers. They might not be the best mates they'd once been but their sometimes tense relationship now was a far improvement on the one they'd had previously—the one he still had with his dad.

It irked, not knowing the reason why they'd done it, and their lack of trust had left a lasting legacy. One he hoped opening the surf school would go some way to rectifying.

Thinking about his family made him pace the shoebox office. He hated confined spaces. Give him the ocean expanses any day. He never felt as free as he did catching a wave, paddling out to sea, with nothing between him and the ocean but an aerodynamic sliver of fibreglass.

Nothing beat the rush.

He heard the determined click-clack of high heels striding towards the office and turned in time to see Calista Umberto enter.

His stomach went into free fall, as it had the first time he'd caught a thirty-foot wave. That rush? Seeing Callie again after all these years topped it.

While he stared like a starstruck fool, she didn't blink. In fact she didn't seem at all surprised, which could only mean one thing.

She'd been expecting him.

In that second it clicked.

CJU Designs.

Calista Jane Umberto.

The fact he remembered her middle name annoyed him as much as discovering the online marketing whiz he'd been depending on for the last three years was the woman he'd once almost lost his mind over.

His Callie.

'I'll be damned,' he muttered, crossing the small space in three strides, bundling her into his arms in an impulsive hug before he could process the fact that she'd actually taken a step back at his approach.

The frangipani fragrance hit him first—her signature bodywash that instantly resurrected memories of midnight strolls on a moonlit Capri beach, long, languorous kisses in the shade of a lemon tree, exploring every inch of the deliciously smooth skin drenched in that tempting floral scent.

Any time he'd hit an island hotspot to surf—Bali, Hawaii, Fiji—frangipanis would transport him back in time. To a time he remembered fondly, but a time fraught with danger, when he'd been captivated by a woman to the point of losing sight of the end game.

In the few seconds when her fragrance slammed his senses, he registered her rigid posture, her reluctance to be embraced.

Silently cursing himself, he released her and stepped back, searching her face for some sign that she remembered what they'd once shared.

Her lush mouth—with a ripe red gloss—

flat-lined, but she couldn't hide the spark in her eyes.

Flecks of gold in a rich, deep chocolate. Eyes he'd seen glazed with passion, sparkling with enthusiasm, lighting with love.

It was the latter that had sent him running from Capri without looking back. He'd do well to remember that before indulging in a spin down memory lane and potentially ostracising his marketing manager.

'Good to see you, Archer,' she said, her tone polite and frigid and so at odds with the Callie he remembered that he almost took a step back. 'Take a seat and we'll get started.'

He shook his head, the fog of confusion increasing as he stared at this virtual stranger acting as if they barely knew each other.

He'd seen her naked, for goodness' sake. For a week straight. A long, hot, decadent week that had blown his mind in every way.

'You're not serious?'

Her stoic business persona faltered and she toyed with the bracelet on her right wrist, turning it round and around in a gesture he'd seen often that first night in Capri.

The night they'd met. The night they'd talked for hours, strolled for ages, before ending up at his villa. The night they'd connected on so many levels he'd been terrified and yet power-less to resist her allure.

She'd been brash and brazen and beautiful, quick to laugh and parry his quips, slow to sa-vour every twirl of linguini and rich Napolitano sauce.

She'd had a passion for everything from fresh crusty bread dipped in olive oil to hik-ing along pebbly beach trails to nights spent exploring each other's bodies in erotic detail.

That passionate woman he remembered was nothing like this cool, imperturbable automa-ton.

Except for that tell with the bracelet he would have thought she didn't remember, let alone want to acknowledge the past.

'I'm serious about getting down to business.'

The bracelet-twirling picked up pace, a give-away that she was more rattled than she let on.

'Plenty of time for that.' He gestured towards her slimline laptop, the only thing on her desk. 'What I want to know is why you've been hid-ing behind your PC all this time?'

Another hit. Her eyes widened and her tongue darted out to the corner of her mouth.

A mouth designed for culinary riches and sin.

A mouth thinned in an unimpressed line so far removed from the smiles he remembered that he almost reached out with his fingertip to tilt the corners up.

'I'm not hiding behind anything,' she said, her tone as prim as her fitted black suit.

Actually, the suit wasn't all bad. Hugging all the right curves, flaring at the cuffs and hem, ending above her knee. Combined with an emerald silk shirt hinting at cleavage, it was better than okay.

He was just grouchy because she wasn't rapt to see him. But then again, considering the way they'd parted...

'You didn't think I might like to know that the marketing whiz I e-mail regularly is someone I...'

What? Once had memorable sex with? Once knew intimately? Once might have given up his freedom for, in another time, another place? If he hadn't still been reeling from his parents' revelations?

Her eyes narrowed. 'Someone you what?'

He should have known she wouldn't let him off lightly. She hadn't back then either, when he'd told her he was skipping out.

'Someone I know,' he finished lamely, trying his signature charming grin for good measure.

Her lips merely compressed further as she swivelled away and strode to her desk. Not so bad, considering he got the opportunity to watch expensive linen shift over that memorable butt.

Damn, he loved her curves. He'd seen his fair share of bikini babes over the years—an occupational hazard and one he appreciated—but the way Callie had filled out a swimsuit?

Unforgettable.

She sat behind her desk, glaring at him as if she could read his mind. She waved at the chair opposite and he sat, thrown by her reaction. Acting professional was one thing. The ice princess act she had going on was losing appeal fast.

'Our fling wasn't relevant to our business dealings so I didn't say anything—particularly after how things ended.'

She eyeballed him, daring him to disagree. Wisely, he kept mute, interested to see where she was going with this.

'I tendered for your account without knowing you were behind the company.'

Her next sign of anything less than cool poise was when she absentmindedly tapped the space bar on her laptop with a thumb.

'When we started corresponding and worked well together, I didn't want to complicate matters.'

'Complicate them how?'

A faint pink stained her cheeks. Oh, yeah, this was starting to get real interesting.

'What do you want me to say? Any shared past tends to complicate things.'

'Only if you let it.' He hooked his hands behind his head, enjoying the battle gleam in her eyes. At last the fiery woman he knew was coming out to fight. 'Don't know about you, but I don't let *anything* interfere with my career.'

'Like I didn't know that,' she muttered, and he had the grace to acknowledge a twinge of regret.

He'd used his burgeoning surfing career to end it in Capri. It had seemed as good as excuse as any. He might as well live down to the reputation his family had tarred him with. Anything was better than telling her the truth.

'Is this going to be a problem for you?'

He threw it out there, half expecting her to say yes, hoping she'd say no.

He wasn't disappointed to see her—far from it. And the fact they'd have to spend time together in Torquay to get the marketing campaign for the surf school off the ground was a massive bonus.

Torquay... Wedding...

It was like a wave crashing over him. He floated the solution to another problem.

They'd have to spend time in Torquay for business.

He had to spend time with his overzealous family at Trav's wedding.

He had to find a date.

A bona fide city girl who'd act as a buffer between him and his family.

Lucky for him, he was looking straight at her.

Not that he'd let her know yet. He needed her expertise for this account, and by her less than welcoming reaction he'd be hard-pressed getting her to Torquay in the first place without scaring her away completely.

Yeah, he'd keep that little gem for later.

Her brows furrowed. 'What's with the smug grin?'

He leaned forward and nudged the laptop between them out of the way. 'You want this latest account?'

She nodded, a flicker of something bordering on fear in her eyes. It might make him callous, but he could work with fear. Fear meant she was probably scared of losing his lucrative business. Fear meant she might agree to accompany him to Torquay even if she had been giving him the ice treatment ever since she'd set foot in the office.

'You know this campaign will mean spending loads of one-on-one time together on the school site down at Torquay?'

Her clenched jaw made him want to laugh out loud. 'Why? I've always worked solo before. and as you can attest the results have been great.'

If she expected him to back down, she'd better think again. He'd get her to accompany him to Torquay by any means necessary—including using the campaign as blackmail.

Feigning disappointment, he shook his head. 'Sorry, a remote marketing manager won't cut it this time. I'll need you to shadow me to get a feel for the vibe I'm trying to capture with the school. The kids won't go for it otherwise.'

Her steely glare could have sliced him in two. 'For how long?'

'One week.'

She sucked in a breath, her nose wrinkling in distaste, and he bit back a laugh.

'From your previous work I'm sure you want to do this campaign justice and that's what it's going to take. You can be home in time to celebrate Christmas Day.'

Appealing to her professional pride was a master touch. She couldn't say no.

'Fine. I'll do it,' she muttered, her teeth clenching so hard he was surprised he didn't hear a crack.

'There's just one more thing.' Unable to resist teasing her, he twisted a sleek strand of silky brown hair around his finger. 'We'll be cohabiting.'

CHAPTER TWO

CALLIE stared at Archer in disbelief.

The cocky charmer was blackmailing her.

As if she'd let him get away with that.

She folded her arms, sat back, and pinned him with a disbelieving glare. 'Never thought I'd see the day hotshot Archer Flett resorted to blackmail to get a woman to shack up with him.'

His eyes sparked with admiration and she stiffened. She didn't want to remember how he'd looked at her in a similar way during their week in Capri, his expression indulgent, bordering on doting.

As if. He'd bolted all the same, admiration or not, and she'd do well to remember it.

For, as much as she'd like to tell him where he could stick his business contract, she needed the money.

'Blackmail sounds rather harsh.' He braced his forearms on her desk and leaned forward, immediately shrinking the space between them and making her breath catch. 'A bit of gentle persuasion sounds much more civilised.'

That voice… It could coax Virgins Anonymous into revoking their membership. Deep, masculine, with a hint of gravel undertone—enough to give Sean Connery healthy competition.

There was nothing gentle about Archer's persuasion. If he decided to turn on the full arsenal of his charm she didn't stand a chance, even after all this time.

That irked the most. Eight long years during which she'd deliberately eradicated his memory, had moved on, had dealt with her feelings for him to the extent where she could handle his online marketing without flinching every time she saw his picture or received an e-mail.

Gone in an instant—wiped just like that. Courtesy of his bedroom voice, his loaded stare and irresistible charm.

'Besides, living together for the week is logical. My house has plenty of room and we'll be working on the campaign 24/7. It's sound business sense.'

Damn him. He was right.

She could achieve a lot more in seven days without factoring in travel time—especially when she had no clue where his house was or its vicinity to Torquay.

However, acknowledging that his stipulation made sense and liking it were worlds apart.

'You know I'm not comfortable with this, right?'

'Really? I hadn't picked up on that.'

He tried his best disarming grin and she deliberately glanced away. Living with him for the week might be logical for business, but having to deal with his natural charm around the clock was not good.

'Anything I can do to sweeten the deal?'

Great—he was laying the charm on thick. Her gaze snapped to his in time to catch his damnably sexy mouth curving at the corners. Her lips tingled in remembrance of how he'd smile against her mouth when he had her weak and whimpering from his kisses.

Furious at her imploding resistance, she eyeballed him with the glare that had intimidated the manager at her mum's special accommodation into giving her another extension on payment.

'Yeah, there is something you can do to sweeten the deal.' She stabbed at an envelope with a fingertip and slid it across the desk towards him. 'Sign off on my new rates. Your PA hasn't responded to my last two e-mails and I need to get paid.'

His smile faded as he took the envelope. 'You're having financial problems?'

If he only knew.

'No. I just like to have my accounts done monthly, and you've always been prompt in the past...'

Blessedly prompt. The Torquay Tan account had single-handedly launched her business into the stratosphere and kept it afloat. If she ever lost it...

In that moment the seriousness of the situation hit her. She shouldn't be antagonising Archer. She should be jumping through whatever hoop he presented her with—adding a somersault and a *ta-da* flourish for good measure.

She had to secure this new campaign. CJU Designs would skyrocket in popularity, and her mum would continue to be cared for.

She had no other option but to agree.

'Just so we're clear. If I accompany you to Torquay, the surf school campaign is mine?'

His mocking half salute did little to calm the nerves twisting her belly into pretzels.

'All yours, Cal.'

She didn't know what unnerved her more. The intimate way the nickname he'd given her dripped off his tongue or the way his eyes sparked with something akin to desire.

She should be ecstatic that she'd secured the biggest campaign of her career.

Instead, as her pulse ramped up to keep pace with her flipping heart, all she could think was *at what price*?

Archer didn't like gloating. He'd seen enough of it on the surf circuit—arrogant guys who couldn't wait to glory over their latest win.

But the second Callie's agreement to accompany him to Torquay fell from her lush lips he wanted to strut around the office with his fists pumping in a victory salute.

An over-the-top reaction? Maybe. But having Callie by his side throughout the Christmas Eve wedding festivities—even if she didn't know it yet—would make the event and its guaranteed emotional ra-ra bearable.

He'd suffered through enough Torquay weddings to know the drill by now. Massive marquees, countless kisses from extended rellies he didn't know, back-slapping and one-upmanship from old mates, and the inevitable matchmaking between him and every single female under thirty in the whole district.

His mum hated the dates he brought home each year, and tried to circumvent him with

less-than-subtle fix-ups: notoriously predict-
able, sweet, shy local girls she hoped would
tempt him to settle down in Torquay and produce a brood of rowdy rug-rats.

It was the same every wedding. The same
every year, for that matter, when he returned
home for his annual visit. A visit primarily
made out of obligation rather than any burning desire to be constantly held up as the odd
one out in the Flett family.

It wasn't intentional, for his folks and his
brothers tried to carry on as if nothing had happened, but while he'd forgiven them for shutting
him out in the past the resultant awkwardness
still lingered.

He'd steadily withdrawn, stayed away because of it, preferring to be free. Free to go
where he wanted, when he wanted. Free from
emotional attachments that invariably let him
down. Free to date fun-loving, no strings attached women who didn't expect much beyond
dinner and drinks rather than an engagement
and a bassinet.

His gaze zeroed in on Callie as she fielded
an enquiry on the phone, her pen scrawling at
a frenetic pace as she jotted notes, the tip of her
tongue protruding between her lips.

Callie had been that girl once. The kind of
girl who wanted the picket fence dream, the

equivalent of his ultimate nightmare. Did she still want that?

The finger on her left hand remained ring-less, he saw as he belatedly realised he should have checked if she was seeing anyone before coercing her into heading down to Torquay on the pretext of business when in fact she'd be his date for the wedding.

Then again, she'd agreed, so his assumption that she was currently single was probably safe.

Not that she'd fallen in with his plan quickly. She'd made him work for it, made him sweat. And he had a feeling her capitulation had more to do with personal reasons than any great de-sire to make this campaign the best ever.

That flicker of fear when she'd thought he might walk and take his business with him… Not that he would have done it. Regardless of whether she'd wanted to come or not CJU would have had the surf school campaign in the bag. She'd proved her marketing worth many times over the last few years, and while he might be laid back on the circuit he was tough in his business.

Success meant security. Ultimately success meant he was totally self-sufficient and didn't have to depend on anyone, for he'd learned the hard way that depending on people, even those closest to you, could end in disappointment and sadness and pain.

It was what drove him every day, that quest for independence, not depending on anyone, even family, for anything.

After his folks' betrayal it was what had driven him away from Callie.

He chose to ignore his insidious voice of reason. The last thing he needed was to get sentimental over memories.

She hung up the phone, her eyes narrowing as she caught sight of him lounging in the doorway. 'You still here?'

'We're not finished.'

He only just caught her muttered, 'Could've fooled me.'

As much as it pained him to revisit the past, he knew he'd have to bring it up in order to get past her obvious snit.

He did not want a date glaring daggers at him all night; his mum would take it as a sure-fire sign to set one of her gals onto him.

'Do we need to clear the air?'

She arched an eyebrow in an imperious taunt. 'I don't know. Do we?'

Disappointed, he shook his head. 'You didn't play games. One of the many things I admired about you.'

Her withering glare wavered and dipped,

before pinning him with renewed accusation. 'We had a fling in the past. Yonks ago. I'm over it. You're over it. There's no air to clear. Ancient history. The next week is business, nothing more.'

'Then why are you so antagonistic?'

She opened her mouth to respond, then snapped it shut, her icy façade faltering as she ran a hand through her hair in another uncertain tell he remembered well.

She'd done it when they'd first met at a beachside vendor's, when they'd both reached for the last chilled lemonade at the same time. She'd done it during their first dinner at a tiny trattoria tucked into an alley. And she'd done it when he'd taken her back to his hotel for the first time.

In every instance he'd banished her uncertainty with practised charm, but after the way they'd parted he doubted it would work in this instance.

'Cal—'

'Us being involved in the past complicates this campaign and I'm not a huge fan of complications.'

She blurted it without meeting his eye, her gaze fixed on her laptop screen.

He wished she'd look at him so he could see

how deeply this irked, or if she was trying to weasel out of the deal.

'You said it yourself. It's in the past. So why should it complicate anything?' He didn't want to push her, but her antagonism left him no choice. 'Unless…'

'What?' Her head snapped up, her wary gaze locking on his, and in that instant he had his answer before he asked the question.

The spark they'd once shared was there, flickering in the depths of rich brown, deliberately cloaked in evasive shadows.

'Unless you still feel something?'

'I'm many things. A masochist isn't one of them.'

She stood so quickly her chair slid backward on its castors and slammed into the wall. The noise didn't deter her as she stalked towards him, defiant in high heels.

With her eyes flashing warning signals he chose to ignore, he stepped back into the office, meeting her halfway.

Before he could speak she held up her hand. 'I'm not a fool, Archer. We were attracted in Capri, we're both single, and we're going to be spending time together on this campaign. Stands to reason a few residual sparks may fly.' Her hand snagged in her hair again and she almost wrenched it out in exasperation. 'It won't mean anything. I have a job to do, and there's no way I'll jeopardise that by making another mistake.'

He reached for her before he could second-guess, gripping her upper arms, giving her no room to move. 'We weren't a mistake.'

'Yeah? Then why did you run?'

He couldn't respond—not without telling her the truth. And that wasn't an option.

So he did the next best thing.

He released her, turned his back, and walked away.

'And you're still running,' she murmured.

Her barb registered, and served to make him stride away that little bit faster.

CHAPTER THREE

CALLIE strode towards Johnston Street and her favourite Spanish bar.

Some girls headed home to a chick-flick and tub of ice-cream when they needed comfort. She headed for Rivera's.

'Hola, querida.' Arturo Rivera blew her a kiss from behind the bar and she smiled in return, some of her tension instantly easing.

Artie knew about her situation: the necessity for her business to thrive in order to buy the best care for her mum. He knew her fears, her insecurities. He'd been there from the start, this reserved gentleman in a porkpie hat who'd lost his wife to the disease that would eventually claim her mum.

She hadn't wanted to attend a support group, but her mum's doc had insisted it would help in the disease's management and ultimately help her mum.

So she'd gone along, increasingly frustrated

and helpless and angry, so damn angry, that her vibrant, fun-loving mother had been diagnosed with motor neurone disease.

She'd known nothing about her mum's symptoms until it had been too late. Nora had hidden them well: the stumbling due to weakness in her leg muscles, her difficulty holding objects due to weak hands, her swallowing difficulties and the occasional speech slur.

The first Callie had learned of it was when her mum had invited her to accompany her to see a neurologist. Nora hated needles, and apparently having an electromyograph, where they stuck needles in her muscles to measure electrical activity, was worse to bear than the actual symptoms.

The diagnosis had floored them both—especially the lack of a cure and mortality rates. Though in typical determined Nora fashion her mum had continued living independently until her symptoms had made it impossible to do so.

Nora had refused to be a burden on her only daughter, so Callie had found the best care facility around—one with top neurologists, speech, occupational and physiotherapists, psychologists, nurses and palliative care, while trying not to acknowledge her mum's steady deterioration.

It was as if she could *see* the nerve cells failing, resulting in the progressive muscle weakness that would eventually kill her mum.

So she focussed on the good news: Nora's sight, smell, taste, sensation, intellect and memory wouldn't be affected. Nora would always know her, even at the end, and that thought sustained her through many a crying jag late at night, when the pain of impending loss crowded in and strangled her forced bravery.

To compound her stress she'd had to reluctantly face the fact she had a fifty-fifty chance of inheriting it too. She hadn't breathed all through the genetic testing consultation, when the doctors had explained that Nora's motor neurone disease was caused by mutations in the SOD1 gene. That tiny superoxide dismutase one gene, located on chromosome twenty-one, controlled her fate.

Insomnia had plagued her in the lead-up to her testing, and the doctor's clinical facts had been terrifying as they echoed through her head: people with the faulty gene had a high chance of developing MND in later life, or could develop symptoms in their twenties.

Like her.

She'd worried herself sick for days after the test, and even though it had come back clear—she didn't carry the mutated gene—she'd never fully shaken the feeling that she had a swinging axe grazing the back of her neck, despite the doc's convincing argument that many people *with* the faulty gene didn't go on to develop MND.

Then the worry had given way to guilt. Guilt that she was the lucky one in her family.

During this time the support group had been invaluable. Artie had been there, just as frustrated, just as angry. He'd lost his wife of forty years.

They'd bonded over espresso and biscotti, gradually revealing their bone-deep resentment and helpless fury at a disease that had no cure. Those weekly meetings had led to an invitation to Rivera's, a place that had instantly become home.

She loved the worn, pockmarked wooden floor, the rich mahogany bar that ran the breadth of the back wall, the maroon velvet embossed wallpaper that created a cosy ambience beckoning patrons to linger over delicious tapas and decadent sangria.

This was where she'd started to thaw, where the deliberate numbness enclosing her aching heart at the injustice of what her mum faced had melted.

This was where she'd come to eat, to chat and to dance.

She lived for the nights when Artie cleared

the tables and chairs, cranked up the music, and taught Spanish dances to anyone eager to learn.

Those nights were the best—when she could forget how her life had changed that momentous day when she'd learned of her mum's diagnosis.

She nodded at familiar faces as she weaved through tables towards the bar, her heart lightening with every step as Artie waved his hands in the air, gesturing at her usual spot.

'You hungry, *querida*?'

Considering the knot of nerves in her stomach, the last thing she felt like doing was eating, but if she didn't Artie would know something was wrong.

And she didn't feel like talking about the cause of her angst. Not when she'd spent the fifteen-minute walk to the bar trying to obliterate Archer from her mind.

'Maybe the daily special?'

Artie winked. 'Coming right up.'

As he spooned marinated octopus, garlic olives, *banderillas*, *calamares fritos* and *huevos relleños de gambas* onto a terracotta platter, she mentally rummaged for a safe topic of conversation—one that wouldn't involve blurting about the blackmailing guy who had once stolen her heart.

He slid the plate in front of her, along with

her usual espresso. 'So, are you going to tell me what's wrong before your coffee or after?'

She opened her mouth to brush off his astute observation, but one glance at the shrewd gleam in his eyes stalled her. She knew that look. The look of a father figure who wouldn't quit till he'd dragged the truth out of her.

'It's nothing, really—'

He tut-tutted. '*Querida*, I've known you for more than seven years.' He pointed to his bald pate and wrinkled forehead. 'These may indicate the passage of time, but up here...?' He tapped his temple. 'As sharp as Banderas's sword in *Zorro*.'

She chuckled. If Artie had his way Antonio Banderas would be Spain's president.

He folded his arms and rested them on the bar. 'You know I'm going to stay here until you tell me.'

'What about your customers?'

'That's what I pay the staff for.' He grinned. 'Now, are you going to tell, or do I have to ply you with my finest sangria?'

She held up her hands. 'I'm starting work early tomorrow, so no sangria.'

How tempting it sounded. What she wouldn't give to down a jug of Artie's finest, get blotto, and forget the fact she had to accompany Archer to Torquay tomorrow.

'Fine.' She pushed a few olives around her plate before laying down her fork. 'CJU Designs scored its biggest account ever today.'

Artie straightened and did a funny flamenco pirouette. 'That's brilliant. Well done, *querida*.'

'Yeah, it'll take care of mum's bills for the next year at least, thank goodness.'

Artie's exuberance faded. 'How is Nora?'

'The same. Happy, determined, putting on a brave face.'

Something *she* was finding increasingly hard to do when she visited and saw the signs that her mum's condition was worsening. While Nora coped with her wheelchair, relaxed as if she was lounging in her favourite recliner, Callie watched for hand tremors or lapses in speech or drifting off.

She couldn't relax around her mum any more. The effort of hiding her sadness clamped her throat in a stranglehold, taking its toll. She grew more exhausted after every visit, and while she never for one second regretted spending as much time as possible with her mum, she hated the inevitability of this horrid disease.

Artie patted her hand. 'Give her my best next time you see her.'

'Shall do.'

That was another thing that bugged her about this Torquay trip. She'd have to give all her

attention to the account in the early set-up—
and to the account's aggravating owner—which
meant missing out on seeing her mum for the
week before Christmas or long drives to and
from the beachside town. Which would lead
to Archer poking his nose into her business,
asking why she had to visit her mum so often,
and she didn't want to divulge her private life
to him.

Not now, when things were strictly business.

'If this account has alleviated some of your
financial worries, why do you look like this?'
Artie's exaggerated frown made her smile.

'Because simple solutions often mask con-
voluted complications.'

'Cryptic.'

'Not really.' She huffed out a long breath.
'The owner of the company behind this new
account is an old friend.'

'Ah…so that's it.'

She didn't like the crafty glint in Artie's eyes
much—his knowing smile less.

'This…friend…is he a past *amor*?'

Had she loved Archer? After the awful
break-up, and in the following months when
she'd returned to Melbourne and preferred
reading to dating, she'd wondered if the hol-
lowness in her heart, the constant gripe in her
belly and the annoying wanderlust to jump back

on a plane and follow him around the world's surfing hotspots was love.

She'd almost done it once, after seeing a snippet of him at the Pipeline in Hawaii three months after she'd returned from Europe. She'd gone as far as logging on, choosing flights, but when it had come to paying the arrow had hovered over 'confirm' for an agonising minute before the memory of their parting had resurfaced and she'd shut the whole thing down.

That moment had been her wake-up call, and she'd deliberately worked like a maniac so she could fall into bed at the end of a day exhausted and hopefully dream-free.

Her mum had been diagnosed four weeks later, and as a distraction from Archer it had been a doozy.

Now here he was, strutting into her life, as confident and charming and gorgeous as ever. And as dangerously seductive as all those years ago. For, no matter how many times she rationalised that their week together would be strictly business, the fact remained that they'd once shared a helluva spark. She'd better pack her fire extinguisher just in case.

Artie held up his hands. 'You don't have to answer. I can see your feelings for this old *amor* written all over your face.'

'I don't love him.'

Artie merely smiled and moved down the bar towards an edgy customer brandishing an empty sangria jug, leaving her to ponder the conviction behind her words.

While Callie would have loved to linger over a sangria or two when the Spanish Flamenco band fired up, she had more important things to do.

Like visiting her mum.

Nora hated it when she fussed, so these days she kept her visits to twice weekly—an arrangement they were both happy with.

The doctors had given her three years. The doctors didn't know what a fighter Nora Umberto was. She'd lasted seven, and while her tremors seemed to increase every time Callie visited the spark of determination in her mum's eyes hadn't waned.

After the life she'd led, no way would Nora go out without a bang. She continued to read to the other residents and direct the kitchen hands to prepare exotic dishes—dishes she'd tried first-hand during her travels around the world, during which she'd met Bruno Umberto.

Callie's dad might not have stuck around long in his first marriage—or any of his subsequent three marriages, for that matter—but thankfully Nora's love of cosmopolitan cuisine had stuck. Callie had grown up on fajitas, ratatouille, korma and Szechuan—a melting pot of tastes to accompany her mum's adventurous stories.

She'd never really known her dad, but Nora had been enough parent and then some. Dedicated to raising her daughter, Nora hadn't dated until after she'd graduated high school and moved out. Even then her relationships had lasted only a scant few months. Callie had always wondered if her mum's exuberance had been too much for middle-aged guys who'd expected Martha Stewart and ended up with Lara Croft.

As she entered the shaded forecourt of Colldon Special Accommodation Home she knew that made it all the harder to accept—the fact her go-get-'em mother had been cut down in her prime by a devastating illness no amount of fighting could conquer.

She signed in, slipped a visitor's lanyard over her neck and headed towards the rear of the sandstone building. As she strolled down the pastel-carpeted corridor she let the peace of the place infuse her: the piped rainforest sounds, the subtle scent of lemon and ginger essential oils being diffused from air vents, the colours on the walls transitioning from muted mauve to sunny daffodil.

Colldon felt more like an upmarket boutique hotel than a special home and Callie would do whatever it took to ensure her mum remained here.

Including shacking up with Archer Flett for a week to work on his precious campaign.

She shook her head, hoping that would dispel the image of her agreeing to his demands. It didn't, and all she could see was his startling aquamarine eyes lighting with a fire she remembered all too well when she'd said yes.

She'd been a fool thinking she had the upper hand: she'd known his identity; he hadn't known the woman behind CJU Designs. However, the element of surprise meant little when he'd been the one who ended up ousting her from her smug comfort zone.

Her neck muscle spasmed and she rubbed it as she entered Nora's room. She didn't knock. No one knocked. Her mum's door was perpetually open to whoever wanted to pop in for a chat.

Vibrant, sassy, alive: three words that summed up Nora Umberto.

But as she caught sight of her mum struggling to zip up her cardigan that last word taunted her.

Alive. For how much longer?

She swallowed the lump of sadness welling

in her throat, pasted a smile on her face and strode into the room.

'Hey, Mum, how you doing?'

Nora's brilliant blue eyes narrowed as she gestured at the zip with a shaky hand. 'Great—until some bright spark dressed me in this today.'

Her defiant smile made Callie's heart ache.

'Buttons are a pain, but these plastic zips aren't a whole lot better.'

Need a hand? The words hovered on Callie's lips but she clamped them shut. Nora didn't like being treated like an invalid. She liked accepting help less.

Instead, Callie perched on the armchair opposite and ignored the increasing signs that her mum was struggling.

'I'll be away next week.'

Nora instantly perked up. If Callie had to sit through one more lecture about all work and no play she'd go nuts. Not that she could blame her mum. Nora loved hearing stories of Rivera's and dancing and going out, living vicariously through her.

Callie embellished those tales, making her life sound more glamorous than it was. Her mum had enough to worry about without concern for a daughter who dated only occasionally, went Spanish dancing twice a week, and did little else but work. Work that paid the hefty Colldon bills.

'Holiday?'

Callie shook her head. 'Work. In Torquay.'

She said it casually, as if heading to the beachside town *didn't* evoke visions of sun, surf and sexy guys in wetsuits.

Particularly one sexy guy. Who she'd been lucky enough to see without a wetsuit many years ago on another sun-drenched beach.

'You sure it's work?'

Nora leaned so far forward in her wheelchair she almost toppled forward, and Callie had to fold her arms to stop from reaching out.

'You've got a glow.'

'It's an "I'm frazzled to be going away the week before Christmas" glow.'

Nora sagged, her cheekiness instantly dimming. 'You'll be away for Christmas?'

Callie leaned forward and squeezed her mum's hand, careful not to scratch the tissue-thin skin. 'I'll be back in time for Christmas lunch. You think I'd miss Colldon's cranberry stuffing?'

Nora chuckled. 'You know, I wouldn't mind if you missed Christmas with me if your trip involved a hot young man. But work? That's no excuse.'

Ironic. Her trip involved a hot young man

and work, and she had a feeling she'd need to escape both after a long week in Torquay.

She stood and bent to kiss her mum's cheek. 'Sorry it's a flying visit, but I need to go home and pack. I'm leaving first thing in the morning.'

To her surprise, Nora snagged her hand as she straightened, holding on with what little strength she had.

'Don't forget to have a little fun amid all that work, Calista.' She squeezed—the barest of pressure. 'You know life's too short.'

Blinking back the sudden sting of tears, Callie nodded. 'Sure thing, Mum. And ring me if you need anything.'

Nora released her hand, managing a feeble wave. 'I'll be fine. Go work, play, have fun.'

Callie intended to work. As for the fun and play, she didn't dare associate those concepts with Archer.

Look what had happened the last time she'd done that.

Archer didn't jerk women around, and after the way Callie had reacted to him yesterday he shouldn't push her buttons. But that was exactly what he'd done in hiring the fire-engine red Roadster for their trip to Torquay.

She'd recognise the significance of the car, but would she call him on it?

By the tiny crease between her brows and her compressed lips as she stalked towards him, he doubted it.

The carefree, teasing girl he'd once known had disappeared behind this uptight, reserved shadow of her former self. What had happened to snuff the spark out?

'Still travelling light?' He held out his hand for her overnight bag.

She flung it onto the back seat in response.

'Oo-kay, then. Guess it's going to be a long trip.'

He glimpsed a flicker of remorse as she slid onto the passenger seat, her rigid back and folded arms indicative of her absolute reluctance to be here. To be anywhere near him.

It ticked him off.

They'd once been all over each other, laughing and chatting and touching, a hand-hold here, a thigh squeeze there. When she'd smiled at him he'd felt a buzz akin to riding the biggest tube.

But you walked away anyway.

That was all he needed. For his voice of reason to give him a kick in the ass too.

But she hadn't been forthcoming during their

meeting yesterday, and he'd be damned if he'd put up with her foul mood for the next week.

If he showed up at Trav's wedding with her in this snit his mum would know Callie was a fake date and be inquisitive, effectively ruining his buffer zone.

Yeah, because that was the only reason he minded her mood…

He revved the engine, glanced over his shoulder and pulled into traffic. 'You know it's ninety minutes to Torquay, right?'

'Yeah.'

Her glance barely flicked his way behind Audrey Hepburnesque sunglasses that conveniently covered half her face.

'You planning on maintaining the long face the entire way? Do I need to resort to I-spy and guess the numberplate to get a laugh?'

'I'm here to work—'

'Bull.'

He swerved into a sidestreet, earning momentary whiplash and several honks for his trouble.

'What the heck—?'

He kissed her, pouring all his frustration with her frosty behaviour into the kiss.

She resisted at first, but he wouldn't back off. He might have done this to prove a point, but once his lips touched hers he remembered—

in excruciating detail—what it had been like to kiss her.

And he wanted more.

He moved his mouth across hers—light, teasing, taunting her to capitulate.

She remained tight-lipped—until his hand caressed the nape of her neck and slid into her hair, his fingertips brushing her scalp in the way he knew she liked.

She gave a little protesting groan and he sensed the moment of surrender when she placed her palm on his chest and half-heartedly pushed. Her lips softened a second later.

He didn't hesitate, taking advantage of her compliance by deepening the kiss, sweeping his tongue into her mouth to find hers, challenging her to deny them, confident she wouldn't.

For what seemed like a glorious eternity they made out like a besotted couple. Then he eased his hand out of her hair, his lips lingering on hers for a bittersweet second before he sat back.

What he saw shocked him more than the rare times he'd been ragdolled by a gnarly wave.

The old Callie was back.

Her brown eyes sparkled, her lush mouth curved smugly at the corners and she *glowed*.

Hell, he'd wanted to get her to lighten up. He hadn't counted on the winded feeling now making his lungs seize.

Being wiped out by a killer wave was easier than this.

But in the few seconds it took him to come up with something casual to say Callie closed off. Her glow gave way to a frown and shadows effectively cloaked the sparkle.

'Happy you sneaked a kiss for old times' sake? Did you want to prove something?'

He shook his head, still befuddled by the strength of his reaction to a kiss that should have meant nothing.

'I wanted to make a mockery of your "just work" declaration.'

She quirked an elegant brow. 'And did you think one little kiss would do that?'

He hadn't. Been thinking, that was. Like feeling the overwhelming rush he got from riding the perfect set on a huge swell he'd done the spontaneous thing. And now he had to live with the consequences: working alongside Callie for the next seven days while trying to forget how incredible she looked all mussed and vulnerable, and how she tasted—like chocolate and coffee.

'I guess I'm just annoyed by your attitude and I wanted to rattle you.'

As much as it turned out she still rattled *him*.

He expected her to bristle, to retreat behind

a mask of cool indifference. He didn't expect her to unravel before his eyes.

'Hell, are you *crying*?'

He reached out to hold her, but stopped when she scooted away.

She dashed a hand across her eyes before turning to stare out of the window, her profile stoic and tugging at his heartstrings.

'It's not you. I'm just juggling some other stuff, and it's taking a toll even though I have a handle on it.'

He'd never heard her sound so soft, so vulnerable, and he clamped down on the urge to haul her into his arms. Mixed messages be damned.

'Anything I can do to help?'

'Keep being a smartass. That should make me laugh.'

The quiver in her voice had him reaching across, gently cupping her chin and turning her towards him.

'I can back off if you're going through stuff. Cut the jokes. No kissing. That kind of thing.'

She managed a watery smile. 'No kissing's a given while we work together. The jokes I can handle.'

As she gnawed on her bottom lip realisation slammed into him as if he was pitching over the falls.

She probably had boyfriend troubles.

'Is it another guy? Because I can kick his ass—'

'Not a guy.'

Her smile morphed into a grin and it was like surfacing for air after being submerged underwater for too long.

She held a hand over her heart. 'I promise to lighten up. I'm just…overworked and tired and grumpy in general.'

'That seventh dwarf had nothing on you,' he mumbled, eliciting the expected chuckle—the first time he'd heard her sound remotely light-hearted since yesterday. 'Maybe you should thank me for kissing you. Because you've had an epiphany and—'

'Don't push your luck,' she said, tempering her growl with a wink, catapulting him back to Capri, where she'd winked at him in a tiny dinghy the moment before they'd entered the Blue Grotto, warning him to be careful because the cave was renowned for proposals and he might succumb.

She'd been teasing, but it had been the beginning of the end for them: no matter how carefree their fling, he'd wondered if Callie secretly harboured hopes for more.

And Archer had already learnt that the price paid for loving wasn't one he was willing to pay.

'Okay, so if kissing's off the agenda, work it is,' he said, holding her gaze for several long, loaded moments, daring her to disagree, hoping she would.

'Just work,' she echoed, before elbowing him and pointing at the road. 'If we ever get to Torquay, that is.'

As he reversed out of the sidestreet he knew he should be glad he'd cracked Callie's brittle, reserved outer shell.

But now he'd seen the woman beneath—the same warm, lush woman who'd almost snared his heart eight years ago—he wondered if he should be glad or scared.

CHAPTER FOUR

OKAY, so Callie hadn't been thinking straight since Archer had strolled into her office yesterday.

She'd been caught off guard by the gorgeous familiarity of him, by his outlandish suggestion to live with him for a week while they work, by his demand to agree or lose the account.

She'd also been worried about leaving Nora for the seven days before Christmas once she'd given in to secure the campaign—a worry that hadn't eased despite seeing her mum yesterday.

Her head had been filled with *stuff*. That was the only explanation for why she hadn't seen that kiss coming.

He'd done it out of frustration. She could see that now. He'd wanted to snap her out of her funk, to prove a point.

So what was the rationale behind her responding?

She'd assumed she could handle their cosy living arrangements for business's sake.

She hadn't counted on *this*. This slightly manic, out-of-control feeling because despite her vow to remain platonic he could undermine her with one itty-bitty kiss.

Damn.

She'd been silent for most of the trip, jotting fake notes for the campaign, needing to concentrate on something other than her tingling lips. Thankfully he'd respected her need for silence until about twenty miles out of Torquay.

They'd arrived, and she hadn't been able to believe her eyes.

As he'd steered up the winding, secluded street and pulled up outside Archer had called it his beach shack.

Massive understatement. *Huge.* Considering she now stood in a glass-enclosed lounge room as big as her entire apartment, with floor-to-ceiling glass and three-hundred-and-sixty-degree views of the Tasman Sea.

This place was no shack.

The pale blue rugs on gleaming ash floorboards, the sand-coloured suede sofas, the modern glass coffee tables—all screamed class, and were nothing like the mismatched furniture in the log cabin *shack* she'd imagined.

Archer had never been into material things when they'd first met. It looked as if being a world pro five years running changed a guy.

'I put your bags in the first guest room on the right,' he said, his bare feet barely making a sound as he padded up behind her.

Another thing she remembered: his dislike for footwear. It hadn't mattered much in Capri, when they'd spent many hours on the beach, and she'd hidden a smile as he'd unlocked the door here, dumped their bags inside and slipped off his loafers.

She liked him barefoot. He had sexy feet. They matched the rest of him.

'Thanks.'

He wiggled his eyebrows. 'Right next to my room, in case you were wondering.'

'I wasn't.' Her heart gave a betraying kick.

'Liar,' he said, snagging a strand of hair and winding it around his finger, tugging gently.

She knew what he was doing—flirting to keep her smiling. But she *sooo* wasn't going to play this game. Not after that dangerous kiss in the car.

'You still feel the buzz.' His gaze strayed to her lips and she could have sworn they tingled in remembrance.

The smart thing to do would be to lie, but she'd never been any good at it. That was how they'd hooked up in the first place—because of her complete inability to deny how incredibly hot she'd found the laid-back surfer.

He'd romanced her and she'd let him, fully aware that their week in Capri was nothing more than a holiday fling. Pity her impressionable heart hadn't caught up with logic and she'd fallen for him anyway. Her feelings had made it so much harder to get over him—especially after the way he'd ended it.

She'd do well to remember their break-up, not how his kiss had zapped her synapses in the car and reawakened a host of dormant memories she'd be better off forgetting.

'As I recall, didn't we have a conversation in the car about focussing on work?'

His finger brushed her scalp as he wound the strand all the way and she suppressed a tidal wave of yearning.

'You didn't answer my question.' His finger trailed along her hairline, skirting her temple, around her ear, lingering on the soft skin beneath it and she held her breath.

He'd kissed her there many times, until she'd been mindless with wanting him.

'That kiss you sprung on me in the car? Out of line. Business as usual this week. That's it.'

'Protesting much?'

'Archer, don't—'

'Go on, admit it. We still share a spark.'

His mouth eased into a wicked grin and she

held up a hand to ward him off. 'Doesn't mean we'll be doing anything about it.'

She expected him to ask why. She expected him to undermine her rationale with charm. Instead he stopped touching her, a shadow skating across his eyes before he nodded.

'You're right; we've got a ton of work to do. Best we don't get distracted.'

'Sounds like a plan,' she said, struggling to keep the disappointment out of her voice.

But something must have alerted him to the raging indecisive battle she waged inside—flee or fling—because he added, 'But once work is out of the way who knows what we'll get up to?'

She rolled her eyes, not dignifying him with a response, and his chuckles taunted her as she headed for the sanctity of her room.

She needed space. She needed time out. She needed to remember why getting involved with a nomad charmer again was a bad idea.

Because right now she was in danger of forgetting.

After what he'd been through with his family, Archer hated dishonesty.

Which made what he was doing with Callie highly unpalatable. He needed to tell her about being his date for the wedding pronto.

They'd arrived at the house three hours ago, and she'd made herself scarce on the pretext of unpacking and doing some last-minute research.

He knew better.

That impulsive kiss in the car might have been to prove a point but somewhere along the way it had morphed into something bigger than both of them.

He'd been so damn angry at her perpetual iciness he'd wanted to shock the truth out of her: the spark was still there.

Oh, it was there all right, and interestingly his little experiment had gone awry. He'd been shocked too.

He'd asked her to accompany him here for work—and the wedding. Nothing more, nothing less.

That kiss? Major reality check.

For there was something between them—something latent and simmering, just waiting to ignite.

Hell.

Way to go with complicating matters.

Best to take a step back and simplify—starting with divulging his addendum to her week-long stay.

He knocked twice at her bedroom door. 'Lunch is ready.'

The door creaked open and she stuck her head around it. What did she think? He'd catch sight of the bed and want to ravish her on the spot?

Hmmm…good point.

'Raincheck?'

He exhaled in exasperation. 'I need my marketing manager in peak form, which means no skipping meals—no matter how distasteful you find my company.'

'It's not that.' She blushed. 'I tend to grab snatched meals whenever I remember, so I don't do a sit-down lunch very often.'

'Lucky for you we're not sitting down.' He snagged her hand, meeting the expected resistance when she pulled back. He tugged harder. 'It's no big deal, Cal. Fish and chips on the beach. You can have your head buried behind your computer again in thirty minutes.'

Her expression softened. 'Give me five minutes and I'll meet you outside.'

'Is this a ploy so I have to release your hand and you'll abscond?'

She chuckled, a welcome, happy sound after her apparent snit. 'It's a ploy to use the bathroom.' She held up her hands. 'No other ulterior motives or escape plans in the works—promise.'

'In that case I'll see you down there.' He

squeezed her hand before releasing it. 'But more than five minutes and I get the best piece of fish.'

'You're on.'

Thankfully she only kept him waiting three, and he'd barely had time to spread the picnic blanket on the sand before she hit the beach running.

His breath caught as he watched her scuffing sand and snagging her hair into a loose knot at the nape of her neck. The actions were so reminiscent of their time in Capri he wanted to run half way to meet her.

Not liking how fast she'd got under his skin, he busied himself with unwrapping the paper and setting out the lemon wedges and salt sachets alongside the chips and grilled fish. Anything to keep his hands busy and resisting the urge to sweep her into his arms when she got close enough.

'That smells amazing,' she said, flopping down on the blanket next to him. 'But you said no sitting down.'

'Trivialities.' He pushed the paper towards her. 'Eat.'

And they did, making short work of the meal in companionable silence. He hadn't aimed for romance but there was a certain implied intimacy that had more to do with their shared past than any concerted effort now.

The comfortableness surprised him. Considering her reservations about heading to Torquay with him in the first place, and then her absentee act all morning, he'd expected awkwardness.

This relaxed ambience was good. All the better to spring his surprise.

'I need to ask you a favour.'

She licked the last grains of salt off her fingers—an innocuous, innocent gesture that shot straight to his groin.

'What is it?'

Now or never. 'My youngest brother Travis is getting married Christmas Eve and I'd like you to be my date.'

She stared at him in open-mouthed shock, her soda can paused halfway to her lips.

'You're asking me to be your *date*?'

She made it sound as if he'd asked her to swim naked in a sea full of ravenous sharks.

'We're not heading back 'til Christmas Day, and it doesn't make sense for you to spend Christmas Eve alone when you could come to what'll basically be a whoop-up party, so I thought you might like to come.'

'I don't have anything to wear,' she blurted, her horror-stricken expression not waning.

So much for that spark he'd imagined when they'd kissed.

'There are a couple of local boutiques, but honestly it'll be a pretty casual affair.'

'Well, you've thought of everything, haven't you?'

Her eyes narrowed, and he braced for the obvious question.

'Why didn't you ask me before we got here?'

Several lame-ass excuses sprang to mind, but he knew nothing but honesty would work now.

'Because I knew you wouldn't come.'

Her fingers clenched so hard she dented the soda can. 'So the business thing was an excuse?'

'No way. I need this surf school campaign to fly and you're the best.' He tried an endearing grin. 'I just figured we could kill two birds with one stone.'

'I could kill *you*,' she muttered, placing her soda can on the sand and hugging her knees to her chest. 'I don't like being taken for a fool.'

'You know that's not how I see you.'

She rested her cheek on her knees, her sidelong glance oddly vulnerable. 'How do I know? It's been eight years since I've seen you.'

Hating the certainty pinging through him that he'd majorly stuffed this up, he scooted closer and draped an arm across her shoulders, surprised when she didn't shrug it off.

'Honestly? I wanted to tell you, but I was pretty thrown at your office, and you weren't exactly welcoming so I took the easy way out and focussed on the business side of things. Forgive me?'

'I'll think about it,' she said, her tone underlined by a hint of ice as the corners of her mouth were easing upwards.

'Is it that much of a hardship to be my date for an evening?'

'Considering I don't know you any more, yeah.'

'Easily rectified.'

Before he could second-guess the impulse he leaned across and kissed her.

It was nothing like his reckless prove-a-point kiss in the car. This time it just felt *right*.

She fought him initially, trying to pull away, but his hand slid around the back of her head, anchoring her, and he sensed the second she gave in.

Her lips softened and she moaned, the barest of sounds but enough for him to deepen the kiss, until the roaring in his ears matched the pounding of the surf crashing metres from their feet.

He had no idea how long the kiss lasted. A

few seconds. An eternity. But when it ended he wished it hadn't.

'You've gotta stop doing that.' She shoved him away—hard.

'Sorry,' he said, not meaning it, and by her raised eyebrow she knew it.

'Hollow apologies after the fact don't cut it.' She jabbed a finger at his chest. 'And neither do those kisses. Quit it, okay?'

'Hey, I'm an impulsive guy. You can't blame me—'

'You want me to be your date for the wedding?'

'Yeah.'

'Then no more funny business.' Her gaze dropped to his lips, lingered, and he could have sworn he glimpsed longing. 'This campaign means a lot to both of us, so let's keep our minds on the job, okay?'

'Okay.'

He wanted to lighten the mood, end on a frivolous note. 'Maybe I wanted that kiss to prove it won't be so far-fetched for you to pretend to be a devoted date at the wedding—'

'You're impossible,' she said, leaping to her feet and dusting the sand off her butt—but not before he'd seen a glimmer of a grin.

'Nothing's impossible,' he murmured to

her retreating back as she marched off in a
semi-huff.

He'd got her to agree to manage the biggest
campaign of his career—and the one that meant
the most. He'd also coerced her into staying
with him for a week, and to be his date for the
wedding.

Considering how he'd ended things between
them all those years ago, he hadn't just pulled
off the impossible he'd pulled off a miracle.

Archer didn't want his family getting wind of
his house-guest just yet.

The Christmas Eve wedding would be bad
enough without the Flett hordes descending on
his place to check her out.

He'd twigged pretty fast that despite Callie
being a Melbourne girl she was vastly different
from his usual choice of date. She didn't need a
truckload of make-up before being seen in the
morning, she didn't need a hair-straightener
or the name of the nearest manicurist, and she
didn't wrinkle her nose at walking on the beach
in case her pedicure got chipped.

Maybe he'd made a mistake asking her to be
his date for the wedding, because from where
he was sitting, staring at the distant dot strolling
on the beach, her hair streaming in a dark cloud

behind her, he wondered if she'd be enough of a safeguard.

Callie was naturally warm and vibrant, not aloof and standoffish, the way he wanted his women to be when he visited home.

He *liked* that his folks disapproved of his dates and kept their distance. That was the whole point. What if they were drawn to Callie like he was and his plan to keep them at arm's length came crashing down?

He had to keep the Fletts away for as long as possible until the wedding, just in case.

He'd managed to fly under the radar so far. Last night had been spent poring over Callie's ideas for the surf school website, thrashing out slogans and content, working late over home-made pizzas and beer.

It scared him, how comfortable it was having her around. He'd never had a woman stay at his place, let alone lived with anyone. It was his sanctuary, away from the surf crowd, the fans, the media.

No one knew he owned this place except his family.

Some of whom were belting down his door at this very minute.

Damn. So much for keeping their distance.

Cursing under his breath, he yanked the door open and glared at Trav and Tom, ignoring the familiar squeeze his heart gave when he glimpsed Izzy, his six-year-old niece, peering up at him from behind her dad's legs.

He hated how out of all the Fletts she was the one guaranteed to make him feel the worst for staying away. The kid was too young to realise what was going on, but she managed to lay a guilt trip on him every visit.

At three, she'd stuck her tongue out at his date every chance she got and bugged him to teach her how to surf. He'd begged off with his usual excuse—only staying for two days, maybe next time.

At four, she'd placed stick insects in his date's handbag and a hermit crab in her designer shoe, while pestering him for the elusive surf lesson.

At five, she'd verbally flayed his date for her 'too yellow' hair and 'too red' lipstick, and had given up asking him to surf.

He should have been glad. Instead it had ripped him in two when he'd said goodbye to her around this time last year.

It wasn't Izzy's fault he had issues with the rest of his family, but he was scared. Getting close to Izzy might let the rest of them in again, which made him angsty. What if he let them into his heart again only to have it handed back to him like eight years ago?

Every trip home it was the same. Initial tension between him and his brothers soon easing into general ribbing and guy-chat, his mum fussing around him, and prolonged stilted awkwardness with his dad. He still wanted the security of Callie as his buffer zone, but maybe this time he'd swallow his pride and make the first move.

He'd wanted to in the past, but every time he made the decision to broach the gap he'd realise two days weren't long enough to make up for the years apart.

This year he was staying for a week. No excuse.

He squatted down to her level. 'Hey, Iz, long time no see.'

She frowned, but it didn't detract from the curious sparkle in her big blue eyes.

The expression in those eyes—guileless, genuine, trusting—slugged him anew. A guy couldn't hide for long from those eyes. They saw too much, knew too much—including the fact he was acting like a recalcitrant jerk in not welcoming his brothers into his home.

He opened his arms, saw the indecision on her face before she slowly stepped out from behind Tom's legs. She hesitated and his gut squelched with sadness.

It shouldn't be like this—his own niece treating him like a stranger. *He'd* done this, with his stubborn pride. He needed to get over the past. For the longer it took the harder it became to pretend nothing had happened and go back to the way it had been before: a close-knit family who supported each other through everything.

Archer waited, eyeballing Izzy, hoping she could see how much he wanted to squeeze her tight.

After another interminable second that felt like sixty, she flung herself into his arms. He exhaled in relief as he hugged her hard, ignoring the flutter in his chest he got every time this kid wrapped her arms around his neck and hung on as if she'd never let go.

'Where've you been?' She released him, stepped back and crossed her arms as he stood. 'You never come see me any more.'

Practically squirming under the interrogation, Archer floundered for words that wouldn't sound like a trite excuse.

Tom placed a hand on his daughter's shoulder. 'You know your uncle travels a lot, honey. We're lucky to see him when he has time.'

Ouch. Tom's barb slugged him like the punches they'd traded as kids, wrestling at the water's edge to see who'd get the long board for the day.

'At least he always brings me a gift,' Izzy

said, pushing her way past him and bounding to the chessboard set up in a far corner, her natural exuberance replacing the reticence that sliced him up inside.

'Manners, Iz,' Tom said, following his daughter into the room and looking around in a not too subtle attempt at sussing out Callie's whereabouts.

'Couldn't keep your big mouth shut, huh?' Archer elbowed Trav as he brought up the rear. 'When we surfed the other day you said you'd keep your lips zipped about me being back early.'

His youngest brother grinned. 'Tom threatened me with bodily harm, and considering he's around a lot more than you, I caved.'

Great—another dig at his absenteeism. Closely following Izzy's reluctant treatment, it made him feel like a heel.

'So where is she?' Tom stuck his hands in his pockets and looked around.

'Who?'

'This mystery woman, of course.' Tom eyeballed him. 'When you make it home for your obligatory Christmas visit your date stays in town. So the fact she's staying here speaks volumes.'

Tom jerked a thumb in Trav's direction. 'We want to check her out, make sure she hasn't got two heads, 'cos that's the only kind of woman who'd be crazy enough to stay here with you.'

Despite another dig from Tom about his obligatory visits, Archer felt his tension fade at his brother's jocularity. 'Wanna beer?'

'Sure.'

Ideally Archer didn't want them hanging around long enough to meet Callie, who'd gone for a walk on the beach to clear her head after a marathon morning brainstorming. But Tom was right; he barely saw his brothers any more and, even though they'd been complicit in his dad's decision to keep the truth secret, he missed the camaraderie they'd once shared.

'I bring a date home every year. This one's no different.' Archer's heart gave a betraying buck at the lie.

'So you're letting some plastic, fake, stick-thin bimbo share your secret hideaway?' Tom snorted. 'Not bloody likely.'

Archer wanted to defend those poor women his brother had just disparaged, but sadly he happened to agree. The women he'd brought home in the past had been exactly as Tom described and not a patch on Callie.

'She's not real, is she? You've made her up so Mum won't go into her speed-dating frenzy in an effort to have you settle for a local girl rather than *those city girls*.'

Archer chuckled at Tom's imitation of their mum, who made *those city girls* sound as if he was dating a brothel's inhabitants.

Tom had followed him into the kitchen, and Archer handed him a beer while uncapping another for Trav and popping an orange soda tab for Izzy.

'She's real. And you'll get to meet her at the wedding like everyone else.'

He held up his beer bottle and Tom clinked it. 'Sure she hasn't got two heads?'

Archer smirked. 'Trust me, Callie's pretty great—'

'Callie? *The* Callie?'

Tom lowered his beer and stared at him with blatant curiosity as Archer silently cursed his slip of the tongue.

He'd had no intention of telling anyone her name until the wedding—let alone Tom, the only Flett who knew how close he'd come to giving up his dream for her.

He'd blurted it out after Tom's divorce had been finalised, sitting on his deck four years ago. That had been one hell of a night. Tom had been miserable, Trav had been blind drunk and clueless how to handle the situation, and Archer had felt like an outcast. The three of them had been in a foul mood and it had almost come to blows. Archer had tussled with Tom and that release of steam and testosterone had opened up a narrow pathway to the truth.

Tom and Trav had told him about dad then—how he'd sworn them to secrecy, how they'd hated keeping it from him but hadn't wanted to stress the seriously ill Frank.

He guessed he understood their logic—who knew? He might have done the same—but it didn't make it any easier to handle when he still didn't know why he'd been the odd man out.

With the air somewhat cleared between them, talk had moved on to Tom's divorce, and Archer had sunk beers in commiseration, alternating between being outraged and bitter on behalf of his brother, who'd done the right thing by marrying the girl he'd got pregnant and yet got screwed over anyway, and determination never to end up like him.

Tom had been morose, berating himself for losing his head over a woman, and Archer had made the mistake of opening up about Callie to make him feel better.

'You're not the only one. We all get sucked in by a memorable female now and then.'

That confession under the onslaught of too many lagers had now come back to bite him on the butt.

He forced a laugh, aiming for casual. 'Turns out my online marketing manager is Callie.

Had no idea 'til we met in Melbourne to tee up the surf school campaign. She's here to work for the week—made sense she came to the wedding as my date. Nothing more to it.'

Archer took a slug of beer after his spiel, wondering who he was trying to convince—himself or Tom.

Yesterday had been tough. Hell, it had been sheer torture, watching Callie come alive as she sketched out ideas, seeing her glow as he approved an early pro forma, seeing glimpses of the vibrant woman he'd once lost his head over many years ago.

Sadly she reserved her enthusiasm for work only. Following that impulsive kiss on the beach she'd reverted to coolly polite and casually friendly.

She might have ditched her initial antagonism, but an invisible barrier between them was still there—one he had no hope of breaching considering how things had ended between them.

Correction: how *he'd* ended things between them.

He didn't blame her for being wary. But late last night, with the woman he'd once been crazy for sleeping in the room next door and insomnia plaguing him, he'd wished they could recapture half the easy-going camaraderie they'd once shared.

He only had a week to get this surf school campaign up and running before he flew out to Hawaii for Christmas Day, so realistically he couldn't afford to stuff around.

He knew what he was doing. Flirting with her as a deliberate tactic to distract himself from the stress of being home and having to deal with his family. It was a distancing technique he'd honed with other dates before her. But none had affected him as much as Callie.

He'd deliberately kept things between them light-hearted and work-focussed, but what would happen if he ratcheted up the heat? Would she release some of that new reserve she carried around like an invisible cloak and resurrect the passion they'd once shared?

Tom pointed his beer in Archer's direction. 'The fact she's the first woman you've ever brought here speaks volumes.'

'It was convenient for work, that's all.'

'Yeah, keep telling yourself that.'

Or course Callie chose that moment to hustle through the back door, wind-tousled and pink-cheeked and utterly delectable.

'Hey, Arch, there's a car out front—' She caught sight of Tom and stopped, her eyes widening, before she crossed the kitchen and held out her hand. 'You're a much better-looking version of Archer, so you must be a Flett too.'

Tom laughed as he shook her hand. 'I like her already,' he said, while Archer shot him a filthy look.

'Callie, meet my older brother, Tom.'

A playful smile teased the corners of her mouth as she glanced up at Tom—a smile she hadn't shot *him* once since they'd arrived.

'Pleased to meet you.'

Something painful twisted in his chest at the way she lit up in the way she'd once used to light up around him.

'Come meet his daughter—and Trav, the groom.'

Tom's goofy grin proved what he already knew: he sounded like an uptight ass.

'You have a little girl? That's great,' Callie said, falling into step beside Tom while Archer brought up the rear, hating himself for feeling petty and out of sorts that Callie had lightened up for the first time since yesterday because of his brother.

'Hey, another girl. Awesome.'

Izzy flew at Callie and a strange, unidentifiable feeling swamped him as he watched his niece hug her, spontaneously and without reserve, the way he'd wished Iz had hugged *him* when he'd first opened the door.

Unfazed, Callie led Izzy back to the chessboard, where she shook hands with Trav, whose goofy grin matched Tom's.

Great—two Flett males she'd slayed. He couldn't wait until she met his dad.

Three.

The number popped into his head.

Three Flett males she'd slayed, including him. No matter how many times he denied it, the fact remained: Callie was the kind of woman who could have an impact on a guy.

An unforgettable impact, considering the schmuck he turned into around her.

When he finally tore his gaze away from the captivating sight of Callie giggling alongside Izzy, Tom's smug smirk greeted him.

'So tell me. What did an amazing woman like that see in a putz like you? And why the hell did you let her go?'

Did.

Past tense.

Having his brother verbalise what he'd been wondering himself since reconnecting with her ticked him off more than the uncertainty plaguing him.

This week was about work and familial obligation, before he fled back to the life he liked. If a little light-hearted flirtation with Callie made it more bearable, so be it.

He hadn't banked on this restlessness, this annoying feeling that he was missing out on something by making the lifestyle choices he had. Worse, having his brother articulate it.

'Leave it alone,' he muttered under his breath, garnering a broader grin from Tom.

'You know I'm the last person to believe in all that romance crap, considering the number Tracy did on me, but have you ever considered this coincidence of her coming back into your life might mean something?'

Archer stared at his brother in amazement. Tom had given up his dreams to turn pro for Tracy, a local surf groupie who'd deliberately got pregnant to snare her man. Tom had foregone his dream to marry Tracy, stay in Torquay and raise Izzy.

Ironically, Tracy had been the one to take off a year into the marriage, leaving Tom with a toddler and a nagging bitterness.

Tom didn't believe in happily-ever-afters, so the fact he'd mentioned the word *romance* and alluded to fate alerted Archer to how badly he must be making a fool of himself.

'You've been spending too much time reading Izzy's fairytales, mate.' His gruff response came out as a snarl, and he immediately realised his reaction had increased rather than eased Tom's suspicions.

Tom held up his hands. 'Just voicing an impartial opinion. No need to get your tether rope in a knot.'

Callie pumped her fists in the air and shimmied her shoulders as Trav made a disastrous move with his queen. Izzy cheered and Callie joined in, her vivacity flooring him in a way he'd never expected.

She'd been so focussed yesterday, concentrating on business and little else. He'd forgotten she could be like this: funny and vibrant and cute.

Well, not forgotten exactly; the memories had been deliberately shoved to a far recess of his mind and ignored. It wouldn't be good for him to recall how good they'd been together for that brief time in Capri. It would only end in tears.

Archer glared at Tom. 'You breathe one word of her staying here to the folks and you're dead.'

A cunning glint lit Tom's eyes. 'Tell you what. I'll keep my mouth shut if you admit you still want her.'

In response, Archer got him in a headlock. He could never stay detached with Trav or Tom for long. Each year when he returned his initial aloofness disappeared a little quicker.

Besides, he didn't really blame them for withholding stuff he should have been privy to. That had been his dad's doing and, while he loved the stubborn old coot, he couldn't forget. Forgive? Yeah, he'd done that a few years back. Now he just had to pluck up the courage to let Frank know, rather than punishing him because he couldn't get the words out to make it all better.

As he tussled with Tom, Izzy joined in the fun by leaping on her dad's back. Her squeals of laughter didn't distract him from the truth.

Denying any semblance of feeling for Callie was useless.

She'd wheedled her way under his skin.

Again.

And there wasn't one damn thing he could do about it.

CHAPTER FIVE

'PEACE at last.' Archer slid Callie a coffee as she lounged on the balcony.

'Your brothers are cool and Izzy's adorable,' Callie said, adding an extra spoon of sugar to her espresso.

She needed the hit, still reeling from seeing Archer in a family environment. The guy she'd known had never talked about family. He had been the quintessential loner who breezed through life without a care in the world. The guy who didn't commit to anything or anyone beyond his beloved surfing.

So to see him interacting with his brothers had thrown her. He'd been reserved at first, as if he didn't want them in his home—which made no sense after the rough-housing she'd seen once he'd lightened up.

When she'd strolled into the kitchen after her walk it had been like walking smack-bang into an invisible glass wall. The tension had been that thick. She'd glimpsed the circumspection in his eyes and the fact she'd recognised it, could get a read on his feelings after all this time, had irked.

She'd masked her discomfort by being bright and bubbly and a little gushing with his brothers and niece. Which had seemed to annoy Archer further.

What was wrong with the guy? As his date for the wedding, didn't he want her to act naturally around his family? *Sheesh*.

And that was another thing that had thrown her: his obvious attachment to his niece. He'd never struck her as the type to like kids. Not with his lifestyle. But he'd been smitten with Izzy, and seeing the two of them together, their heads bent close as they mulled over a jigsaw puzzle, had unlocked a host of feelings she'd rather not deal with.

She didn't want to remember how attentive and caring he'd been in Capri. And she sure as hell didn't want to acknowledge his consistent flirting, slowly chipping away at her necessary resistance.

She wouldn't give in—not when she knew his overt displays of charm came as naturally to him as catching a wave. She'd been sucked in by it once, and had been let down beyond belief.

She knew that feeling well. Bruno Umberto

had made an art form of building up hopes only to let down his daughter.

As for the rare glimpses of unguarded admiration—first when she'd been playing chess with Trav, then when she'd made lemonade for Izzy—she didn't like that at all.

He'd used to look at her like that in Capri, as if she were the only woman in the world, and to see the same look seriously perturbed her. She couldn't afford to get involved with Archer again—not when her emotions were already bruised and fragile from the rollercoaster ride with her mum.

Living life in the moment was one thing. Setting herself up for another dose of heartbreak was another.

She'd given in to his request to be his wedding date for one reason only: to keep the peace between them so they could get the surf school business done and dusted this week.

That kiss on the beach had been just like the one in the car on the way down here yesterday morning. Archer being Archer. Impulsive. Rash. Selfish. Doing what he wanted regardless of the consequences.

Harsh? Maybe, but all the kisses in the world couldn't turn back time and erase the way he'd ended things between them, and that was what she had to focus on if she were to keep any residual feelings at bay.

And doing that was imperative. She couldn't afford to acknowledge how incredible his kisses were, how alive they made her feel.

Uh-uh. She needed to focus on the one reason she was here: business.

'Yeah, Izzy's the best.' Archer held up a hand, wavered it. 'Tom and Trav? Not so much.'

'Your mum must've had a handful with three boys.'

He stiffened, as if she'd asked an intensely personal question rather than making conversation. 'Yeah, we kept her on her toes.'

She wanted to ask about his parents, about his childhood, but she couldn't get a read on his mood.

They were sprawled on comfy cushioned sofas—she'd studiously avoided the love-seat—on the glass-enclosed balcony, overlooking an amazing ocean tinged with sunset. It reeked of intimacy, yet Archer's perfunctory answers and shuttered expression weren't encouraging.

'Do you want kids?'

And then he went and floored her with a question like that. A question far surpassing intimacy and heading straight for uncomfortable.

'Not sure.'

She cradled her coffee cup, hoping some if

its warmth would melt the icy tentacles of unease squeezing her heart.

After the genetic testing, when it had been proved she didn't have the mutated gene that sounded a death knell for her mum, she'd undergone counselling to get a grip on her rioting emotions: relief, guilt, happiness, fear. Yet for all these years, deep down where she hid her innermost fears, she hadn't been able to shake the irrational dread that somehow those doctors had made a mistake and she'd contract the disease after all.

Crazy and illogical. The odds were in her favour to have perfectly healthy kids. But why tempt fate when it had dealt her such a rough hand so far?

'The opportunity hasn't come up?'

Surprised by his line of questioning, she eyeballed him. 'If you're asking if I've been in a serious relationship since Capri, no. I've dated. That's about it.'

She half expected him to flinch at her bluntness in bringing up the past, but to his credit he didn't look away.

'Why?'

'What is this? Pry into Callie's soul day?'

She placed her coffee on the nearest table and her hands unexpectedly shook.

'Callie, I—'

'Sorry for snapping your head off, but if you're hoping to hear I've been pining for you all these years, and that's why I'm not involved in a serious relationship, you're delusional.'

His eyes widened in horror. 'Hell, that's not what I want.' He rubbed the back of his neck in a familiar gesture that added to the poignancy of the moment. 'I just feel like we've been doing this avoidance dance, concentrating on work, making polite small talk, retreating to our rooms. Then I saw how you were with Izzy and it got me thinking...'

She shouldn't ask. She really shouldn't. 'About?'

Yep, she was asking for it.

'About why the beautiful, vibrant woman I met in Capri hasn't been snapped up by some smart guy?'

A guy smarter than you? she wanted to say, but silently counted to five before she blurted it out.

'Maybe I don't want to be snapped up? Maybe I'm happy with my life the way it is?'

'Are you?'

She stiffened as he reached out and traced a fingertip between her brows, eliciting a shiver.

'Because you've got this little dent here that tells me otherwise.'

Touched he'd noticed, annoyed at his intuitiveness, she swatted his hand away. 'How did you get so perceptive?'

'Honestly?'

She picked up her coffee cup, cradled it, hiding behind it as she took a deep sip and nodded.

'The way you lit up around Izzy was the same way you used to be in Capri. Carefree. Quick to laugh. Like nothing fazed you.' He paused, as if searching her face for approval to continue. 'At first I thought it was me and the way I treated you in the past that was bugging you. But it's something else—something that runs deeper.'

He snaffled her hand and squeezed it before she could protest.

'You know you can tell me, right?'

Uh-oh. Callie could handle teasing, charming Archer. She couldn't handle this newer, sensitive version, who'd honed in on the emotional load she carried daily like an invisible yoke.

'We should finish off the home page of the website—'

He gripped her hand tighter. 'Tell me.'

'Wow, you're bossy.' She blew out a long, slow breath, not wanting to do this but knowing he'd keep badgering until she did.

He'd been like that in Capri: badgering her to have dinner with him that first night; badgering her to stroll along the moonlit beach afterwards; badgering her with his loaded stares and sexy smiles and wicked ways.

Now, like then, she was powerless to resist.

'It's my mum. She has motor neurone disease.'

Shock widened his eyes and sadness twisted his mouth. 'Aw, honey, I'm sorry.'

'Me too,' she said, gnawing on her bottom lip and willing the sudden sting of tears away.

She'd cried enough to fill the Tasman Sea but it didn't change the facts. The horrid disease was eating away at her mum's nervous system one neurone at a time.

'There's nothing they can do?'

She shook her head, grateful for the strong hold he had on her hand. She would have bolted for the sanctity of her room otherwise and not come out for the next few days.

'They initially gave her three years. She's lasted seven.'

Quick as ever he did the math, and understanding flickered in those aquamarine depths. 'Did you find out soon after you got home from Europe?'

She nodded, remembering the far-reaching consequences of that diagnosis.

Despite the way they'd ended, would she have booked a flight to join Archer if her mum hadn't fallen ill? Would her life have been filled with sunshine and sand and surf rather than a rented box-like office space? Would she have been blissfully unaware of the potential gene landmine pumping through her veins and had Archer's kids?

Stupid thinking, considering Archer hadn't wanted her back then, let alone a commitment that could lead to kids.

'So she's undergoing the usual rounds of physiotherapy and occupational therapy to keep her as mobile as possible?'

'Yeah, though her muscle wastage is advancing pretty rapidly.'

How many times had she gently massaged those muscles in the hope they'd somehow miraculously regenerate? Too many. The sight of Nora wasting away before her eyes broke her heart.

'She's confined to a wheelchair, though the special home where she lives is fabulous in taking care of her.'

'The staff in those facilities deserve a medal, considering the range of healthcare they provide.'

'How come you know so much about it?'

'I sponsored a charity benefit for Lou Gehrig's disease in LA. Thought I'd better know something about it before rocking up to the shindig.'

Callie eyed him speculatively. Sportsmen around the world attended charity benefits, but she doubted many of them cared enough to delve into the details of the fundraiser's disease.

'Is there anything I can do?'

Touched he'd offered, she shook her head. 'Thanks, but I've got it covered.'

At least she would have once she got paid for this surf school campaign. Which meant getting back to work, despite the urge to linger in this intimate cocoon where the guy she'd once loved seriously cared.

'We should get back to work—'

'Tomorrow,' he said, scooting alongside her and draping an arm across her shoulders before she had a chance to move. 'We've been pushing it pretty hard since we arrived yesterday. Let's just chill tonight.'

Chilling sounded good, but sadly there was nothing cool about being snuggled in the crook of Archer's shoulder. The opposite, with her body warming from the inside out until it felt as if her skin blistered.

She should move, should head inside and collate a few more ideas for the website's link page. Instead she found herself slowly relaxing into him, wanting to savour this moment.

The irony of being cradled in Archer's arms after she'd rammed home the fact that this week was just about business wasn't lost on her. It felt good. Great, in fact. But temporary—a comforting hug from an ex. An ex who'd ended their all-too-brief relationship in no uncertain terms.

She wouldn't get used to it, but for now, with his solid warmth seeping through her, she couldn't help but wonder what it would be like if she made the most of their remaining time together.

Was she a glutton for punishment to contemplate another short-term fling? Heck, yeah. But considering the road ahead—the uncertainty of her mum's illness, her lifespan, and the ensuing pain when the inevitable happened—would it be so bad to take a little bit of happiness while she could?

Logically, she'd be an idiot to contemplate it.

Emotionally, her heart strained towards him, eager for affection, knowing how sensational they could be together even for a scant week.

He kissed the top of her head and she sighed, appreciating his sensitivity in not pushing her to talk any more.

Besides, she'd said enough. She hadn't told any of her past dates about her mum—hadn't let them get close enough. Yet in two days she'd let Archer march back into her life—and a little corner of her heart if she were completely honest—and trusted him enough to divulge the truth about her mum.

At least she hadn't told him all of it. Some things were best left unsaid.

The memory of her genetic testing sent a shiver through her and he tightened his hold, conveying strength in silence.

Yeah, she could do worse than have some fun for a change over the next week.

In the lead-up to Christmas surely she'd been a good girl all year and Santa owed her big-time?

The next morning Callie had to admit spending the week in Torquay had been a stroke of genius on Archer's part.

She'd worked uninterrupted for the last three hours, perched on his balcony, enjoying the sea air and the view, inspired in a way she hadn't been for a long time.

She didn't know if it was being away from the office for the first time in years that had sparked her creativity, but she'd added some amazing touches to the surf school website today. Ideas to build on when he gave her the grand tour this afternoon.

It helped that he'd made himself scarce since dawn this morning. She hadn't been looking forward to having him hover over her work-space after her confession last night.

Sure, it had seemed as if telling him about her mum had been the right thing to do at the time, while they were relaxed and cosy at dusk, but in the harsh light of day, after a sleepless night spent second-guessing herself, she hadn't wanted to face him.

Shared confidences bred intimacy, and that was one thing she couldn't afford with Archer. She'd been foolish enough in testing herself by being here this week. For while he'd demanded she come to Torquay to secure the campaign she probably could have weaselled her way out of it if she'd tried.

But the moment he'd strutted into her office, spouting his terms, she'd wanted to prove to herself once and for all that she was over him, that he had no hold over her despite spending seven days in her company.

She'd been doing a good job of it too—those kisses he'd sprung on her notwithstanding—until last night.

Following their break-up, she'd tarred Archer with the same brush as her dad: selfish, self-absorbed, a man who followed his whims without regard to anyone else. It had been a coping mechanism, labelling him so harshly.

Yet last night—the way he'd comforted her,

the way he'd been attuned to her mood and content to sit in silence—had seriously undermined her lowly opinion of him and made her seem childish in lashing out in the past because she'd been foolish enough to feel more than he had.

Laughter drifted up from the beach and she sheltered her eyes with her hand to focus on the group by the water's edge.

A bunch of teenagers surrounded Archer, their boards stuck vertically in the sand like sentinels. He stood in the centre, gesturing towards the ocean, demonstrating a few moves, while the teens jostled and elbowed for prime position in front of their idol.

Embarrassment twanged her heart. A selfish guy wouldn't give up his precious schoolset-up time to hang with a bunch of kids. Just as a selfish guy wouldn't have taken the time to comfort her last night.

Feeling increasingly guilty, she shut down the webpage program she'd been tweaking, scooped up her paperwork and dumped the lot inside.

Another bonus of working here. She could take a head-clearing walk along the beach any time. And right now, remorseful, she wanted to let Archer know he wasn't so bad after all.

Not that she had any intention of confessing such a thing to him, but she'd been pretty remote, deliberately maintaining an invisible distance between them. Considering how great he'd been with her last night, it wouldn't hurt for her to lighten up a tad.

She slipped off her sandals at the bottom of the steps, loving the gritty sand squelching between her toes as she strolled towards him.

The closer she got, the more she could see the rapt expressions on the teens' faces, and hear Archer giving a pep talk. The guy was usually a livewire, but she'd never seen him so animated. Which made her wonder why he'd been so reticent with his brothers when he was obviously a people person.

The pep talk must have worked because the teens let out a rousing cheer before grabbing their boards and heading for the surf.

Archer's eyes glowed with pride and satisfaction as he waved her over.

'Did you see that?'

She smiled and nodded. 'Those kids think you're a surf god.'

'I just gave them a few pointers. But the way they responded...' He shook his head, staring at the wetsuited blobs bobbing in the ocean. 'They were blown away to hear about the surf school and asked a million questions. They're going to tell their mates.'

He pumped his fist. 'I'm stoked.'

'You did good.' She touched his arm, an impulsive gesture to convey her approval, but one she regretted when he snagged her hand and tugged her close.

'Your approval means a lot.'

'Why?' She eased away, needing to put a little distance between them, overwhelmed by his closeness.

'Because I hate to have you think badly of me.'

Still wrestling with her recent revelation as to his true character, she aimed for levity. 'Come this time next week it won't matter what I think. You'll be hanging loose in Hawaii or Bali, and I'll be doing an amazing job maintaining your surf school website.'

'You're wrong.'

She pretended to misunderstand. 'No, really, I'll be working like a maniac on your website—'

'Your opinion matters.'

She glanced away, unable to fathom his steady stare, almost daring her to—what? Argue? Agree? Analyse?

'Aren't you going to ask me why?'

She bit down on her bottom lip. No, she didn't want to hear any of the deep and meaningful reasons he'd concocted. However much she regretted misjudging him all these years, she didn't want anything from this week beyond a successful campaign.

'Fine. I'll tell you anyway.' He released her arm, only to capture her chin, leaving her no option but to look at him. 'You're the only woman I've ever known who gets me. And, while it scares the hell out of me, I kinda think it's cool.'

Oh, heck. Trapped beneath the intensity of his stare, with his praise like a soft caress, she felt the inevitable pull between them flare to life.

She couldn't look away, couldn't resist as their lips inched towards each other, couldn't think of a rational reason why she shouldn't kiss an old flame on a pristine beach.

Old flame… Those two words penetrated her dazed fog.

What the heck was she doing? She could blame his first two kisses on impulse, but this? This was something else entirely.

If her opinion mattered to him, his praise mattered to her. She basked under his admiration, but letting it go to her head would be beyond foolhardy.

She couldn't do this. Fall under his spell. *Again.*

She wasn't the same naïve girl any more.

This time she had no doubt if they had another fling it would end the same way.

All the whispered words in the world wouldn't change the facts: Archer lived for his freedom; she lived for making Nora's lifespan—what was left of it—as comfortable as possible.

Their goals were worlds apart.

With their lips almost touching, she wrenched out of his grasp and took a few backward steps.

'Callie—'

She couldn't bear the confusion warring with something deeper in his eyes, so she did the only thing possible.

She turned and ran.

CHAPTER SIX

'WHAT do you think?'

Callie stared at Archer's 'little' surf school, not quite comprehending how the plans and architectural impressionist photos she'd used for the pre-website had morphed into this sprawling complex perched on a sheltered bluff metres from the ocean.

'It's absolutely breathtaking,' she said, doing a three-sixty, taking in the whitewashed main building, the dorms with bright blue doors, the storeroom large enough to house her apartment three times over, and the supplies shop tucked to the left of the entrance.

'You designed all this?'

His mouth quirked. 'Don't sound so incredulous. I'm not just a pretty face.'

She grimaced at his lame line. He laughed. 'Come on, I'll give you the grand tour.'

He snagged her hand as if it was the most natural thing in the world, and she clamped down on her first urge to ease it away.

She'd done some hard thinking after she'd bolted from the beach earlier. Confiding in Archer about her mum's illness last night, allowing him to hold her, welcoming his comfort, followed by their closeness on the beach that morning, had solidified what she'd already known deep down.

That spending time with him, albeit for work, had the potential to crack open the protective wall she'd erected around her heart.

The fissures had appeared with his kisses, and they'd well and truly fractured last night, when they'd sat on that damned deck until the sun set. Throw in that *moment* on the beach today and…trouble.

That was another thing. He'd been quiet last night, attuned to her need for silence while still holding her. He hadn't prattled on with small talk designed to distract. He'd just held her, his arm wrapped solidly around her waist, his cheek resting lightly on the top of her head.

He thought she *got* him? The feeling was entirely mutual and that was scarier than any reawakening feelings she might be experiencing.

He'd been like that in Capri—attuned to her moods and desires after only just meeting. It was as if they'd fitted. She didn't believe in love at first sight, or great loves, or romantic kismet—her pragmatic mum and selfish dad had ensured that—but her connection with Archer eight years earlier had defied logic.

He'd anticipated what she'd wanted back then—more Chianti, a cotton shawl for their evening walk, another swim—but his intuition beyond the physical had impressed her the most.

He'd tuned in to her emotionally, on some deeper level that had made her truly comfortable with him in a way she'd never been with another guy. They'd talked for hours. Usually about inconsequential stuff, childhood anecdotes, secret dreams, and she'd never recaptured that magic with any date.

It had made their break up all the harder.

They'd both had open-ended travel tickets and hadn't discussed moving on. While the end of their holiday idyll had been inevitable, she'd expected to stay in contact. And a small part of her had hoped they'd reconnect in Melbourne one day.

But all that had ended when he'd told her the blunt truth: she'd read too much into a holiday fling. What they'd shared was nothing more than a bit of fun and she needed to lighten up before she scared off more guys.

His harsh words had hurt. Devastated her, in fact, and she'd never understood how the guy she'd grown so close to in such a short space of time could shut down emotionally and walk away without looking back.

She'd do well to remember the past before those cracks and fissures around her heart disintegrated completely.

Thankfully he hadn't mentioned her bolt up the beach after their almost-kiss, and she'd been working double time to pretend everything was fine.

She'd finish out this week without him knowing how he still affected her if it killed her.

She pointed at a sign with her free hand. 'I still can't believe you called it Winki Pop Surf School. Sounds like something out of a kid's fairytale.'

He feigned indignation. 'I'll have you know Winki Pop is one of the best surf breaks around here.' He chuckled. 'Besides, it has a better ring to it than some of the other breaks around here.'

'Like?'

'Southside. Centreside. Rincon.'

'I see your point. It does have a certain charm.'

''Course it would, with me as the owner.' He winked. 'Mr Winki, that's me.'

She groaned at his terrible joke, his carefree laughter reminding her of another time they'd swapped banter like this, a time she'd treasured before reality set in.

She listened closely as they toured the school, taking mental notes. The smart thing to do would be take out her iPhone and dictate ideas, or pull out the trusty notepad she kept in her bag.

But both activities would involve releasing Archer's hand, and for now her blasé act depended on it. Easing her hand out of his would probably have him asking what was wrong, and if it was connected to earlier on the beach, and yada, yada, yada. She just didn't want to go there.

When they reached the store shed he unlocked the door and flung it open. 'Ready to put the master touch on the online forums you suggested?'

Confused, she glanced inside the shed lined with surfboards and wetsuits of all shapes and sizes. 'Not sure what you mean.'

His wicked grin alerted her to an incoming suggestion she wouldn't like.

'If you're going to be the moderator of the school's online forums, you need to know what it feels like to surf.'

The incoming missile detonated and left her reeling. 'Me? On a surfboard? Out *there*?' Her voice ended on a squeak as she pointed to the expanse of ocean a short stroll away.

'Yeah. And no better time to start than now.'

Like hell. She loved swimming, loved the ocean, but no way would she klutz around like a floundering whale in front of him. Learning to surf had always been on her life's 'to do' list, but here, now, with *him*?

No flipping way.

She snapped her fingers. 'Sorry, no bathers. Maybe next time—'

'I'm sure we stock your size.'

His gaze roved her body, assessing, warming, zinging every nerve-ending along the way.

Before she could protest further he placed a hand in the small of her back and propelled her forward.

'Come on. You said surfing was on your bucket list. No time like the present to tick it off while getting first-hand experience for work.'

Stunned he'd remembered her bucket list, she allowed him to lead her into the dim interior.

A pungent blend of new fibreglass, rubber and coconut-scented wax tickled her nose, but through all that she could smell the potent male beside her: sunshine and sea air and pure Archer.

He was right, of course. Knowing what learning to surf entailed would give her more credibility when she manned the surf school online forums, so technically this classified as work.

But the part where he sized up her body, his glance as intimate as a lover's caress, went beyond work. Way beyond.

Her skin grew clammy as he flicked through the suits on a rack before unhooking a black wetsuit with a fuchsia zig-zag and handing it to her.

'Here—this should fit.'

A little tremor of excitement shot through her as her fingertips brushed the rubber. How long since she'd done something spontaneous and fun and just for her? Too long. And as he handed her a practical navy one-piece, she suddenly couldn't wait to get out there.

He jerked a thumb over his shoulder. 'Changing rooms back there. But first let's get you set up with a board.'

'Whatever you choose will be fine.'

He folded his arms, making his biceps bulge beneath the trendily frayed ends of his designer teal T-shirt. 'Don't you want to get a feel for the board in here before we head out?'

Feeling one hundred percent novice, she wrinkled her nose. 'Um, I'm guessing I'm supposed to say yes?'

'Yeah. You need to connect with your board.'

'Oh, brother,' she muttered, rolling her eyes as they moved across to the other side of the shed, where boards stood vertically in racks. 'Next you'll be making that hand sign and telling me to hang loose.'

He smirked. 'The *shaka* sign is part of surf culture.'

She extended her thumb and little finger while keeping the middle fingers curled. 'So does this make me cool?'

'Nah. You have to stay on a board longer than thirty seconds for that.'

She laughed, watching him run his hands over the boards, sliding down the smooth surfaces, his rapt expression almost making her jealous.

He'd once looked at her like that.

Before he bolted without a backward glance.

She'd do well to remember that rather than wishing she were a surfboard right about now.

'This one.' He slid a monstrous cream board etched in ochre swirls from the rack. 'This is your board.'

'Did the fibreglass speak to you?'

His eyes narrowed in indignation. 'Are you mocking me?'

'A little.'

'Let's see who mocks who when you're face-planting the waves,' he said, beckoning her closer. 'Here, you hold it.'

The thing weighed a tonne, but she managed to hold it upright—just. 'Feels like this thing's made of stone.'

'The best epoxy resin, actually, which makes it stronger and lighter than traditional boards.' He took hold of her hand and ran it down the board. 'This is called the deck.'

He edged her hand towards the side of the board in a long, slow sweep that made her bite her lip to stop groaning out loud.

There was something so sensual about having him stand close, his body radiating heat, warming her back, his arms outstretched and inadvertently wrapping around her, his large fingers splayed across hers as they'd once splayed across her belly.

She swallowed and prayed he didn't expect an answer, for there wasn't a hope she could speak with her throat constricted.

Her heart pounded like a jackhammer, the blood coursed through her body like liquid wildfire.

The heat suffocated her, making breathing difficult, making thinking impossible, making her crave the insane…him shoving the board aside, ripping off her clothes, and taking her right here, right now, on the sandy floor.

'The back is the tail, the forward tip is the nose, and the side edges are the rails.' He guided her hand back to the middle and she swayed a little. 'The concave surface from nose to tail is the rocker.'

He moved the board side to side and she almost whimpered.

She must have made some giveaway sound, because he wrapped his arms around her from behind, making holding the board steady impossible.

She could feel his heat, feel how much he wanted her pressed up against her, and she'd never felt the urge to forget sanity as much as she did at that moment.

Correction. She'd experienced the same insanity the first night they'd met—the night he'd romanced her and charmed her and convinced her that tumbling into bed in the early hours of the morning, with the Capri moonlight spilling over them and accentuating the beautiful craziness of the night, was the only possible thing she wanted.

Which begged the question…what did she want now?

While her mind tussled with the dilemma, her body gave a resounding response by leaning back into him.

She heard his sharp intake of breath, felt his arms stiffen.

She had no idea how long they stayed like that, suspended for an incredibly tension-fraught moment in time, and if it hadn't for the beep of her darn phone indicating she had a message she had a fair idea of what might have happened.

'Better get that in case it's about Mum,' she said, instantly missing his warmth as he released her and stepped away, managing to hold the board upright and disentangle herself from her simultaneously.

'I'll meet you outside when you're done,' he said, his voice husky and laced with the same passion pumping through her veins as he picked up the boards as if they weighed nothing and marched outside.

With a sigh of regret she shook her head to clear it, fished her phone out of her pocket and checked it. The message from a client could have waited.

This all-consuming yearning, making her want to run after Archer and drag him back to the sanctity of this shed to finish what they'd started, was not so patient.

Torn between wanting to indulge her newly awakened cravings and wanting to slap herself upside the head, she marched over to the change rooms.

The sooner she got back behind the safety of her computer screen and away from sexy surfer, the better.

Archer jammed the surfboards into the sand and took off for the ocean at a run.

He needed the clarity only the sea could bring. And the chill to ease his inexorable desire.

He'd had a close call back there. So close to giving in to the relentless drive to possess Callie again, to see if the resurfacing memories were half as good as he remembered.

Who was he trying to kid? Those hazy memories were becoming sharper by the day. Even the most trivial things, like watching Callie snag her hair into a ponytail or jot down notes, would resurrect memories of how she'd done the same thing years ago, and he'd be catapulted back to a time when they'd had no responsibilities, no pressures, and were free to indulge their passion.

A time he'd deliberately screwed up to avoid feeling the same way he had when he'd discovered his family had withheld the truth about his dad: as if he wasn't good enough.

He'd trusted his family and they'd let him

down, seriously interfering with his ability to trust anyone.

If he couldn't trust them, who could he trust?

Walking away from Callie back then had been inevitable. Early days in a burgeoning career taking him straight to the top. So when she'd got too close, when he'd started to think beyond Capri, when those trust issues had raised their ugly head, it had been easier to sabotage and run without looking back.

That didn't stop him wanting to have that time again.

Now.

The waves broke around his ankles as he sprinted into the sea and dived through the break, the invigorating brace of cold water slicing through his musings but doing little to obliterate his need for her.

He should have known this blasé flirting as a ploy to distract himself from the impending catch-up with his folks would morph into something more.

He had a feeling nothing would dull this ache for Callie. Nothing less than indulging in a mind-blowing physical encounter designed to slake his thirst and get this thing out of his system.

He could have damped down his need, could have kept things friendly and continued on his casual flirting way, if she hadn't blown his mind in the shed.

She wanted this too.

She'd had a choice and she'd made it, leaning back into him, pressing against him, showing him she felt the buzz too.

He'd been stunned, considering the way she'd aborted their kiss a few hours ago. This time, why had *he* bolted?

As he sliced through the water, free-styling as if he had a shark on his tail, he knew.

Last night, when she'd divulged all that heavy stuff about her mum and he'd held her for ages comforting her, he'd started to feel something. He'd felt that sitting on the deck of his home for ages, with a woman he seriously cared about, content to just sit and not talk, was kind of nice.

It was the first time he'd ever been in Torquay and felt like staying. And that terrified him more than any Great White. He wasn't a stayer. Even for a woman with doe eyes and a soft touch.

He rolled onto his back, letting the swell take him. He closed his eyes, savouring the sun warming his body.

This was where he felt at home. In the ocean, with all the time in the world to float, far from people he'd trusted who hadn't returned the favour.

This was where he belonged.

Then why the urgent pull, like a rip dragging him where he didn't want to go, that said belonging to Callie mightn't be so bad after all?

Callie felt like a trussed-up turkey in the wetsuit. She hated the way the rubber stuck to her skin. She hated the way it moulded and delineated every incriminating bump, and she particularly hated how it made her feel.

Like a novice floundering way out of her depth.

She didn't like floundering. She liked staying in control and staying on top and staying in charge.

She'd lost control once before. And the reason was staring at her with blatant appreciation as she trudged towards him.

'By your foul expression, I'm guessing a wisecrack about rubber and being protected isn't in my best interests?'

She glared at him. 'I'm here under sufferance and you damn well know it.'

She could have sworn he muttered, 'You weren't suffering in the shed,' but didn't want to call him on it.

She didn't need a reminder of the heat they'd

generated in the shed. Not if she wanted to stay upright on this stupid piece of fibreglass for more than two seconds.

Errant, erotic thoughts of Archer were guaranteed wipe-out material.

She yelped as something brushed her ankle—only to discover Archer grinning up at her.

'How about a crack about keeping a wild woman on a leash?'

She let him fasten the cord attached to the board around her ankle before nudging him away with her foot. 'How about I crack you over the head with one of those boards?'

He laughed, straightened, and unkinked his back. 'Just trying to get you to loosen up.' He added a few side stretches. 'The looser you are, the easier it'll be to get the feel of balancing on the board.'

'I'm loose.'

She took a step and tripped over the leash in the process. His hand shot out to grab her, and even through the rubber his touch sent a lick of heat through her.

'You okay?'

An embarrassed blush flushed her cheeks. 'Let's do this.'

Concern tinged his glance before determination hardened his mouth, and she wondered if this was his game face—the one he used precompetition. If so, she wasn't surprised he'd won the world championship five times.

He pointed towards the sea. 'We're in luck. Surf's up today and the waves are off the hook.' She raised an eyebrow and he winced. 'Habit. Surf-speak for the waves being a good size and shape.'

'Gnarly dude,' she muttered, earning a rueful grin.

'We'll concentrate on the basics today, and see if we can catch a wave or two.'

Basics sounded good to her. Basics wouldn't involve tubes or rips or drowning, right?

'I'll break it down into steps and you copy, okay?'

She nodded and he dropped down on the board on his front, leaving her with a pretty great view of a rubber-moulded butt.

'You'll need to be in this position to paddle out.'

Got it, she thought. *Paddling...butt...*

'Cal? You planning on joining me down here?'

With an exasperated grunt at her attention span—not entirely her fault, considering the distraction on offer—she lowered herself onto the board and imitated paddling.

'Nice action,' he said, and her head snapped up to check for the slightest hint of condescension.

Instead she caught him staring in the same vicinity she'd been looking at a moment ago, and a thrill of womanly pride shot through her.

'Next is the pop-up.' He demonstrated going from lying on his board to standing, all in one jump. 'And gaining your balance.'

He held his arms out to his sides, looking so perfectly natural on the board it was as if it was an extension of his feet.

'Now you try.'

And try she did. Over and over again. Until her arms, knees and back ached from her lousy pop-ups and her pride absolutely smarted.

Though she had to hand it to him. Archer was a patient teacher. He praised and cajoled and criticised when needed, eventually getting her from the sand into the water. Where the fun really began.

'Don't worry if you get caught inside,' he said, paddling alongside her.

'Huh?' she mouthed, concentrating on keeping her belly on the board so she didn't slip off as the swell buffeted.

'It's when a surfer paddles out and can't get past the breaking surf to the calmer part of the ocean to catch a wave.'

'Right.' She tried a salute and almost fell off the board.

'If you do, you can try to duck-dive by pushing the nose of the board under the oncoming wave, but it's probably easier just to coast back into shore and we'll try again later.'

She nodded, knowing there wouldn't be a 'later'. She reckoned she had enough first-hand experience now to facilitate the online forums. Perching on top of a wave wouldn't give her much more beyond a momentary rush of adrenalin.

'Follow me.'

And she did. Until she got caught inside, just as he'd predicted, and ended up paddling back to shore, where she gratefully dragged the board onto firm sand, plonked her butt, and watched Archer strut his stuff.

The guy was seriously good—cresting waves, twisting and turning on his board with precision, looking like the poster boy for surfing that he was.

She could have watched him for hours, but a few minutes later he coasted into shore, picked up his board, tucked it under his arm and jogged towards her.

For some inexplicable reason she felt compelled to get up and run to meet him halfway. Last night when he'd comforted her might have been the catalyst, or maybe his admission on the beach earlier today, but whatever it was she felt she wanted to be close to him.

As he drew near the urge intensified, and when he smiled at her, with tiny rivulets of sea water running down that impossibly handsome face, her heart twisted like one of the fancy manoeuvres he'd pulled out there.

She wanted him.

With a desperation that clawed at all her well-formulated, highly logical reasons why she shouldn't, shredding them beyond repair.

'You're looking at me like I'm Red Riding Hood and you're the big bad wolf.' He laid the board down and sat beside her. 'My showy moves impress you?'

'*You* impress me,' she said, sucking in a deep breath and covering his hand with hers.

His questioning stare snagged hers, and with her heart pounding loud enough to drown out the breaking surf she leaned across and did what she should have had the guts to do earlier that morning.

She kissed him.

Archer had pulled some pretty fancy moves out there. Show-pony stunts: fins out, a sharp turn where the fins slide off the top of the wave; soul arch, arching his back to demonstrate his casual confidence; switch-foot, changing from right to left foot forward, and hang-ten, putting ten toes over the nose of his long board.

Usually when he hit the waves he surfed for himself, for the sheer pleasure it brought him. It was that enjoyment that gave him the edge in competitions, for he concentrated on fun and not his opponents.

Not today. Today he'd surfed to impress Callie.

By that lip-lock she'd just given him it had worked. And how.

If he'd known that was all it would take he would have hit the waves the first day they'd arrived.

'You're grinning like an idiot,' she said, nudging him with her elbow.

'It's not every day a guy gets a kiss like that for balancing on a few waves.'

She rolled her eyes. 'Give me a break. You get smooches from bikini babes every time you win a tournament.'

'Congratulatory kisses.' He traced her lower lip with his fingertip, exploring the contour, feeling the faintest wobble. 'Nothing compared to that lip-smacker you just planted on me.'

She blushed, but to her credit didn't look away. 'You wanted a date for the wedding. I'm just trying to make it look authentic.'

'How authentic do you want to get?' He puckered up in a ludicrous parody and she chuckled.

'How important is it for you to convince them I'm the real deal?'

His smile faltered as her innocent question hit unerringly close to home. 'Hold my hand, gaze adoringly into my eyes, smooch a little. Well, actually, a lot. That should do the trick.'

'So why would you need a date to your brother's wedding anyway?'

He'd been waiting for her to ask that for days, but she'd been so hell-bent on burying her nose in business and avoiding him that they hadn't strayed into personal territory. It looked as if last night had well and truly changed all that.

'Things with my folks are a little tense when I come home for flying visits. It's awkward.'

He waited for the inevitable *why* but she surprised him, tilting her head to one side as if studying him. 'I'm surprised a tough guy like you can't handle a little *awkward*.'

He should have known she wouldn't buy his trite answer. But how could he tell her the rest without having to answer a whole lot of other questions he'd rather left unsaid?

'It's easier this way.' He snagged her hand and pressed a kiss to her palm, enjoying the flare of heat in her eyes. 'And much more enjoyable with a date I actually like.'

Her nose crinkled adorably. 'You *like* me? What are you? In fifth grade?'

'You'll be pleased to know I'm a lot more experienced than I was in fifth grade,' he said, tugging on her hand until she almost straddled his lap. 'I like you, Callie. You know that. And I'd like nothing more than to spend the next few days showing you how much.'

He expected her to bolt again. To revert back to business mode. To resurrect the invisible wall she'd steadfastly maintained since they'd arrived.

Instead, she surprised him.

She captured his face between her hands and gently bridged the distance, whispering against the side of his mouth, 'Then what are we waiting for?'

Callie didn't want time to second guess her impulse.

She wanted Archer.

Now.

'Let's get cleaned up, grab some dinner, then head home—'

'No.' It almost sounded like a desperate yell, and she laughed to cover her nervousness. 'I—I want this to be like in Capri.'

His eyes widened at the implication.

He remembered. Remembered that hedonistic time in a sheltered alcove on a deserted beach. Remembered the frantic hands and straining mouths and incredible eroticism of it.

'You sure?'

'Never been surer of anything in my life.'

And then she promptly made a mockery of her brave declaration by stumbling as she tried to stand.

He steadied her, his gaze never leaving hers. 'Cal, do we need to talk about afterwards? Because nothing will change. Our lives are separate—'

'Since when did you talk so much?'

She silenced him with a kiss—a hot, open-mouthed kiss designed to distract and titillate and eradicate any lingering doubts they might harbour.

When they finally came up for air, he held her hand as if he'd never let go. 'There's a bunch of deserted dunes just over that hill.'

She liked how he didn't spell it out, how he left the option up to her with his silent challenge.

Tilting her head to meet his heated gaze, she tried her best sexy smile and hoped it didn't come out a grimace. 'Lead the way.'

After making a detour to the sheds, where they struggled out of their wetsuits and Archer snagged his wallet and a throw rug, they ran, their feet squeaking on the clean sand, their soft panting in rhythm with her pounding heart.

When they crested the hill and she saw the pristine dunes stretched out before them tears stung her eyes.

It was so beautiful. A perfect place to resurrect incredible memories and to create new ones.

They didn't speak as he led her by the hand to a secluded spot sheltered by an overhanging rock, laid out the rug, and knelt.

She'd never felt so worshipped as she did at that moment, with the guy she'd once had serious feelings for kneeling at her feet and staring up at her in blatant adoration.

When he tugged on her hand she joined him on the rug and in a flurry of whispered endearments, sensual caresses, and mind-blowing passion they came together.

Afterwards, as Archer cradled her in his arms and she stared at the seagulls wheeling overhead, Callie wondered one thing.

What the hell have I done?

CHAPTER SEVEN

'SHOULD'VE known you two bozos couldn't keep your big traps shut.'

Archer glared at Trav and Tom, who merely grinned and raised their beer bottles in his direction.

'What do you mean? This barbecue's in lieu of Trav's rehearsal dinner. You had to come.' Tom smirked and gave a less than subtle head-jerk in Callie's direction. 'And you couldn't leave your wedding date at home. That just wouldn't be right.'

Archer punched him on the arm. 'I had to tolerate Mum's interrogation on the phone for thirty minutes this arvo, and I've spent the last hour dodging her since we arrived, thanks to you.'

Tom raised his beer. 'You can thank me properly when she's presiding over *your* wedding.'

'Like hell,' Archer muttered, the thought

of marriage making his chest burn like he'd scoffed a double-pepperoni pizza.

'It happens to the best of us, bro.' Trav nudged him and Archer frowned. 'You lot are a poor example to bachelors the world over.'

'Hey, *I'm* a bachelor.' Tom thrust his chest out and beat it with his fists like a gorilla and they laughed.

'With behaviour like that I'm not surprised,' Trav said, pointing at a group of his fiancée's friends clustered around the chocolate fountain. 'Shelly has loads of nice single friends. Why don't you go chat up one of them?'

Tom shrugged, his nonchalance undermined by the way his fingers gripped his beer. 'Not interested.'

'Not every woman's like—'

'Trav, Shelly's calling you,' Archer said, earning a grateful glance from Tom.

'Think about it. Izzy needs a mum.'

Archer stiffened, expecting Tom to fire a broadside at Travis, but he merely muttered 'Punk' under his breath as Trav headed for his bride-to-be with the swagger of a young guy in love.

'At the risk of being bashed over the head with that bottle, maybe Trav's right.'

As expected, Tom bristled. 'Izzy and I are doing just fine.'

'I know you are, mate, but she's growing up.'

He glanced at his niece, her blonde pigtails streaming behind her as she raced across the lawn in pursuit of a rabbit. 'She's six going on sixty, and one day soon you'll find her asking a bunch of questions you'd rather not answer.'

To his surprise, Tom seemed to deflate before his eyes. 'She's an amazing kid.' He dragged a hand across his eyes, blinking as if he'd just woken up. 'She's my world.'

'Then maybe you should think about joining the land of the living again?' Archer hoped to lighten the sombre mood. 'When's the last time you had a date anyway?'

Old hurts darkened Tom's mood and his usually jovial brother frowned. Archer felt like a jerk for probing his wounds but Trav was right. Tom needed to start dating again—for his own sake as well as Izzy's.

Not that he had a right to butt in where his niece was concerned, considering his deliberate distancing over the years. But this visit was different. Seeing Callie interact with his family made him appreciate them in a whole new light. And made him feel like a first class jerk.

How long would he keep his own old hurts locked away inside where they festered? How long would he let wounded pride get in the way?

Tom's turbulent gaze focussed on his daughter as he placed his bottle on a nearby table and folded his arms. 'You ever wish you had a different life?'

Never. Discounting the hash of a relationship he now had with his family.

Archer loved his life: the freedom, the buzz, the adrenalin. He liked being his own boss, and valued his independence as much as his trophies. Though he'd be lying if he didn't admit to wondering more and more these days why he was so hell-bent on the single life.

At the start it had been about striving for success and not needing ties to hamper him. Emotional ties that ended up causing pain.

His family might not know it, but in their decision to ostracise him from his dad's illness and not trust him enough to cope they'd solidified his life choices.

Better for him not to connect emotionally with anyone, to enjoy his lack of responsibility and savour the single life. No strings attached; a motto that had served him well over the years.

Callie's laughter floated on the breeze and something in his gut clenched.

No, he didn't regret a thing, but for a moment he wondered how different his life would have been if he'd put his trust issues aside and taken a risk on their relationship.

'No use wondering about maybes, mate. All we can do is make the best of what we've got.'

Pensive, Tom nodded. 'I don't regret marrying Tracy for the sake of Izzy, that's for sure. But sticking around here with its same-old, same-old has its moments.'

Tom wouldn't get any arguments from him. The monotony of living in the small town he'd grown up in would've driven him nuts.

'What about surfing?'

Tom's frown deepened. 'What about it?'

'Do you resent not going pro?'

'Hell, no.' Tom guffawed. 'I was never as driven as you, squirt. No way would I have spent years traipsing the world chasing the next big wave.'

'It was all you talked about growing up. I think it's half the reason I wanted to go pro—because you did.'

Tom shook his head. 'You always wanted it more than me. I couldn't hack all the training and moving around.'

'But I thought…'

'What?'

'That you gave it all up when Trace deliberately got pregnant. That she trapped you and you hated it and that's what eventually led to the marriage falling apart.'

Tom slapped him on the back. 'Not that it

matters now, but to set the record straight—
yeah, Tracy fell pregnant on purpose, but
she didn't trap me. I didn't have to propose.
I wanted to, because I was young and dumb
and idealistic.'

He glanced towards their folks, toasting each
other with champagne at a quiet table at the rear
of the marquee, oblivious to the family bedlam
around them. 'I guess I secretly wanted what
they had.'

A familiar sadness enveloped Archer when
he glanced at his folks. The Fletts had always
been a close family, and his folks seemed more
devoted now, following the health scare that
had so shocked him when he'd eventually found
out.

He envied them that closeness. It was like
standing on the outside looking in at an exclusive club.

Tom's mouth twisted into a wry smile. 'I'd
give an arm and a leg to have a relationship like
that. A woman who adores me, who's content
to be with me and doesn't need all the fancy
trappings of a big city.'

Liking the fragile bond of reconnecting with
Tom on a deeper level than mock-wrestling,
Archer delved further. 'Is that why Tracy left?
Because she wanted the high life?'

''Course. Once she had Izzy it was all she

talked about. I wanted a future that focussed on building a stable environment for our child to grow in, and she couldn't leave fast enough.'

Archer rubbed the back of his neck, wondering if Santa would make an appearance to dispel any other myths he'd once believed in.

'Wow, I didn't know.'

'Because some things are best left unsaid. Besides, I don't want Iz hearing bad stuff about her mum, just in case Trace grows a conscience one day and wants to see her daughter.'

'Where is she?'

'Sydney, last I heard but who knows? She sends the obligatory birthday and Christmas gifts. That's about it.'

While Tom's tone didn't hold an ounce of censure, guilt niggled at Archer.

Was that how the Fletts talked about *him* when he wasn't around? Saying that he should *grow a conscience* rather than sending *obligatory* birthday gifts and making an *obligatory* Christmas visit during which he couldn't wait to escape back to his life?

Considering how he'd withdrawn from them, he couldn't blame them.

He *wanted* to forgive and move on.

He *wanted* to shelve his pride and bring the whole thing out into the open.

But every single time he wanted to broach

the painful subject of how he'd felt at being shut out, and how their rebuttal of his overture had hurt, one image stuck in his mind.

His dad, elbows braced on his precious piano, head in his hands, crying. Big, brusque Frank Flett never cried, and to see his father so broken had left a lasting legacy.

It had been just after they'd finally told him the truth—a year after his dad had been given the all-clear. Twelve freaking months, on top of the six months Frank had battled the disease that could have claimed his life, when his family had shut him out because they didn't want to distract him, or thought he couldn't handle it, or some such rot.

He'd been livid, and seeing his father's tears had reinforced what they thought of him as nothing else could.

If his dad could still cry when he was cancer-free, how bad must it have been during the long battle of surgery, chemo and the rest?

A battle *he'd* been excluded from because they'd deemed him not responsible enough to handle it.

His hands unconsciously clenched into fists and he inhaled, forcing himself to calm down before any of his bitterness spilled out.

'What's wrong?' Tom's perceptive stare bored into him and he glanced away.

'Nothing.'

'Like hell.' Tom paused, made an exasperated sound. 'Is that why you keep running? Because you think I got trapped, gave up a dream, and you don't want the same to happen to you?'

Archer's tension eased as he saw Callie strolling towards the bar, her pale lemon floral dress swishing around her calves, making her look ethereal and pretty and all too ravishing.

What could he say?

The truth?

That he didn't dare trust an incredible woman like Callie? That even now, after the incredible reconnection they'd shared last night, first at the beach and later at his house, he was absolutely terrified of giving in to the feelings she evoked?

He settled for a partial truth. 'You know I wanted out of Torquay, and surfing was my ticket out. No harm in following your dreams.'

'Unless it interferes with what you really want.'

Archer glared at his brother, not liking the direction this conversation was taking.

'How would you know what I really want?'

'Because I see the way you look at Callie.'

He hated Tom's condescending smirk as much as his homing in on his innermost fears.

'And I'd hate to see you throw away a chance at real happiness because you're stuck on some warped idea that being in a relationship means giving up your freedom.'

That was not the only thing being in a relationship meant. Reliance, trust, love, they were all a part of it too, and those were the things or, more to the point, the loss of those things that ensured he'd never let Callie get too close.

She'd almost made him slip once before.

Not this time.

'You've been watching too many chick-flicks after Izzy's in bed,' he said, wanting to wipe the infuriating, know-all expression off Tom's face. 'I *like* my life. I'm doing what I want to do, so lay off.'

'Truth hurts, huh?'

Archer swore. 'How about you concentrate on getting your own love-life in order and leave me the hell alone?'

He stalked off a few paces. Not far enough to escape Tom's taunt.

'Who said anything about love?'

He strode faster. He might be able to outrun his brother's annoying chuckles, but he couldn't shake the insistent little voice in his head that focussed on that one little L-word and its disastrous implications.

* * *

Callie's head ached.

Bad enough she'd spent the last twenty-four hours over-analysing her impulsiveness in tumbling into a physical relationship with Archer—now she'd inadvertently joined the unofficial Archer Flett Fan Club.

Ever since she'd arrived at the party she'd been bombarded with glowing recommendations from every female family member. And the interrogation from the Flett females was truly frightening.

They wanted to know *everything*.

And she didn't know what to tell them. What could she say? That she'd handed Archer her heart eight years ago, he'd trampled it, and now she'd foolishly come back for more?

Uh-uh. So she'd glossed over her relationship with Archer as being old friends catching up while he was in Melbourne. Interestingly, Shelly had revealed what a refreshing change she was from Archer's usual dates, '*snobby, plastic, citified bimbos*', who wouldn't mingle let alone talk to his family.

She'd wanted to pry, but Archer's mum had shot Shelly a warning look and she'd clammed up. Not that Callie wanted to acknowledge the twinge of jealousy, but considering how warm and welcoming Archer's family had been towards *her*, she was surprised he'd bring that type of woman home.

That was another thing. His interaction with his family. Something was definitely *off*.

He'd been nervous about attending this party. She'd seen it back at his place, subtle signs that his usual confidence was rattled: pacing the balcony while she'd been getting ready, sculling caffeine drinks, absentmindedly changing TV channels without watching any show.

When she'd asked him about it he'd laughed it off, but she'd known there was more to it when he'd taken his sweet time getting out of the car when they'd arrived and then remained on the outskirts the entire party.

She'd seen him talking to his brothers, but beyond a perfunctory greeting for his parents he'd kept his distance from them.

Which begged the question *why*?

She'd ask later—add it to the million other questions buzzing around her brain. Questions she should have asked before falling in lust with him all over again.

One thing was for sure: Archer's family wanted him to stick around for a change. No way would she break the news to them that there was more chance of her winning the next surf pro classic than Archer Flett putting down roots.

He was a confirmed nomad, and in a way it added to his charm. His impulsiveness, his spontaneity, his live-for-the-moment attitude. What they'd done on the beach…the memory had her running a chilled glass across her forehead. It did little to cool the scorching images replaying like a naughty film.

Archer peeling off her swimsuit, exploring every inch of her body with strong, sure hands, kissing her everywhere…

'You can get arrested for looking like that.'

Archer's whisper fanned her ear, sending little pinwheels of sensation ricocheting through her as his arm slid around her waist, anchoring her to him.

As if she'd want to run. Her surname wasn't Flett. More was the pity.

'Like what?'

He growled at her *faux* innocence. 'Like you've spent the day in bed and you can't wait to get back there.'

She glanced up at him from beneath her lashes. 'Who said anything about a bed? As I recall, the beach served us just fine—'

'Stop, you're killing me.'

His grip tightened as he swung her around, protecting her from prying eyes and backing her towards the rear of the marquee.

'Like you haven't been thinking about it,' she said, challenging him to open up a tad.

They hadn't talked much since the beach, and had fallen into a physical relationship as easily as they'd tumbled in Capri. It had suited her yesterday, not discussing much beyond the present. She'd been on a high, wallowing in the decadence of being in Archer's arms again.

But today reality had set in.

Considering their proximity, living together, it had been all too easy—almost inevitable— sliding back into a physical relationship with the underlying attraction still sizzling between them.

It shouldn't mean anything. Sadly for her it did.

Getting physical with Archer had thrust her right back to the same place she'd been eight years earlier: knowing there'd be an expiration date and not liking it.

She also didn't like being vulnerable to him, and that was exactly what she'd made herself in opening herself to him again.

Incredibly foolish, considering Archer hadn't fundamentally changed. Footloose, fancy-free and loving it.

The situation reminded her of the many times she'd taken a chance on her dad, when he'd blown into her life, swept her off her feet with gifts and empty promises, only to forget her when he left.

It had been such a buzz being around him. But later the let-down and disappointment and devastation had sucked.

With Archer in Capri she'd made the mistake of masking her feelings, pretending a fling was no big deal. This time she wouldn't be so stupid.

At the start of this week they might have agreed that spending time together in Torquay was about work and being his date in exchange for the surf school campaign, but getting physical had changed the boundaries.

Their futures weren't intersecting, but this time she deserved more. She deserved answers.

Why had he really asked her to be his date for the wedding? How could he be so caring with her, especially about her mum, and shut down around his family?

What were his plans? Because from all accounts the guys at the surf school she'd spoken to had collectively mentioned that Archer would be around more often. What could that potentially mean for them?

Because she wouldn't let him walk away this time. Not without a fight.

She wasn't the same idealistic, naïve girl she'd been in Capri. Life was short—too short—and second chances were rare, so if she and Archer had a remote shot at making some kind of relationship work she'd take it.

She didn't want deep and meaningful, but something casual and fun to lighten her days in the tough time ahead with her mum. She was all for that.

Ironic how she'd changed in a few days. She'd initially thought Archer wasn't a keeper, wasn't the kind of guy who'd support her when the going got tough.

Maybe he still wouldn't, but the more she saw him interact with his brothers, Izzy and the teenage surf crew, the more he held her and talked to her about her mum's illness and what he could do to raise awareness of her horrid disease, the more she realised she'd misjudged him.

He might have broken her heart eight years ago, but she'd changed. Why couldn't she believe he had too?

Only one way to find out.

Ask the hard questions.

Archer nuzzled her neck. 'I've been thinking of getting you naked again ever since we got here, but there are children present.'

Those questions she needed to ask were momentarily put on hold. 'Stop. People might see.'

'Let them,' he said, his lips trailing down

her neck towards her collarbone, nipping along the way.

Her skin rippled with sensation as she arched towards him, wanting whatever he could give.

A low wolf-whistle signalled the arrival of company and Archer swore as they disentangled. 'If that's Tom I'm going to kill him,' he said as Callie readjusted her skewed dress straps.

'Sorry to interrupt, but we're doing speeches.' Travis grinned, not sorry in the least.

Archer shot him a death glare. 'Can't you leave that boring stuff until the wedding?'

'Why? Got better things to do?'

The corners of Archer's mouth curved up and Callie's heart gave a little kick. She loved that half-smile, as if he was genuinely amused and loving life.

'Yeah, and if you had any sense you'd be doing the same thing rather than getting caught up in all this wedding nonsense.'

'Hey, why not add to the Christmas festivities with a rousing Flett shindig? Keeps the folks sweet, that's for sure.'

'It's a sad day when a Flett male turns into a romantic sap,' he said. An odd expression Callie couldn't fathom flitted across Archer's face as he released her waist to snag her hand.

'We'll be there in a sec,' he added.

A little frown creased Travis's brow but he merely nodded and walked away, leaving her the perfect opportunity to discover what it was about his family that made Archer tense up.

'I've ordered a whole lot of online gift cards for your family for Christmas. Think that'll be okay?'

'Fine,' he said. But clearly it wasn't. That little exchange with his brother had left Archer edgy and reticent and standoffish.

She preferred him laid-back and happy, but she wanted answers and there was only one way to get them.

'Why do you do that?'

He shot her a confused glance. 'What?'

'Close off around your family.'

His brow instantly furrowed. 'That's bull—'

'Is it?'

His lips compressed as he stared at his parents, in deep conversation with Tom on the other side of the marquee.

When he didn't answer, she continued. 'When your brothers showed up at your house and I walked into the kitchen I could feel the tension. Since then you've spent all your time either working or surfing and haven't visited your folks.'

The slash between his brows deepened.

'And tonight, rocking up to this party seems

like the last thing you wanted to do.' She blew out a long breath. He was still here, listening. She took it as a good sign. 'Your family can't speak highly enough of you, so I don't get it. Maybe—'

'Maybe you should butt out.'

Hurt slashed her hopes. Hope he'd changed, hope he'd trust her with the truth, hope they had a future.

She tugged on her hand, but rather than releasing it as she'd expected he held on tighter and swore under his breath. When he finally looked at her, the pain in his eyes made her breath catch.

'Sorry for snapping at you.' He gestured towards his family with his free hand. 'None of this is your fault.'

'Want to talk about it?'

'Not really.'

But he did. She could see the turbulent conflict tearing him up inside as his wild gaze swung between Tom, Trav, his folks and Izzy.

It was as if he waged some great inner battle before his stare softened, fixed on Izzy.

'I'm not around much any more. I feel like a stranger.'

He said it so softly she had to lean into him to hear, and the underlying sadness in his reluctant admission tore at her heart.

'My fault, not theirs,' he added, his hand gripping hers as if he'd never let go. 'It's like once I hit the surf circuit I didn't belong here any more.'

Silence stretched as she tried to come up with something to say that didn't sound trite.

'Your lives are so different. Maybe having less in common made you feel like that?'

'It's not that,' he said, his eyes bleak as he tore his gaze away from his family and refocussed on her. 'They kept something from me. It changed everything.'

Oh, heck. She could see it was big from his shattered expression. She'd wanted answers; she hadn't wanted to cause him this much pain.

'What happened?'

He sucked in a deep breath and blew it out in a long stream.

'Dad had prostate cancer. They didn't tell me for eighteen months.'

Stunned, she stared at him in disbelief. She couldn't comprehend the enormity of how betrayed she'd feel if her mum hadn't told her the truth about her disease. And in that moment she understood everything: Archer's discomfort around his family, his unwillingness to get too close.

'I'm so sorry,' she said, pulling him in for a

comforting hug that didn't convey half of what she wanted to say.

'It sucked.' He disengaged, the slight catch in his voice underscoring his vulnerability. 'Apparently he was diagnosed around the time I first started making a name for myself on the pro circuit. A couple of years before we first met.'

His gaze swung back to his family.

'They didn't want to burden me with something I could do little about. They waited to tell me once he'd got the all-clear so I would follow my dream.' He dragged a hand through his hair. 'Damn it, do you have any idea how shallow that makes me sound?'

Wishing she could do something to ease his pain, she captured his chin and made him look at her.

'Don't judge them too harshly. I've been where they are, sitting around helpless and frustrated, waiting for results. It's a relentless, mundane task that eats away at you, and there isn't one damn thing you can do about any of it.' She released him, shaken by the vehemence of her response. 'I know how hurt you must've been at being shut out, but did you stop to think they did it because they love you?'

Confusion clouded his eyes and she continued. 'You told me in Capri that all you'd ever wanted growing up was to be the best surfer in the world. You said that every night you poured into getting your degree part-time was because you wanted to *be* something. Something beyond a local Torquay guy with big dreams and little else.'

She grabbed his arms and gave him a little shake. 'You wanted it so badly I envied you that certainty of what you wanted and how far you'd go to get it. If I picked up on that in a week, don't you think your family knew how much your dream meant to you?'

He opened his mouth to respond and she placed a fingertip under his chin and gently closed it. 'Think about this. If you'd known and given up everything to be with your dad, would you have ended up resenting your family because of it?'

''Course not. I should've been here, supporting them.'

She shook her head. 'You're telling me the independent, driven, determined guy I know would've been happy giving up his dream to stay in Torquay?'

His frown was back. 'It was my decision to make, and they didn't give me a choice.'

His hurt was audible and she cupped his cheek. 'They love you, Arch, and your dad's fine. That's all that matters. Don't waste time on regrets, because life's too short.'

She saw the moment some of his load eased. His confusion cleared and clarity shone through.

'Is that why you gave me a second chance?'

His question came out of left field and stunned her a little. Of course her 'seize the day' mentality had a lot to do with her mum's illness and her approach to life, but him being intuitive enough to pick up on it—and call her on it—really surprised her.

He slid his arms around her waist and rested his forehead against hers. 'I'm sorry for the way things ended.'

Her heart stalled. There was so much she wanted to say, so much more she wanted to ask, but she'd made great inroads in getting him to open up about his family—who were now gathering for speeches and sending curious glances their way. The rest would have to wait until later.

'Me too,' she said, easing away, needing to lighten the mood before she started bawling. 'You know, the faster we get the speeches over with, the faster we can get out of here.'

'I like the way you think,' he said, dropping a quick kiss on her lips.

CHAPTER EIGHT

ARCHER'S guts griped the way they had the time he'd eaten too many jalapeños in Mexico. Sadly, what ailed him this time wouldn't be fixed with a dose of alka selzer.

This was what opening up did to a guy: it made him feel as if he'd be sick at any moment.

How the hell had Callie done that? Wormed some of the truth out of him? He hadn't told anyone about his dad's illness for fear it would paint him in a bad light. Not that he'd been deliberately uncaring. He just hadn't been given the chance to care.

But having Callie articulate his family's possible motivation in keeping such a momentous thing from him had gone some way to assuaging the pain.

Maybe it was time to swallow his damn pride and try to start building a few bridges again?

'Come with me.' His grip tightened on

Callie's hand, and as she smiled up at him a new pang twisted his gut.

This one had nothing to do with old regrets and everything to do with a new realisation.

That Callie meant more to him than he'd like to admit.

'Sure. Though if I have to listen to one more anecdote about you guys terrorising Torquay by running around naked as kids I'm bailing.'

'I don't hear you complaining about seeing me naked *now*,' he said, his low voice making her eyes widen. The molten depths urged him to head home with her right this very minute, bridges be damned.

'I'm assuming we're heading over to your family to say goodbye?'

He grinned at her cool delivery, spoiled by her healthy blush.

'You assume right.' He ducked down to whisper in her ear. 'The sooner I get you naked the better.'

Her blush intensified and he was chuckling, as Izzy bowled up to him and careened into his legs, almost upending both of them.

'Hey, Iz, where's the fire?'

'You're leaving,' she said, hanging off his leg in a similar way he'd seen her do to her dad. 'And I don't want you to go.'

Hell.

Intuitive as usual, Callie squeezed his hand and released it so he could squat down to Izzy's level. She transferred her death grip from his leg to his arm.

'I'm not going far, Iz, just up the road.'

Her blue eyes narrowed, pinning him with the retribution of a child he'd let down too many times in the past. 'You sure you're coming to the wedding on Christmas Eve and everything?'

'I'm sure.'

Her wariness didn't ease, and he half expected her to give him a kick in the shins for all those times he'd sidestepped her too-astute questions about his early departure.

'Okay, then,' she said, but she didn't let go, and as she stared at him with wide-eyed suspicion it hit him.

Izzy didn't believe him.

And that more than anything Callie had said or his family could say got through to him. He needed to stop thinking about making amends and actually start doing something about it.

'Hey, Iz, I know things are kinda busy around here, with everyone getting ready for Uncle Trav's wedding, but if it's okay with your dad why don't I take you surfing tomorrow?'

She stared at him in disbelief for a good five

seconds before an ear-splitting grin indicated he'd done the right thing.

With a loud screech that had every guest in the place looking their way, she released him and ran towards Tom, about six feet away, yelling loud enough to be heard in Melbourne. 'Uncle Arch is taking me surfing! Yay, yay, *yay*!'

His family stared at him in unison.

Tom's warning glare spoke volumes: *You'd better not let my kid down this time*.

Trav was giving him a thumbs-up of encouragement.

His mum's soft smile was warm and appreciative and hopeful.

His dad gave a brief nod of approval before he glanced away, unable to look him in the eye as usual.

Well, he'd *make* Frank Flett look him in the eye before he left this time. If the surf school didn't show his dad he was worthy and responsible he'd face this situation head-on regardless.

Callie's pep talk had got him thinking. He'd spent too many years being an outcast in his own family—his choosing. Time to discover the truth about what had happened during his dad's illness, and why they hadn't deemed him fit to know at the time.

And he had Callie to thank for giving him the push he needed.

'Thanks.' He caressed her cheek with his fingertips, a fleeting gesture he hoped conveyed even half of what he was thinking.

'For what?'

'Everything,' he said, pulling her in for a quick hug to the sound of embarrassing applause from his family.

She laughed as they disengaged, and as he took in her flushed cheeks and sparkling eyes and smiling mouth he realised how much he'd given up in walking away from her all those years ago.

And he'd end up doing it again.

He didn't want to lose her, but he didn't trust himself to make her happy. He'd analysed it at length: if his family didn't trust him when the going got rough, was it *him*?

Was it because he didn't inspire trust in people? And if his own family didn't trust him, how could he connect emotionally with a woman like Callie?

Where did that leave them?

Damned if he knew.

While Izzy alternated between dancing around Tom and tearing towards him, he grabbed Callie's hand and tugged her towards his family.

He made arrangements with Tom to pick up Izzy in the morning, slapped Trav on the back and hugged his mum.

When it came to Frank, the inevitable questions bubbled to the forefront of his mind.

Why didn't you tell me, Dad?

Why didn't you let me be there for you?

Why did you trust the others and not me?

He didn't ask. Now wasn't the time. But before he left this trip he'd discover the truth behind all the pain.

They stood there, self-conscious and ill at ease. Archer wanted to say so much, yet he was plagued by the same discomfort that inevitably occurred around his dad these days. When Frank tried a tentative grin Archer shook his hand and mumbled something about seeing him at the wedding. He wanted answers, but right now he was plain exhausted.

This emotional re-bonding took it out of a guy, and hot on the heels of his realisation that he didn't want to lose Callie...well, Archer knew he had some serious thinking to do.

When Archer had invited Izzy to surf he'd envisaged the two of them having a little uncle-niece bonding time.

What he *hadn't* imagined was the entire Flett clan descending on the beach for an impromptu picnic. Izzy loved the attention and the mayhem and the laughter. Him—not so much.

As he watched Trav elbow their dad and share a laugh with him on the foreshore, regret strengthened his resolve to put the past behind him and move on.

Regret that he'd missed out on being there for his dad when he'd needed him most.

Regret that he'd missed out on so much with his family because of his deliberate withdrawal.

Regret that he hadn't confronted the issue sooner because of his damned pride.

'Hey, you're not watching me!' Izzy's yell refocussed his attention on where it should be: refining her pop up technique.

'I am now, squirt.'

As she sprang from her knees to a standing position, arms stretched out sideways, her grin wide and proud, some of his residual tension whenever his family were around eased.

He'd wasted enough time hanging onto old hurts, and he had missed out on spending time with Izzy as a result.

No more.

'You're a natural,' he said, sweeping her into his arms and tickling her until she squealed.

'I wanna go in the water,' she said, grabbing both his ears and twisting until he released her.

Rubbing them, he tried to frown and failed,

his mouth twitching with suppressed laughter instead. 'Ow, Iz, that hurt.'

'Wuss,' she said, poking out her tongue, mischief sparking in blue eyes the colour of the ocean behind her.

'That's it. Lesson's over.'

She giggled and ran into the shallows, kicking water at him as he followed. They dodged and weaved and splashed until he tackled her, scooped her in his arms and made for deeper water.

'My daddy will get cross at you for taking me out so far.' She pouted, but there was no denying the mischievous twinkle in her eyes or mistaking the devious machinations of an intelligent, conniving child who'd say anything to avoid a good old-fashioned dunking.

'Your daddy's laughing as hard as Nan and Pop,' he said, laughing when she glanced towards shore and saw he spoke the truth.

'Put me down,' she said, pummelling his shoulders, so he obliged, chuckling as a wave swamped them and Iz resurfaced, a wide-eyed, bedraggled imp with a grin as wide as the stretch of beach.

Archer lost track of how long they frolicked in the waves—duck-diving, playing tag—and he didn't care. The longer he stayed out here with Izzy, in the one place he felt truly at home, the easier it became to let go of the past.

He'd recaptured some of the magic with his niece and he'd be damned if he lost it again.

Now if only he could do the same with his dad.

'I'm hungry,' Izzy said, flinging her arms around his neck and hanging on tight. 'And thirsty.'

'Okay, kiddo, let's go attack that mountain of food your nan brought along.'

As he waded into shore with Izzy in his arms and strode towards his family their collective expressions gave him hope for the future. Approval, warmth, relief and optimism—the latter on his dad's weather-lined face as admiration lit his smile.

Yeah, it was definitely time to put the past behind him, and he owed it all to Callie.

As if on cue she popped out from the main office of the surf school, where she'd been putting a few finishing touches to the website.

He saw her glance towards his family, sprawled across a picnic blanket on the sand in casual unanimity, and back to him, as if unsure whether to join them or not.

Later. For now he had to thank her.

He lowered Izzy until her feet hit sand, savouring her hesitation to let him go. 'Save me a Vegemite sandwich, kiddo, I'll be there in a sec.'

'But I get the last brownie,' she flung over her shoulder, already racing towards the Fletts, where she flung herself into Tom's arms.

Archer had never envisaged himself settling down, let alone having kids, but watching his brother and niece rub noses in an affectionate greeting he damn well wanted what they had.

'You did a good thing today.'

Callie touched his arm, and the immediate lick of heat made him wish he could drag her back to their sand dune for a repeat performance of that time earlier in the week.

'What? Take my niece surfing?' He shook his head. 'I should've done it a long time ago.'

'It's never too late,' she said, and the barely audible quiver in her voice reminded him that for her, for her mum, one day it *would* be too late.

'Thanks.' He rested his hands on her waist, enjoying the way they seemed to belong there.

'For?'

'For giving me the kick up the ass I needed.'

Her gaze darted towards his family and a small, satisfied smile curved her lips. 'It's hard when you're too close to a situation. Sometimes all it takes is a little objectivity to help clear through the fluff.'

He chuckled. 'The fluff?'

Her gaze met his and it was as if he'd been dumped beneath a massive wave and couldn't catch his breath.

'The extra stuff that weighs us down and clouds our vision and makes us go a little crazy.'

She was something else.

Her beauty, her warmth, her wisdom.

And he'd let her go.

'I think I had some of that fluff clouding my judgement in Capri.'

Understanding sparked in her eyes and she opened her mouth to respond just as Izzy bowled into them like an out-of-control dervish.

'I've saved a sandwich for you, Uncle Arch. Come and get it.'

'Now, how can you refuse an offer like that?' Callie said as she ruffled Izzy's damp curls.

Izzy's nose crinkled in consternation. 'I don't think there's any more Vegemite ones for you, Callie, but I reckon you can have a piece of my fairy bread.'

'Sugar sprinkles? My favourite.' Callie slipped out of his grasp to hold Izzy's hand, but he snagged her arm before she could leave.

'You're amazing.'

He ducked down for a swift kiss, which resulted in a blush from Callie, an excited whoop from Izzy, and cheers from his family.

Yeah, he definitely had some talking to do later—with his dad and with Callie.

Christmas this year wasn't looking so bad after all.

'This place is awesome, dude.' Trav slapped Archer on the back as they entered the supply store at the end of the tour.

He'd been hyped, taking his family around the surf school while Callie entertained Izzy—who was demanding sandcastles—on the beach.

The Fletts' opinion of this place mattered.

He wanted them to like it. He wanted them to tell him he'd done good. Most of all he wanted them to realise he had a lot to give and was a guy of substance—not the flake they'd wrongly presumed.

'Great job, bro.' Tom shook his hand. 'Torquay needs something like this, a place where the kids can hang out.'

'Yeah, that's what I thought.'

They shared a conspiratorial smile, remembering their own tearaway teenage days and some of the mischief bored kids could get up to at the beach.

'I'm so proud of you, son.' His mum enveloped him in a squishy hug, the familiar lavender and fresh bread scent clinging to her so reminiscent of his childhood he felt choked up.

'Thanks, Mum.'

He hugged her tight, saddened by how much he'd missed over the years through the choices he'd made. Distancing himself from his family had probably hurt them, but he'd been the one to suffer the most.

They'd had each other.

He'd had no one.

He planned on changing all that.

When he released his mum, she moved over to the doorway, where Tom and Trav were deep in conversation. It gave Archer the opportunity to seek out his dad, who'd been hanging back during the tour.

While his brothers' and mother's opinion meant everything to him, it was Frank's he prized most.

Over the years they'd fallen into a pattern of mutual gruffness and avoidance that seemed impossible to breach.

Every time he made the slightest effort to reconnect his dad would brush it off as unnecessary in his usual jovial way. And Archer would let him. He never pushed the issue, his pride reiterating that there was only so far he could extend the olive branch and it was up to his dad to grab it.

Frank never had, and he hated the distance between them. He'd once idolised his dad. He'd always reckoned him, Tom and Trav had been super-lucky, having a hands-on dad who took them fishing and camping and hiking. Frank had attended every one of their footy matches, had never missed a training session either.

It made what had happened later all the harder to accept, and made Archer doubt himself as nothing else could.

Tired of second-guessing himself, and buoyed by the shove in the right direction Callie had given him, he had every intention of ensuring the gap between them wasn't irredeemable this time.

'What do you think, Dad?'

He hated having to ask, wished Frank had volunteered some faint praise without prompting, for it signalled that the divide between them was bigger than he'd anticipated.

'Good for Torquay.' Frank glanced around, stuck his hands in his pockets, shuffled his feet as if he couldn't wait to escape. 'Though it's a bit rough putting your name to something around these parts when you're going to be AWOL all the time.'

His dad's aloofness stung, but not as much

as the barb behind his words. Frank hadn't acknowledged the good thing he'd done in setting up the school; he'd said it was good for the town.

As for the dig about him being away all the time, it might be true, but why couldn't his dad admit he was proud of him, rather than chastising him for having a school in his name?

'I may be around more often,' Archer said, making it sound blasé when in fact he was hanging on his dad's response.

Frank turned away, but not before he'd seen the scepticism twisting his mouth. 'Uh-huh.'

How two little syllables could hold so much doubt he'd never know.

Archer swallowed his disappointment. His pride in showing his family around and his hope for the future was shattered by his dad's continued standoffishness.

If Frank didn't get why he'd done this, couldn't bring himself to offer one word of positive encouragement, why the hell should he keep busting a gut trying to build bridges between them?

His pride might have kept him from being truly a part of this family all these years, but they'd wronged him first. Was that a childish way to look at it? Yeah, but as years' worth of hurt bubbled up from deep within it obliterated his intention to heal the rift between them.

'Why, Dad?'

Frank stiffened. 'Why what?'

Disgusted, Archer shook his head. 'You know what.'

'Frank, come take a look at this.'

Archer glanced at his mum. Her worried expression was a dead giveaway that she'd sensed tension and was trying to avoid a messy confrontation.

Uncertain, Frank hesitated.

With disappointment warring with his bitterness, Archer said, 'Go.'

Which was exactly what he intended to do on Christmas Day, as planned.

Go back to his life, far from Torquay and the ghosts of the past haunting him.

'Come back to bed.'

Archer slid his arms around Callie from behind, resting his chin on her head.

'Just let me finish this.' She'd like nothing better than to slip back into his arms, but she had less than a day to get this website done and she didn't want to leave any loose ends.

Once Archer left she wanted a clean break. No contact.

It might be idealistic to hope for a stress-free

resumption of their previous working relationship, where they e-mailed each other as needed,
but she had a feeling Archer wouldn't mind.

Since Izzy's surf lesson and the impromptu
Flett picnic at the beach this morning he'd withdrawn. Nothing overt, but she could tell.

She'd been here before.

In Capri it had been that silly joke she'd
made about proposals in the Blue Grotto. Now
she had no idea what had prompted his emotional shutdown.

From what she'd seen this morning he'd been
closer to his family than he had all week. He'd
been demonstrative and open and carefree—
in his element.

Something must have happened during the
tour of the surf school, because when they'd
met up afterwards the tension between him and
his dad had been so thick she was surprised it
hadn't clouded the sky.

And he refused to discuss what was happening on Christmas Day with his family, despite her subtle prompting this afternoon. She
had plans of her own to make, and the least he
could do was let her in on what the heck was
going on.

The Christmas holidays might not be a big
deal for him, considering he lived his life on the
road, but his youngest brother was getting mar-

ried, for goodness' sake—surely this Christmas would be different?

'We've got all tomorrow morning to work on the website.' He ducked down beside her and kissed her cheek. 'Now's the time to play hooky.'

'Won't you have to do last-minute Christmas stuff before the wedding tomorrow night?'

Shadows darkened his eyes to indigo. 'Not really. Like you, I do all my shopping online, so stuff will get delivered direct to the family tomorrow.'

Knowing she was treading a hazardous path, she pushed away from the laptop and swivelled to face him.

'Don't you do other stuff?'

'Like?'

'Help your mum chop veggies for the roast on Christmas Day? Set the table? Fill stockings? That kind of thing?'

He stared at her as if she'd suggested he dress up as Santa and prance around Torquay lugging a sack for the day.

'I don't do that stuff.'

'Why?'

A part of her was dying to know, while the realistic part knew he'd never divulge the truth in a million years.

Guys like him didn't share deep, dark truths.

They hid them away beneath a veneer of charm and practised wit.

She should know. Her dad had been the same.

A quick smile and a clever quip for everybody. Loving the world, but not staying put in one place long enough to form any real emotional attachments to anyone.

Including his own daughter.

She'd thought Archer was like that too until she'd seen the way he'd connected with those teenagers on the beach. And Izzy.

He genuinely cared about people, willingly gave of his time expecting nothing in return. That generosity came from within. It wasn't something you could fake; kids—especially teenagers—picked up on that kind of thing. She had with her dad.

Seeing that side of Archer, giving himself freely to those teens on the beach, had opened her eyes to his deeper facets—the ones he kept hidden. And it had made it pretty darn impossible to resist him.

Even with his complicated family history, why didn't he want to show that side of himself to *them*?

'I'm not around enough to warrant that kind of involvement in the rituals,' he said.

His jaw was clenched so hard she was surprised she couldn't hear his teeth grind.

'I fly in each year, stay a few days, then I'm outta here. Why disrupt their routine?'

'Maybe because they want you to?' She kept pushing, her previously undiscovered sadistic side wanting to prod an obvious wound. 'I know it's tough on you, after what you told me at the party, but your family light up when you're around.'

His sceptical glare indicated that he didn't believe her for a second. 'Prodigal son syndrome.'

She touched him on the arm. 'Why do you do that? Pretend your family isn't important to you?'

'That's bull.' He leaped to his feet as if she'd electrocuted him. 'They know how I feel about them.'

'Do they?'

She stood, wanting to see his reaction when she continued peppering him with bombshells. 'From what I've seen, Travis hangs on your every word, Tom looks out for you, and your folks think you walk on water rather than surf it.'

She reached for him, but he stepped away on the pretext of shutting a window, when in fact he was shutting her out.

'It's like they're vying for your attention and you don't want any of it.'

A tiny vein pulsed just below his ear, in the spot she loved to kiss. By his formidable glower, kissing was the last thing on his mind.

'You've met my family only a few times. A few more than any other woman I've known. What gives you the right to judge when you don't know them?'

Or me. The words hung unsaid between them and she resisted the urge to rub her chest where his barb had hit.

Because it was true.

She didn't really know him.

They'd connected for a brief seven days in Capri, but that had been mostly physical— as articulated by the man himself when he'd walked away.

As for their time together here… She'd fallen into the old trap of believing physical closeness implied intimacy, when in fact Archer didn't want to share anything with her. Not the stuff that mattered.

She wanted him to open up to her about what had happened earlier today to make him retreat—wanted him to trust her enough to do it. She'd thought they'd made major inroads in their developing relationship when he'd divulged the truth about his family at the party.

She'd been wrong.

For all she knew nothing had happened with his family during that tour this morning and he was deliberately closing off to *her*.

Maybe she'd been getting too close, and this was his way of cluing her in that come Christmas Day, when he dropped her home, they were finished.

Well, newsflash, surfer boy. She already knew they were over, but this time she wouldn't walk away with a whimper.

'So I'm supposed to be grateful you let me meet your family?' She slow clapped. 'Well done. You took the monumental step of letting a woman get closer than your bathrobe and a kiss on the cheek on her way out the next morning.'

Stricken, he paled, staring at her as if she'd morphed into a monster, and she knew she'd gone too far.

He was so infuriating, standing there in his emotional cocoon, holding everyone at bay when all they wanted to do was love him.

Her included.

Damn, she *loved* him.

Fine time to realise it. Her shock mirrored his.

'Sorry, that was way out of line. I'm just so mad at you for—'

'What, Callie? For walking away from you

in Capri? For blackmailing you into being my date for the wedding? For sleeping with you again?' Anger radiated off him like a nuclear cloud. 'You've been mad at me since the day I stepped into your office.'

He jabbed a thumb at his chest. 'You've done such a great job of dumping home truths on *me*, why don't you take a look at yourself?' He took a step towards her, the air crackling with tension. 'Go on—admit it. You're still mad as hell for something that happened eight freaking years ago.'

She shook her head, close to tears. 'It's not that…'

He gripped her upper arms. 'Then tell me why you're so mad.'

She could have lied, could have made up some lame story, but that was what she'd done in Capri. Put on a brave face and lied when he made light of their week together.

Not this time.

'I'm mad at a lot of things, most of them beyond my control, but I'm mostly mad at myself.'

Confusion creased his brow and his grip on her arms eased now he was convinced this crazy woman wouldn't slug him. 'Why?'

'For being a hypocrite. For making light of what we share now, for calling it a fling and pretending I'm happy with it.'

Archer stiffened as she'd expected when she confronted him with the truth.

'I'm mad I let you walk away in Capri belittling what we'd had. I'm mad at you for not trusting me enough to tell me what's going on with you now. And most of all I'm mad as hell you're going to do the same thing this time around.'

Shock slashed his brow. 'I don't know what you want me to say.'

Saddened that even now, when she'd laid it on the line, he couldn't open up, she touched his cheek. 'That's the problem between us, isn't it?'

Fierce determination lit his eyes as he hauled her close. 'Callie, I don't know what you want me to say because I'm clueless here. I've never felt this way about anyone, but I can't change who I am.'

'I'm not asking you to change.'

Though inadvertently she was, and that wasn't fair. She didn't want Archer to give up his life.

She wanted him to love her the way she loved him.

And she couldn't make him love her. Just as she hadn't been able to make her dad love her.

That was when it hit her how alike the two really were. On the surface Archer appeared to be more giving of his time, but only with those not close to him. Why, she had no idea and she wouldn't waste time figuring it out.

How many years had her mum wasted trying to decipher her dad? How much time had Nora spent hoping Bruno would change, that he'd actually commit to something, even if it were only regular visits with his daughter, before being disappointed repeatedly?

She'd hated being second-best in her dad's affections, and no way in hell would she put herself through that with another guy who couldn't commit.

She'd finally told Archer the truth and, while he did care, he could never be the guy she wanted him to be.

So she had two choices.

End things now and spend the next day and the wedding being miserable.

Or make the most of their remaining time together.

Her mother's 'seize the day' attitude flashed through her mind.

'I'm not expecting anything from you.' She stepped into his personal space, almost treading on his toes, to whisper against his mouth. 'But it's Christmas Eve tomorrow and I have a few wishes I need to come true.'

Archer was too smart to buy her excuse completely, but she knew he wouldn't push it. She'd given him an out from the heavy, confrontational stuff and he'd take it. No doubt.

'Want to be my personal elf?' he said, a moment before he kissed her.

She loved this infuriating, emotionally repressed guy, and she'd be anything he wanted for the next twenty-four hours.

For come Christmas morning they'd be saying goodbye, and this time she didn't want to have any regrets.

CHAPTER NINE

ARCHER spent the morning at the surf school.

He'd always done his best thinking at Winki Pop, his go-to place when he'd been a kid. It was like home.

He owned property near Mavericks in Northern California, Pupukea on Oahu's north shore near the Pipeline, and Jeffreys Bay on the Eastern Cape of South Africa. Perfectly nice houses situated near the world's surfing hotspots—houses where he chilled at regular intervals.

But none brought him the peace of Winki Pop.

He'd surfed at dawn, eager to escape the house and Callie's all-seeing eyes.

She'd got close last night, too damn close, homing in on areas of his personal life strictly off-limits.

Hell, he could hardly go there himself.

He didn't get it. One minute he'd been coaxing her to come back to bed, the next she'd seen into his soul.

The thing was, she'd been right about some of it. He knew his family wanted more from him than he was willing to give. He saw it every time he came home—which was why he rarely did.

But this time he'd tried, damn it. Although he'd already made inroads with his brothers, his mum and Izzy, he'd finally done what he'd been yearning to do for years: tried to bridge the gap he'd created with his dad. But the way his dad had reacted at the surf school had demonstrated there was nothing he could say or do to mend metaphorical fences with him.

Because of that he'd been edgy since, and Callie had noticed. She hadn't pushed him and he'd appreciated it—until she'd blown up in his face last night.

When she'd admitted to considering their relationship more than a fling—then and now—he'd wanted to say so much, to lay it on the line: how he was feeling, what he was thinking. But with his dad's rejection fresh from the morning he hadn't been able to do it. Hadn't been able to take another chance with his jumbled, messed-up feelings.

Until he sorted out his options for the future, what would that mean for Callie? A casual relationship with benefits whenever he happened to be in town?

He doubted she'd put up with an arrangement like that, and he wouldn't want her to. She deserved more. More than he could give.

But for one infinitesimal moment, as he stared at the surfers bobbing like buoys on the ocean, he wondered what it would be like to have Callie on a permanent basis.

A woman to come home to.

A woman to love.

Shrugging off the terrifying thought, he resumed his final inspection.

As far as he could see the surf school was in tip top shape and ready for business.

Which was more than he could say for himself.

He was in lousy shape, and considering he not only had to face Christmas Eve but a Flett wedding too things could only go downhill.

Callie dressed with particular care.

She wanted to make this a night to remember.

She'd bought a knockout dress for the wedding from a local boutique expecting to show Archer what he was missing out on. Considering what they'd been up to the last few days, the strapless maroon chiffon cocktail dress with its flared skirt had become redundant.

Archer hadn't been missing out on anything.

Except the one thing she could never give him.

Her heart.

The realisation that she loved him shouldn't have come as any great surprise. She'd fallen hard during their week in Capri all those years ago—had only been saved from pining by her mum's diagnosis. But this time around it had hit her harder, and the constant slightly breathless feeling she had when he was near was beyond annoying.

She knew the score: there'd be no romantic proposals under the mistletoe for her this Christmas.

They were leaving first thing in the morning, apparently. Considering how his family had shut him out during his father's cancer battle she shouldn't be surprised he didn't want to spend Christmas Day with them.

She understood what it felt like when family let you down. She'd put up with it from her dad for too long, until she'd wised up and learned to expect nothing from the selfish, self-absorbed guy who valued his carefree lifestyle more than his only kid.

But from what she'd seen the Fletts were

a close-knit, loving bunch. His parents had been married for yonks and still held hands, his youngest brother believed enough in romance to get married on Christmas Eve, and even Tom, who should be disillusioned after his wife had run off after less than twelve months of marriage, was keen to settle down again, according to Travis.

But, despite professing a wish to build bridges with his folks, Archer was still refusing to commit to them.

And her.

Foolish to think that way. Once he'd crept under her guard again and they'd fallen into a physical relationship she'd gone into it with her eyes wide open. In it for a short, good time, not a long time. A self-indulgent fling filled with amazing memories to sustain her through the tough times ahead.

In that respect getting involved with Archer again had exceeded her expectations. Every kiss, every touch, every whispered endearment had been imprinted on her brain to resurrect on a cold winter's night, when she was huddled over her computer working at midnight with a cooling coffee and a bowl of chocolate almonds for company.

Archer had been attentive, charming and altogether gorgeous over the last few days. Little wonder she'd fallen in love.

Her diaphragm gave a little spasm and she dragged in a deep breath and rubbed under her ribs. It didn't ease the stitch that grabbed her every time she associated the words 'love' and 'Archer' in the same thought.

She might be a realist, but the thought of spending the evening at a romantic wedding, the night in his arms and waking up together on Christmas morning made her want to bawl.

She had every intention to farewell him tomorrow, but it wouldn't be easy. Now she finally understood why her mum had secretly pined for Bruno's love all those years ago. *'We always want what we can't have,'* Nora had once said, in relation to Callie's pony request one Christmas, but by the tears in Nora's eyes Callie had known there was more to it.

Nora had led a full life, the epitome of a single mum who was loving it, but as a child Callie remembered hearing muffled sobs late at night, and seeing the way Nora lit up when Bruno returned home for a rare visit.

Callie empathised with her mum, but she didn't want to be that person. She didn't want to cry over lost love. She wanted to remember the good times and celebrate the second chance she'd had with Archer—even if it ended in tears like the first.

Snatching a tissue from the dresser, she dabbed under her eyes, absorbing the seepage. No way would she cry. Archer would be knocking on her bedroom door any moment and she wanted to wow him—not send him back to the surf school where he'd hidden out all day.

On the pretext of work, of course. A final inspection or some such guff. But she knew better.

He'd opened up a little last night and then emotionally closed down a lot. To the point where, when she'd shut down the program she'd been working on and backed up her work, he'd been asleep when she'd returned to bed. Or pretended to be.

She'd been too drained to care, but when she'd woken this morning to find a terse note and no Archer she'd had her answer to any silent questions she might have been contemplating.

Questions like had the last few days meant anything to him beyond a fling?

Did he feel their connection on a deeper level?

Would he walk away again without a backward glance?

Pointless questions, really, for even if he

came up with the answers she wanted to hear it wouldn't change a thing. Her life was in Melbourne for the foreseeable future; his was traipsing the world. The closest they'd be was in cyberspace, where she'd contact him on a need-to-know basis. End of story.

A loud rap sounded on her door and she blinked rapidly, ensuring her eyes were sheen-free.

'Be right there.'

The incongruity of the situation struck her. They'd been intimate, this was *his* house, and yet he wouldn't open the door to her room.

Yeah, the barriers were already up, and the sooner she got used to it the better.

Attending this wedding, pretending she was happy, would be tough. Then again, compared to what she had to face in the future, she could handle it.

She could handle anything. It was what she did. Capable Callie. Canny Callie. No one ever saw lonely, emotionally fragile Callie, a woman who craved love and affection and a foolproof guarantee that she wouldn't end up like her mum.

'Damn,' she muttered, swiping a final slick of lip gloss across her lips and staring wide-eyed at the mirror so she wouldn't cry.

She didn't like feeling edgy, as if she'd snivel

at any moment. Considering their impending goodbye she'd have plenty of time for that tomorrow.

Until then...*time to put her game face on.*

Archer held onto Callie's hand through the ceremony, the congratulations, and most of the reception.

He caught her wary glances several times and squeezed her hand in response, as if he never wanted to let go.

The truth was he was absolutely freaking terrified.

Weddings scared him.

The Fletts *en masse* scared him.

Combine the two? Guaranteed scare-fest.

Thankfully, having Callie meet his family at the barbecue and on the beach guaranteed he was safe from his mum's matchmaking for once. But holding onto her hand was more than a gesture, and only he knew it.

She anchored him.

Her ability to socialise with ease, to smile and laugh and be absorbed by his family's mayhem, to make everyone around her feel at ease, was a gift.

Maybe it was all the romantic claptrap in the air? Maybe it was Christmas working its magic? Whatever it was, he found himself strangely reluctant to let her go.

And not just her hand.

Even now, after she'd survived the Flett females' incessant teasing when she caught the bouquet, after dancing with Izzy and the kids until she hobbled, after being ribbed by his brothers, she stood tall, surrounded by the bride, the bridesmaids and his mum, laughing and exuberant and glowing.

She'd never looked so beautiful.

It was more than her brown hair hanging in a sleek curtain down her back, her lush lips slicked in gloss the same colour as her dress, her bare shoulders glittering with a dust of bronze.

It was *her.*

When they'd met in Capri she'd blamed her spontaneity on her Italian heritage and he'd loved her impulsiveness. But it was more than that. She was alive in a way many people weren't. People who dragged their bored butts to work every day, doing a job they hated to pay the bills, returning to equally dead-end relationships at the end of a day.

By the way Callie glowed she'd never had a boring day in her life.

What would it be like to be close to that vitality on a daily basis? Would it rub off?

He loved his life, loved the constant travelling and challenges and business success, but he'd be kidding himself if he didn't admit some of the gloss had worn off lately. Now that he wasn't competing as much he felt jaded, as if his lifestyle wasn't all it was cracked up to be.

Having someone like Callie along for the ride would brighten his days, that was for sure. But with her mum terminally ill would she go for it?

'That's some young lady you've lucked in with.'

His dad sidled up to him and Archer inadvertently braced for another confrontation.

'No such thing as luck, Dad. It's the legendary Flett charm.'

Frank's tentative guffaw sounded as if he had something stuck in his throat. Probably his conscience.

'Whatever it is, she's a keeper.'

'Thanks. I'll take your advice into consideration.'

Archer silently cursed his hint of sarcasm when Frank stiffened, hesitated as if weighing his words.

'Don't let her get away,' he said.

Archer swallowed his annoyance at being given relationship advice from a father who'd deliberately shut him out years ago.

Frank cleared his throat. 'We worry about you, son.'

Yeah, right. His dad was so worried that despite the times he'd made tentative overtures these last few years he'd been brushed off or shut down every time.

'Don't. I'm having the time of my life.' Archer made the *shaka* sign. 'Living the dream.'

Frank's scrutiny almost made him squirm. 'Are you?'

'Hell, yeah.' His response came too quickly, sounded too false. 'I like what I do. It's better than—'

He bit back the rest of what he'd been going to say, on the verge of saying more than he should.

'Better than what?' Frank swept his arm wide. 'Better than being stuck near your family?'

Archer took a steadying breath. Another. 'Do you really want to do this here? Now?'

Frank shook his head, sorrow deepening the creases around his eyes. 'I've only ever wanted what's best for you.'

Archer knew he should walk away now. Make a flippant remark to cover his profound anger and walk away.

But he'd had a crappy day, he was confused

about Callie, and he'd had a gutful of being on the outside with his dad for leading the life he did.

'What's best for me is staying true to myself. What about you, Dad? What's best for you?' Years of suppressed anger and pain bubbled up and he couldn't have stopped the questions even if he'd wanted to. 'Having your family around you while you battle a life-threatening illness? Being able to rely on your sons to take care of business while you're juggling chemo? Trusting your family to support you no matter how ill you feel or how bad the diagnosis?'

Frank recoiled as if he'd struck him, but Archer wasn't finished.

'I saw you, Dad, that day you finally told me about being given the all-clear.' He sucked in a breath. The vision of that day was embedded deep, yet so clear. 'Eighteen freaking months too late, you finally deemed me responsible enough to handle the truth about your prostate cancer. After I stormed out you sat at the piano, slid your sheet music into a folder, and you cried. You sobbed like you'd been given a death sentence rather than the all-clear. And right then I knew how big a battle you must've faced, and it acted like a kick in the guts all over again.'

Hating how his voice had clogged, he lowered his tone. 'You should've told me earlier, Dad. I should've been here!'

'You're wrong.' Frank stared at him as if he were a stranger. 'I cried because I knew I'd done the right thing in not telling you, despite how damn furious you were. Even though seeing you hurting almost killed me more than the bloody cancer.'

Stunned at his dad's words, Archer pinched the bridge of his nose. It didn't help ease the headache building behind his eyes.

'You still think you did the right thing in not telling me—?'

'Son, you were a world champion when I finally told you. You'd done it. Followed your dream. Achieved the ultimate. I was so proud of you.'

Frank blinked, and the sight of possible tears tempered Archer's disbelief like nothing else.

'That's what I wanted for you. Success. It kept me going all through the illness: watching your competitions, charting your stats, following every mention on the internet. It gave me focus even when I felt like giving up.'

Frank gripped his arm and gave it a little shake.

'*You* did that. You helped me in ways you can't possibly imagine. And no way in hell would that have happened if you'd known about the cancer.'

Shock peppered every preconception about his dad Archer had ever had, and he couldn't formulate a word in response.

Frank gestured towards the family. 'As much as I love those guys, and the support they gave me, their constant hovering became smothering.' His rueful grin eased the lines bracketing his mouth. 'Some days I'd fake fatigue just so I could get into bed with my laptop and check out what you'd been up to.'

'Hell, Dad.' Archer dragged a hand through his hair, wanting to say so much but still floundering.

'Did you know I could've toured with the Melbourne Symphony Orchestra?'

Whiplashed by the change of topic, all Archer could do was shake his head.

'I would've liked performing to large crowds, living on the road.' Frank squared his shoulders and gazed fondly at his wife. 'But I met your mother and my dreams changed. I ended up teaching local kids and looking forward to your mother's slow-cooked lamb and apple pie and long walks along the beach every night.'

His dad rested his hand on his shoulder.

'While I don't regret staying in Torquay and giving up on my dream, I didn't want you to give up yours, son. I wanted you to have the chance I never had.'

Stunned, Archer stared at his dad—really looked at him for the first time in years. 'That's the real reason you didn't tell me?'

Bashful, Frank nodded. 'I'm sorry for being a jerk at the surf school yesterday. The distance between us over the years has been rough. We both have too much pride for our own good. And the bigger the divide between us the guiltier I felt about what I'd done, and the harder to breach the gap became. Then I saw you rebonding with everyone and I wanted to do the same, but things were so damn awkward between us all the time. I just didn't know how to express half of what I was thinking.'

'Honestly, Dad, I don't know what to say.' Archer blew out a long breath, knowing he had to exorcise the past and move forward. 'I tried a few times but you always shut me down, pretended nothing was wrong. Now you tell me all this stuff and I'm having a hard time dealing with it.'

'Deal with it. Move on. Life's too short.' Frank nodded towards the dance floor, where the mayor was treading on his mum's toes for the umpteenth time. 'I'm happy with the life choices I've made.'

What about you?

Though his dad didn't say it, the question was there, lurking in his shrewd stare.

Archer had led a charmed life. No regrets.

A peal of laughter floated on the air and he turned, seeing Callie as if in slow motion, with her head thrown back, her hair streaming behind her. Her laughter was loud and boisterous and genuine, and he could have sworn his heart turned over.

He'd lied. He did have one regret in his life. Walking away from this incredibly striking woman.

The real question was, would he make the same mistake twice?

'Settling down isn't all bad.' Frank's genuine smile alleviated the tension between them. 'Happens to the best of us. Just ask your brother.'

Archer winced as he saw Travis doing the Time Warp with his bride. Trav gawky and awkward, Shelly laughing so hard she clutched her sides.

'Think about what I've said, son.' Frank nodded towards Callie, who glanced up at that moment and waved. 'You'd be a fool to let a woman like that slip through your fingers for the sake of a footloose, fancy-free lifestyle. Times change and so do we. We move with them or get left behind.'

As Callie moved towards them, Frank chuckled and nudged him in her direction.

Archer didn't know what to think. His head was spinning with what he'd learned; his heart was reeling from the possible truth.

Did he dare give up one dream to trust his heart and follow another?

CHAPTER TEN

'I'VE never had a Christmas like this,' Callie said, staring at the table in amazement.

Covered in crisp white linen, crimson tealights, vases filled with decorative baubles, sparkling crystal, shiny silverware and tiny handmade wreaths sprinkled with silver glitter, it stretched from one end of the marquee to the other.

'Trav and Shelly wanted a combined Christmas-wedding theme, but I think Mum commandeered the decorations.' Archer pointed overhead at the liberal mistletoe hanging from strategically placed hooks. 'She's always gone the whole hog with Christmas. It's the same every year.'

'It's beautiful.' Callie cleared her throat, embarrassed by the sudden surge of emotion making her want to cry. 'You're lucky.'

He must have caught her hint of whimsy and

he clasped her hand. 'How do you usually celebrate?'

'Low-key,' she muttered, instantly ashamed of her bitterness.

She'd tried to take her mum on day-trips, especially on special occasions like birthdays and Christmas, but Nora had deteriorated so fast over the last few years it had become easier to stay in.

Her mum had been so distressed last Christmas that she'd made Callie promise not to do it again.

So celebrations these days consisted of snuck-in takeaway Thai and luscious chocolate cake from Brunetti's, carols on her iPod and a lot of forced cheerfulness when neither of them really felt like celebrating.

Even their gifts had gone the way of practical rather than indulgent. That hadn't stopped her buying an e-reader Nora could swipe with a fingertip, special organic cream for her crêpe-like skin, and her favourite chocolates this year.

She'd ordered online a few days ago, when she'd been flushed with happiness after her escapades with Archer at the beach.

If she was going to live in the moment, she wanted her mum to also.

Now, with her heart deliberately sealing itself off and her impending departure in the morning, she wondered if she'd been foolish and frivolous.

'Guess it's hard celebrating when your mum's so sick.'

'Yeah.'

He stared at her with blatant curiosity and she wished she'd kept her mouth shut. What better way to ruin their last evening together than to rehash her dysfunctional family's past? Especially in the face of his familial warm and fuzzy perfection.

'You don't want to talk about it?'

She shot him a grateful smile. 'I'd rather focus on this.'

She waved towards the table as the first guests trickled in from the other entry. 'It's really beautiful.' On impulse, she kissed him on the cheek. 'Thanks for coercing me into accompanying you to this wedding.'

He had the grace to look sheepish. 'Sometimes a guy's gotta do what a guy's gotta do.'

That motto applied to girls too, and for tonight she'd drink, dance and be merry. And later, she'd spend an incredible night in Archer's bed, hoarding away memories she'd always cherish.

She hadn't had the opportunity last time, had deliberately banished their time together courtesy of his abrupt break-up. And she'd had more important things to worry about since, like her mum's illness.

Yet for all her reservations about getting involved with him again this week she was glad she'd done it. The last seven days had shown her that the guy she'd thought she'd known in Capri she hadn't known at all. Archer was caring and intuitive, and he had vulnerabilities like the rest of them, and discovering his hidden depths had guaranteed she fell for him.

That was another thing she was glad she'd done: confronting him with her feelings. While she still wished things could have been different, the outcome wasn't unexpected. How could a guy who'd been emotionally shut off from his family for years commit emotionally to her, when realistically they'd known each other for only two weeks eight years apart?

'There is a way you can thank me properly.'

'How?'

He slid an arm around her waist and tugged her close. 'Look up.'

'Beautiful hand-crafted wood beams, red-gum panelling—'

'Mistletoe,' he murmured, a second before he kissed her—a ravishing, soul-reaching melding that left her breathless and clinging to him when he eased away.

It was only then that she registered the hoots and claps of the Fletts.

She blushed, while Archer waved towards the clan, squared his shoulders and escorted her to pride of place with the rest of the family at the head of the table.

As he pulled out her chair and caressed the back of her neck, a sliver of longing lodged in her shielded heart.

What would it be like to belong to a family like this? To be surrounded by love and laughter? She'd never known it, and she'd never felt her deprivation so acutely as now.

Her dad had done that to her—taken away any semblance of a happy family upbringing—and while she'd given up on him a long time ago it was moments like these when she could easily throttle Bruno Umberto.

She could thank him for her dark hair and eyes, her love of pasta and her quick-fire temper, but there was little else Bruno deserved her gratitude for.

The self-absorbed man who'd now married four times, who lived life on the edge and loved the same way, had breezed in and out of her life like a flitting butterfly.

Since Nora had been diagnosed he hadn't been near them, and the odd e-mail didn't cut it.

The genetic testing had proved she hadn't

inherited the mutated gene from her mum. Luckily she hadn't inherited something far more deadly from her father.

His selfishness.

She'd be there for her mum whatever it took, whatever she had to sacrifice, however much it hurt.

'You're kinda spaced out.' He waved a hand in front of her face. 'Everything okay?'

She dredged up a dazzling smile to fool him. 'Fine.'

She'd ensure everything was fine tonight, for come tomorrow their dalliance would be over. But for a fleeting moment she wished she had Bruno's selfish streak and could demand this wasn't the end.

'Hey, surf dude, when are you going to introduce us?' A tall, broad-shouldered guy who had the Flett blond good-looks sat next to Archer and jostled him.

Archer grinned and elbowed him back. 'Callie, this is my cousin Jonesy.' He draped a proprietorial arm across the back of her chair. 'Jonesy, this is my friend Callie.'

'You're a stunner.' Jonesy reached across Archer and shook her hand vigorously, his smile goofy rather than leery.

'Thanks,' she said, grateful when Jonesy

started interrogating Archer about wave conditions for the upcoming season.

Friend.

He'd introduced her as his friend, and while it might be the truth it sounded so distant after what they'd shared.

All her one-on-one pep talks with her voice of reason meant nothing in the face of reality.

Mistletoe kisses, passionate love in the sand dunes and cuddles on the balcony aside, she was right back to where she'd been in Capri.

Wishing for a miracle.

Wishing for him to love her.

After what she'd been through with her mum, she'd given up on miracles a long time ago.

What could be so different now?

But she wouldn't waste her life pining. She'd move on ASAP.

Starting first thing in the morning.

Archer couldn't figure it out. One minute Callie had been kissing him with all the passion and exuberance he'd come to expect from her, the next she'd retreated.

Not that it was obvious to anyone but him. She danced and giggled and ate two pieces of red velvet wedding cake, apparently having a ball.

But he could tell. Every time she glanced his way he saw the shadows. Fleeting, willow-o-the-wisp flickers of…what? Pain? Regret? Disappointment?

He'd wanted to ask what was wrong on their drive home, but she'd been trying hard to fill the awkward silence, chatting non-stop about his family and the ceremony and the exchanging of gifts. And he'd been happy to let her talk, still trying to assimilate the truth behind his dad's secrecy all those years ago.

He'd wanted to thank her for encouraging him to swallow his pride and give his family a go, for making him see beyond his anger and resentment. But she hadn't stopped talking. Anything to avoid silence.

Yeah, there was definitely something wrong. Or maybe she just felt weird about their impending departure tomorrow?

Not that she should. He had it all figured out. Make tonight a night to remember, wake up with her in his arms Christmas morning, then talk to her when they arrived back in Melbourne.

He had a rough plan that he'd come up with over the last few hours.

His dad was right. His pushy brothers were right.

Callie was a keeper.

He'd be a fool to let her go.

He hadn't figured out all the logistics yet. He'd never done a long-distance relationship. Hopefully with a little help from her they'd figure out how this would work.

The thought of having her in his life made him want to ditch the tux, grab his board and head for the beach—but to celebrate, not to escape. He wanted to crest a wave, ride a tube, to see if anything could beat the adrenalin rush of realising he didn't have to lose Callie.

Not this time.

'I know you said no gifts, but I've got you something,' she said, strolling towards him on the balcony before sliding onto the love seat next to him.

He shook his head. 'Should've known you wouldn't listen,' he said, wondering what she'd think of his gift when he presented it to her tomorrow.

He'd arranged it online ten minutes ago, as part of his grand plan, while she'd been 'turning back into a pumpkin'—her words, not his—exchanging her dress and up-do for T-shirt, leggings and a loose ponytail that left tendrils curling around her face.

She looked tousled and tired and casual, and she'd never looked so beautiful.

'It's nothing big. I brought it with me. Didn't want to be caught empty-handed. It's not much.'

She was bordering on babbling, and he covered her hand with his to calm her. 'It's from you. I'll love it.'

Darting a nervous glance at him, she gnawed on her bottom lip, her nerves puzzling. It was only a gift. Then again, considering the yearning he'd glimpsed when his family were handing out gifts after the wedding, and the way she'd clammed up about her family celebrating the Christmas holidays, he figured maybe presents were a big deal for her.

He took his time, tugging on the gold ribbon, fiddling with the knot, sliding his finger under the sticky-tape.

'Hurry up,' she said, practically squirming with impatience.

'I see you're a rip-it-off-in-one-quick-move girl,' he said, putting her out of her misery by tearing the paper in three broad strips to reveal something that snatched his breath with the same surreal, suffocating sensation he'd had being caught in a rip once.

'What—? How—?'

He remembered the day they'd stumbled upon the tiny glassblower's cottage as if it was yesterday. It had been their third day together in Capri—a day filled with swimming in a pristine ocean, sharing grilled calamari and fresh bread for lunch, indulging in a decadent session of afternoon delight, before strolling hand in hand through the cobbled streets.

They'd laughed and jostled and snuggled, typical holiday lovers, and discovering the cottage with exquisitely made glass figurines had made Callie's day. She loved that kind of thing, and he'd indulged her by going in, surprised by the wizened old guy who looked about a hundred creating mini-masterpieces.

The porpoises had caught his attention because he'd seen some during his first major competition, and he'd labelled them his good luck charm ever since.

He'd commissioned a Californian artist to carve a replica of these little glass guys a few years ago, and it took pride of place in the entry hall of his Malibu home.

A home that, like the rest of them, he barely visited.

'You thought it was cool when we went into that glassblowing shop in Capri, so I went back and bought it. I was going to give it to you that last day, but...' She trailed off, not needing to finish.

He'd acted like a jackass, deliberately saying stuff he didn't mean before he let another person get close. Easier to depend on no one and avoid the ultimate let-down.

'Reading too much into a holiday fling... nothing more than a bit of fun...lighten up before you scare off more guys.'

The words came back to haunt him. Come tomorrow he'd make amends and say the words she wanted to hear.

He had all night to work on his delivery. When he wasn't making love to her, that was.

'I was a jerk.'

'Yeah, but you were right.'

He didn't like her emotionless tone, or her shuttered expression as he turned over the delicately intertwined frolicking porpoises.

'I can't believe you've kept them all these years.'

She ran a fingertip along their fins, a soft, wistful sigh escaping her lips. 'I actually forgot I had them. Then, when you showed up and bossed me into coming here, I thought they'd make an okay Christmas gift.'

'An okay gift?' He stared at her in disbelief. Was she being deliberately blasé or did this really not mean anything to her?

She'd kept something so special all these years, something he'd specifically wanted, and she was acting as if she'd given him a pair of woollen socks.

'It's a trinket from the past. Nothing more.'

She shrugged, and the first fingers of doubt crept around his dream of a relationship and strangled it.

'I'm glad this time we had the foresight to know this was a fling and nothing more. No expectations that way. No feelings get hurt. Nice and clean.'

Her brittle laugh set him on edge.

'What did you say back then? A short time and a good time?' She interlaced her fingers through his. 'It's certainly been that, Archer Flett. Consider this a thank-you gift too.'

Gobsmacked, he let her take the porpoises and place them on the glass-topped table beside them before clambering onto his lap. Her arms snaked around his neck, tugging his head towards her, her lips meeting his in an explosion of need.

There was nothing tender about the kiss. It was pure desperation, heat and passion and fear. Fear of the future? Fear of farewell?

Whatever, now wasn't the time to dwell on it. He had a million questions to ask her.

In the morning.

For now he wanted to show her how much she meant to him.

He might not be able to eradicate the immature stuff he'd said in Capri, but he could sure as hell let his actions do all the talking now.

CHAPTER ELEVEN

CALLIE wasn't proud of what she'd done.

She should have told Archer the truth last night. And she shouldn't have snuck away in the early hours. Or made Tom complicit in her deceit.

She had to give him credit for not spilling her secret. She'd half expected Archer to confront her about her plan to abscond once she'd asked Tom for a favour at the wedding.

But Archer hadn't suspected a thing.

She'd had her chance to say goodbye and she'd taken it. Several times during the night, with each erotic encounter surpassing the last.

It had been subliminal, knowing it would be their last time together. She'd imprinted every whispered word, savoured every caress, treasured every touch.

If Archer had been surprised by her wild enthusiasm he hadn't shown it. He'd responded in kind, taking her to heights she'd only ever read about in novels.

And then she'd left, creeping out at 5:00 a.m.

Thankfully Izzy had been asleep in the back of the car, and after a few less than subtle questions Tom had given up interrogating her.

The Fletts were a loyal bunch, for not once had Tom discredited his brother, apart from saying he was a nong for letting her get away again.

She'd had to give him something to shut him up, so she'd settled for a semi-truth. They'd already said their goodbyes last night. They were happy to resume their respective lives, and she had to get back to her mum on Christmas Day.

All perfectly respectable, perfectly legitimate reasons…for running out like a chicken.

The truth was she couldn't face the long car ride back to Melbourne with Archer—couldn't face the awkwardness of another goodbye.

This way they could resume their old relationship—e-mailing for business—and avoid any mess.

He was flying out today, so he wouldn't have time to worry about her early departure anyway. He had things to do, places to be.

Things and places that didn't include her.

That was why she'd given him the porpoises.

She'd lied about that too, telling him she'd forgotten about them.

As if. She might have banished her memories of their time in Capri, but every now and then, when her mum had a particularly bad day and Callie felt lonely, she'd take them out of their recycled cardboard box, cradle them in her hand and remember…

Remember that special time in Capri, wishing she could have one ounce of it again.

Well, now she had, and where had it left her? Worse than before. Seriously in love with a guy who had no clue.

To his credit, his reaction to her gift had blown her away. She hadn't expected to see him emotional, and for a few tense moments beforehand had half expected him not to remember that day in Capri at all. But he had. And it had made her wish things could be different all the more.

Instead she'd go back to working on his lucrative campaigns—with the bonus of having Nora's medical bills taken care of—and he'd hit the surf on some exotic island far removed from Melbourne and the memories they'd built.

Memories that would have to last a lifetime.

For now, it has time to get on with her life, starting with a quick visit to Rivera's to wish

Artie a Merry Christmas and then spending the day with her mum.

The Spanish bar was jumping when she arrived, with revellers in Santa hats and flashing reindeer noses spilling out onto the street. Many locals came straight from mass to get a taste of Artie's special virgin sangria on Christmas morning, before heading off to their respective hot roast lunches with family.

It had become a Johnston Street tradition, and one she enjoyed, because it gave her an all too brief taste of what a normal Christmas should be.

Not like the understated days she'd had growing up, where she'd wait for her dad to show up with the pony he'd promised only to be disappointed yet again.

Or the recent Christmases spent with Nora, forcing cheer when all she'd felt like doing was holding her mum fiercely and banishing the disease slowly sapping her life.

She slipped through the crowd and entered the main door, her despondency lifting when she glimpsed Artie taking pride of place behind the bar, his costume this year more outlandish than the last.

He'd gone for monstrous reindeer antlers that threatened to take a person's eye out when he turned, a big red nose made from a dyed tennis ball, and a fake white beard that reached to his belly.

It made her happy to see him enjoying life, a far cry from the devastated man he'd been following his wife's death.

He caught sight of her and waved, calling her over.

Determined to put on a brave face, she wound her way towards the bar, where he swept her into a bear hug.

'*Hola, querida.* Merry Christmas.'

'Same to you.' When he released her she tweaked his nose. 'How can you breathe with that thing?'

'I can't,' he said, in a fake nasally voice, and she laughed. 'Come. Have some sangria.'

For a moment she wished it was the alcoholic version, despite the hour.

'Tell me about this new business.'

Great. Just what she felt like. Talking about her week in Torquay. *Not.*

He poured her a drink, garnished it with a strawberry, slid it across the bar and winked. 'And tell me more about this old *amor.*'

She remembered contradicting Artie a week ago. *I don't love him.*

This time she didn't have the energy to lie.

'The business is exciting. I've developed an online marketing campaign for his new surf school, including online forums and interactive sessions on his webpage, and a social networking page unlike anything anyone's ever seen.'

'Sounds impressive.' Artie topped up her glass even though she hadn't taken a sip. 'Now, tell me about when you weren't working.'

She blushed and Artie patted her cheek, his smile indulgent.

'You're in love. I can tell.'

'How?'

'You have the look.' He pointed at her eyes. 'You have a sparkle dampened by sadness.' Artie frowned. 'This *amor*, he broke your heart, *sí*?'

'No, nothing like that.'

More like she'd broken her own heart by being foolish enough to fall in love despite knowing the expiration date on their seaside fling, knowing he couldn't emotionally commit, and knowing he had traits of her dad she'd rather forget.

Artie cupped his ear. 'You want to talk about it? I'm a very good listener.'

'Don't I know it?'

Artie had listened to her deepest fears and regrets after their unofficial support group for two had formed. He'd been just as forthcoming in his sorrow, yet strangely this time she didn't want to talk about Archer.

Besides, what was there to say? They were headed in different directions, their lives on different paths, without a hope of colliding.

Artie snapped his fingers. 'I can see you don't want to talk to an old man about your *amor*. I understand.' He shrugged. 'If you do, you know where to find me.'

'Thanks,' she said, making a big show of drinking the refreshing fruit sangria as he was called away, when in fact her favourite Christmas drink had already lost its fizz.

With Artie shooting her concerned glances in between mixing drinks and plying his customers with Christmas cookies, she sculled her sangria and gave him the thumbs-up sign.

She had to leave. Before she took him up on his offer to listen. For she had a feeling once she started talking about her relationship with Archer she wouldn't stop.

Archer stared at the note in disbelief.

Sorry to run out but had to get back to Mum.

Tom & Izzy heading to Melbourne to visit Izzy's mum, who unexpectedly dropped into town today so I hitched a ride.

> Thanks. Had a lovely time at the wedding.
>
> Will be in touch about the surf school campaign when needed.
>
> Merry Christmas!
>
> Callie

'What the—?' He slammed his palm on the kitchen benchtop, barely registering the pain of hitting marble so vigorously.

His first instinct was to punch something. The second to grab his board and hit the surf.

He settled for pacing. It didn't help. After several laps of the balcony he flung himself onto the soft-cushioned couch where he'd once sat with Callie and uncurled his fingers to reveal her crumpled note.

He reread it, no closer to understanding.

She sounded so cool, so remote, so untouchable after all that had happened over the last week. They'd reconnected on so many levels, to the point where he'd been about to reveal his thoughts for the future to her this morning.

Schmuck.

This was his family all over again.

Trusting someone with his heart, only to have them hand it back with a *Thanks, not this time, maybe another,* and having no clue as to why.

To make matters worse it catapulted him back years, to when his family had first told him the truth. The same insidious doubts were creeping in, making him wonder what the hell was wrong with him that the people he trusted the most with his feelings didn't return the favour.

How could she up and leave without saying goodbye? Leaving a freaking note?

He glared at the offending piece of paper in disgust, bitterness twisting his gut into knots.

Growling in frustration, he shoved it in his pocket and headed for the storage room under the house where he stashed his gear. He had to hit the waves. It was the place he did his best thinking.

However, as he stomped around, grabbing a wetsuit and his favourite board—the one with more dents than a dodgem—a funny thing happened.

Some of his initial anger faded, to be replaced by a clarity that left him shaken.

He paused mid-step, halfway between the storage room and his car.

What the hell was he doing?

It was Christmas morning—a time for warmth and caring and happiness. Emotions he'd been lacking lately, if he were honest with himself.

Not this last week with Callie, but before that.

Riding the tubes hadn't held the same buzz in a long time, crashing in fancy hotel rooms after a competition had lost appeal, and the string of meaningless dates left him feeling faintly empty.

The real reason behind the surf school had been to make his family sit up and take notice, see he was more than a sport-obsessed surfer, to show them they'd done wrong in not trusting him with his dad's illness.

But another underlying reason was that he'd wanted to give something back to the sport that had given him everything, and connecting with the kids at the beach last week had made him feel worthy in a way he hadn't in for ever.

That had been the hardest thing to realise over the years following his dad's cancer disclosure—that somehow he hadn't been worthy. He might now understand his dad's motivation for secrecy, but it would take a while for his old beliefs to ease.

Hanging with the teens had helped with that. Callie had too. He'd felt rejuvenated this last week, had truly felt close to a woman for the first time ever.

She'd made him reassess the way he treated his family, made him see things in a new light.

And he'd been happy in a way he hadn't for a long time. So what the hell had happened?

Buoyed by his overture towards his dad, he'd taken another risk and told her he had feelings for her. Why had she run?

After she'd given him that gift last night he'd thought she felt the same way... Well, he'd thought wrong.

The way he saw it, he had two options. Forget about the gift he'd bought her, then head for the surf before boarding that plane this afternoon and heading back to the life he knew.

Or quit running and confront Callie.

He headed for the car, the board tucked under his arm suddenly weighing him down. When he stowed it in the back, the weight didn't shift. Then his gaze landed on the red Roadster he'd driven Callie here in—a replica of the car they'd explored Italy's south coast with.

He remembered the thrill of taking the curves of a spectacular scenic route, laughing and teasing, and later he'd explored *her* sensational curves in minute detail.

He'd wanted to resurrect the past—this car was testament to that—but was he willing to try a different outcome this time?

What would his life be like if he didn't walk away second time round? If he made a full-blown declaration and truly trusted her with his heart?

Terror made his hands shake, and he stuffed them into the pockets of his board shorts.

He had his answer right there.

He'd re-established a bond with his dad and he'd never felt so relieved. Taking a risk on people wasn't all bad. And he wouldn't be feeling this sick unless he really felt something for Callie. Something that went deeper than caring.

The question was, how far was he willing to go to prove it to her?

Callie had put on a brave face for her mum. She'd made a show of savouring the cardboard-tasting turkey and dry Christmas pud, she'd sung the loudest through the residents' carolling, and she'd fake-laughed over each and every corny joke pulled from a cracker.

She'd thought she'd done a pretty good job of pretending there was nothing wrong. Until she wheeled her mum back to her room and Nora snagged her hand, concern deepening the fatigue lines in her sunken cheeks.

'What's wrong?'

Callie opened her mouth to protest but Nora shook her head.

'Do me a favour, sweetheart, and let me be a mum to you in whatever way I can.'

As a guilt trip, it worked. She'd been taking care of her mum for a while now, and she knew it irked the once independent Nora.

Nora had relished her role as a single mum, not once complaining. When a job had needed doing, she'd got on and done it, so to have her mobility and her dignity curtailed by this dreadful disease... Callie couldn't begin to fathom how awful it must be.

'Work pressures. Nothing major,' she said, not wanting to worry her mum—not today.

Nora had always loved Christmas with all the trimmings: roast turkey and stuffing, trifle, pudding—the works. They'd always had a fresh tree and stuffed stockings, and a day made all the more special by a mother who'd do anything for her only child.

It might have been understated and only the two of them, but it had meant a lot to her mum.

Now those Christmases were in the past, but the least Callie could do was not ruin this Christmas for Nora. Not when she'd already ruined her own.

Nora searched her face, as if seeking the truth, and Callie ducked down to give her an impulsive hug. 'Don't worry, Mum, I'm fine.'

And then she glanced over her mum's shoulder and saw Archer hovering in the doorway.

'What the?'

'Callie?'

She straightened and laid a comforting hand on her mum's shoulder, hoping her glare conveyed what she wanted: for Archer to turn around and leave the way he'd come.

Following her line of vision, Nora slowly swivelled until she too faced Archer.

'Can I help you, young man?'

He hesitated a moment, before squaring his shoulders and stepping into the room. 'I sure hope so, Mrs Umberto.' He held out his hand to her. 'I'm Archer Flett, a friend of your daughter's.'

The way he gently shook Nora's hand eased Callie's anger somewhat. Though she couldn't figure out why she was so angry. Was she upset at him showing up here, or upset at herself for wanting to fling herself at him despite a definitive goodbye?

Well, on her part anyway. It looked as if he hadn't taken too kindly to her brief farewell note.

'Sorry to barge in on you like this, but I need to see Callie before I fly out later today.'

Callie frowned but he blithely ignored her, his dazzling smile deliberately taunting.

'Merry Christmas, by the way,' he said.

He produced a box from behind his back, in crimson shiny paper bound by gold ribbon.

'Not very original, I'm afraid, but if you're anything like your daughter I thought you might enjoy a sweet treat.'

'How thoughtful.' Nora's hands shook as she took an eternity to undo the ribbon and rip the paper.

Callie had to stop from reaching out to help. Not from pity for her mum but the desire to see Archer leave.

'Dark mint, my favourite.'

Nora's grateful smile made Callie's heart ache. She hadn't wanted to tell her mum anything about Archer, and now the rat had left her no choice. Nora would want to know all about the nice young man who knew her favourite chocolates and how he knew and…the rest.

She'd kill him before she sent him packing.

'I hate to intrude, but do you mind if I have a quick word with Callie?'

Nora shot her a quick look—a very perceptive look by the mischievous gleam in her eyes.

'Not at all. Go ahead.' Nora rattled the box. 'And thanks for these. I'll enjoy each and every one.'

'My pleasure.'

His smile was genuine, without an ounce of pity, and Callie grudgingly admired him for it.

'We can talk outside,' she said, with a subtle jerk of her head towards the door. The last thing she needed was for her mum's gossip radar to prick up. Any *more*, that was.

Callie couldn't figure out what Archer was doing here. She'd given him an easy out with that note, and she'd assumed he'd jump at the chance to fly off into the blue yonder and resume his life.

The last thing she'd expected was to see him rock up here. It made her angsty and uncertain and decidedly edgy.

She'd had this all figured out—end fling; resume working relationship—and now he'd messed that up.

She waited until they'd stepped outside Nora's room before jabbing him in the chest. 'How did you find me?'

Her snappish tone only served to make him lean against the wall, arms folded, grin cocky.

'Not all that difficult. You said you'd be spending the day here, so I checked redial on the phone at the beach house for the number, rang it, discovered where your mum was staying.'

'Nice one, Sherlock,' she muttered, still clueless as to why he was here.

'Actually, I'd make a lousy detective, because I have no clue as to why you ran out on me in the middle of the night.'

'It was early morning. Tom and Izzy were

heading to Melbourne, so I thought I'd get a head start on spending Christmas with Mum.'

'Bull,' he said, his grin replaced by thinly compressed lips and an unimpressed frown. 'You couldn't have rung Tom at four a.m. on impulse to hitch a ride, which means you must've organised this last night.'

Why couldn't he be all brawn and no brains?

'Tom's wisely not answering his phone, but I have no doubt you coerced him into aiding and abetting your little escape.' For the first time since he'd shown up a flicker of uncertainty creased his brow. 'I don't get it, Callie. I thought we had something going—'

'*Had* being the operative word.' She shook her head, wishing her heart would stop flipping all over the place and slamming against her ribcage at the thought of him showing up here because he genuinely cared.

No use wishing for the impossible.

Fact: he was still getting on that plane later today.

Fact: whatever he said wouldn't change a thing. They led different lives, a world apart.

Fact: she loved him, and seeing him again only drove the knife in that little bit deeper.

'Look, we had a great time, Arch, but it's over.'

His glare turned mutinous. 'Doesn't have to be.'

He rummaged in his jacket pocket and pulled out a folded piece of paper.

'Here. This was supposed to be your Christmas present.'

When she made no move to take it, he placed it in her hand and curled her fingers around it.

'Go on, take a look.'

More than a little curious, she unfolded the paper and gasped.

A computer printout for an open-ended, first class, round-the-world air ticket.

In her name.

'We've got a pretty good thing going, Cal, I don't want it to end. This way you can join me wherever I am. We can hang out—'

'No.'

She crumpled the paper ticket and let it fall to the floor, her gut spasming with sorrow.

'Don't you get it? I can't just jet off whenever I feel like it. I have obligations.' She jerked a thumb over her shoulder. 'I can't leave Mum and you know that.'

His face fell. 'I thought… Well, I hoped you might want to explore…a…relationship—'

'On your terms?'

Pain lanced her resolve, making her waver.

Was she being too harsh? Was she annihilating any chance of a possible future of happiness?

She shook her head. 'If you're so keen to explore what we have, why don't you stick around? Stop running? Commit to something for once in your life?'

A flash of anger sparked his eyes. 'I've committed my life to being the best in the water—'

'Yeah, but what about out of it? What about your family? You can't bear to spend longer than a few days with them once a year. How the hell do you expect to maintain a relationship?'

She knew what she was doing: deliberately sabotaging his attempt at a relationship. Fear clogged her throat at the thought of continuing what they had, growing closer, only to discover he hadn't really changed after all and she'd end up pining and waiting for someone she couldn't rely on. Been there, done that, still waiting for her dad to bring her the T-shirt as a present.

She might have foolishly wished for a happily-ever-after with Archer this past week, but at the time she'd recognised her pie-in-the-sky dream for being just that. That was why she'd indulged in another week-long fling, confident of the end date.

She'd never take the risk of a full-blown relationship knowing she was opening herself up to further heartbreak.

'Just go.'

She expected him to run as he always did. The fact that he was still standing there, a vein pulsing in his neck, shoulders rigid, only served to rile her further.

What was he waiting for?

'I'm not the one running scared this time, Callie. You are.'

Sadness seeped through her, making her want to curl up in a corner and sleep for a century. 'Shows how well you know me. I'm not running anywhere. I can't.' She jerked her head towards Nora. 'And the fact you'd give me an air ticket expecting I'd follow you on a whim proves it.'

Tears prickled at the backs of her eyes. She had to drive him away before she collapsed in a wailing heap in his arms.

'You don't know me and you never will.'

When he didn't flinch, didn't move, her mum called out, '*You* should go, dear.'

Callie did the only thing possible.

She fled.

CHAPTER TWELVE

FOR the second time today Archer wanted to punch something.

Frustration made his head ache as he watched Callie run away from him.

Again.

He should follow her, try to make her understand… His gaze landed on the crumpled plane ticket at his feet and his resolve hardened.

He'd wanted to explore the spark they shared. She'd rejected him.

Best to walk away and not look back.

'Archer? Could you please come in here a minute?'

Great, just what he needed. For her mum to berate him for messing up her daughter's life.

He snatched the ticket off the floor, jammed it into his pocket and entered the room.

'I have a plane to catch—'

'"Later" is what you said.'

The woman before him might have a terminal disease which left her stoop-shouldered and shaky and fragile, but the determination in her intelligent eyes was pure Callie.

He sat on the footstool opposite her wheel-chair. 'I'm not comfortable discussing my re-lationship with Callie.'

'From what I overheard, seems like you're not comfortable with a relationship period.'

'Harsh.'

Nora's eyebrow rose. 'But true?'

When he opened his mouth to protest, she held up a trembling hand.

'This is none of my business, but if you want a chance with my daughter I recommend you listen.'

He remained mute.

'Good. You want to know why Calista re-fused your offer?'

He nodded.

'She's scared.'

'Of?'

'It's not my place to tell you, but I think you need to ask her if you want a future together.'

He let out a breath he'd been unaware he was holding, his fingers relaxing from where they'd dug into the footstool's leather.

Damn right he'd ask her. If Callie's mum thought he still had a chance, no way would he waste it.

'You might be interested to know that when Calista returned from Europe she was glowing. She had a bounce in her step, she smiled constantly, and she hummed Spanish tunes under her breath. Then I was diagnosed and her exuberance faded.' Tears glittered in her eyes. 'I hate this disease for doing that to my beautiful Callie.'

Archer didn't handle emotion well, tears least of all, and he sat there like an idiot, searching for the right thing to say and coming up empty.

'Interestingly, when Calista came to see me last week, before her trip away with you, she had some of that old spark back. Which leads me to believe you were more responsible for her post-Europe glow than geography.'

If acknowledging emotions wasn't his forte, discussing them sent him into full-blown panic.

'We shared something special.'

The simple truth, and the right thing to say by Nora's nod of approval.

'My advice? If you want to share that same spark again, don't give up. Go after her. Convince her how you feel. Make her trust you. Trust is everything to my little girl.'

He knew the feeling.

To his surprise, a lump wedged in his throat,

and no matter how many times he swallowed he couldn't dislodge it.

'As for her fear of leaving me in case I die—don't worry. I'll fix that.' Nora's smile turned wicked. 'If she doesn't spend some of her time on the road with you I'll threaten to live out my time in the smelly nursing home up the road—the one with roaches the size of rodents—and donate the exorbitant fees she pays for me to stay here to the lost dogs' home.'

The lump of emotion in his throat eased, and his admiration for this feisty woman skyrocketed. 'I'm glad you're on my side.'

She pointed a bony finger at him. 'I'm only on your side because I can see you're head over heels in love with my daughter. Hurt her—you die.'

He laughed. 'Got the message, loud and clear.' He stood and ducked down to kiss her cheek. 'Thanks.'

A faint pink stained her cheeks. 'I may not be around much longer, but while I'm here I'm going to be the best damned mother-in-law you could ever wish for.'

It took him a good sixty seconds to process what she'd said, and by then he'd reached his car.

Him? Head over heels in love? What were the chances?

As for a mother-in-law...that involved marriage...

By the time he'd hit Alexander Parade some of the initial shock had worn off and he found himself heading for Johnston Street.

He needed answers.

Only one woman could provide them.

Callie texted her mum an apology as soon as she pulled into a parking spot at home.

She'd cooled off by the time she'd walked through to the foyer, and had headed back to Nora's room. But when she'd got there she'd seen Archer in the room. It had looked as if her mum was telling him off so she'd left. She hoped Nora had flayed him alive.

The guy didn't have a clue, thinking she could traipse around the world while Nora was stuck in that home dying.

Selfish. Unthinking. *Male.*

She thumped the steering wheel. It did little for the resentment simmering like a dormant volcano. She wasn't footloose like him. She couldn't jump on a plane whenever he snapped his fingers. She wasn't impulsive and selfish. She wasn't her father.

But as her anger faded a sliver of clarity glimmered through. Maybe she was looking at this all wrong. Archer had walked away from her once without looking back. This time he wanted to continue seeing her, to explore a relationship. And, while she didn't want to risk her heart again, she'd been harsh. She'd said some pretty nasty stuff at the end, accusing him of being a shallow, emotionless commitment-phobe.

And what had he done? Gone and copped more from her mum. Not many guys would do that. The Archer she'd once known would have headed to the airport without hesitation.

But this older, more mature Archer wasn't the same guy he'd once been. He was wiser, more responsive, more willing to see past the end of his surfboard.

And the thing was, if a guy like him had taken a monumental risk in tracking her down to lay his heart on the line should she consider taking a risk too?

Was her lack of trust worth a life of misery in losing the love of her life?

She rested her hands on the steering wheel and her head fell forward, her eyes closed.

She couldn't leave Nora, that was a given, but maybe she could compromise in some way? She wouldn't expect him to wait for her, but the thought of having Archer in her life—to support her, to care for her when the dreaded inevitable happened with her mum—was pretty darn appealing.

She knocked her head repeatedly against her forearms.

Yep, she'd been a fool.

The rev of an engine penetrated her misery, punctuated by three short blasts on a familiar horn. She lifted her head, daring to hope, just in time to see Archer kill the engine of the red Roadster, unclip his seatbelt and vault over the door.

He strode towards her, determination lengthening his strides, and she got out of the car, waiting for him to reach her.

'We're going for a ride and I want you to promise me you won't speak the whole way.' He snagged her hand and tugged.

She resisted. No use giving in too easily. 'As an apology, that sucked.'

She bit back a grin at his comical disbelief.

'*Me* owe *you* an apology?' He shook his head. 'Not. Another. Word.'

This time she let him lead her towards the Roadster, open the door and buckle her in. His familiar fresh air and sunshine scent wrapped around her like a comforting hug.

She gritted her teeth to stop herself from nuzzling his neck, and curled her fingers into her palm to stop herself reaching for him.

He took a deliberately long time, taunting her, and she almost capitulated. Almost. He straightened, his grin smug, and she wanted to smack that smugness off his face.

As they wound through the heavy Christmas Day traffic she snuck glances at him, her heart giving an extra kick when they locked stares for a long, loaded moment at some traffic lights.

All her mental pep talks to get over him, all her determination to move on, vanished in that one look. The sizzle of heat was invisible yet unmistakable.

She'd never been more thankful when the lights turned green.

Ten minutes later he'd pulled into a rare parking spot in Lygon Street and his intention hit her.

He'd brought her to Melbourne's Little Italy. Was he aiming to soften her up by resurrecting memories of Capri?

They were so past Capri it wasn't funny, and she fully intended to tell him so. But the hint of vulnerability in his questioning gaze caught her completely off guard and she bit back a smartass remark.

She saved it for when they were seated in a tiny trattoria so reminiscent of their favourite place in Capri she half expected Luigi, the owner, to come strutting out to welcome them.

'Can I talk yet—?'

'No.' He made a zipping motion over his lips and proceeded to order: linguine marinara, fresh bread, Chianti.

Their meal.

Yep, he was trying to schmooze his way into getting her to change her mind. As if a fabulous Italian meal would do that.

She had obligations.

She had responsibilities.

He snuck his fingers across the table, snagged her hand, lifted it to his lips and kissed her knuckles.

She had it bad.

He released her hand and she reluctantly, perversely, snatched it away.

'You can talk soon, but only after you listen first.' She rolled her eyes and he chuckled. 'I had a plan. Wake up next to you Christmas morning, make all your Christmases come at once—' she winced at his corny pun '—and then tell you how I feel.'

Her pulse stuttered, before pounding like a jackhammer.

'But you robbed me of that opportunity and I wanted to run. I was all set to head to the airport early 'til I realised something.'

His gaze dropped to her hands, clasped on

the table, before slowly raising to eyeball her, and what she saw snatched her breath.

Adoration? Hope? Dared she think it...*love*?

'I figured this time I wanted to run *towards* something and not away from it.'

Some of her resentment melted as she gnawed on her bottom lip, wanting to speak, afraid of saying too much.

'That airline ticket was my lousy way of saying I want to be with you.' He cleared his throat. 'I can't lose you, Cal. Not this time.'

The silence stretched between them and she took it as her cue to speak.

'I can't traipse around the world after you, even if Mum says it's okay.'

He nodded. 'I know. I was thinking maybe I should stick around for a while—teach classes at the surf school, give back to my home town and the sport that's given me everything.'

Shock ripped apart her carefully constructed defences.

'You're staying in Torquay?'

'If you make it worth my while.' His mouth kicked up at the corners in a cheeky dare, and she could have sworn her heart kicked right back.

Wow.

Renowned nomad and confirmed gypsy

Archer Flett was willing to put down roots. For her.

It was what she'd dreamed of—what she would have traded anything for eight years ago. But despite the urge to be selfish for once in her life, grab what she wanted and damn the consequences, she couldn't do it.

Archer was willing to stick around now, but for how long? What about when the going got tough with her mum? What about when they had to live apart for months because of his work commitments and her emotional ones?

Constant pressures on a relationship would wear it down and she'd be right back where she started. Loving Archer, her trust shattered.

'So what do you say? Think you can handle having me in your life?'

Her heart wanted to yell, *Hell, yeah*.

Her mind froze with the implications of losing him. This time around it would be so much worse, because he was willing to give it all up for her.

And she had to push him away.

'I—I can't. I'm sorry.'

She had a second to register his open-mouthed shock before she bolted from the restaurant, dodging a family of boisterous children brandishing crackers and a bedraggled Santa who looked as if he'd been doing overtime all week.

She couldn't head for the car, and both sides of the road were lined with outdoor chairs and tables filled to overflowing with Christmas revellers.

Her hesitation cost her dearly. A hand clamped around her upper arm.

'I've asked the waiter to hold our meal until we've had a little chat. In private.'

She could have struggled, but with people casting concerned glances their way and reaching for their mobile phones she acquiesced to him leading her to the car, where she slouched in the front seat like a recalcitrant child.

'Nora told me you have trust issues and that you'd tell me the rest. Is that what this is about?'

Way to go, Mum, she thought. *Traitor.*

She folded her arms and glared. 'Maybe I'm just not that into you?'

He laughed. 'Not buying it. Try again.'

She clamped her lips shut in the hope that he'd tire of the silent treatment and give up.

'She said you were scared. Has some guy done a number on you? Because I can emasculate him if that'll help.'

The corners of her mouth curved upwards before she could stop them.

'You know I'll keep throwing out outlandish suggestions 'til you tell me the truth, right?'

And he would. If the guy had been determined enough to win the World Championship five times, odds were he wouldn't let up.

She took a deep breath, blew it out. 'My dad let me down repeatedly. Rarely followed through on promises. Popped in when he felt like it. Paid more attention to his next three wives than he did to Mum and me. Then when Mum was diagnosed he stopped contact altogether.'

Archer swore.

'Yeah, I think I've used that expletive a few times myself.' She shrugged, hoping he'd back off and she wouldn't have to divulge the rest—the real reason why she was petrified of a relationship with Archer. 'Guess I'm reluctant to trust people because of that.'

'There's more.'

She should've known he'd be too smart to let this go.

'Cal, look at me.'

But she couldn't. Couldn't risk him seeing her real fear.

'Your dad sounds like a selfish jerk, but that's not what has you so scared.'

When she still wouldn't eyeball him, he swore again. 'Thanks to you, I sorted things out with my family. I stashed my damn pride and took the first step in rebuilding the gap I created.' He jabbed a thumb at his chest. 'I've got trust issues too, because they didn't trust me enough to confide in when they should've. I often wonder if it's me, something about me that made them do that. But I'm not wasting time second-guessing myself any more, Cal. It's not worth it. I'm going out on a limb here because it's *you*. I'm scared like you are, so there has to be more.'

Damn him for being so intuitive.

'Is this about the motor neurone disease? Are you scared you'll inherit it?'

Her gaze snapped to his, and in that instant she gave away her final fear.

'Because it's natural to be scared, but whatever happens in the future we'll face it together.'

'Are you crazy? You saw my mum. And she's only going to get worse. You think I want you to…?' She trailed off in horror, tears blurring her eyes at how close she'd come to blurting the truth.

'Tell me.'

He placed a fingertip under her chin and gently tipped it up so she had no option but to look at him.

She wanted to fob him off, to lie, but the love blazing from his intent stare was her undoing.

'You think I want you to be stuck with something like that? For you to give up your freedom for me?' She shook her head, dislodging his touch. 'If the disease didn't kill me, the guilt would.' A great sob tore from her chest. 'I want more for you.'

'*You're* all I want—'

He broke off, and for one horrifying moment she thought he might cry.

'Look, I'm new to this emotional stuff. I don't know what to do or say to prove I love you.'

He dropped his head into his hands, his defeatist posture so far removed from the confident guy she knew it got through to her as nothing else could.

He loved her.

He wanted to be with her.

How many people got a second chance at their first love?

Tentative, she reached out and laid a hand on his shoulder. 'Genetic testing says I don't carry the mutated gene, but that doesn't mean I can't get it. My chances are still elevated.'

He lifted his head, his bleak expression tearing at her inside. 'Life's full of risks, Cal. I take risks every day. Sharks. Rips. Getting on a plane. In a car. If we don't take risks we're half dead anyway. And that's not you. The woman I remember in Capri was vivacious and bold and lived life to the max. I've seen glimpses of that woman the last week and she's magnificent.'

She couldn't speak if she wanted to. Her throat was constricted with emotion.

'I won't pre-empt your mum, but she's going to tell you the same thing I just did. She wants you to make the most of your life, to embrace it, not run from it for fear of losing it one nebulous day that may never come.'

'I don't want you to give up who you are for me. I won't be that selfish, like Dad—'

'He's a callous bastard and you're nothing like him. You're standing by your mum. You're doing everything in your power to show her how much she means to you. As for your trust issues because of him, I can deal with them.' He jabbed a hand through his blond spikes. 'I can deal with anything as long as I have you by my side.'

When it came down to it, that was what convinced her to give their relationship a go.

Having Archer by her side, through good and bad, was a pretty potent attraction.

'What about kids? I'm not sure I could take the risk. They may inherit—'

'Enough. You're reaching for excuses, probably terrified to commit like me.'

Damn straight she was.

He tapped his chest. 'If you're feeling half as vulnerable and open wide in here as I am, you're grasping at whatever you can to avoid taking a risk.'

He was good. He'd homed in on exactly how she was feeling: raw and vulnerable and shell-shocked.

And downright petrified.

He was right. She was grabbing at any old excuse, hiding her fear behind it.

But in opening her heart to him a second time around hadn't she already taken the biggest risk of all?

He snagged her hand, squeezed it. 'You're worrying about the future when we need to live in the present.'

When her mum had been diagnosed, and later when Callie had been given the all-clear following genetic testing, she'd made it her mission to make the most of every opportunity.

Archer had proved how much he loved her by his willingness to give up what he treasured most: his freedom.

He wanted to be with her for ever. It was the greatest opportunity of a lifetime.

What was she waiting for?

He enveloped her in his arms and she finally let go, her emotion spilling out in torrents of tears as she drenched his shirt.

'Kids, marriage, the works, we'll face it. Together,' he murmured, smoothing her hair, stroking her back until her sobs subsided.

Stunned that this incredible man was willing to give up so much to be with her, she eased back and gazed into his eyes.

'I love you. I always have.'

He kissed her, long and slow.

By the time they made it back to the restaurant their Christmas dinner was cold.

EPILOGUE

'WE SHOULD HAVE eloped to Hawaii,' Archer murmured in Callie's ear after the umpteenth back-slap and congratulatory kiss.

Callie elbowed her new husband. 'And miss out on sharing another Flett Christmas Eve wedding with our families? No way.'

'You're such a romantic sap,' he said, sliding an arm around her waist and holding her close.

'So sue me.' She sighed and snuggled into him. 'Thank you.'

'For?'

'This.'

She waved towards the festivities in full swing on the beach foreshore in front of the Winki Pop Surf School.

Artie, resplendent in tux and Santa hat, was mixing up another batch of his secret sangria.

Izzy, too cute in an eclectic Christmas elf-fairy costume, was racing around Tom in a demented version of Ring-a-Rosie. Travis and

Shelly were canoodling, and Archer's folks were sitting hand in hand alongside Nora, watching the fun with benign smiles.

Even the recalcitrant Bruno had made a rare appearance, resurfacing from the Middle East *sans* wife, and trying to make it up to Nora and his daughter.

Let him keep trying. Callie wasn't buying it, even if she'd generously agreed to let him come to the wedding and to Christmas lunch tomorrow.

The wedding ceremony on the beach had been incredible, but it had been earlier, when Archer had carried Nora in his arms and gently deposited her in a front row seat, that Callie had lost it.

He'd wiped away her tears to a chorus of sniffles from their small crowd of guests and she'd managed to hold it together for the vows. Just.

The fact that she'd married her first love, her only love, was so surreal she kept smoothing her strapless calf-length ivory silk wedding dress to ensure it was real.

Lucky for her, Archer rarely released her hand, and his solid presence was all the reassurance she needed.

His gaze followed hers. 'You sure your

mum's going to be okay while we honeymoon in Capri? Because I'm happy to stay here—'

'She'll be fine.'

Callie had had a long talk with her mum when she'd almost lost Archer twelve months ago, resulting in her letting go of her residual fears and starting to live life in the moment.

Sure, watching her mum deteriorate a little every day sliced her in two, but Nora was making the most of the time she had left. The least Callie could do was the same.

It was what Nora had wanted—to see Callie happy—and they'd brought the wedding forward for that very reason.

Not that she or Archer minded. They'd been living together anyway, spending Monday to Friday in Melbourne and the weekends in Torquay.

He didn't mind the commute, and she didn't mind a sexy surfer crowding her space. They hadn't decided on permanent living arrangements yet. Time enough when they returned from Capri.

She couldn't believe they were returning to the beautiful town where they'd met, where this amazing guy had wooed her with wine and moonlight and sea.

'What are you thinking?'

She glanced into her husband's deep blue

eyes and smiled. 'I'm thinking about old memories of Capri.'

'Well, I'm thinking about creating new ones.'

His exaggerated eyebrow-wiggle made her laugh.

'You know we're going to have an amazing life together, right?' He cradled her face in his hands, his thumbs caressing her cheeks.

'You bet.'

For whatever they faced in the future she'd do it with her incredible husband by her side.

Life didn't get any better than this.

He lowered his head and kissed her, a soft, tender melding of lips that quickly escalated into heat and passion and need.

Maybe it did…

* * * * *

LET'S TALK
Romance

For exclusive extracts, competitions
and special offers, find us online:

- facebook.com/millsandboon
- @MillsandBoon
- @MillsandBoonUK

Get in touch on 01413 063232

For all the latest titles coming soon, visit
millsandboon.co.uk/nextmonth

MILLS & BOON
MODERN
Power and Passion

Prepare to be swept off your feet by
sophisticated, sexy and seductive heroes, in
some of the world's most glamourous and
romantic locations, where power and
passion collide.